"Reynolds Price's place in the affections of his readers is justifiably secure, and so is his place in contemporary literature."

—*The Boston Globe*

"Reynolds Price has always understood the particular rhythms of Southern life. The best characters in his fiction are people who follow the thrum of everyday routine, but keep one ear tuned to distant, secret music, always a haunting song."

—*USA Today*

"During a distinguished and prolific career, *Blue Calhoun* is an impressive demonstration of just how subtle and complicated Price can be when exploring his themes of pain and redemption."

—*San Francisco Chronicle*

"It is the candor and true-sounding voice that gives depth to the character and provides this novel with a stature that grows."

—*Detroit Free Press*

"This is the voice of a good storyteller—Price's characteristically energetic prose, the very Southern, almost biblically cadenced voice."

—*The Washington Post Book World*

"Reynolds Price has written a beautiful novel that remains in the reader's mind and heart long after the final page is read."

—*Chattanooga Times*

"Price is in top form . . . clear, clean prose that captures perfectly the rhythms of the South and of the human heart."

—*Orlando Sentinel*

BLUE CALHOUN

BOOKS BY

REYNOLDS PRICE

REYNOLDS
PRICE

BLUE
CALHOUN

SCRIBNER PAPERBACK FICTION
PUBLISHED BY SIMON & SCHUSTER
NEW YORK   LONDON   TORONTO   SYDNEY   SINGAPORE

SCRIBNER PAPERBACK FICTION
Simon & Schuster, Inc.
Rockefeller Center
1230 Avenue of the Americas
New York, NY 10020

First Scribner Paperback Fiction edition 2000
SCRIBNER PAPERBACK FICTION and design are trademarks of Macmillan Library Reference USA, Inc., used under license by Simon & Schuster, the publisher of this work.

Manufactured in the United States of America

1   3   5   7   9   10   8   6   4   2

The Library of Congress has cataloged the Atheneum edition as follows:
Price, Reynolds, 1933–
Blue Calhoun / Reynolds Price.
p.   cm.
I. Title.
PS3566.R54B55   1992
813'.54—dc20   91-22877
CIP

ISBN 0-684-86782-6

FOR

ROBERT CHEATHAM

BLUE CALHOUN

M

Y DARLING,

I have to leave you tonight, and it could be for good if fate says *Quit*. You're deep asleep and I can't stand to wake you after what we've gone through again today. But I'm convinced you're safe here now, and I've asked Luna to read these pages and pass them to you when she believes you'll understand. Wise as you are, that may be soon or years away. I'll let Luna choose since what's down here in black and white is much of your family's waste and pain but also devotion and the best kinds of pardon. Because I've meant to tell the whole truth, I've had to write it for a person older than you are now, a good deal older—the person you'll be in time, I trust. So even if you don't read them soon, store these pages for when you're further on in time. It may well take you most of your life to give me the mercy I'm asking for.

See, once I thought I'd rescued you—and then you turned so hard against me—the principal thing that's mattered to me is leaving behind a means to help you weigh my love and what it caused us: mainly your pitiful father's death and a break in the bonds we'd built between us, you and me. And however long you take to read and ponder this, remember please—I'm leaning deep on the hope you'll see how I did what I could at the time, which was dark all ways—what I *thought* I could, what any man might try to do for the dearest person he knows on Earth and is desperate to save.

I knew from the instant I found your father's lifeless body that I'd provided a crucial hand in the solemnest deed a human can do. But I saw no way to tell you straight that, yes, I'd truly stopped him forever and that you were free from his demands, though I'd be punished in my mind the rest of my days. So all these months from Stuttgart to Raleigh, and now out here in the warm green country, I've had to survive some endless nights. And what I did was work long hours, some nights till dawn, to tell the story that actually says where your life came from and why—once your dear mother was gone and I looked through that final door and saw the hell you were trapped in— I was able to let your father die alone and helpless ten steps from me with no kind understanding word, though of all the men he'd ever known, I had old reasons to share his anguish.

I hope I see you again on Earth. I even hope it will be soon if I get back. I hope your eyes can meet mine then with some kind of welcome. If not, I hope any child you bear in years to come will live in a family that's stronger for what I had to do. At the very least, may you hereafter dream in a peace you've yet to know.

Your one grandfather,
Blue Calhoun

ONE

THIS STARTS with the happiest I ever was, though it brought down suffering on everybody near me. Short as it lasted and long ago, I've never laid it all out yet, not start to finish. But if I try and half succeed, you may wind up understanding things, choosing a better road for yourself and maybe not blaming the dead past but living for the here and now, each day a clean page. At least you'll see how certain things in my long life have gone down fast as one of those Japanese domino shows where two million pieces trip each other in hot succession and set off the unexpected jackpot—an exploding mountain or a rocket blast that hurls men farther than they've yet gone, to Neptune or worse.

The time I'll tell about ran its course when I was thirty five, then thirty six. Till then I'd lived a fairly normal life, if normal includes some badly drunk years—and I think it does in America still. So honest to God, I doubt you need to know much about me before the latter half of that day when everything started streaking downhill. Of course I'll add the odd event that feels worth knowing or tells a good story. Stories are something I'm better at than life; and that one year was built like a story, whoever built it. It had a low start that stoked up fast to such a heat that hinges on doors were melting away; and pent up people were tearing loose and running for what looked like daylight till, at some weird invisible signal, everything started cooling again.

And everybody slowed to average speed and drew deep breaths to treat their burns and wonder if they could stand the sight of each other's faces from then till death or just for that day. Some said Yes; a few said No; and everybody thought I'd caused the wreck, which may have been true. Even my mother, a certified saint, called me out to the country house and said "Now, son, you've ruined two lives— your own blood child and the girl you claimed to love so strongly. How do you plan on living the rest of the time you've got with that on your mind, that blood on your hands?"

Blood was a figure of speech at the time, and she well knew it. I'd almost certainly killed four Germans in the Second War but nothing since. So I said what I believed was true, "Look, Mother. Nobody's dead." I was technically right.

But her deep blue eyes never flinched, and she said "Far worse than dead—far worse."

Then I saw that the thing I dreaded had happened. I'd badly harmed three worthwhile souls that trusted me; and I knew no way on Earth to mend them—not till your and my past months together, thirty years on. Know this first though (it's some of the worst you'll know about me)—I drove myself back home from Mother's that late spring night in a tardy frost with my face grinning each mile of the way. I could see it in the mirror, dark as it was. My *body* was still that pleased with the memory; it still is today. Maybe my mind and heart just figured I'd taken enough from God or fate, my family and the U.S. Infantry—not to mention the Nazis—to earn me some substantial relief and nourishment. Whatever, I flat-out gorged myself for twelve full months. So here much further on in time, I'm hoping to make my slim amends by telling this history that's all but true.

I'm Blue Calhoun as you well know; and wild as I've been, I still like the sound. The full name's *Bluford* and the middle name's *August*, but there can't be more than ten people left who know that much about me still—to the world I'm *Blue* and have always been. Except for the war and the times I was wild—and our hard time overseas just now—I've mostly stayed near my birthplace: a capital city, Raleigh,

N.C. When I was a child, Raleigh called itself "The City of Oaks." But don't try to find an oak these days in the criminal mess that money and the chloroformed City Council have made from innocent fertile dirt and what grew in it.

I'm drifting already but here's the start. As I said, I'd climbed the sizable hill of my thirty fifth birthday—a rough time for men, the downhill side. I think I was sane; people from all walks of life assured me I was not bad to see. I'd been stone sober for nineteen months—the longest ever up to that point—and as it turned out, I've stayed sober the rest of my life to this night now. I worked the best job I'd had in years; and to my knowledge, no part of my life was starved or frozen. I didn't stare off at sunsets and grieve. I thought I cherished my only spouse, born Myra Burns, a friend since childhood and your grandmother that you'd have prized.

We'd been married for fifteen years, and Myra had tried her absolute best. As you well know we had a daughter that I near worshiped named Madelyn (called Mattie or Matt from the day of her birth, according to how we felt at the moment). Matt was the finest influence on me of anybody yet. I owed her the world and was aiming to give it, minute by minute from here on out—upright kindness and every decent thought and act I could see she needed. But then that one day fell down on me from a clear spring sky, no word of warning. It tore the ground from under my feet, and everything round me shook the way a mad dog shakes a howling child.

April 28th, 1956 was an early scorcher; and I met my fate when a girl turned up in the midst of my job. The place I worked was on Fayetteville Street near the Capitol building—Atkinson Music Company, a long narrow store with high old ceilings, gentle light and air that smelled antique and soothing. Up front was the sheet music department, then the phonograph records and concert tickets. From there on back it was musical hardware of every description. First the small things—fiddles, accordions, ukuleles, flutes. Then you worked your way through banjos and mandolins, the big band instruments, tall gold harps and sets of drums you prayed your neighbors would never buy. Then you finished up with Steinway grands, Hammond organs and one enormous church size console with pipes enough to sweep back the roof and blow you skyward if a person that knew how to play it lit in.

I truly liked the actual job. For a man with no enormous mind and what he thought were normal ambitions, it offered a peaceful eight hour day, a respectable paycheck every two weeks and music around him, dawn to dusk—real music made by live human beings, not piped-in syrup. As for making music I myself never got that far past whistling, despite my mother's early dream that I wind up as what she called "a poet of the keyboard." I took piano from the fourth grade on into early high school when baseball got me, but I seldom practiced and learned next to nothing except what music really is—far and away man's best creation—and how it can help when nothing else will.

When I flunked out of college at nineteen, and hadn't begun to lean on liquor, I and my thumb made numerous tours of the U.S. east of the Mississippi. In those free years I'd often end up wet or cold in the night with nobody near but a small harmonica that my dad gave me when I first pushed off. However gruesome or lonesome I got, there were very few times when even a talentless boy like me couldn't improvise a song or hymn and wind up glad to be on Earth plus ready to sleep. But I quit that too when I came back and grounded myself.

To this day now I regret that laziness. Even more often after I got married, I'd sink very near the floor of this world—the black sub basement—and every one of those desperate times, I'd hear some mangled piece of my mind start begging for music—any music on Earth from nursery rhymes to opera on the radio that all but etches the window glass. If only I'd learned some lapsize instrument like the guitar, I might well have spent less time in Hell than I've since done.

Speaking of Hell, on the day in question, the whole world still wasn't air conditioned. And dim as it was, the store was stifling. Business was slack, the staff was mostly dozing upright; and I was on the verge of sleep behind the pianos. Then the street door opened and played its chime. A woman walked in, broad in the beam. The sun on the glass was blinding bright and I'm nearsighted, so I couldn't see her face right off. I gave her no thought anyhow. Somebody up front would help her if needed, and I could still doze.

But in maybe a minute, a voice sang out—a woman's unashamed high sound in one long line of a song new to me, then a laugh and silence.

I thought right off how strange it was that, after these months of work among children blasting away on saxophones and pounding drums, I'd yet to hear a human voice sing so much as part of a tune and it sounded grand. I stepped forward five yards and tried to see if that broad woman had done us the favor—she plainly had the chest to do it. It took a few seconds to realize she was more than one person. There were two females and they must have walked in single file. The other one looked like a slender child and was close beside the broad one at the sheet music counter. One of them must have been demonstrating the tune of a song she didn't know the name of. The singing voice had sounded grown, and I edged onward another few steps before I saw that the child was still—still as a post and watching me. And not a child.

I was pulled right on another few yards. The girl never blinked or turned aside. I was maybe twenty feet away; and her look was so strong, I had to glance down. On the showcase beside me was a pear-wood mandolin perfectly made. I strummed it once and tried to pretend I knew how to tune it. When I had it sounding halfway right, I looked again. Now the girl was smiling, and her mother was striding on towards me as if I'd made some last mistake.

The mother was ten feet off, and mad, when I recognized her as somebody I'd known centuries past in grammar school—the very same scared old-time girl was hid in this stout woman's body. I held up a hand to slow her and said "Rita, old flame, you've kept your *figure*."

No brick wall could have stopped her faster. Her three chins shivered and her eyes went flat but stayed right on me. Then her thin mouth said "I'm way too stout and I don't know you."

I said "I've known you, down to the *ground*, for thirty five years" (not strictly true, more like twenty nine). By then the girl had come up behind her but I still watched Rita.

And Rita kept hunting my face for a sign. Old as I was and badly behaved, I hated to think my face had aged past recognition.

That instant a stock boy passed, bumped me and said "Old *Blue.*"

Rita said *"Blue?"*

I held in place.

"Not Blue Calhoun?"

I nodded and grinned. "—His cold remains."

She stood a second, then made a little graceful skip and a glide, then took my hands. "If you're cold, child, then cool *my* skin."

She was hot as a stove and had always been, even in the old days back in school. I could still see her eyes the day she quit the seventh grade—all of us knew she was far gone pregnant (she'd failed a grade and was one year older).

I let Rita hold me as long as she would, and I looked beyond her now towards the girl. She was tall for what I guessed was her age—seventeen or a little more—and she had great handfuls of dark brown hair that looked as pliant and strong as cable. In the midst her skin was a perfect white; and her eyes were bluer even than my mother's, so deep you thought they were purple or navy. Her lips were full and wide—wider still since she went on smiling.

Then Rita faced her. "Luna, say hey to one fine gentleman."

I couldn't think why Rita said that much. But it touched my heart—whether I was any sort of gentleman or not, she'd likely known few in her hard life. I'm always too susceptible to joy, and I was scared I'd pour out a tear there on the spot where the staff could see me. I was also scrambling back through memory, trying to know what kindness I'd done to Rita Bapp (I suddenly knew that was her maiden name).

Young Luna said "Hey—"

It hit me bullseye, square in my chest. I put out my hand and said "Luna what?"

The girl looked puzzled but Rita said "Tell him Absher—*Absher.* I'm a widow, Blue." Then she sailed right on. "This boy—Bluford

Calhoun—in this nice suit: he gave me an arrowhead the last day I saw him. Recall that, Blue?"

I suddenly did—the best belonging of my whole childhood, a spear-point big as a pullet egg that one of my uncles brought me from Mexico after he'd fought some banditos down there with the National Guard. I'd had it with me the day our class got final word that Rita was *out*; and when she looked my way that noon as she emptied her school desk forever, I wrapped the point in a sheet of lined paper and held it towards her. I couldn't think what on Earth I meant, but Rita Bapp reached out and took it last thing and *left*. Today I nodded and said to her bright eyes "Sure, I recall. I hope it helped."

Rita said "Oh more than you'll ever know. My son's got it now, or he will once he's out; and Blue, he needs all the help he can get."

I thought I'd read a few years back that Rita's son had gone to prison for something earnest like killing a highway patrolman or worse. Luna though—was she Rita's daughter or what? The girl's face and body were so much finer, I was trying hard not to meet her eyes. So I said to Rita "I know you're proud of this girl here."

Rita glanced at her, then back at me. "You truly think pride's called for here?" She seemed dead serious.

I said "Absolutely, you've outdone yourself."

Rita still didn't smile. She asked how many children I had.

"A daughter—just one child, age thirteen."

"Ain't they a heartbreak?" Rita said.

Luna said "*Mother*—" and looked to me.

So I said "Maybe I've had better luck."

Rita smiled. "You always had scads of luck." She took Luna's elbow. "Here, look at this man. I knew him back when he was bad off as me; and he's bettered himself—fine job, nice shoes." That was not strictly right, but I didn't stop her, and she looked my way. "You tell her, Blue. I've about give up."

I'd been a fair joker most of my life, and I tried to think of some funny advice. But while I waited my eyes caught Luna's again and held. From the day I was born, I'd also been a soul that loves women—

most everything about them, day and night—but for all my past adventures among them, I'll have to say I never felt so caught before. Not trapped but held. My whole body felt like a child a-borning, pushed helpless down a dim long tunnel towards strong new light.

Suddenly Luna said "Come on."

I barely heard her and I understood less. *Come where, for what?* Luna said "Please—" and Rita slapped her arm.

So I pulled my mind back into my body and said "Set eyes on your mark and run, girl—*run.*"

Rita nodded like I'd offered a blessing.

Luna tried not to smile; but those slant eyes—that looked out at you from a cool dark recess far in the woods, that deep at least—those eyes couldn't hide the powerful joy she took in watching me hang out there in the helpless air beyond her. She said "Yes sir, I'll run when I can." By now her eyes burned nearly too high.

I could see she was serious as any bonfire, but you can't say that to a near rank stranger as lovely as night. I was just guessing but I said "You were singing up front just now."

Luna didn't quite blush but something way inside her huddled, and her eyes nearly shut.

Rita said "Best voice you ever heard. Sing him a song."

Honest to God I thought to myself *Don't, girl, please don't. I'm doing so good in this new life.* If that was prayer it got a quick answer—*No no no.* At the time I didn't think who from—fate or worse— and I'm still not sure.

Luna gazed at the ceiling, her mouth came open, her chin rose slightly; and out rolled the first slow line of "Abide With Me"—

Abide with me; fast falls the evening tide.

It was nearly everything Rita promised. But I still had memories in those days of how my mother's voice had sounded when I was a boy across her lap in the white porch swing on summer nights with always a moon part-hid in the elms—

Moonlight shines tonight along the Wabash;
Through the fields there comes a breath of new mown hay—

and other such magic. Luna Absher ran my mother's voice a beautiful race and barely lost.

When she finished she looked down at me and said "Thank you, sir."

I couldn't think how I'd earned her thanks. But like a green fool, I said "You bet."

Before I could beg the girl's pardon for that, Rita stepped on past me. She said "I'm hoping you sell used Autoharps."

Autoharps were rare back then, in the piedmont anyhow—a strange combination of harp and guitar that lay on your lap or was propped upright against your chest. You mostly found them up in the mountains with blind old women that sang like fingernails scraping on slate. In younger hands they could sound like news from behind the moon, that keen and silvery. I looked to Luna and said "Oh yes—auto, steam driven, neon lit: harps in every shape and size."

Truth to tell, there was just one Autoharp; and it was new—inlaid with mother of pearl and jet—but when I brought it out from the storeroom and held it towards Luna, she accepted it calmly as her rightful due and took the hymn up where she'd left it—

The darkness deepens; Lord, with me abide.
When other helpers fail and comforts flee,
Help of the helpless, oh abide with me.

At the end to hide how deeply she'd touched me, I said "You get our best discount."

Rita said "We'd better or you lose a good sale. This girl is *headed* somewhere, let me tell you. She'll be so famous she'll send *you* business."

But when I quoted a price that truly was under cost, Rita said "Lord God—" and staggered a step.

Luna faced her mother, took a real pause and said "I earned every penny of this"—she didn't say how. Then she met my eyes, held right on them and—when I thought one of us would break—she finally smiled, though she wouldn't play the popular song she'd sung up front. She said "That would be sacrilegious now."

But still her eyes were close on mine, and I had to wonder where *sacred* began and stopped in her life.

The rest of the day, I felt fairly normal. Business picked up. By closing time I'd sold not just the Autoharp but a metronome and a spinet piano with a nice commission. So I didn't have much time in those hours to think about Rita's growing child. Still I'd been a salesman of one sort or other for many years, and faces and names are our life blood (nobody but criminals want to be strangers). Naturally that whole afternoon then, Luna Absher's face would drift up into view and wait, smiling or saying again how she thanked me.

And though I hadn't been able to coax her to play a popular song on the harp, I kept on hearing the actual sound of the one she sang— "Abide with me; fast falls the evening tide." I couldn't think of those last three words without the cold shakes in that hot day. For several years I'd understood what short lives most of my male kin got (most of them drank liquor hard as me). So sure, once I'd passed thirty five I felt every day the pull of an evening tide on my tired mind and my long legs that for nineteen months now had walked a neat circle.

I drove straight home at six o'clock. We'd lived for years in my parents' house where I grew up. When my father died, Mother pulled up stakes, went back out to the country place (her dead parents' home) and left the big brick house for us on Beechridge Road—crape myrtle bushes the size of trees in every yard, a lot of healthy mischievous kids with their comfortable parents. And as I turned into the drive that evening, there was Madelyn on her parked bicycle, talking in earnest to a loud boy from the next street down. By my strict standards he was more than a year too old for Matt—that saddle of bumps across his nose and the hair on his legs.

But he wasn't all dumb. However drawn he was to the scent, he gave me a quick wave and trotted off. (If this is getting too tame to read, bear with me a minute. I'm trying to lay out the day and night that changed my life and all lives near me from then till now—three full decades, no gentle stretch—and the clues to even a normal day are in the details, the nods and moans that most people miss, being blinder than any blind beggar with a dog.)

Anyhow I sat in the car a minute and watched my child. Since her mother's hair was a dark blond and mine nearly black, we'd never known how Matt came by her splendid chestnut ringlets. But her deep blue eyes were straight from my mother (it took me awhile to notice how their eyes all but equaled Luna's in darkness). And now she was thirteen, all the rest of Mattie was rushing to be a woman, too fast for me. She was poised so near the edge of that peak, it was scarey to see her—the peak or the pit, Heaven or Hell. Her body was that near ready to break on the visible world and start its full grown fun and work. Natural and *due* as it all was, it hurt me more by the week to watch her. She meant that much to my head and heart. I used to have two pictures of Mother in high girlhood, a local beauty. I'd study them in my own early years and try to picture my mind inside her, waiting for whatever life her body would choose to give me.

And lately as Matt was rushing on, I'd catch these glimpses of her alone and realize what a sizable thing I'd partly made and how many times I must have crushed her, what permanent sights she'd stored of me in my worst drinking and doping days (barbiturates) and how I'd never catch up now and pay her back with appropriate care. Hardest of all to face someway—she'd never blamed me and never given the trace of a hint of whatever mess she'd seen me do. I'd try to press my eyes through her mind and find the hurts I needed to ease; but once you have your own first child, you'll know how I failed.

Mattie was as loyal a Catholic as her mother. Of course I wasn't (native Catholics in the South back then were scarce as good sense and regarded as weird, if not suspicious)—and the main thing on her mind this April were the coming events at parochial school. She'd all but finished the seventh grade, and in a few days she'd wear a long white dress and veil and march up the aisle with other girls to crown the Virgin Mary with flowers. She'd only just got to the point of guessing that, while I'd go to church with her and her mother, I couldn't share her feelings on the subject—Christ and his mother and

poor St. Joseph, the old spare wheel, were as urgent for Matt as nourishment. More so at times but it got her through.

In all my desperate former days, I'd prayed to what most people
call God—the standard moody Santa Claus that does, or doesn't, love
the world. Every now and then I'd get some help that seemed like an
answer but nothing steady enough to win my long term worship or
endless thanks, not then at least, in that much trouble. But Madelyn
got more answered prayers than the average pope (she got me sober
for one main thing, or so she believed and I didn't doubt her). That
achievement marked her as thoroughly strange in my glad eyes—
grand but strange and almost spooky except when she laughed, which
was luckily often.

So as I sat behind the wheel that April evening, Matt stayed on her
bike and watched me seriously.

Finally I smiled, beckoned her near and turned my cheek out the
window towards her.

She rolled over slowly, gave me a rub with her own dry cheek, then
sat back to watch me another long while. I met her eyes and waited
her out till she finally said "May Day please—you'll be there won't
you?"

I nodded I would and thought I meant it.

She rolled in closer and leaned to my ear. In all her life I'd never
seen her whisper to her mother, but she made me the gift of numerous
secrets. Now she said "You think I'm truly worthy?"

I understood but I said "What of?"

She looked behind her—we were still safe alone. So she whispered
again "You know—this crowning."

I knew that the nuns had leaned hard on her for the past three
years—*pure, worthy* and even *spotless* were words with a white hot
meaning for Madelyn. But proud as I was of her looks, her brain and
her generous heart, I sometimes knew she was being tormented past
her years with the hopeless dream of spotlessness. So I spoke out
plainly. "They ought to be crowning *you*—you've won it."

She thought about it anyhow and looked again for signs of her mother. Then she shook her head like she watched a spreading stain inside that even I could never be shown.

Wild as I'd been for much of my life, I wanted to rush Matt into the car and flee west with her that minute for good. I'd wanted it more than once here lately. And now she looked so ready to save herself and me that I might well have said "Let's *go*" and vanished with her.

But Myra suddenly stood on the side porch, fanning her neck in the heat and smiling.

And what I saw that instant—plain as a flare at night—was Luna Absher, back of my eyes in the evening tide.

In those years TV still hadn't totally captured Raleigh. So after supper on a warm spring night, you had a whole different set of choices to make—old time choices and not so bad. You could visit the neighbors and talk on their porch, they could visit you (neither one of you phoned, just turned up raw). You could ride the family up to Five Points and eat hand dipped ice cream at the drugstore or sit in an air cooled movie theater, watching or dozing. If the heat was heavy, you could drive awhile longer out to the country and sit with your mother or just roll on through narrow roads and deep night shade with no sign of lights to warm you up, telling each other the news of the day, which was generally tame but occasionally funny.

On the night in question, the heat was letting up by eight; Mattie was upstairs doing her school work, and Myra's sewing machine was bearing down on the famous homemade May Day dress. I'd finished the newspaper, knew there was nothing worth hearing on the radio and really didn't feel like riding out as far as Mother's and answering every question she'd stored since my last visit. But I still felt normal— remember that. I didn't feel miserable, tired or trapped.

I knew I wasn't deprived of love, I wasn't roadhogged by sex as badly as in younger days, and I had no sign of the craving for numbness that ran my young years down the rathole of liquor and pills. At eight o'clock though, for no known reason, I hollered upstairs to Myra and Mattie that I was going to drive downtown and buy us some magazines at the newsstand run by the blind. If either one had asked to join me, I'd have calmly said Yes. But this one night they each requested their favorite magazine and said hurry back, be sweet—stale prayers.

Since you weren't here in the 1950s, I doubt you'll believe how good it felt to drive through the streets of a shut down city with your windows open and not once think of danger or death. To be sure in those days Raleigh was smallish—fifty thousand, give or take—but that was a lot of people then; and noon or midnight, the streets were safe. Worst thing you'd see was a harmless drunk, the black transvestites in long red wigs or an old white girl too eager to share the leavings of her native charms. Otherwise you moved through the darkest streets like somebody welcome on this Earth and urged to stay by people that had their own safe homes and clean warm beds. Even the free-roaming crazies, with dressed up cats in baby buggies, went home to their mothers at night or some other kin.

Nowdays for instance no blind person could hope to sit alone in a nighttime newsstand and not get held up, whipped or shot. But till far on down in the 1960s, every weekday night of the year, Miss Alma Nipper was there on duty in the midst of Raleigh by the old post office. Nothing less than a smile ever crossed her face as she heard you tell her what you'd selected, from *The Wall Street Journal* to the timid peep magazines of the time. She'd count your handful of change in an instant and say either "Thank you" or "Three cents more"— with paper money she trusted the public and still seemed to prosper. Unless you were blind too or otherwise afflicted, she'd leave you feeling lucky to have two working eyes and also much less nimble than she at walking life's various windswept tightropes.

That night as I browsed through the loaded racks, for some odd reason I picked up that day's *Raleigh Times*, the evening paper that wasn't worth reading and we never got. On the back of the single flimsy section, my eye caught a small headline down low—HIGH

SCHOOL GIRL WINS MUSIC SCHOLARSHIP. It said that Luna Absher, a junior at Broughton, had won a fifty dollar scholarship to music camp this coming June in the Blue Ridge mountains—it gave Rita's name, no father was mentioned, and then an address behind Peace College in a section of town that was starting downhill.

That caused it, that instant—plain as that, that sudden and reckless. Luna's face rose up again in my sight—clearer than even today in person—with body heat and a curling odor that reached my skin. And this time I didn't hear the sound of her song but the baffling thanks she'd mentioned more than once when I'd done nothing, good or bad, in her direction. I recited the names of my choices to Alma, and she shot back the cost plus tax. Then while she made change from my five dollars, she said "You're the dad to a lovely girl."

That was a shock and I must have balked.

Her smile slacked off and milky eyes rolled up in her head. She said "Am I badly mistaken?"

I said "Oh no" and thanked her sincerely before I wondered how she knew about Madelyn, or was she wrong for the first time yet? I said "I'm buying this *Photoplay* for her; she loves Hollywood."

Alma said "She's a starlet."

I suddenly thought Alma must be Catholic—you Catholics know each other better than howling Baptists—but my new mind was hurrying on. I said "Then we may see you May Day."

She looked confused—what was May Day please?

But whatever thing was hounding me had turned my body hard away with the strength of great hands. I wished Miss Alma pleasant dreams and trotted on.

Once I cranked the engine and aimed the wheels, the car took over and moved itself at legal speed through streets that were stranger than they'd ever been—to me anyhow, a native son. The shortest way would have been no more than a five minute drive, a long mile from where I'd parked to Rita's street (I kept thinking of it that way—*Rita's* house). But maybe the car went a roundabout way, or maybe some other hand entirely was holding me back in hopes I'd cool.

I seem to recall I passed the locked gates of Oakwood Cemetery where my father was buried long since on a knoll below the Civil War vets, both sides, gray and blue. The site was now in a Negro section way off any course I should have taken to get home or wherever else I was steered. And I even had a quick idea of climbing the iron fence and finding Dad's stone in the heavy dark, but I'm almost sure I barely slowed. I know I passed a lighted phone booth and thought *Call Myra and tell her you'll be back directly.*

Then the car turned into her street—Rita's street still (I didn't let myself think *Luna*). What was the number? My mind was blank; there were no street lights. Most of the houses were already dark and shut for sleep but on I went. The pavement was broken and, by the time I was almost down at the black dead end, I hit a pothole that shook me so I stopped and spoke out loud in the car—"What in the name of Christ are you after?" Though as I say, I was far from believing, I seldom used Christ's name in vain. It was not vain now; I was that concerned.

I even thought *Find a drink—anywhere, any kind. Back out of here, son, and steady your nerves.* The thought slid off me like harmless rain. By then my eyes had opened to the dark. And there in the midst of the narrow street, something made me switch off my lights. On the right twenty yards ahead was a dim gold shine. I fixed on that till suddenly down the length of my spine from some trapdoor in the quick of my brain fell a rush of desperation so hot I had no choice but to curb the car before I passed out. Slowly I got outside, then stood and tried to breathe.

The air by then was cooler still. So I propped there, leaning hard on the door and waiting to calm. It was maybe thirty seconds till I heard anything but the creak of my engine and a small bat hunting. Then in a space just a notch above dreaming, I heard what seemed like a slow set of chords—almost wind chimes, that high and pure, except there was not so much as a breeze. I knew. I knew who they came from and how they were made, and I dreaded the news. That pitiful light was on Rita's porch, and the music had to be coming from there.

I sat back sideways on the car seat with my feet outside, and I tried again to picture a drink. Young as I was, I was still the man who'd bribed the guard that oversaw me in the worst drunk tank of the State Hospital to buy me small cans of shoeshine wax. I'd set a can on the ward radiator; and when the wax melted, an eighth of an inch of alcohol would suddenly rise to boil away. I'd stand there eager as Judgment Day and suck that bitter blessed drug before it could vanish and leave me pounding my head on concrete one more time. In fifteen minutes from where I sat in my car now, I could find a bootlegger or a friendly druggist, buy me a pint or a few capsules and have my mind turned safely in on my sick soul before anything worse got a real grip.

Tonight though drink meant less than God, who was thoroughly gone. The same strong hand that drew me here was hauling me still (and I don't mean to claim I was forced—the hand was all but surely my soul, my own faulty mind). I stood back up and walked towards the light. Every step of the way, I told myself *Go home; you're grown. Your life's back on its own two rails and aimed for home. Go home, son—home.* And I tried but couldn't make myself say my wife's name or even my child's. Myra and Madelyn might have been dots on an old lost map that failed to guide me. My mouth was stuck half open in a smile.

They had a porch as wide as the house, which was two rooms wide with six steps up. Both front windows were open but dark. And all I could see from where I paused was some kind of motion on the dark right side, a swaying shadow and no more music. I tried to think out what I knew—no husband or father mentioned in the paper, I was almost sure the older son was still in the pen, this had to be Rita or Luna herself or maybe both. Or was I lost on some other planet this much like Hell? I tried not to grin.

Understand, I'd known several women in my youth—more than several and it's nothing I brag on, oh far from it. I'd fouled my marriage vows more than once in our early days when I was confused, and all Myra knew to do was watch with a bone white face and steady eyes. But I'd taken real pride in good behavior these last few years. I'd even half convinced myself that the storm-tossed Blue had come to rest in a peaceful port. But now all that seemed gone for good—and sweet good riddance. That April night it felt like the trip took at least an hour from my car door to the foot of the steps. And by the time I got in reach of the feeble light, I felt myself on the boundary line of a whole new country with a thick black ocean between me now and the home I'd left just to buy magazines. I said to myself *You're not gone yet. You're on the safe side.*

But Luna's voice said "I dreamed it was you."

It burned but not because it scared me. The time those five words hit my ears, I knew I'd waited all my days—and double my nights—for that one message from that one throat. I took a few steps and then I saw where she really was.

Far on the right she sat in a porch swing, hardly moving; and what looked like the Autoharp was up at her breast—it had been her music that brought me on. What dim light reached her showed just her face and the color she wore. This was long before phosphorescent dyes were used on clothes, but that spring night Luna Absher's clothes seemed live and pouring out rays—a deep vermilion.

I got somehow to the bottom step and said "I knew you had a good voice, but you never told me you were this fine."

She waited, pushing back on her heels till her face was dark. "*I'm* not fine," she said, "not a bit."

Like a child I pointed behind me towards town—the evening paper, the news on her. Then I said "Congratulations, Luna." I hadn't said her name till then, and it shocked my ears.

She was still far back in the shadows, past seeing. "They took several pictures; must not have come out."

"They spelled your name right." When she didn't seem to answer, I said "Where's your mother?" I thought I meant to congratulate her too.

"Gone to the doughnut shop, I bet. She says I won't talk to her enough. So she sits down there on her nights off, drinking coffee till they close up."

I said "Then tell her Blue's proud to know she's done this well. I understand how much she's paid—" I stopped, unsure of what Luna might know about older days.

She waited silent, then stood and walked towards the top of the steps. The light was behind her now; and her face was hid again, however badly I needed to see it.

But enough of her was lit at the edges, and now I could see she was neater dressed than she'd been in the store—a straight-cut linen dress, dark as I said, with the color bleeding out in the yellow light, swimming on the evening. She wore no stockings, her feet were bare, and the crown of her head was almost flaming. I had no idea what would come next.

Luna said "Doesn't everybody?"

She'd thoroughly lost me. I said "Beg your pardon?"

"*Pay*," she said. "You said Rita *paid*. But people in general pay for things, don't they?"

I was still no closer to understanding. I said "I don't often steal things, no. Not anymore." I thought of the bad days strewn behind me, and more words came of their own accord. "I've paid heart's blood—sure, child, I paid." I must not have heard my tongue say "child."

But Luna said "I'm sixteen now—sixteen and two months last Thursday night."

"Got your driver's license?" These idiot words were pouring out— surely Rita couldn't pay for a car.

And Luna knew better than to answer that. She slowly turned, went back to the swing and settled herself with the self respect of a practiced lady. Then she said "Nobody's here. You can stay if you want to—" It sounded as high and clean as her song in the public store (the afternoon seemed ten years back). And what she meant was surely politeness, *Rest yourself.*

There were no porch chairs though, and she was square in the midst of the swing, so she must have meant me to sit on the steps.

I climbed to the top and was halfway seated, ready to ask about her harp.

But then she said "You got *your* license?"

"Ma'm?" I was utterly lost by now.

"You're bound to be a legal driver."

I tried but couldn't hear a smile in her voice. I said "Best driver in the tri state area"—I didn't even know what states I meant.

"How about we cool down then on the open road?"

I actually went so far as to make one serious try at holding us back. I said "How about you play me a song?"

She seemed to take me up for a minute—she reached in the dark, found the harp, held it against her chest and strummed the same set of chords I'd heard from the car.

When she stopped I said "Come on—one song."

And with no more urging, she played a verse of "Beautiful Dreamer" perfectly.

All through, I waited for her voice to start; but she got to the end with just the harp.

I said "Near perfect but again now please—and *sing* it this time." I realized I'd issued an order like father to child, but I left it there.

And she started over but where the words would normally start, she stopped in midair and said "I'm stifling. Let's find me some air."

A half hour later we were parked on the far outskirts of town, eating ice cream at a dingy drive in. Since it was a weekend night, I'd driven that distance so we wouldn't see any kin or friends. And sure enough the lot was empty except for us and a carload of school boys younger than Luna. All we'd talked about on the ride were things we passed on the street and her music. In a lot of ways her questions and answers were simpler and even more innocent than Madelyn's. Music was so far all that brought out Luna's age and outlook, and even then she seemed not to know much or care about popular music, the truly dumb songs of those late '50s—Matt knew far more about them than Luna. Luna finally said "See, it's just my *dream*—music lasting all my life."

So I had to say "Where will this dream take you?" I meant the thing she'd called a dream as we left town—to sing elsewhere (she'd mentioned New York, Tampa and Hollywood).

She went on drinking her jumbo Coke, not facing me.

I'd finished my coffee and was watching the side of her face, maybe too hard and steady. It was that good a sight.

So still not looking, Luna put out a hand and said "Slow down"— no smile now; this was no place for jokes. She took a long bite; then said "It's no kind of dream, if you need to know. It's what will *happen* and no way to stop it." She looked as likely to fail as a bullet in dead straight flight.

I tried to respect her. "Then I'll know a star."

Apparently that was worth facing me for, even me (as old as her dad—wherever he was, above ground or under). Her face was solemn as Justice in a courtroom, and her voice went low. "Mr. Blue Calhoun, you *know* a star—no waiting required."

And then she began to dawn on me. I mean that literally. Up till then her voice, that strong dark hair, her eyes and her odor had fired the obvious parts of my body, the ones that lead most men astray— I'd used her that way once already in my mind, no fault of hers (and from here on out, at whatever age you read these lines, you're going to have to brace yourself—truth, as I mentioned, is all I'm after, that and your mercy). But now here well past nine o'clock on a warm spring night in the midst of an asphalt parking lot with garbage and dogs and teenage cacklers staring our way, I watched this gift rise up for me at a two foot distance across a car seat.

I had no idea what the gift was (beyond a body I ached to touch). And I sure God had no idea who sent it. But for then and a year of months ahead, I never doubted it was some kind of blessing. I had no notion of how it would change my life and family or who it would harm and how long it would last. I just knew this—one human being was *here* for *me*, the right one at last. She would do things for me, unheard of before (and that didn't only mean for my body). I'd help her more than anyone yet, past her best dreams. In no time now we'd be one new thing—body and soul—and God damn the doubters.

Through however long the process took, Luna sat very still, not quite watching me. Then she finally said "Homework now."

I must have looked stunned—it was Saturday night.

"I'm an honor roll student like the newspaper said."

I didn't know if she meant to stop me. But for fifteen seconds I thought I just might cool down to safety and drive us both our separate ways, polite and finished forevermore.

But she said "Mr. Blue, you know as much about music as you claim?"

She was still dead earnest but I had to laugh. "I don't recall I've claimed a thing."

Luna said "Hold your horses—the place you work, the way you showed off on this harp" (I'd strummed a few chords).

"I love it, sure. I'm a helpless fan."

"You're about as helpless as a Sherman tank" (the big tanks then).

I suddenly knew she was perfectly right. Never in all my days till now had every volt of my main strength—a strength I never knew I owned—stood up in me and howled its name. The thought of any promise I'd made outside this car was long since gone. What I needed to do first—and here I doubt I was that unusual for men my age—was find a dark back road right then and try this out, this brand new chance the world was giving. And Luna's eyes were still on me as flat as a doll's—no Yes or No. How much of this did she understand? My hand went out to the engine key, and I heard myself say "Home or what?"

"I told you," she said.

"Home?"

She waited what felt like a lonesome month. "If that's what you heard Luna say, sure—straight home, right now."

I almost thought the Luna I'd known these seven hours had vanished and left this mystery here, better than any question yet that I'd been asked. I started to say "*You* say right now—"

She stopped me fast, her hand on my mouth.

We'd never touched, her skin felt normal; but all these years on—
and all that pain—I can set myself in a quiet room, take two seconds
to bring her face up out of my mind, and there will be her feel again
on my dry lips—the strong smell of a clean child's skin that's run too
hard in the darkening yard but dreads to sleep.

I almost didn't know our house when I got near it. It was past ten
thirty; the upstairs was dark. And I went on beyond the drive and had
to back up. Till I cut the engine, I hadn't thought of a story to tell.
Maybe because of my worst years, Myra seldom pressed me for a list
of my actions (they might alarm her). But I might need some slight
explanation of where I'd been since eight o'clock. So I sat in the drive
and tried to think—names of my men friends at work, car trouble,
Mother. Nothing clicked. Forget it; fly home blind. I was that relieved,
that sure of myself.

She was in the den—Myra in her blue housecoat, sewing by hand
in too weak a light; and when she saw me, she halfway smiled.

At least I had the magazines. I set them down on the table beside
her and leaned to watch her patient fingers.

Finally she said "Pearls, just seed pearls—this is her veil."

At first I couldn't guess what she meant—*pearls, her, veil?* But
then I recalled and reached to touch the warm surface of one of
the seeds.

While my hand was still there, Myra took my fingers and pressed.
"Welcome back," she said. "It's still *tonight.*"

I understood—Myra used to beg me, drunk as I might get, to be
home safe in bed by midnight. And bad as I got, I seldom refused
her that much at least. Now I checked my watch and, not pretending,
whistled low at how late it was but said no more.

Myra said "Hungry?"

"Thank you, no. Is Mattie asleep?"

Myra's eyes had barely met me still. Looking down she said "Long
since. She sent you her love."

That sat me down on the piano stool across the room. "*Sent* me her
love?"

Myra faced me then. "That's the way Matt put it—'Send Sky my love.'"

Sky was the nickname Matt chose for me because I was *Blue*. I suddenly felt like a killer caught in crossed floodlights with blood on his lip. "Where's she think I'm going?"

Myra said "Search me" but then half smiled. "I guess there's something we better talk over—it's nagging me."

Myra had never caught me fresh-guilty. Any lie I told her about my body and its few betrayals never came to light till days or weeks later. Again I couldn't think of a decent way to hide. So I just said "Shoot."

"You saw her this evening with Talmadge Alphin?" She waited for me to nod that I heard her. "He's on Matt's mind pretty much all the time."

I waited for more but she went back to sewing. "That's all?—her *mind?*"

"Blue, I'm slaving on this white dress for our one child to wear in church; and dogs are already ganging our yard, dry humping each other."

If Myra had pulled out a roll of pictures of me and Luna dark on Ridge Road an hour ago, I couldn't have been any worse amazed. She was no big prude. And when we were starting life together, she'd sometimes say sweet things to my body. But I'd never heard such words as these on her lips before. The pressure inside my head zoomed down and I nearly laughed. "Myra, I'll grant you poor Tal's too loud; but I don't see him as a gang of rank dogs." I could see her blush but she didn't agree. So I said "Once Talmadge left her this evening, Matt came to me and made me swear to be on hand when she crowns that statue."

Myra looked up finally. "It's not just a statue. And what does that prove for her future life?"

I thought about it. "It proves Matt's aimed in a clean direction anyhow."

"She's thirteen years old; she could turn any way."

I couldn't believe this. Myra, for all her Catholic schooling, had never showed this brand of fear (and that was a time well before you needed to guard your children like cash in the road). I pointed towards what I always called the Magic Department—a corner cupboard where Myra and Madelyn kept their creepy Catholic magic. There were pictures of various groggy saints and a boneless Jesus, a statue of Mary broken three times and badly mended so her eyes were crossed. But the focal point was a "genuine" relic of some old priest the Mohawks butchered two centuries back. Myra and Matt were praying the pope would canonize him; and what they had, embedded in the midst of a plastic star, was a barely visible flake of bone that for all they knew belonged to a cat.

When I'd thought awhile I said "Miss Myra, welcome to Earth." I was trying to smile.

And she gave in. She almost laughed, then looked me over for a long slow minute. She lacked my mother's X ray eyes or maybe she knew to blind herself at certain times.

So I didn't cringe like a crook in a lineup. Truth was, I didn't even feel like the man that had gone with Luna. He'd hung back with her when she left the car, and her strong mind had somehow sent this imitation Blue Calhoun to stalk through life in his former home. I chuckled and said "I'm tired as man's first wheel at least."

Myra said "Me too," then finally laughed and corrected herself in a high class voice—"I also, sir."

Single file we climbed on up to sleep.

I confounded myself by sleeping deep with no known dreams, from the second my head touched the pillow till I woke at four thirty when Myra slid out quietly to pee. Right off I knew I'd satisfied my tiredness but would have to lie there two more hours or make a big scene by rising early. I also knew I shouldn't think of Luna, and I knew my reasons. It was Myra's bed, the room we'd shared since before Matt's birth. I didn't mean to bring in a stranger, even in thought. I might be back in my old bad life or launched on a new one, worse than any.

But the least I could do in my wife's presence was control my mind. I also didn't want to rouse myself and then make Myra play the part of a teenage girl, with musical gifts, to my stiff body.

But Myra stayed gone a good while; and my mind claimed the rope I'd given it all that evening. So I lay there on a pillowcase embroidered by a woman I owed my existence to (Myra had played the lion's share in hauling me back from self destruction), and I lived through every instant again of Luna Absher taking me in. A virgin woman that showed how near she was to childhood by all she did and said to please me—watching me every move of the way in near full dark, then asking politely if *that* was right or if *this* felt better, done this way? And when I finished, hadn't she said the strangest thing I'd ever heard at any such time—"I'm glad to oblige"?

Had she obliged me? God knew she *had*—to the dry hid sockets. But was it for life? And hadn't I broken in quick and bloody on too young a girl and marked her forever? Had I fed my soul one more mean drug, finer than liquor or any pill since, that I'd never quit? And whatever answers those questions had, hadn't I already swamped this house—this home we'd almost learned to balance—and drowned it deep? Weren't Myra and Madelyn already gone from me at least, past watching me, not to mention forgiving?

Then Myra was back, settling the covers lightly around us.

She plainly thought I was still asleep, but I knew her head leaned close over mine—I felt her clean breath. And something made me whisper one sentence. "I'm scared as hell."

Myra waited a long time before she leaned back to her own place. "I know you are."

"You can't know why." Lord, what was I after—piling fire on her kind head?

"You're lonesome again. I can feel it, strong." *Lonesome* was Myra's explanation for ninety percent of this world's woe, and these years later I don't contradict her.

Far as she went that night, she was right; and I dreaded now she'd reach to touch me. I was scared if she did, I'd board her and take my hot little piece, to calm my brain. And in my fouled up head, I thought that would hurt her even worse—coming to her that soon after Luna.

But she didn't reach out, though she didn't lie down. In a while she said "Oh Blue, you can do anything. You can *be* anything you want to be—you've got that strong in these last months. Why not be glad of what we've got?"

I'd understood since age maybe twelve that any man who's fed and warm and dry at night and lives near a woman that likes his presence is a miserable baby to cry for more. I wanted to say it out for Myra— "I'm thoroughly glad." But then I knew a worse thing still. There that instant awake in the night, I was gladder than I'd ever been in my life. A girl I wanted like clean sunlight had reached inside my chest just now, dark hours ago, and gripped the cold remains of my heart. I hoped I'd done the same for her. And I meant to keep that steadily happening all the rest of my and her days.

I've said how seldom Myra pressed me, but now she spoke in the night again. "Blue, listen, friend—just relax and *live*. We've got time now."

And then I knew she was dead on right—I was glad, there was time, but all because of this new reason I'd hid from her and would keep hid for good. So I actually reached to touch her shoulder, and I said "I'm glad. I'm truly glad. Now finish your rest." I thought I meant it as gently as if she was my child too, just taller than Matt. I was already crazy but calm as any saint they had in the Magic Department.

TWO

Madelyn's may day celebration fell on Saturday the 5th that year—perfect weather, balmy and dry. The store gave me the morning off to keep my promise and see my daughter crown a statue that she believed was holy and helpful. So we got downtown to Cathedral School well before time and even managed to park on the back street next to the convent. Since she woke at dawn, Matt had been truly fit to tie. I kept wanting to whisper to her "It's just a statue and we're just people." But Myra was nearby and anyhow I always tried to remind myself that they might be onto something bigger than I'd ever seen, even in my drunk visionary days (Matt had made me sit through *The Song of Bernadette* twice in the same week a few years back).

When she and her mother ducked into school to get Mattie dressed and practice the show, I made a quick choice. Within two hundred yards of my car were two tall churches—the Catholic cathedral and the First Presbyterian. I'd grown up in the Presbyterian, though I'd seldom been there lately but for funerals; and my natural thought was to take a short hike and wait over there in the clammy air conditioning. But then I thought *No, it's Madelyn's day. Sort your soul out on your own time* (not that I felt a trace of guilt that early on—to the contrary, I felt safe all over like somebody dressed in seamless armor). So I stepped into the hot dim cathedral and found a pew.

I'd been there numerous times before—my wedding of course,

Matt's christening, her first communion, assorted shindigs for the living and dead—and I've always granted that if there turns out to be one God, then you Catholics have almost surely cornered the market on how to deal with him, her or it (if I were God I'd sure as hell not spend Sunday mornings with the hardshelled Baptists, staunch Presbyterians or shouting Methodists, not to mention the licensed howlers, stompers and Episcopal bankers. In America still and for my whole life, it's Catholics who've always outright said the glaring truth, that the world is far more than halfway a game—mostly a midnight sports event—and magic's the only way to play it. *Don't ask questions; don't look left or right. Pull the damned string we tell you to pull. Likely as not, you'll pull down a rose, though sooner or later you'll pull down a pig iron statue of God on your paper thin skull. Then so much for you and both your dimples, though we promise to bury you in style with soothing tunes and sufficient smoke to cure your hide for durable wear*).

Those years, recall, were still the dark old glory days before the Vatican ruined everything they'd worked to keep for two thousand years and overnight turned their hideous new glass and toothpick churches into Rotary Clubs with excess pink fluorescent lights, busy glad-handers and prayers that sound like hemorrhoid commercials but work less well. In the late fifties though, the average Catholic (Matt and Myra were way past average) was still an amateur detective, hot on the trail of a dangerous mystery and rightly scared of one false step.

So when my eyes adjusted to the dim cathedral that morning, there were maybe fifty women in sight—all on their knees—and a man and boy beside the confessional with faces grim as if they'd melted a family of girls in sulfuric acid and come for pardon. I also knew—if that was the case and they truly asked—well, sweet Christ, they'd truly *get* pardon, God or not. Like most Protestants in those days, I was always scared I'd make a false move in a Catholic church and set off bells or raise up a demon gnashing his fangs—the same way you feel at high priced auctions.

Catholics' hands and heads, knees and legs, would make these curious nifty moves—crossing themselves, bowing at the sound of unexpected words, dipping their thumbs in holy water and scrubbing small crosses between their eyes. All of it came with their magic kit. And as I mentioned, far be it from me to say it was foolish. Hadn't Myra and Madelyn saved me almost singlehanded from decades more of a life so selfish I'd got crosseyed just watching myself? Wasn't Madelyn Calhoun a full satisfaction? So I did that morning what I always did—sat near the back on the aisle, set to run if panic hit me (which it hadn't since three months after my last drink)—and tried to make myself invisible but still keep watching.

The organ above me was noodling around in the bass department. Two nuns appeared up front in the flowers and made minute adjustments to the leaves that banked a pedestal in front of the altar. Everything plainly moved on plan. And since that April night with Luna, I'd wandered miles off any honorable plan for my life, I found my eyes beginning to sting. At first I fought it. Then I thought *All right, son—let it out. Let it pour if need be.* In fifteen seconds I was leaking tears and letting them fall. I could barely see. But I thought *Now pick a focus point and calm yourself.* I'd heard that technique recommended more than once from doctors, nurses, chaplains and cranks in my locked up days.

I picked the brass pedestal way down front, assuming they'd set the statue there any minute now. I tried to concentrate on the shape—four straight legs ending in lion feet and all of it polished bright as the day. I let that shine rush into my head, and I hoped somehow it would find the place where Luna Absher's feel and taste ate me away like battery acid—me wanting her now so hard my teeth had ached in the sockets through each long minute since I left her that first night and hadn't seen or talked to her since. I'd been to regular A.A. meetings and tried that hard to change my course. Each time I told them "I'm an alcoholic," I actually meant "I crave one girl more than drink or drugs" (don't let any expert try to tell you that sweet warm bodies are any less of a maddog craving than all the liquor east of the Rockies or mainline coke).

I wasn't praying. I used no names and I called on no power other than mine. But well before my eyes went dry, I could see my recent deeds and thoughts like they had happened in deep cold space. What in the name of all that mattered had I thought I was doing? Wasn't it all as sensible as stuffing my ass with dynamite sticks and lighting the fuse? Worse than that—I'd risked destroying everybody near me, Matt worst of all, not to mention young Luna and the parts of her I'd forced into bloom. In thirty more seconds, I thought *You're loose.* I meant I was free and it felt that fine. It felt everlasting. I wasn't inclined to fall to my knees on the plush bench there. But I did hear, over and over inside, the one word *Thanks.* I thought I was thanking myself for horse sense.

I'd thought for so long, I hadn't noticed the people start coming for the ceremony. When I looked up there were crowds around me. And soon I felt as lonesome as Myra had said I was. So I stood and aimed for the sunny door to find my family and come back in the normal way with a wife beside me. As I took the first steps, I felt tons lighter, though decades older—and both felt good. When I passed the holy water basin, without even looking to see what Catholics might be watching, I cupped a palmful, scrubbed both hands, then rubbed both palms across my eyes. I might have been way out of line in how I did it, but in my heart I felt dead right. I was ready now to watch the child, of which my body was half the cause, as she set a crown of live flowers on top of a statue she truly believed was a speaking likeness of the actual girl who mothered God.

Outside I paused on the steps to get my bearings in the sun. On my right by the school, children were lining up with the nuns. I looked but couldn't see Myra or Matt. On my left a huddle of altar boys were having their vestments arranged by a priest (young Father Scanlon, Matt's chief idol). It came to mind that my family had *run*, run off from me—they'd learned the truth about this past week and had finally vanished in thin air for good. Then I felt, if so, there was no way to blame them. I ought to just send them checks and best wishes and let them be. So I actually stood there with people swarming and thought through that like a realistic plan.

But then somebody touched my back and said "I made it."

I turned slowly and it was my mother, Ashlyn Hampton Calhoun herself in a spotless grass green linen suit and a broad white panama hat, set rakish. In general she showed the world her best side, but somehow today she'd done even better. If she'd just been a skim of water on the alkali flats, she couldn't have been more welcome to me. I said "Well, you did. Who on Earth drove you?"

"My able self." She was already smiling.

Cataracts were her main problem, but we never spoke of those in public. I chose her second worst ailment and said "Then your leg got well." Her right knee and ankle were subject to stiffness; and when they flared up, she wouldn't drive.

She gave a high laugh. "Not at all," she said. "They hurt like hell. I drove with my teeth."

I had to think *More truth than poetry*. Very few days of Miss Ashlyn's life had passed without her taking the bit in her fine teeth— her bit and everybody's around her—and streaking ahead on the track she picked, regardless of you. But I just told her how good she looked, the absolute truth. She was sixty one and her black hair now was entirely white, but her face was firm on its lovely bones, her eyes were clear and deep as mines, her shoulders straight, and she still looked very much like the thing I'd loved forever and always would.

She said "I guess Myra's dressing our star."

What was all this *star* business lately? I said "Yes ma'm. We'll save her a seat" and reached for Mother's arm to guide her. She balked and I looked.

Her eyes were set on the long line of children.

I followed her gaze and there was Madelyn, last of all with Myra beside her smoothing the veil. I thought the word *Luck* and kept on feeling it. Who had I known, in all my years of honest watching, as lucky as me? Who'd been given this so far endless string of chances to be a good man and count for something?

Matt's eyes found us and quickly looked down. This business here was way too earnest for grins or waves.

And in the next minute as I kept watching, Matt all but turned my mind around and sent me to my knees in the light (her hot fixed eyes right then *convinced* me the portable plaster statue of Mary beside her was an adequate picture of God's kind of woman, if he'd ever picked one).

My mother said "Can you really believe we had a hand in such a child?" She was smiling again.

I told her I could—I finally could. And I felt that genuinely worthwhile.

So Mother took my offered arm and we moved inside.

After the crowning and all the congratulations we got on Matt's good looks, her dignity and dress, I assumed I'd drive her and Myra home; then come back to work till closing time. But when Mother heard I had to work, she offered to take the girls to lunch, then drive them home. So I kissed the crown of Madelyn's head and thanked her for being what she was.

She took a step back—she was still in white—and met my eyes. "Someday will you tell me what that is, what I am to you?" I guessed she meant I'd told her similar things for years, and now she was old enough for details. But her face went solemn and she said "Now please."

At first I thought *She's found me out.* Then I thought it wasn't that strange from Matt; she'd run that deep from the time she could talk. So I grinned it off, winked, kissed Myra's cheek and told her again how fine the dress was.

Myra just said "Now I can cook you some decent meals—I've been so busy."

"It's way too hot to eat," I said. But I thanked her again and walked away, leaving the car beside the convent. The store was just a two block walk.

As usual nobody seemed to have missed me. Something about the air in the store—the cool gray light and the tall oak cabinets of music and violin strings and rosin kept most of us in a courteous daze, drifting among the untouched instruments. I'd drifted well past three o'clock and hadn't sold but one harmonica when Brantley, the organ salesman, came over and said "That old girl ever call you up?"

I laughed. "You'd better name the girl. There's too many calling." Then I felt like a jackass and said "No, who?"

"The one that bought the Autoharp."

Maybe it was just because he said *old*, but honestly I didn't think of Luna. And I stood awhile, still empty headed.

So Brantley said "The lady wrestler with the mad red face—Juanita something?"

Maybe I was still under some kind of spell from Madelyn's service and the heavy flowers. "Can't help you," I told him.

"*Rita*," he said. "Mrs. Rita somebody."

You couldn't have stunned and scared me more if you'd walked up with a bush axe and swiped off both my legs at the knee. *Old Rita—Christ. What does she know?* Brantley's face was blank so I had to say "Did she leave any word?"

"Just to tell you she'd asked."

"Asked what?"

He gripped my shoulder. "Easy, sport—she ain't the police."

"Was she by herself?"

"Well, you know old Rita looks like a *squad*."

"No daughter?" I said.

"Sorry, no—just the beauteous mother."

I told him she and I went to school together—he was ten years younger, so that shut him up. But through the shank of the afternoon, I fought my mind like me and a ten foot snake in a sack. *What could be up?* Had Luna told her and made Rita mad, was Rita after blood money now, was Luna hurt or had she run off, did they somehow know she was already pregnant?—*No way for that surely.* All week I'd kept myself from checking the phone directory—could they pay for a phone?—but as my May Day trance broke up, by five o'clock I'd gone to the stockroom and looked up *Absher*—not one in the book. At that I leaned on a new crate of metronomes. And all of Luna streamed up from my depths—the finest chance I'd come in sight of, somehow badly harmed by me and calling for help.

*

I trotted the last half block to the car and got there, sweaty with my tie undone. As I turned the key in the hot doorhandle, a priest came down the convent steps and looked straight at me—Father Scanlon, Madelyn's pet. He was also some years younger than me; and when he waved, grinned and headed towards me, I finally saw what Matt had mentioned—he was made out of ovals like a child's first drawing. An egg head with circular gold rimmed glasses, egg body, curved arms, short legs and straw colored hair cropped down to a stubble.

"Ah Mr. Calhoun, we owe you thanks." He was ten yards off and had stopped in his tracks, an odd space between us.

I thought I well knew what he meant, so I said "You people have done right by her. She's a joy on Earth." Again I heard my last words echo—A joy on Earth: *what can that mean now, bound where I am?*

The Father kept smiling. " 'We people' are just as proud as you." He seemed to be at the end of his point, though he stayed in place there grinning away.

For Matt's sake I covered the ground between us and offered my hand. It clearly surprised him but he gave me a small hand, tender as veal. I pointed to the car and said "I'm sorry—a friend of mine's sick. Come see us sometime."

The Father's Irish finally showed. "You *sher* you mean it? I've got horns, ya know, and a pointed tail—"

I suddenly thought of the holy water. And as I stepped on backward to leave, I held up both my callused hands. "I washed in your best-grade holy water, Father, today at noon. You don't scare me."

His face went slack and I thought I'd hurt him. But then he broke into schoolboy giggles, clapped his own palms—they *woofed* like pillows—and I was gone with a hard little thrill between my eyes, back of the bone, like a cold lead slug.

Milder air had drifted in. So when I'd rolled my window down and pulled away, I could take deep gulps of sweet dry air. The way to Rita's was also one of the ways towards home. And since the car was already aimed in Rita's direction, I told myself at the first stoplight

Roll on and take the signals that come. I'd long since sunk my teeth in believing that this new thing was managed past all human control. My notion of being swept along was not a fresh error, as I said before. I had let myself be carried down the length of my life, with few exceptions, by whatever river moved beneath me, whatever people manned my oars—family, doctors, women, the Law (I'd been arrested more than once for drunk driving, though back when drunks were let off light). And while I was past the midpoint flag of three score and ten, in my bad times I still suspected that all our lives were worked someway by iron invisible strings that we couldn't touch or change (it's a drunk's philosophy and saves on guilt). So what I watched for now in traffic was any clue to my next stop. No Indian brave ever searched the guts of a butchered doe any harder for help.

And what I found at the second light was a Michigan car with a license plate that showed—among others—the letter R. *Rita, Rita*—plain as my hand.

Rita was on her porch with a broom, sweeping down cobwebs as I pulled up. She saw me right off and came to the head of her steps to wait—I could literally see her blood pressure rise. But not till I was fully stopped and leaned to the window was I sure she knew me. Then her natural frown got deeper still. And for the first time, I had a flash that—whatever else had happened here—it was past me mending. Anything I'd torn was *torn*, and I'd never been much good at repair. I know I took five seconds to think *Haul ass out of here.* For once in my life, it made good sense.

But still not breaking her red frown or moving my way, Rita waved me in with a big slow arm like time's windmill.

I stopped in the dinky bone-dry yard, ten feet from her porch, and said "Good evening."

She looked it over, especially the sky, and said "Not yet."

"You waiting for something?"

She met my eyes. "Ain't you waiting, boy? Well, aren't we all? *Rain*—we're parching."

We'd been in a desperate drought for weeks—was that all she

meant? I gambled on it and said to the sky "Please rain for Rita." Then I walked to the steps.

She stood at the top for one more look dead on at my eyes. Then she took her strange little skip again—surprisingly graceful for so big a frame—and went to the swing.

This time I saw she'd added a chair, a low straight chair close by the swing.

She said "Bluford, sit down and hear me out." Her face was clearing, with no sign of anger.

But before I took the first step up, I asked her "Where is Luna now?"

"Sit yourself down. Luna won't hear me—she hasn't for years."

"But she's inside?"

"Luna's nowhere near this house and won't be till bedtime or later. She's *my* duty, Blue—nobody else's, not yet nohow."

I left it there for the time being, then climbed up and sat. If anybody recognized my car on this side street, I'd have an excuse—I met an old school friend downtown and gave her a ride home, warm as it was. When I turned to Rita, I tried to start us at some cool distance—"You and she live here by yourselves?"

Rita nodded hard like that cut deep.

"You mentioned your son—you're a widow too?"

It took her awhile but then she laughed once, a high outcry. "Widow?—child, I've buried *two*." And she laughed again but her eyes looked raw.

"Anybody I knew?"

"I hope not, *Lord*—the sorry fools, not six years of schooling between them. Neither one of them fit to tie good shoes, but didn't I bury them both in style?—Georgia pink marble with their names spelled right for once in their lives." Her forefinger seemed to write in the air. I could read several letters.

"Which was Luna's dad?"

Rita's eyes flashed off me and onto a fence beyond the street with honeysuckle already putting out leaves and the threat of its odor,

strong as a need. When she turned back, her eyes were set and her
mouth was hard. "I asked you to hear me out, about *me*."

"Yes ma'm. I've got exactly five minutes."

"That's more than I usually get from the world." Then she pressed
both broad palms hard on her thighs like that would press her meaning out. "You and I already mentioned the past—me kicked out of
school with my first baby. That was Marvin Ray's child, my pitiful
boy. Maybe you did know Marvin Ray. He was four grades ahead of
us—a stumpy sweet boy from out near Millbrook?"

I said I recalled him, though I wasn't sure.

"Once I told Marvin what him and me'd done—and we hadn't
done it all that many times—it scared him sick. But he married me,
for about ten minutes (we had to drive to South Carolina and lie in
spades about my age—thank God, I was tall). Then the bigger I got,
the farther across the room Marvin drifted till he just joined the
damned Coast Guard that, right off, steamed him to parts unknown.
Still his baby turned out to be Luther Ray—best behaved boy the
world ever saw till sex broke on him at age about twelve. It gouged a
great black hole in his head that he had to stuff with other people's
skin. So he ate up every girl he could find till the ground was bare
all under his feet. He'd burned up the *world*, of girls at least. No sane
girl would go anywhere near him, not to mention touching his lanky
body that was hot just to feel—even to my hand, combing his hair. So
he turned to stealing expensive *dead* stuff—silver trays, cars, whole sets
of dishes—till he accidentally killed an old man for one gold ring no
bigger than mine." Rita held up her left hand, a ring thin as wire.
"Not this one, understand. I bought this one honest."

"Bought your own wedding ring?" I was trying to smile and lighten
her up.

"My second husband made three monthly payments. I took it from
there."

"Would I have known him?"

Rita said "Not unless you've crawled on your gut through the
world's worst sewers. He was that low down in filth and meanness."

By then her eyes were burning again; she meant every word.

I noticed she still hadn't mentioned his name—the last name surely had to be Absher—but all I said was "I hope he didn't last."

Rita said "Thirteen endless months, till Luna came." Then she seemed to regret she'd said the girl's name. "The child was three weeks old to the day, and a born wailer, when he stepped into this same kitchen while I was frying country sausage and said 'Miss Rita, need anything from town?' I'd tried to like him right along—he grinned good as you—so I said 'Sure, one mended heart and a working brain. Then slice this pitiful body up and start me over.' I thought I was joking—I know I laughed—but all I can figure these long years later is, he took it wrong (he took a *lot* wrong). He strolled out the front door, whistling 'Ma-rie, the dawn is breaking'; and that was *it* till four years later when a man come by from the Coroner's Office and said my husband was dead and boxed, and did I have a grave? Well, I did—bought and paid for, Oakwood Cemetery near your dad. I planted him there and then—my Jesus—didn't three years pass; and here came Marvin, sweet Marvin of old, in a box from the Coast Guard with a covering letter from his commander saying Marvin expressed the deathbed wish to lie by me? So what I've got in the way of family—after all my struggle—is two dead husbands that barely stayed here long enough to part their hair, one son in the pen with vicious neighbors, and the girl you know."

I'd understood from the start of her tale what Rita meant—she'd hoed a hard row; I should step back now for good and spare her. And while I listened it seemed a wish I could easily grant. But what I said was "Where do you work?"

It set her back and her eyes prowled over my face again. "Anywhere a decent woman can work. I've done everything but peddle my monkey, if you take my meaning. Right now I'm nursing a broke down widow, rich as cream, on North Blount Street with stained glass windows. I stay with her all day and sometimes the night—mostly her son sleeps there, a mean drunk." Rita searched me again. "Why—you got some good job to offer?"

It had been just a question, no special reason. I laughed. "No, I was just curious." Then I suddenly noticed tears in her eyes and streaks down her face. You know by now I've caused strict havoc in several lives—and before I quit you'll know even worse—but I need to say I can't face tears: I can't or won't. Some of my farthest runs have been set off by nothing but tears—my mother's, Myra's, even young Mattie's, I'm sad to say. Anybody trying to hold me with *water* is far more likely to drown themselves. So I got up slowly and said to Rita "I wish you the very best on Earth." In those days I kept my cash in a money clip; so I reached in my pocket and took off the top bill—a five or ten— and held it out to Rita, folded. It didn't cross my mind to think I was paying for my one use of Luna. I thought I was making a good will effort towards easing their path.

Rita's eyes looked down but her hands stayed put, and again she looked me hard in the eye. "I'd rather you beat me."

I showed I was baffled.

And Rita seemed almost ready to break, to smile and be my old friend again. Then her upper lip stretched tight, and it took her awhile. "Blue, ask me to eat dog shit off the street; but don't go begging to rent my child." Her cheeks were still wet.

So I went down the steps. But by the time I got to the bottom, my inner mind could see Luna's dark face trying to find my face in the car that splendid night a week ago. Anything else, on Earth or under it, seemed worth risking to own those eyes, even one more time. I looked up to Rita then—"What if I love her?"

Quick as it hit her, she seemed to give the question a chance. But then she rose and came to the steps. "You don't. You can't. No way on Earth you can truly love a girl that's young enough to be your kid, with a white trash daddy behind her brain that tore her *down*."

"You said he left when she was three weeks old—"

Rita gave herself a long wait, then shook her head like I wasn't worth a second story. Her big right arm rose and waved me off. "Go home and wipe this slate *clean*, Blue."

"Then what did you come to the store to say?"

"It's already said. Nothing's left but to shoot you." No trace of a smile.

I understood she thought she meant it. With jailbird Luther for an only son, Rita likely had a gun or two on her bedside table. All my life I'd shown profound respect for guns; so I thanked her now and—with my mind still watching Luna, just Luna by night—I cranked the car and turned it slowly. Before I even stopped at the corner, I knew I couldn't go home, not yet. And for the first time, I thought *Maybe never.*

I drove down Peace Street till I saw a phone by Economy Cleaners. I put my nickel in and told Matt a lie—she answered, one ring. First I told her the truth again (how fine she'd looked in church that morning), but then I said that Mother had called and asked me to drop by, so I might not be home till late and please tell Myra.

Mattie heard me out but just as I was ready to quit, she said "I need to talk to you."

"All right. I may well see you by bedtime." When she didn't speak I said "You'll live till bedtime, won't you?"

She finally said "I'll try but—"

For a flash I thought she knew too much—Luna had told some girl who'd told another girl and so on to Mattie. But then I knew how thoroughly private Matt's school was from the public schools. That got me off the hook for now, so I calmed Matt down and made my next move.

I drove a wide circle back through town and parked on a side street overlooking Rita's. I was close enough to watch her porch but far enough off to hide from her eyes. The plan of course was to wait for Luna if she passed my way and catch her before she went indoors. As I crouched in the seat, I gave myself a self respecting deadline. *It's quarter to six. If you don't get her by quarter past, then that's your sign that Rita's right.*

You already know how thirty minutes can feel like a week. It felt like a month that May evening. I sat there with my windows down but the radio off, and I found one point—an old political poster on a light pole at Rita's corner. I saw right away that it was nailed at Luna's height. I'd focus on it and if she broke across my view, I'd finally know

I was right—*Go take her*. But in that much time, nothing passed but a pack of street dogs, the normal cars and a doughnut truck from the shop nearby where Rita parked her pitiful hulk and waited at night.

When all but three minutes finally passed, I asked out loud "Blue, what are you *after*?" And one more time all I could think was *Feeling the way you felt with her that one short night and making it last as long as you can.* (These next pages may well be harder for you to read than for me to write, and that's very hard. I've thought a long time but see no way to leave them out and still tell you the truth you'll eventually need to know about me and your family's life in the world. So if you're trying to read them now at your young age, they'll almost surely be as strange and awful to you as words in *Bat*—or whatever language black bats speak inside their brains when they hang themselves head down in caves and relive their nights.)

Whether my hopes were good for Luna too or my own family, or whatever decent spirits might watch me—the thought of others came nowhere near me, not my fixed mind, not then at least. I was that drunk now on the hot hope to touch her and that sick to see my clock run down and Luna not come. But some last scrap of dignity made me keep my deadline down to the second. At six fifteen I rolled to the corner, turned the car away from my home and passed through a block of deep oak shade. I'd make good on my lie to Mattie and sit with Mother awhile in the cool.

I've said that Mother had moved from Raleigh to her home place some four miles east in open country. Before her own dad could plan to marry, he built the two story long frame house with the help of three old former slaves "and two blind mules." He let the plaster walls dry out through one hard winter of low banked fires. Then he proposed to his childhood sweetheart, a fine eyed girl with a lovely voice who died the day I turned eleven, Christmas eve 1931. The young couple moved in, first day of spring. My mother came a quick ten months later and spent her whole first twenty three years in the south bedroom with floor length windows on three sides. Just when everybody thought she'd be an old maid, my dad passed by, a traveling

photographer with roots in Raleigh. He couldn't persuade her to sit
for a portrait till he showed her, over the course of six weeks, how he
could recite all Shakespeare's sonnets by heart to perfection. Just give
him a subject—love or sorrow—and off he'd go: "Shall I compare thee
to a summer's day?"

Mother took his hand "to shut him up," they moved to Raleigh, I
and my sister came in time, though she died at five of encephalitis
(the sleeping sickness of those bad days before strong drugs). They
built the house I lived in now on the west edge of town in a green
suburb, and Dad did well as a portrait photographer with his own
studio on St. Mary's Street—those airy old time portraits where nobody came out blemished or poor. What I watched them have for
years together was something approaching an ideal marriage till Dad
walked in through the kitchen door one winter evening, said "Glory
be" and pitched down dead, half smiling still with a handful of proofs
of your own mother's portrait he'd taken that very week—Matt's
seventh birthday.

The night of the funeral, Mother drew me aside and said "You
take this house now, Blue. I'm going home." I told her we were doing
all right in our duplex there on Glenwood Avenue. She said "You're
lying" and off she went, not ten days later, with barely a suitcase full
of what she chose to save from her former life.

By the time I got to her this May evening, it was on towards seven.
Dusk was even starting to rise from the bottom slope of her quarter
mile yard, but I could see her out on the porch in the wicker rocker
she'd loved all her life—dark green with a green canvas cushion. Her
eyes were on my car as I turned, her head was still and her hands were
empty—she claimed she never read outdoors or worked with her
hands in the open air ("Too much else to watch—I might miss a
trick"). Lately I wondered how far she could see.

Her eyes were showing a haze from the cataracts I already mentioned. But when I'd asked about them twice in recent weeks, she'd
said "Son, mind your own outlook please. I'll tell you when I need

your arm—and pray I don't." Every time I urged her to see the eye doctor before her normal six monthly date, she'd say "My darling, leave this to me. If I have cataracts at all, they've got to 'ripen,' as my pa said. You can't just slice in a live eyeball till the lens has gone completely milky. Then you see where to cut. So 'Ripeness is all,' as Shakespeare says—in eyes as in all else on Earth."

Lately she'd even turned to me—on the porch, full dark, a month ago—and said "I mentioned ripeness to you. Old Blue, you're ripening handsomely, aren't you?" We hadn't said a word in maybe three minutes, so I couldn't guess what set her off. But I understood she meant my life, not drinking or doping for so many months and trying to start my reparations. We two were alone—the only way we could be together and not cause envy in other eyes—so I said "Mother, I hope you're right. I feel nearly grown." I shot her a smile as if to say I'd been grown for years; we knew I was lying.

Who knew then whether she'd seen my car as it parked by the well or whether my face was reaching her before I changed my voice and said "Miss Ashlyn, that man up the road said you might buy a white leather Bible illustrated with Jesus in colors and big black print. I'm a poor afflicted boy selling Scripture to pay my way—" (Like my dad I called her Miss Ashlyn as often as not).

"Where you headed?" she said.

"Beg your pardon?"

"You claimed you were paying your way—where to?"

"Heaven, I hope, ma'm—but not too soon. Man up the road said you might *need* one, being so set in your habits and all."

She said "My darling, come take my hand. I'm too blind to meet you even halfway."

At that my throat nearly shut down on me. She'd never before come anywhere near that grim admission of helplessness. So I said "Ma'm, man up the road says you drove to Raleigh this morning, *today* like you had good sense."

"I did," she said. "I did and I do. I can see in the day. You've come too late."

I knew I was licked. I cleared my throat and went on towards her to take her hand and kiss the palm. She'd known right along but just the same I said "It's Blue."

She held on to me. "It always was."

I sat in a cane bottom rocker beside her. Then I thought that through—*It always was.* I said "You've known me way more than half of your sweet life and all of mine."

She still hadn't faced me but looked straight out to the empty road. "Don't undersell yourself, old Blue. You were in my mind when I was a girl and my dry body was flat as a dime."

"Before you knew Dad?"

"Whole geological *ages* before. Girls in my day had good sense."

"You were better than good."

She faced me at last and gave a quick wink. "Glad you noticed it— few men have."

"Dad knew it. You painted rings around him."

"I loved him though." I'd never heard her say it, though I'd always wondered.

Remember I'm speaking of years ago, the later 1950s now, when men hadn't even begun to think such things about women; so I don't know where I got the next question. "Didn't you feel too good for us? God knows you were."

She gave it some thought. "Not too good, no—too different maybe. I had this notion from about age five that I was meant somehow for music." She faced me again. "A life in music." Then her blue eyes smiled.

I'd heard her play most days of my childhood, the old piano in the musty parlor. There'd be songs from her girlhood, occasional hymns, simple pieces mostly by Schubert and—strangely—scales. I've heard her just play scales for long minutes when she thought she was all alone in the house. But this declared ambition was new; and because Mother always held my attention, I hadn't yet thought of Luna's dream and how the two matched. "You saw yourself at center stage in Carnegie Hall? Or some smoky dive and you in ruffles, cranking out tunes for beer and pickles?"

She said a cool "No. It was stranger than that. And a good deal better."

Long ago when we'd sit here with me as a child, I'd see Miss Ashlyn drawing lines on her narrow lap with just a finger. At times I'd think she was writing words, and I'd ask what was on her mind. She'd laugh and say "Sawdust!—for all you know." I hadn't remembered that for years, hadn't noticed it happening lately either. But here tonight she was drawing again, not looking down.

Then she turned back towards me. "When I was a girl—oh up till I was maybe fifteen—I could hear what they call the music of the spheres."

Till then I doubt I'd heard the phrase. "Who's *they*, please ma'm?"

"Poets, you know, in ancient times. Only the pure in heart can hear it. So there for a while it seems your mother was pure in heart—ain't that a relief? No, swear to God—when summer came in my early years, I could run down this same yard to the road and cross on over into woods that were thicker then than now. And on some rare dry thrilling days, I'd hear this music high in the trees like Heaven sifting down on me. There were no words ever, just slow enormous perfect chords—I was no Joan of Arc; I was given no definite mission to serve. But I understood that the music itself was sent my way. I told myself I was meant to learn to pass this on to the needy world the best I could. And the only means I saw for that was to learn some way to play in public, some instrument that could imitate chords. I went on and took piano for years; I even got to where I could strike enormous chords of my own, nearly right. But you know how I let that slip out of my reach once you were born." She waited, then grinned and lowered her head. "I'm a misspent arrow that failed of its mark."

I said "Maybe not. Think of it this way—look where I work. I'm responsible for sending music through the world every day of my life—the stuff I sell."

By now the dusk was closing in fast. But when Mother faced me I saw the frown. "Oh no, my darling. I mean something else."

All her life she'd always meant a great deal more than Dad or I could understand with the minds we had at the time at least. And all my life I'd felt that burden of never quite giving her what she needed. More than half of all I tried to hand her when I was a boy and then a man, it also just fell a yard or two short and struck her feet—it almost never reached her hands. Not that she was so hard to please—she'd laugh a dozen times a day in ways that made you feel supreme on Earth. But you mostly got the feeling she lived elsewhere and had strayed in here and stayed too long, which must have been why I loved her so deep and still did now.

We were quiet awhile, she watched whatever she saw of the road like some entirely unexpected happiness would come round the curve, I just watched her. And in no time I was back in boyhood watching her here in this same space when we would visit out here in the summer; and she'd step out after supper dishes and sit a little nearer to me than my poor sister or even Dad, and she still in her dark best dress that very nearly matched her hair and the night around us.

She'd watch this narrow piece of the world—or whatever bigger world she saw and the music she heard—and I would lay all the love I had against the side of that one face and beg the sky to let me die before she did, so I didn't lose her. And to this day I'd never grown past feeling like a privileged child to be this near her. I was well on into my later teens, and starting to drink the landscape dry, before I thoroughly understood that my young mother would never be mine in any one of the thousand ways I longed to know her.

And this May night 1956, I more than halfway felt it again. In fact here lately the world was teaching me an old slow truth—anything you ever feel in your life, really *feel* in your sockets, will never leave you (which is one more reason to watch what you feel). Like learning to swim or roller skate, once you've truly learned to care about something, you'll cherish it on to the grave—maybe farther. And I realized on this same porch that even now, so far in life, I'd never told my mother what she'd meant to my heart and mind. So with raw adultery and deceitful lies festering in my heart, I reached and touched the back of her hand with one light finger.

She looked up smiling like all these years had never been—near four decades since she and I had been one peaceful thing in one body.

I said "You deserve a lot more than this."

"What's *this?*" she said.

"Waiting out here alone this way, your eyes going dim, nobody but me—and me the pitiful fool I've been."

Miss Ashlyn took a long pause to study me—was I drunk or cracked? Then she smiled again. "I wasn't aware I was waiting for something. I've had most everything I planned and a lot I didn't. What I've got for my late age is a normal life, old Blue—Lord, it's more. It's precious *luck*. And you're much less than pitiful now. You're very nearly what my pa called 'value for money.' I like to see you."

"You can't really see—"

Her smile was lasting but she said "Don't blame me for cloudy eyes."

I touched her again, then felt I had no right to that. "Mother, I've slewed way off the road."

"You're sober tonight—I'll swear an oath."

"Yes ma'm, cold sober. It's worse than drunk."

"Nothing on Earth is worse than drunk unless it's tearing innocent children limb from limb."

"I may yet do that. I may have already."

She said "Not Mattie. Matt was happy this morning."

That burned me almost harder than the sight of Luna which rose up now in this old place she'd never touched. When I'd clamped my eyes to clear them, I said "Matt doesn't know yet."

"Does Myra?"

"Not really. She sees I'm *off*."

Miss Ashlyn still looked straight ahead at the night. "It's a woman?"

"A girl."

"Is she pregnant?"

I said a hot "No," then realized we'd never talked this way—liquor, jobs and money, yes; but never like this with both gloves off, just the bare white bone. So how much further should I go, here and now? *What help can your half blind mother be when a middle aged man has failed himself, and everybody round him is likewise helpless to break his course?* I valued Ashlyn Calhoun enough, and I hurt enough, to tell her the truth like I saw it at least. "You remember Rita Bapp, a girl in grade school with me back when?"

"Big Rita that was pregnant and got expelled? Tall flat-faced girl with beautiful hair?"

I didn't remember the beautiful hair, but I said "That's her. And that first baby's a man in prison for killing somebody."

"Anybody named Bapp might well bear watching" (Mother always called the Baptists "Baps" and had told outlandish tales about them to tease my dad, an earnest member).

I said "No, the boy's last name is Ray. And poor Rita's an Absher now—so's her next child, a girl named Luna."

Mother said "Luna—that's a long lost name, haven't heard it for years. You remember Miss Luna Pittman? Turned wild at the end and called her preacher a son of a bitch at the church door on Easter morning. They hauled her off unfortunately, and none of us ever saw her again—I miss her still."

This was our normal way to talk, a looping road with plenty of time to stop and stare. Now I needed to push ahead, but all I could think to say flew out. "Luna may be somebody I want for life."

Mother waited a moment. "You can't have her though."

"I've had her, Miss Ashlyn, once already."

"Son, you can have any number of creatures. Hard as you tried to ruin your face, you're a strong light still; and the moths *flock* to you."

"This is different," I said.

"It always is." But then she put a hand out towards me, not for me to take but with her palm outward to mean *You wait*. Then in the full dark, I saw the line of her head turn my way. "Darling, I've got ten words to say—Myra's been broken and mended over till she's strong as me. Myra will last. It's Madelyn Calhoun that's on your back. Matt's yours to carry for some years yet." Again Mother waited. "That was more than ten words. But each one's true in letters of flame." She stood upright in place, no warning. Then she wavered slightly and put both hands on the railing before her.

I stood and moved close. "You feeling bad?"

Her head shook hard. "That's it," she said. "I don't feel a thing.

You've told me something utterly tragic—or soon to be—and all I'm thinking is, how's that lemon pie I left on the table to cool?"

I knew she felt as awful as she should, but I knew she'd rather eat glass than show it. "You made yourself a whole lemon pie?"

"You said I deserved it—"

I suddenly also knew I was starving—not a bite since breakfast. "You do, all of it. But spare me a slice?"

She waited and then declined to speak, but her left hand hooked my right elbow, and I led her in.

We both got through wide slices of pie and cup after cup of powerful coffee, but all we mentioned were trifling things. The main subject was the big block of salt she meant me to buy and put out back to draw the deer closer (everything Mother planted got nibbled by deer, which was fine by her—she loved the deer better). But just the peaceful muttering between us was nearly enough to soothe me down to where I might stand up, slap myself in the face and head back into a decent life.

Then finally Mother reached for my hands. She spread both of them palm up on the table and studied my skin. Mattie had run through a palm reading phase some months back, but Mother had never trucked with such stuff. Still I let her look just to know what she meant. After a while though—with her fingers naming various lines of my "Fate and Future"—she simply quit and stepped to the sink with both our plates.

"Is it truly that awful?" When she looked unsure I said "My hand?"

She nodded Yes firmly and then said "Hopeless."

As a staunch but merciful Presbyterian, she believed in predestination of course, far more than me with my drunk's reliance on an alibi-fate. But she'd never turned her belief on me this strictly before, and it slowed me some—I still leaned on her that hard for hope. Then I must have looked back at my hands.

"Not there," she said. She tapped her skull. "Your mind's still wild, still trapped in your *self*. You never have learned to deal with the humans."

"Hell, Mother, what am *I*?"

She searched my face like she'd never seen it. Then she came back slowly and sat at the table. "When you were just born, I was too scared of you. I thought I'd break you—had terrible dreams where I'd touch you and a bruise would slowly take your whole body. Or I'd pick you up gently and snap your neck. But old Jett Bass, that worked here with me, finally said 'Miss Ashlyn, truth of it is—this Bluford here ain't nothing but a mouth and a belly beneath it and one more hole at the dirty end. You feed him every time he cry; and he'll be fine, he'll grow more parts.' " Mother stopped and rubbed on a dent in the table.

"You saying I never grew more parts?"

She faced me again. "Not a full set, no."

"Does anybody?"

She knew right off. "Oh surely yes. Your father, my Aunt Clement, your excellent wife."

"But I'm still a mouth?"

"Or a belly," she said. She tapped her skull again, harder still. "I'm all *mind*, Blue. I'm turning, fast, into nothing but thoughts—old women do that."

I had to smile. "For a mind, you made quick work of that pie."

But she was past joking. "How old is the girl?"

My own mind gave me a strong order—*Leave*. But I stayed to give my mother her due. I said "Sixteen and some few months."

"Then she's truly a child."

"Your own mother married at sixteen, I know."

"She did but that was back when people grew up. No other choice. She had to tend to her two young brothers when her own mother died—she was just Mattie's age."

"Luna's full grown."

"And you're convinced that Luna needs you?"

"No, Mother, I'm not."

"Then what's this about? What's the worry here?"

"I told you. I want her. I want her for good."

Whatever Miss Ashlyn's eyes could see, they were calm as the air. "And will Luna have you?"

When I saw how, just this quick, my mother had reached to the heart of the thing and shook it hard, it chilled me deeply. I said "I don't know what Luna wants."

Mother's face stayed calm as a field commander's. "What's Rita think?"

"She's told me to quit."

"Why?"

It was such a strange *why?* that I nearly laughed, but I saw I was wrong—Miss Ashlyn actually wanted the facts. "Rita came by the store while we were at church and asked for me. So I went by her place after work; and she told me the tale of her life—two dead husbands, her boy in the pen, a girl sixteen with dangerous looks who's just won a scholarship to study at a music camp up near Boone."

"Then you *let* her." She drew a deep breath. "Blue, there's your out. Shut your mind tonight, go home and thank your Madelyn for all the good she's trying to give you—trying so hard it's aging her fast. Thank Myra for helping you through years of torture—yours and hers. Then let Rita's pitiful girl go sing to the rocks and rills forevermore, no help from you."

Of course it felt like a sane prescription—the one I'd tried to give myself more than once already—and I tried to see how much of it Mother could really mean, but she'd already shut her face on questions. So I said "You know that cannot be."

She'd cut the pie with her favorite knife, an ancient blackened eight inch blade. Now she took it up by the blade end and held it towards me.

"Ma'm?"

"Be kind." She was almost smiling as she shook the blade. "Finish me off quick and let me sleep."

I took the handle to spare her hand. But I said "You'll see *me* into the ground and plant the grass."

She waited, then nodded hard again. "I will. Oh Christ. You're punishing me."

I said "Miss Ashlyn, I'm not and you know it. This is not about you—"

But she bore down. "Bluford, you're giving your best imitation of scalding me; and it's working, son. You hurt my mind worse than any soul yet in all these years."

It was nothing but true so I just nodded.

It was past nine o'clock when I got back to town. You maybe can guess I was still affected by Mother's words. With all my meanness I'd respected her feelings more in my life than anybody else's barring my own. And my reason was bound up in her true bravery, not just living unscared alone through nights. No, ask her a question—a question that mattered—and if necessary she'd answer in words sufficient to strip the paint off a battleship. To be sure, she seldom reached me in my addled years, which was no fault of hers. By the time I was eighteen, and had that taste for sweet confusion burned deep in my tongue, nobody human could come between my hand and mouth and what they wanted. It was past my mother's understanding to come anywhere near reaching me then, though nobody else came nearer than she.

The time we both laughed about so often in the good years since was one black dawn when I'd been drinking two weeks and was raving. Myra had left to stay with her mother who was sicker still, and the liquor stores were closed. So at four a.m. I went to Mother in desperation. Dad was asleep or was too smart to rise. But Mother stayed there and held my head while I retched up, time after time, the few little scraps I'd eaten all week. Then when she saw I couldn't stop and that blood was coming, she crept away and came back in with a pint of bourbon, still sealed and full. I was weeping hard—my life was saved—but my hands were jerky, so I asked her to hold it while I sucked a drink. And she said "Oh darling, just smell the cork." Kind as she was, that was all she knew, all the help she could be.

Still as I said, her words were on me this May night, hard as a fist, when the town lights hit me. But I've never been a truly deep thinker, one that quietly plots a course or weighs two choices. I think I know where right and wrong live, most days at least. And I try to head their way when I can, weather permitting. But you well know how things come at you in the actual world—you're riding smoothly, a tire blows out, you swerve or wreck or hold it in the road. Or a wall goes up, and I try to dodge it.

Common and stingy and sad as it sounds, that's me—the literal way I've worked most days of my life. So I was holding no cards in my hand, no big resolutions. The most I thought was *I'm heading home from seeing my mother.* Then I saw a bright show of lights up the street; and wasn't it the doughnut shop, full blast? I didn't slow down and had almost gone too far to turn when I thought *If she's in there, tell her right now.* I thought I meant Rita—I'd ease her mind, and I pulled in to do it.

The place was empty of everybody but a spotty kid working the counter and a Negro man frying doughnuts behind him. I stayed in the door and looked again—empty tables and chairs. So I said to the kid "You seen Rita Absher in here tonight?"

He said "Who's that?"

But the Negro man turned. "Big heavyset white woman, eyes too close?"

"Sounds like her," I said.

"Not tonight, not yet. If you a betting man though, I bet you she be here before ten o'clock."

That news and the good smells made me recall that, even with Mother's lemon pie, I was short on food for such a long day. So I ordered coffee, three glazed doughnuts and sat as far back from the light as I could. While I waited I tested my mind again and rethought everything Mother had said. She was mostly dead right, but that was no news. Without ever trying to act know-it-all, Miss Ashlyn had hit more nails on the head than any ten builders. And it wasn't her perfect aim that hurt. From early boyhood I'd understood that she could give me ideal plans for every deed I was called to do.

But where she always failed me lay in the lonesome place all parents fail you—once she'd set my feet on what she thought was the track, she couldn't walk with me to the goal she'd set, which was nothing but life—the sensible decent life she meant me to get and hold. Even as late as age nineteen when I flunked out of college and came home awhile, I remember feeling two opposite things, both as urgent as live steam—*Why in God's name can't she just let me breathe on my own?* and *Look at her cut these last lines to me and shove me off.* Still what the hell?—I was way past grown. I knew the rules of the road and could drive; I could get odd jobs at any crossroad, long as my mind continued to roam. Miss Ashlyn was something to watch and respect as time weighed on her.

I'd already finished the three doughnuts. I'd finish the coffee, harsh as it was, and head on home—Rita or no. And I had the last bitter slug in my mouth when the door pushed open.

A boy walked in, an outright hood with a duck's ass haircut and a face as lean and cold as an ax. He stopped on the doorsill and looked around—nobody he knew—so he turned back outside and gave a big scooping wave with his hand.

You already know it was Luna behind him. She must have been lurking in hopes her mother wasn't inside. And when she came on into the glare, her eyes nearly closed. She hugged her bare arms tight to her chest and shivered once in the cooler air before she sat beside the boy in the booth he picked (their backs were to me, hid by the seat).

In those few steps before she vanished, I saw the grass green blouse that made her hair and eyes look strong and rank like parts of nature. I saw her pale skin burning high on her broad cheekbones; and to this day I can safely swear her odor rushed towards me, sharp and magic. But I knew she hadn't looked my way, and neither had the hood. I was truly as clear as I needed to be—I'd already seen the fire door behind me. The way I felt in the first half minute—swamped like a tidal wave had passed and snapped my spine—I thought *Son, get your hulk out of here.* And I pushed my chair back silently to stand.

But then the kid at the counter spoke out to ask if I could use more coffee. He was bound towards Luna's booth with menus.

I shook my head No.

But Luna's head rose up from the seat and turned my way. For an instant her face snagged on mine—she had to know me—but she gave no clue, her look never changed and slowly she swept the rest of the room with those dark eyes, and then she sat back against the trainee felon.

I might as well have been on the rack. The room and everything in it felt like one drastic bruise, that ugly and tender. I sat there telling myself again that I was grown—a responsible man with a paid for home, dependent kin and a useful job that brought people pleasure. I even heard my mind reciting a poem I'd learned in the tenth damned grade and won a prize for—

> *Look in my face; my name is Might-have-been;*
> *I am also called No-more, Too-late, Farewell.*

It was one that used to come to me daily in the various drunk tanks, plush or desperate, that I frequented. Tonight I guess I was bucking myself up for what came next—creeping out that fire escape like a cold kidnaper or some war victim with a melted face.

It didn't work. I couldn't make myself accept such pitiful pay for all the care I'd spent today in healing myself. I took my check, stood up and walked past Luna's booth. As I got to the counter, the kid was humming a popular song I knew but couldn't name. So when it took what felt like an hour to pay my forty two cents and leave, I kept on dreading that Luna herself would take up the tune and put it to words.

But no, the hood broke out in a laugh that she didn't follow, though she watched him close.

And I was out in the night again, thinking at last I was aimed on home.

But in the time it took to walk from the door to my car, this smothering cloud fell over me. It felt as real as poisoned gas, though I knew straight off it was just my mind—my mind or whatever outside hand had seized my throat. I balked in place with my back to the shop. And I could hear as plain as if I screamed it out, *You cannot leave here without Luna. Claim her.* Claim her?—Christ, she was no way mine. What could I do with a girl this young that had no better self respect than to put her body and all her gifts in the miserable hands of this small a creep?

But then I thought *Make her see you though. Make her nod she knows you.* And for no saner reason than that, I turned and walked towards the left side window, right where she sat watching the hood. At first I stopped a yard away, and my mind tried to make her look. They were watching each other too close for that. So I came on farther till my feet knocked the wall itself, and my right hand went up and rapped once hard on the glass.

The hood was still involved in her face. But I knew Luna heard me—she had to be waiting. And didn't she wait a long two seconds, then roll round slow as a glacier rolls and meet my eyes straight on, first try? She didn't frown. God knew she didn't smile. Her face was blank like she saw nothing else but night and traffic. Then she turned on back to the boy. By then he'd poured a low hill of sugar on the table before him and was licking grains off his long wet finger.

I figured I'd die. My heart shut down. I couldn't find any air to breathe. And next my eyes were seeing nothing but sheets of light like nothing I'd seen since fire bomb flares way east of the Rhine. For nearly the first time since I passed it, I saw again in the front of my mind the strangest thing I saw in all my fighting days. We'd shelled a town on the west edge of Germany two whole days before we advanced, thinking the Nazis were dug in there. We crept in though to nothing but *quiet*—the deadest air I've ever breathed, no soul in sight.

And as I came round one last curve expecting fire, there stood a tall rock house beside me and what seemed like a dummy kitchen with three real looking human dolls in chairs at the table with bountiful food on every plate. Their heads were level with all eyes open. The man had a fork in his big left hand—he had a star tattooed on his thumb. The older woman was holding a black iron fork in the air with a slice of bacon. But nothing was ever that still before. It took me maybe half a minute to know they were corpses, not lifesize dolls. We'd blown a wall of their house away, sheared it quick and clean as a sickle. And that concussion had sucked the breath out of these six lungs and frozen three corpses bolt upright and natural as breakfast.

Bad off as I was in the parking lot, I actually thought *Let that kid at the counter see me and call for help.* But he was busy with his two new customers, and then my blood lurched on again and led me back alive to the car and in it and someway on to my home.

When I got to the drive, it was quarter past ten; and all the front of the house was dark—early for that, if they were home. I thought *I can't go in a dark house.* I didn't know what might wait for me there. But I still hurt so hard I had to make some move towards help. I turned in and edged my way to the back. There the kitchen lights were blazing, though I couldn't see any sign of life at the open windows. Well, I'd try to walk in. *But first I need a story to tell.* Like most of the humans born south of Baltimore, I was seldom without a story to meet the occasion. All I could think of now as I walked through the cool wet yard was Mother again upstairs in this house, telling my desperate mind to please just "smell the cork." *What else has anybody ever said to me but "Sniff at the lid, wait at the door, don't come in the room"? Christ, I want the room and all the goods, the whole nine yards.*

I climbed the back steps and paused at the screen. Plentiful light, no sound whatever. I could see the screen was loose, not locked; but I tapped anyhow with my knuckles softly. Still no sound and I stood there, not craning to see till it almost felt like a great dark beast was slowly coiling itself inside and waiting to strike at the sight of my eyes. I know I even turned to leave. But I heard bare footsteps moving my way.

And then it was Madelyn framed in the light with both hands spread out open on the screen. Her face was dim and she looked like somebody facing a gun, trying hard to surrender and live. I couldn't see her eyes, but what she said when she saw me was "Are you all right?" Her body was tense with serious worry, the way I'd seen too many times in my bad years.

I tried to grin but my lips were stuck on chalky teeth. So I said

"I've seldom been gladder, my love." Then I thought how true that was—true and awful.

"What happened?" she said.

My story fell in place on my tongue. It seemed appropriate anyhow. "*You* happened, dear child—so fine this morning."

She took a step back, and the light struck her face.

Then I knew that the words I'd used were actually true. This late, in shorts and a torn sweatshirt, Madelyn Calhoun looked like somebody fit to crown the statue of God himself in flames. I said "Where's your mother?"

Matt thumbed behind her. "Sitting right here."

"Can I still come in?"

Matt hung there quiet like she hadn't heard me.

But Myra called out. "He owns the place. He can go and come at his sweet will."

That wasn't the warmest greeting I'd got. Myra seldom used that brand of punishment. But since there was nowhere else to go; and since somehow I needed to see them, I climbed inside and hugged them both. Quiet as they were, they both seemed ready to take me back. And cold as it was, they'd been shelling and roasting peanuts; the air smelled good. Again I knew I hadn't eaten a sensible bite since eggs that morning, so I sat between them at the alcove table and helped them shell out pounds of peanuts, eating half of all I shelled. Myra wasn't skulking or edgy, but she and I said very little. Matt did the talking and she was wound up.

First we went through my trip to Mother's or a laundered version. Matt asked me a lot about Mother's eyes. She said when she got to the altar this morning, she could see Grandmother seated by me and that both of her eyes looked milky at a distance.

I explained how the cataracts still had to ripen. And then I could see Matt thinking her way through the subject of eyes—she rubbed at her own.

Finally she said "Now you two listen—here's my summer plan. I'll move out there when school ends in June and stay with Grandmother through the summer at least—she'll need a guide by then, just to walk." Matt had never looked this strong before, like the kindly owner of me and Myra, issuing orders.

So I rushed to say "That's a kind idea" (both Myra's parents had died too young).

But Myra said "Miss Ashlyn won't want you." Mattie looked shocked and I must have looked puzzled, so Myra went on explaining to her. "Your grandmother Calhoun would starve in a chair before she'd take steady help from us. We well know that."

A day ago I might have agreed. But after tonight, leaving my mother in that empty house, I was much less sure. I said to Matt "If your mother says Yes, then call Grandmother up in the morning, tell her and see how she feels about it."

Matt just said "I already have."

Then it was Myra's turn to look slapped.

It turned out Mattie had managed to get alone with Miss Ashlyn for a minute after church, had made the offer and been accepted with thanks on the spot.

I asked her if Mother had said she'd need to ask our permission.

Myra looked me in the eye and laughed. "Of course she didn't. Miss Ashlyn takes what the poor world offers."

It didn't sound bitter, it was nine tenths true, but I knew that Myra was already aimed for her old standard envy of Mother and how much Matt and I plainly loved her.

I said "Well, June's a long way off." Then I looked to Matt and said a thing I hated at once. "You and your ma start praying now, and Mother's eyes could be healed by June."

Myra narrowed her own eyes and shook her head at me, too late a warning.

Mattie showed nothing for several minutes. She shelled another handful of peanuts, then stood up quietly and walked to the refrigerator. She took out a frozen Eskimo Pie, peeled off the wrapper and laid it in the garbage as carefully as if it was a human baby. Then she was climbing upstairs, still quiet.

I called to her. "Good night. And thank you again—"

She said "Uh huh."

Myra took my wrist to stop me saying any more. She was generally right at such tense times.

But I whispered to her. "I need to tell Madelyn—I was just kidding."

"She's worn out, Blue—all her stage nerves today and then waiting up to see you back and get your praise." Myra lowered her voice. "See, we've been praying for your mother's eyes three times a day. It was Mattie's idea. She asked me to join her."

So I reached for Myra's idle hand; and with no real notion of what I meant, I made a small cross in the midst of her palm. She'd done that for me many times in the old days when I needed blessing. And now I had quick tears in my eyes. "I'm bitterly sorry," I said. *Sorry for what—your whole sad past or this new shadow barreling down?* Whatever I meant, it felt sincere, though no six high priced criminal lawyers could have sorted out why.

When we got upstairs twenty minutes later, Mattie was flat in the dark on her bed. I knew by her breath she was truly asleep, but her legs and arms were thrown out loose from her body like rags. I stood beside her a long hard time, trying to wish her back awake for just the time it took to say how much she counted all over my heart.

But what she did was finally turn her face to the wall and sound as dead as any member of that cold German family I passed, eating their huge perpetual breakfast.

THREE

Y**OU'LL UNDERSTAND** I didn't sleep. I kissed Myra good
night and lay flat beside her, touching her arm, till she fell off. Then I
turned to the cooler side and waited, halfway thinking and howling
out in my hot skull. I can sympathize if you wonder why I didn't go
down and drag myself through the gravel naked or roll the car on into
the shed, shut the door, crank the motor and go to sleep in what I
knew was the only economical way. The three women near me—
Mother, Matt, Myra—would grieve sincerely and always ask if they
were the cause. But they were each clear minded enough to recall my
past and know I'd made my own last bed, no help from them.

Mother would never tell my secret but would fix her eyes and last
till ninety to keep a good watch on Madelyn's future. Myra would
finally get the job she'd talked about since Matt could walk—in children's wear—and her sweet dignity would be more widely known than
now. Matt's church would tell her I was chained in Hell, but she'd
pray for me anyhow the rest of her days. And Luna Absher would
read about me in the evening paper, or Rita might keep the news to
herself till Luna went in the store one day to buy harp string and
finally heard.

Wasn't that it?—the sensible course. Or could I do what Rita and
Mother had already begged and I'd attempted? Could I just someway
stretch my mind, and any remnants of my tired soul, to live here sane
with Myra and Matt from this night on and not keep throwing my

mind and body these endless cuts of fresh smelling meat? I got that mean but realistic on myself and Luna, not to mention on fate or blundering life.

By one o'clock with the whole street quiet and nothing but tree frogs neeping away, the only thing I could think to do was clear my head and try to run behind my eyes a kind of movie—Mattie and Myra finding me gassed cold in the morning and no word of why. *Christ, what could I write to say farewell?—invent a cancer or say I was starting to drink again?* They watched me close enough to know those were lies.

No, in fact it might be Matt that found me. Myra slept till the clock went off at seven, so she might not even miss me till then. Matt would come to say good morning right off; and when I was missing, she'd look out the kitchen window and see the shed door closed. She wouldn't speak. Young as she was she'd want this news to herself for the few bad minutes till Myra followed her down and saw me. And when my mind imagined Matt's face as she touched my hand and felt the chill, then I knew I'd spare her that much pain this morning at least, whatever I might yet pour on her in times to come.

Three out of any five men would say "Ease up on yourself. You spent two hours with a sixteen year old girl big enough to call her own shots—a girl your wife knows nothing about. You joined her body that one short time, and now you're planning to wreck three lives and end your own for a quick hot cheat that you can forget or, God knows, won't ever need to repeat?" And I well understand there's a world more to say by way of judgment on my brain and body, my brutal treatment of several women (despite the fact that to this day I've never laid an actual hand on woman or child in anger or hate—and your tragic father was the only man I truly hurt, though again I didn't actually touch him).

What might be more worth noticing here is all that's happened in American minds since the 1950s. The thing I'd done had a one word name back then—adultery. That's nothing but grinding your hot body with somebody else's when you've sworn a vow to keep yourself clean and aimed at your mate. You may recall it's Commandment Seven in a short list of ten. In America back in my boyhood and right till the seventies, adultery was still as low a crime as any offense but torture and murder. That was not to say it was never done.

Of course it was but when you finished and dried yourself off, you knew the name of what you'd accomplished; and you smelled the stench of your household crime (even if your wild brain still felt magic). You didn't go on network TV and talk it out calmly with some flip host and a standup comic sex expert who made you feel as normal as leaves and reassured you that nothing truly precious was torn by your treachery—not to mention that you had maimed several people for life and thereafter.

No indeed, in the 1950s with divorce barely heard of outside Hollywood, you most likely went on living with the mate and children you'd fed lies to. And your mind either grew a thick yellow callus, or it slowly poisoned itself and rotted from the core on out. More often than not it also poisoned everybody you touched. To be sure, it still does and will forever, though it's far more common than courtesy now and is likewise fatal to all concerned plus the standby kin, whether they ever know it or not.

So running that movie through my eyes, I promised myself one more time that I was clear and back on my best rails ready to roll. The air in our bedroom was chilly by then, and I reached down to pull up the spread. Myra moaned in her sleep but stayed unconscious. One of the joys of her life was sleep; and though she'd stay awake for weeks if a loved one asked her, she'd sleep like a lead fishing weight if allowed—a strange trait in any grown woman.

I'd checked the radium glow of my watch a minute ago. So I know it was past one o'clock when the telephone rang. *Mother,* I thought, though she'd never called this late before. The upstairs phone was out in the hall. I hit the floor and beat it to the third ring, but all I heard was a long live silence—somebody was there. *Mother—a stroke—and now she can't speak.* I said "Mother?" clearly. Nothing came. "Miss Ashlyn?" Nothing again. I could see her stunned face trying to speak. She'd be dead soon. And all at once I needed to tell her I'd followed her wish, I'd made my choice, I was here with my family.

But a high voice said "I hope you know I'm sorry by now." It didn't sound like man, woman or child. It was more on the order of wire cranked out of a small machine with a high pitched wail.

Then it stopped and I could hear cars through the phone—light traffic far off. This was long before the telephone system fell into the hands of nuisance salesmen and anonymous crooks. But still I knew not to speak out yet. And a long wait started with just those far off cars behind it.

Then "Mr. Blue. You know me, don't you?"

Honest to God, I didn't yet.

"I don't want to say my name this late." The voice had lowered a little.

I all but recognized her. So I said "Thank you" and moved to hang up.

She rushed on, saying "I'm by myself outside at the phone where you last saw me—"

It was Luna, Luna—no way to doubt it. *Luna out there alone by the doughnut shop with late cars passing—cabs and cops, and where's the hood?* Please understand I'm telling a fact—not aiming to win your hero award—when I swear it felt like I was raking my naked face with razor blades, but I said "Good night" and held the receiver out in the air for maybe ten seconds. I thought I heard "Blue—" but then I quit and cut her off. I left the receiver off the hook and stood in place, much colder still. A natural expectation blocked me seeing Luna in my head. I thought any instant Myra would come and start the questions. Or even Mattie, who was on the near outskirts of teenage slavery to telephones. But no, nobody. Just me and my choice, which right that moment was the empty air I sucked up my dry nose and mouth.

Under twenty minutes later I was back at the shop, that was long since dark. I actually got out and searched through the lot, the whole

dark rear by the garbage cans and the phone booth. Then I drove off
in Rita's direction, creeping along in case the girl had somehow fallen
down by the road or was hurt in the shadows—after my stunt at the
window glass, the hood could have beat her (he'd looked low enough
to pound on women). But again no sign. So I stopped at the corner of
Rita's street and asked myself if I had the guts or the lunatic strength
to drive on down there, knock at the door and ask was Luna safely
home? Or would I tap on Luna's window and hope Rita slept as deep
as Myra? *What window though?* Luna hadn't told me. I thought of
the locked up murdering son, and again I figured Rita was armed and
wouldn't take too much foolishness now.

Then I figured I knew her way to school, down Peace Street and
up that nearly vertical hill and then straight on to Broughton High
at Peace and St. Mary's (Broughton was the place I'd got one blessing,
whatever I failed—a taste for reading any sensible words, whatever the
subject). Something told me Luna was walking that stretch, a road
that led to a spacious building where clean smart people would gather
at daybreak. Again I nosed on past the college, the poor-white houses,
then the baseball diamond down in the meadow. The stop lights
worked and I obeyed; but in those long blocks, I never saw a live thing
move. So when I got towards the crest of the hill, I told myself if the
red light caught me, I'd just turn right and be back home in under
ten minutes.

I drove at a measured legal speed and slid through a green with
seconds to spare. In the next short block, somebody was walking in
what looked like a ground length cape or an old time duster. At first I
thought it was some late tramp, but then I switched my bright lights
on. And the body turned—a woman in a long raincoat and Luna's
face, white as any lit candle. I veered to the right and nearly stopped.
She's got to be alone like she said—no public meeting.

Nobody else was in sight around her; and whether she knew my car
or not, she turned again and aimed on forward like school would open
in the next two minutes and be her rescue.

I moved towards the center line and called her name to let her
know she was safe by now, whatever had hurt her. At first she kept

going but I tried again. In a low clear voice, I said more or less what she'd told me—"I want you to know I'm sorry too."

That slowed her at least. We moved on parallel another few yards; then I lowered my lights and stopped.

She stopped and faced my way but stayed put. Dim as she was I could see her arms bolt-straight at her sides. Her fists were clenching and loosening fast.

And what I could see of her face was something no iron wall would have kept me from trying to save and mend. I said "They don't have night school, you know."

She nodded as hard as if I'd asked did she want world peace but she seemed paralyzed.

I had to ask the urgent thing. "Has somebody hurt you?"—old Rex Hospital was five blocks off.

She didn't nod again or speak, though she held in place.

So I got out and walked the six yards. She didn't come towards me, but she didn't draw back. And when I took her right hand gently, she moved on with me like a child sleepwalking and relieved to be caught. As we got back to the passenger door, I leaned down closer to check her breath—had the hood fed her liquor to drive her like this? But the smell I caught was warm and fresh.

For one of the rare times in my life, I didn't have a word to say. I didn't want to know who the hood was or where he'd gone. Or did Rita know that Luna was out here wild as this? My mind was blank as a mile of sand—no gladness, no pain, no thought of day. I must have figured if she was bleeding, she'd say as much.

But Luna made no sound at all till we were back off Ridge Road again in the same grove of trees.

I'd switched off the motor but left on the parking lights, so we could see each other's eyes. Still I didn't face her. *Let her start, son; then follow her lead.*

She finally drew a long breath and said to the windshield "I lost my mind. I—" It didn't sound like she was crying. It was more like she'd just told the truth—her mind was gone.

And I knew I'd done it. The deepest wrongs I'd done till then were the times I showed myself drunk and sick to Madelyn Calhoun when she was too young to know what had changed me. Now I'd ruined something more than a mind. Luna was bruised from crown to toe. *Worse. I've* torn *her.* Of course I wanted to take her hand and find some way to lead her back to where this started in a music store a week ago that felt like a year. Then I'd sell her the harp and forget her, and that would cancel this stifling nightmare she was locked in.

But then she turned. Her eyes were dry and clear as they got (they were always too deep to fathom safely). And when she'd found whatever it was she hunted for in my tense face, she said "Nobody since I drew breath has treated me half as kind as you."

It felt like the grandest compliment my life had earned, and it thrilled me deep. I said "Who's been unkind to you?" I guess I was halfway thinking of the hood and hoping to further blacken his name.

But Luna took it seriously and thought a long time. Then she said "If I was to give you a list, it would start just a few steps out of my cradle and run till tonight. They've hurt me, ass-over-tit, so bad I may not last—somedays I doubt it."

I couldn't hear a trace of pity in her voice—she got extra strength from the fact that she'd used words scarcer then than now. But something told me not to ask for more news now, not yet tonight. All my life—to this night here—if you lay out your honest pain where I can see it, I'm likely to try to spare you more. It came in my blood from Ashlyn Calhoun.

All I knew about Rita's life and her awful luck—it all rose up in my mind now and told me I could believe every syllable this girl said. At least I could think she truly meant it tonight out here. And that thought spread on down my body like a broadcloth cotton fine nightshirt. I was warm but not too warm. I thought I was safe. I'd help this girl, whatever came, to know a better life than this—maybe even her dream of music. I still hadn't thanked her. But I couldn't think of adequate words for the best human news I'd heard in years or ever before. Times like this, before and after, I reach for a person's hand or arm and let that say what my voice can't. I knew I ought not to touch Luna now, even this late and deep in the country. Her thanks, and whatever pain she felt, had put her past me. But finally I said "I thought I'd harmed you."

"Who told you that?" Again she was looking ahead at the night.

"My conscience, I guess."

She said "Rita Absher, I'll bet you ten dollars."

"Not really, no."

She didn't believe me and her head shook twice. "Mother tried to shame you today—I know."

"Were you in the house when I stopped by?"

Luna looked at me like I was a miserable child in the street. "No, say no—you didn't lower yourself to come meet her, didn't let her do it on her own mean ground." Any rock could have heard the hate in her voice.

So I tried to let her know I was here—still here unshamed. I said "Your mother stopped by the store this morning when I was out. That got my curiosity up, and I looped by at six o'clock to see what she meant. Neither one of us raised our voices once."

"My precious mother means for you to *vamoose*." Dark as it was I could feel Luna's strength rising beside me, almost like her years were speeding fast on a gauge till she'd have her own wings to fly.

I smiled. "I all but suspected she hoped I'd *fade*."

Luna waited a long time, then put out her left hand and touched my arm—I was in a raincoat over pajamas. "Will you ever pardon me?"

"For what on Earth?"

"Getting you tangled in white-trash mess and spoiling your life."

I barely believed I'd heard the words. Back then *white trash* didn't mean *poor* or *lazy*. People saved it to use on vicious families of white cutthroats that beat their children mercilessly or plowed their mule till it died in harness. But in Luna's voice the words sank through me like those first notes I'd heard her sing in the store, first time. And harsh as they were—they felt as good. I said "No need for pardon, sweet child. Your mother is right."

"Your daughter's the only *child*, Mr. Blue." Her voice was gentle and accurate.

Again I had this sudden thought Luna might someway know a friend of Matt's. "How do you know Mattie?"

"I read the paper. I know this was May Day, and she was the queen."

"She crowned a statue at the Catholic church."

"I wish I'd seen it. I know she was lovely."

Luna sounded entirely sincere, but you'll understand that the name and sight of Mattie right now was as painful to me as it should have been. I took a long pause—*Why in Christ's name are you out here, son? Take this child home and honor your own.* Then I knew what next, and I said it straight at her. "Luna, I've made a bad mistake— me, just me. It was none of your fault. I beg your pardon now and in your life to come. I vow I won't ever touch you again or even try. I'm not a rich man, and I've got my family, but I'd like to give you fifty dollars to help you at that music camp." I'd brought my wallet and I thought I had sufficient cash. Back then fifty dollars was no insult; you could ride the all night Silver Meteor from Raleigh to New York for slightly less and still buy your breakfast.

Luna waited too; the entire feel of her body changed in some new way I couldn't name. Then she turned towards me and poured her certainty at my eyes. "I *gave* you all I gave, Mr. Blue, because you were kind and I meant to thank you. Don't try to ruin it here this late." I'd seen her mad. She wasn't mad now. She was like a girl in algebra class at the board exploring a hard equation that you could solve just one right way.

And when she'd worked to the end of her problem, it seemed to me she'd found the answer—the absolute answer—to every quandary I ever faced. In a second my body had jolted on like a new trans- former, and all the sad regrets I'd felt in my full life were joined in a single high long wail inside my head. It was what I could hear, not to mention *think*. However plainly I knew the future wrongs I'd cause and the people I'd crush, I wanted Luna Absher now and for all time to be. I thought it was plain she wanted me. I also thought I needed to test it. So I held my right hand out in the space between our bodies—open and palm down, quivering hard.

It hung out there till the shaking got so bad I thought *I'll take it back in three more seconds.*

But Luna met it halfway with hers. She held it lightly, then brought both hands to rest on her knee. Then she looked at them, not back at my face. Finally she said "You play the piano?"

"No ma'm. Why?"

"You've got these endless fingers, see?" She laid my fingers out full length and stroked them gently.

I said "I've struck a lot of wrong notes with those but not on a keyboard." I meant to smile but she still wouldn't face me.

Then she did the strangest thing I'd seen. With both her hands she lifted mine right up to her face and spread my fingers like a mask between us. Wherever her skin touched mine, I could feel her young blood beating out a message in code. Her eyes looked at me like an animal caged or like herself behind strong bars. My palm hid whether she smiled or frowned, but I let her keep it there a few seconds. Then she folded it slowly, moved it down to her mouth and kissed it— brushed it really with clean pale lips.

From age eleven my sexual body had been stoked high as any blast furnace. Even there lately, loyal at home, I'd wondered if I ought not to see a doctor and ask for some kind of pill or shot to cool my jets and let me *think*, not just be steered through a lot of my life by a hard blind rudder between my legs that had no destination but joy—thirty seconds' worth and the lifetime memory. Not that Myra had really complained. Whatever had gone bad between us before, my wife and I still tended to meet on good common ground where sex was concerned (whenever I doped I'd get sick or sleepy, so I very seldom leaned on her drunk). Now what came next was even stranger than Luna gazing through my hand. I was suddenly calm as a baby dozing in safe sunlight. I felt like this was *enough* right now. *Don't grab for what you don't want and can't use.*

She wanted more—Luna, that night. And that's the God's truth or whoever else's. She didn't turn coarse or ugly or give some imitation of a screen star frying a gutted man. She leaned back slightly against her door and just watched me—my eyes, nothing else. She didn't quite smile, not quite but nearly.

I kept on thinking *She's promising something.* And it went on so long, it seemed like she had a giant reason to memorize every fact she could see, which was not much more than my two brown eyes—still 20/20 and always grateful to beautiful sights. For all I know we stayed there quiet like that for months.

Then she finally said "When you were in school, did they call poor children 'underprivileged'?"

I couldn't imagine what that meant. But I said "No, we just called them paupers."

She said "I've been underprivileged every day of my life till now, till you." Her face made it look like the truest thing any soul had said, to Bluford Calhoun anyhow.

So when she bent again to brush my hand, I had no choice—by my own lights that instant then—but to ask if we could get out now and walk on deeper into the grove and lie down there in clean pinestraw.

Luna said "Thank you."

The last thing you need, or that I want to give, is a full replay of the next half hour. All I can ask in the way of mercy is for you to listen to just this much. I've already mentioned a fact I don't brag on at all—far from it, *far*. But an unavoidable truth of my young life had run like this—I'd more than tasted several bodies (unlike numerous men I've known, I don't have a list of names and dates). And from the knowledge I got in those times, I can try to tell you that Luna this night was, past all dreaming, an answer to questions I'd never dared ask—questions I'd never known existed. *Will you go where you've never gone, on risk of killing yourself and all you've loved till now? And if you love whatever you find, will you stay there through whatever pain the world flings at you, whatever blame?*

She started slow like we both were fragile. But when she saw I didn't refuse, she moved on through every deed and word, again not like some movie vamp or even a seasoned decent soul but some entirely new creature on Earth. You could tell she barely knew what

next, but just when you were about to lead her—or pull back short of
something you'd craved for thirty years—she'd flow right on to that
perfect place, just before you, and make it pay you triple the gain
you'd gambled on. And when we'd both run all the race and were
quiet and separate, she looked up through the ragged holes in the
black pine limbs and said "I feel like you're not even a man."

I was too near sleep to say any more than "What am I then?"

She seemed to take the time to find out. Then she finally said "Oh
Lord, *Lord*—I doubt I know. I hope I know someday. But for now
I'm guessing you're something better than I ever planned." And then
to show she didn't mean anything cheap about money or our two
separate stations in life, she reached out to touch my resting skin.

I knew right then, *She's true as light*. And though, as I've said more
than once, I leaned on no one brand of God, I aimed my own mind
towards the sky and said a short thanks to the Milky Way if nothing
else. I thought *Please let this last for good*. Even now ashamed as I
am, I can taste exactly why I thought it. It was not that crazy. I felt
that fine and no other creature alive on Earth at that late hour meant
a plugged nickel to me.

When I left Luna outside her place, it was past three o'clock in
the morning. I asked her if she was scared of Rita. She said that Rita
could sleep through earthquakes. And when I parked in my own drive-
way, crept upstairs, washed myself and slid back into my place by
Myra, she muttered something about a dream she was having right
then; and I think she asked was I all right. I said I was and, strangely,
next I fell through sleep like a rock down a well. If I dreamed, it was
nothing bad—no threats or judgments, no sights of your mother tortured by pain like she would be years on from now. I know I was
spared because, when I woke up that Sunday morning, I felt clean
and rested all down my body. I lay there after just four hours' sleep
and tried to interpret shadows on the wall, knowing that Myra and
Mattie would doze till the last minute before late mass if I didn't
move, which I didn't do.

Once my mind had cleared its cobwebs, I lay on still and thought about nothing but the river I rode down long years back on a truck innertube. A friend that was older than me, with a car, had found this shack that rented the tubes. You launched yourself at a little pier, and the easy current took you along as far as you might need to go, yards or miles through low hanging trees and occasional otters. Then you walked back. Even that first day I said "*All* the way—hell, the damned Gulf Stream." My friend said "Sure" but of course he stopped us after three miles. There's still no doubt they were three of the finest miles I've traveled—riding clear water and facing the sky through tame song birds and red tailed hawks—but of course at the end we had to walk back. In spite of the fact that it set a pattern for the rest of my life—*Wherever you sail you're bound to walk back*—the memory still can soothe my mind and give a new day a peaceful start.

There were six more weeks till Luna left for music camp. I fully intended for her to go and better her chances at some kind of life. But after that second night together, the two of us thought of very little except the next way to meet and *feel*, one more time, that fine and free. I'm trusting you—if you're full grown—to understand this much at least: that brand of joy, all down your skin and through your mind, can have you under its spell in no time. Not even a *spell*—it'll have you raw in the palm of its hand in less than a week, and then it will slowly close around you. At first you'll just feel the warmth and safety, and that can last indefinitely. But one hard hour down the road, you come to yourself and know your bones are pulverized; your good mind's been pressed like an orange, and you've been left with rind and seeds.

That runs me way too far ahead. For those six weeks of warm spring days and cool nights, Luna and I felt very little but joy and thanks and the steady hope to make that last for the rest of our lives. I'm confident in speaking for her, even this late, because her finest trait was this—she told you minute by minute how she felt. And all those early weeks, she was happy—at least as happy as I knew I was, or so she claimed with an honest face. We mostly talked on the phone during lunch.

She'd walk to the soda shop near school, which was strictly off limits, and call the stock room at the store. I'd take my lunch and eat it there. Hobe Pierce, the Negro in charge of stock, was my old friend. So when he'd answer the phone and hear Luna, he'd hand her on to me with no question. Maybe two or three times, I got so restless or she got worried; and I drove towards the school at lunch. I'd park a block south; Luna would meet me. And we'd ride out Hillsboro Street almost to Cary, twenty minutes together, just talking and gazing and breathing each other.

The only other way we were reckless in public anyhow was our weekend meetings. I've mentioned Oakwood Cemetery where my dad was buried with hundreds more of Raleigh's older natives plus all the Rebel and Union soldiers who fell nearby in 1865. It stretched over maybe sixty acres of oaks and streams four blocks downhill from Rita's place. Luna said right off that Rita never went there despite her dead husbands. So the second weekend in May, we'd agreed to meet in the afternoon up on the hill by the Rebel graves. I was a little late getting there, about four o'clock; and all the widows had propped their flowers and gone on home. Luna had named the spot to find—she'd wait beyond the Rebel graves by one particular family tomb. I'd known and admired it all my life, a small Greek temple in nearly black granite with wrought iron doors and just the one name BONAVENTURE.

By the time I got there, the light was slanted through new yellow leaves. And the whole place one more time had started its weird nightly trip—from childhood I always imagined it took a pitch dark sail through outer space to let its various bones revisit their happier souls. And the tomb stood there in a pool of strange light but no sign of Luna. Empty as the place was, I didn't want to hang around with no clear purpose. So I started counting the Rebel names, never losing sight of the Bonaventures. A quarter hour passed, still nobody. And I knew the iron gates closed at six. I moved back nearer the Bonaventure tomb, took out a pencil, a scrap of paper and started drawing the line of the roof. In maybe half a minute, I heard a high thin note. I looked behind me, nothing again. I stayed in place and thought I'd give Luna three more minutes, then leave and hunt the neighborhood streets.

Again the voice took up that note. And then it glided down into words—an actual song, "Abide With Me," the actual first words Luna ever sang me. It had to be her, but still she was hid.

So I tried to track it and wound up soon at the door of the tomb. I stopped just short of the sill and called her gently.

The singing paused but she didn't speak.

So I said "I very much hope it's you, not a dead Bonaventure."

She finally said "I'm a spirit at peace," but then she showed behind the glass and iron grille of the door. She'd got inside and her face was grim.

My skin went through some serious crawling. But I managed to say "Come out of there. That's not a joke."

And the door slipped open, slow and quiet. She'd somehow unlocked it and she waved me in.

I shook my head and stepped well back.

But Luna held her ground. "It's *safe*. I've broke in here nearly all my life."

Since my World War I've had enough to dread from the living; I've never bothered to fear the dead. But out of respect I didn't mean to upset the Bonaventures' rest.

So Luna slid out and beckoned me to step around back where the shrubs were thick. She said "I found this door open years ago when I was a girl, and I've been coming in here ever since. Nobody else has touched the latch in all that time—at least nobody's locked the door. I figure all their children are dead. So I bring flowers Christmas and Easter, which gives me rights the way I see it. I come up here real often and think. It's just two coffins, a man and wife; and they welcome the company or have till now."

My hope had been to lead her to the car, then out to the country and back by supper. But though I still felt sacrilegious, Luna kept saying it was no disrespect. And of course her eyes kept hauling me on. Finally I took her lead and followed.

It was just a small room maybe eight by ten with long stone benches where two coffins rested—Maurice and Marguerite Bonaventure dead since the 1920s and "Joined Still on the Higher Plane," or so the chiseled inscription believed. In the back wall a circular stained glass window let in enough frail rosy light to set our bodies trembling like foxfire and showing us each other's eyes. That was enough, far more than sufficient, to aim me hot towards our first full meeting indoors by day. Like stunned kids peeling off their clothes for a Saturday bath, Luna and I rushed down to our skins and stretched on the floor. So in that spooky purplish glow, between the dried up Bonaventures and with only an unlocked clear glass door between our love and the world at large, we plowed ahead.

Notice I used the word *love* just now. I didn't foresee that my hand would write it. But out it came and I'll keep it in place. That mid May Sunday afternoon, especially after I left her at five, was surely the time my mind bit down on a new idea—*Here you are in actual love for the first time maybe in all your years except with Mother when you were helpless*. I didn't try to think what love really was. How many people do?—don't we just duck our chins and charge at something we guess we might want for good? (I always have). I still had a lot of affection for Myra and a world of thanks. I still thought Matt stood an excellent chance of being the finest woman of both her time and place. And of course I've mentioned other girls before my marriage and a few women later in my bad times. But in under a month from the day I met her, I understood that the present fact of Luna Absher had saturated my mind and body like a drop of blood in a glass of water.

The fact gave me a steady feeling that my whole body—my willing hide—was in a mighty high-step *strut* at this strong taste of happiness. My skin and every other part of Blue Calhoun were wanted and used like never before and never since. And every taste I got of Luna and of Luna's praise just left me howling for the next quick taste. I could barely think the commonest thoughts—when to rise and sleep, shave or breathe. I'd forget where I parked the car at work, in a daze I wandered off from a lady buying a banjo and she got mean, I seldom ate the lunch Myra packed because I'd wait so hard in the stock room for Luna's calls.

Worse still, I seldom thought of Madelyn unless she stood two feet in front of me calling my name. I still didn't doubt she'd been the main thing that stopped my drinking—me wanting to spare her any more pain. And all through these past sober months, I'd used Matt's face as a pilot light to travel by. Now though I never stopped to realize I'd nearly forgot her and all her cares. At home I wanted to be else-where. Like everything to do with obsession, it was just that simple. I steadily longed to be on the moon with somebody else who'd soon make me a different man—a respected creature, *wanted* the way he's hoped to be and *used* right down to the smoky sockets.

I went on living my nights at home, I never missed work, I strained to give my best imitation of who I'd been before this total change broke on me. Luna never called the house again, never came to the store; we only met on late afternoons at the Bonaventures' or there-abouts, though once or twice on weekend evenings, we got a half hour of country love in the mild spring dusk. Nights in bed I responded to Myra whenever she showed she expected me, and I thanked her for it. But I don't want to tell you the scenes I had to run inside my mind to help me bring off Myra first and then manufacture some thrill of my own like a buckshot pellet deep in my brain.

Myra had known me most of my life since grammar school, and she'd watched me closer than a ticking bomb, but the strangest thing in the air of those weeks was the way Myra never asked one question or showed one sign of guessing my news. Like all old drunks and similar friends, I told myself I'd learned perfect camouflage long before I joined the Army (like the poor Army had taught me much besides beer slugging and talking trash). Luna even told me time and again that Rita was likewise lost in the dark about our meetings, much less my love. And since I had no further visits or words from Rita, I chose to believe she also lived in ignorance of a thing that big and bright in her midst.

*

So those short weeks till Luna headed to music camp were the time I warned about when I started. I was outright happy night and day, the way I'd never known before. I thought I hid it from all the world but me and the girl I craved to join. I'd catch myself any time of the hot day shivering slightly, and then I'd wonder had I caught a cold. Never, no. I was just that endlessly stunned and glad to be who I was—and to be me while I was young enough to hope for long years at that same rate. Even from here three decades later, working to mend what little I can of so much waste, I can't in honesty say I don't recall that time as a paradise and still the only one I've known.

Maybe I can help you understand it—and also see that sex was not the sole engine that drove us—if I say what moved me most in those weeks was a thing as simple as Luna's questions about my life. Some edgy fear kept me from wanting details of her short past, but we couldn't be together ten minutes before she'd start in quizzing me about everything from the day of my birth till adolescence (she always stopped at my teenage years like she suspected I went hog wild at the stroke of thirteen, though it took awhile longer). She'd ask if I'd been born blond headed (I was brown haired now), were my eyes born blue like normal babies' or brown like now, what was my first sentence and spoken to who, and what were my good childhood dreams—the actual dreams, not just ambitions?

It was some years after we moved apart before I guessed that Luna focused on my childhood in some instinctive try at bringing me closer down to her age and trimming the rind off nearly two decades that lay between us. Whatever, in a month she knew more about my deep foundations than Myra herself, who'd watched me nearly my whole life. And those shared facts through those spring weeks of '56 brought Luna and me so close to being one joined mind that every hour I dreaded her leaving more and more.

She meant to leave on Saturday morning June 16th and planned to stay gone most all summer. However much I feared us parting, I also knew that both of us secretly wanted the chance to test ourselves and catch our breath. Since nobody in her family had a car—and I could see no safe way to drive her—Luna planned to ride the bus through the mountains up to Boone and be met there by people from the camp who'd drive her farther on up in the Blue Ridge.

Our goodbye would need to be said on the Friday somehow. There was always the cemetery, though we'd tried to ration our visits and not get known to the one-eyed guard that roamed the graves. All that week I'd thought of lies I could tell at home and get my freedom for most of the night. But I'd got through the recent weeks with very few lies to Myra, Matt and none to Mother; and I felt like it was nearer to decent if I kept on just telling the truth but leaving parts out.

So what I did was to say I'd sold a spinet piano some months ago to an elderly lady near Rolesville and that she was after me to drive out now and hear her play and say whether I didn't think it was "off." The story was true but I made the trip right after lunch on the Friday in question. That left me free for a good two hours after work, maybe three. And Luna was waiting where I'd said, well on past the dough-nut shop on North Person Street. Two blocks off I saw her before she spotted me. Just the pure unfiltered sight of her there in the public world nearly stopped me cold.

If *pure* seems wrong, believe me it wasn't. She sat on a waist high fieldstone wall and stared across the road at times; so I got her full profile, very still. She had on something new to me—dark blue shorts and a matching blouse—and she'd pulled her hair back tight someway so it thinned her face close down to the bones and made her look like a girl who chose to stand in the path of a strong headwind. I'd never known her to wear anything but a skirt or dress, and seeing that much of her skin in sunlight hit me hard. I mean it scared me watching her lay that much of herself on view to the world (remember this was years ago before girls flung themselves mother-naked all over TV). And it also stunned me seeing how young she looked like that—how far behind me, green in her childhood.

In those short weeks, with all her questions, I'd gone past thinking about the gap between our ages, how Luna could easily be my daughter. She'd long since felt like the perfect match to every hope, and age had nothing to do with the way we joined together like broken halves. Now though, edging forward on her, my scalp burned cold with what felt like her absolute impossibility. *What on Earth ever made you think she's meant for you? Who would send you this big a gift, and haven't you already wronged her as badly as your own family? What in God's name have you got to give her? Take the next left here, and let that child go her own way for good.*

Her head turned then and she saw the car. With the liquid bones of a natural dancer, she slid to her feet and faced my way. Then I could see she was holding a suitcase in her left hand, a small black case. She didn't wave but her eyes never quit till I'd pulled up beside her and leaned to open the passenger door. She didn't get in. She also leaned and faced me straight. "You wanted to quit up there. I saw you"—she pointed back the way I came.

If I'd slowed or braked, I hadn't known it. And anyhow then she was turned away. I figured her travel nerves were talking (she'd already said she hadn't slept two consecutive nights away from Rita in her life till now). So I just said "I wanted to see you quick as I could. I must've got nervous." I patted the empty seat to urge her.

She stayed outside. "I've got to be home by eight o'clock. My mother thinks I'm taking a lesson" (she'd only mentioned the previous week that she told Rita how an elderly lady in Boylan Apartments was giving her free harp lessons daily). She was plainly waiting some signal from me that I'd yet to give.

I said "You've taught me precious news." It had come to my lips from I-knew-not-where. And at first I thought *What the hell does that mean?* But then I knew it was unvarnished truth.

It seemed to ease her. She reached across the seat to the back and set her bag there. Then she climbed in neatly and shut the door. Before I popped the clutch, she said "You always ushered me into the door."

I always had. Till then I'd seen her into the door and safely seated. I thought she was teasing, and I said "That was when you wore long dresses."

We were underway and had gone two blocks before she spoke, to the windshield again. "I understood you liked my skin."

"I prize you, lady, skin and bone."

Her eyes were full, I was almost sure. She didn't turn and I didn't force her. It sometimes took her half an hour to get her mind right when we met; and my general policy concerning tears—with her or the world of weepers in general—was *Say you don't see them for the first three minutes or until blood shows*. And Luna managed to swallow hers before she said "I'm here to thank you and to say please stop."

It hit me so rough, at first I didn't feel it. I thought we were taking a normal ride. I drove awhile until I could say "What you got in the suitcase?"

She looked ahead. "It's not a suitcase."

"A machine gun then?"

"You know," she said. She met my eyes and saw that I didn't. "It's just my harp."

That seemed to cancel her telling me to stop. All through those weeks I'd begged her to play her new harp for me. She'd always refuse, saying how she'd wait till after camp when she could play right. But now she must be planning to play as a farewell gesture. I thought I knew enough about her not to say any more but to let her lead me. I drove on quietly, catching quick sights of her hair and skin and trying not to show how scared and happy I was together, to be that near her.

By then the fringes of Raleigh were past us. We rode in a cool dim stretch of pine woods. And finally Luna said "Where are you going?"

"I'm going to tell you a nice goodbye." What I'd done two days ago still burned my mind. I'd called a Mom and Pop motel well out in the country and booked a room. We'd spend at least an hour there, and that would be our first chance alone in natural walls. It would also serve as a reassuring memory for Luna while she was gone. And for me it would lay down indelible pictures of a person I treasured who was leaving awhile but might return.

She said "Whereabouts?" and looked in earnest—nobody was hijacking this strong a girl.

Then I was embarrassed. I felt like a stiff fraternity boy on a fall weekend, all but chloroforming his date and shacking up in a tourist court to use her body through a drunk black night. But if my plan would halfway work, we'd both feel more dignified looking back. It felt like rolling a hand grenade towards a child who might well pull out the pin, but I said "I got us a clean private room."

"In a private home?"

"A motel."

"No—" Luna said. And it wasn't clear if she meant *Forget it* or was just expressing calm surprise.

So I said "A small one, three miles ahead."

She threw it straight at me. "I could tell you to let me out on the road. My thumb could get me home before dark."

I lifted both hands off the wheel to show I meant it. "I'll turn both of us around right now. You say the word."

But she eased back and didn't even seem to breathe through those next miles. She watched the trees race past her window. And when they suddenly stopped and next came a wide deep pasture with black cows resting and one white horse, she faced the road again, not me.

When the low-slung brick motel appeared round the next long curve, I saw Luna's eyes clamp shut for three seconds. And her lips made words I couldn't hear and knew not to question, though every cell of my body knew it was blessed beyond compare to be this close to knowing this much fineness again.

She didn't say another word through the whole next hour. Neither did I, partly in respect to her silence but mainly because words turned out quickly to be the last thing we needed. Again I know every instant by heart and could run them past you at natural speed and maybe even change your life—that much kindness between two people, that much pure skill and purifying heat. I'll spare you though and try to describe my deepest thoughts as we worked together like one grand creature to ease ourselves for that one hour and maybe the entire rest of our lives (I think both of us were that realistic).

Anyhow when we lay back separate and waited to cool, I asked my mind what time it was. My watch was on the bedside table, but I hated to pick it up and sound a warning note. I thought it was not quite seven thirty; and I thought we might stay twenty more minutes, then bathe together for the first time yet and go our ways. Still I felt no cause to speak, but slowly I turned to my left side and laid my hand on Luna's ribs.

She was facing the roof, and again her lips were making what had to be silent words. I kept on watching; my hand kept still. And after what felt like a slow month later, she let the words come out in a whisper. "I - want - to - love - you."

You recall I mentioned thinking of love some weeks before at the Bonaventures'. But I'd never said it out loud to Luna, and God knew she hadn't said it to me. I thought we'd each just tucked our skulls and plunged ahead till now we lay here sapped and safe but maybe ten trillion miles apart. If I'd heard her right, the whole world was changed. She'd outraced me and the backwash was steep. I might well drown. At first though, sprawled there in reach of my dream, I knew I must have heard her wrong. She was still faced upward. I remember thinking *She's talking to God.* But I knew not to ask. If by any chance it was meant for me, she'd find her time to say it again. And oh it felt like another long month before she turned.

Her eyes were almost too dark to watch—you thought you might get hauled in and lost. And the hair that she unclasped when we started, it set her face off—so pale beside me—that it seemed like a face thrust out of the night to lead me home, the true real home I'd waited for but never found till I met Luna. I knew the only brave thing to do was *answer* the words I thought I'd heard and wait again. I said "Luna Absher, I hope to love you every day of my life." The words took a long time to bridge the ten cool inches between us. And when she didn't move, I said "Signed, Blue Calhoun."

Her face stayed calm but she said "And *after?*—what then?"

"After what?"

"Your life."

We'd never mentioned God or our souls, but I said "If we outlast the grave, then—sure—I plan to love you better right down the ages as my soul grows and you play better and better songs on the heavenly harp."

She shut her eyes and shook her head.

I said "What's wrong?"

She still didn't look. "There's plenty of *after* and don't you doubt it—God's waiting at the gate. But he'll have us on the far side of Hell, both staked down dry on a flat iron grill, no drop to drink and not recalling each other's names."

I stroked her shut eyes gently with my thumb. "You don't think that. Think how we *feel*." I meant the goodness that all but swamped us minutes ago and still poured through me, tamer now.

Her eyes split open and her normal voice said "I got no clear idea on Earth how you feel about the least thing you do, not to mention these awful things *we've* done."

How can she lie here naked to me and think like that? My hand was still on her face, that looked peaceful. I traced the neutral line of her mouth. *Which part of all this can she really mean? Does she even know if she's serious?* I said what I truly believed at the time, "You know you don't believe that."

She said "I don't know nothing *but* that." Yet then I almost thought I could see the thinnest trace of a smile die out along her lips.

"Don't scare me," I said.

"I'm the scariest thing you know and vice versa in coal black spades." Her smile made a second try to break.

By then I was starting to see she meant her actual words. "Don't smile and say what you don't mean."

She said "I don't know what you mean from instant to instant. Why should you know me?"

"Ask me any question on Earth."

That set her back some, but then she said "Tell me the worst that's happened to you and the worst you've done." As I said, she'd never gone near my crimes and misdemeanors; but when I laughed she shut my mouth with her hand. "Blue, you promised."

So I tried to boil the worst truth down. "I spent nearly twenty years of my life hid in liquor and doctor pills. I either did it to numb my mind or to give me courage to treat my people like ignorant filth— I'm fairly sure I meant to do both. I strowed my body on several women that volunteered for a night or two. To my sure knowledge I've never drawn a drop of blood from a woman I touched; but sometimes blood might have cost them less than my slow meanness finally cost." I watched the words pass over the narrow space between us to Luna's eyes; and I tried to think *You're hard on yourself, son. Tell her so.*

But before I could she said "Ask me."

"What?"

"My worst—turnabout's fair play."

It actually scared me. *You don't want this. Stop her right on a dime.* But how many humans call a halt at those dark doors?—few men anyhow, though some wise women might. So I just stayed on there beside her, hoping she didn't plan to end us in the next few minutes.

Luna shut her eyes and rolled to her back (we'd faced each other). And she had it ready. "I've grown up dirt poor with my sad mother. I've lacked anything you'd recognize as a decent home. I've thought black hateful thoughts forever against my mother, though I guess she's *tried.* Till I knew you I wouldn't have crossed a sidewalk crack to see any human alive but my brother—" It sounded like she meant to push on; but the quiet stretched and she lay on there, still as the Bonaventures on slabs.

So I told myself *If that's her worst then you're home free.* And when Luna still didn't look or speak, I finally said "What was that all for?"

"That what?"

"Those questions."

Her eyes came open and slowly she turned to meet my face. "I said I wanted to love you, remember?" When I waited till I could thank her for that, she said "I also want to be Luna and *fine* at it, Blue—really good at *Luna.* Everything else can wait on that."

I braced myself up and looked all down her breasts and belly, her wiry fork. The plain outlandish fact of her being that real, that close, seemed too big to bear. I wondered if I'd ever breathe again, but of course I did. So I tried again to meet those steady amazing eyes. And

I said the one important thing. "Luna, I'm waiting at the head of your line—whoever's in it, wherever it ends. I beg you please, love me when you can." I never meant anything more sincerely in the years after that, except when I told your mother goodbye with a world of thanks and now tonight in asking this present mercy from you.

A look of kindness like none I'd seen—not since my mother would smile and watch me nurse her dry—came on that girl from some new place in her hid mind. She took my wrist and pressed the veiny side to her lips. Then she said "Don't beg."

I tried to ask "Why?" but her eyes forestalled me.

She whispered "Don't beg" and then frowned hard. "Don't beg, never beg. I tried to beg when I was a kid—don't ask me why—and it made things worse. Nothing in this poor world's worth begging."

"But you," I said. I thought I knew what she'd begged for—to move off safe from her own father. So I begged again for her best love. I meant it then and—seeing my simple lost *wrong* face in memory now and hearing me say the words again—I mean it all still, wrong or right (and it's too late to choose), here thirty years on. My only regrets are who I burned; and now I'm working to heal who I can, though some are dead—as you know, to your grief—and are far past my reach now in this life.

FOUR

WHEN WE'D GOT BACK in the car that evening and were halfway to Raleigh, I asked Luna for one more thing—"Take up your harp and sing me just one simple song." To my everlasting thanks she did it—short and simple the way I requested. She didn't pout or ask to be begged. She reached to the back seat, took out the harp, held it up against her bosom—not stopping to tune it—and strummed the chords to start her tune. When the first words came, I almost wrecked us.

Moonlight shines tonight along the Wabash.
Through the fields there comes a breath of new mown hay.
Through the sycamores the candlelights are gleaming
On the banks of the Wabash far away. . . .

I racked my mind to know if I'd ever mentioned that one song to her—how it was what my mother had sung me so many nights in the dark porch swing when the world was still enough for me. But even Miss Ashlyn's clear high voice couldn't match this magic girl's beside me. I've mentioned music as far my favorite blessing on Earth. So more than ever, once she'd sung that song of Mother's, I knew that Luna was sent to me—for me somehow to help and serve. I was sure I couldn't have given the hint. So I didn't tell her how right it was at this time now, how close I was to breaking down and begging her to stay in Raleigh, at hand. But I kept fairly calm and got us safe to a spot three blocks away from Rita's.

on as I stopped, Luna reached for the door and said "Well, thank you and so long now—"

It felt like she was flinging herself down an endless hole, not caring for what we'd made in these weeks. I had to take her arm to slow her. Then I gave her the only tangible thing I'd ever heard her say she wanted—a thin gold chain with a small heart-locket, no picture inside (it only cost me seven dollars but no big diamond could have showed the feeling I intended). I'd meant to give it while we were still alone in the room. But then I'd thought it might sit wrong there, like too quick a payment for what she'd agreed to. Anyhow I'd left it just in the box with cotton around it, no wrapping paper. I didn't mean to stage a dramatic event and leave her glad to go. So I just set it in the palm of her hand and said "In memory—now you study hard, enjoy yourself, don't fall off a mountain and know I thank you."

But Luna wouldn't open it, even when I said I'd gladly exchange it for something else. She said "I love to surprise myself. I'll wait till I'm on the bus tomorrow—I may need it then." Still she gave the broadest smile in all the weeks I'd known her. I doubt I've seen a serious rival on any face since except your mother's when she held you towards me, two weeks old, at our first meeting. Then Luna said "Thank - you - Blue" again, with just her lips in the air, no sound. And she was gone in another instant, no backward turn.

You can guess the next few days were rough. At first I thought I finally knew how amputees feel—your right leg's gone but you still feel pain in the ball of your foot. By the second day I knew I was different. I wasn't the amputee himself. I was the leg, the hacked off leg—no hip, no torso, lungs or heart, alone in space but hoping to walk. Again I got on through my job and laughed when I could. I sat at home and watched TV with Myra and Mattie and heard their stories. I took out garbage and pruned the shrubs. I scoured the papers morning and night like the smallest buried ad might tell me the secret of peace. I was hunting news that a Raleigh girl on scholarship at music camp had dropped off a mountain trail, breaking her back, or had drowned in an ice cold lake by night with no one to save her.

Several days before she left, I'd given Luna the store's address and said she could drop me a note or two if she really felt like it. I specified plain envelopes marked *Personal* and no return address. She'd nodded and put the card in her wallet. In those first days once she was gone, I calculated the mail schedules between home and the mountains a hundred times. If she got there Saturday night on time, she likely wouldn't write till Sunday at the earliest, by Tuesday maybe when she'd learned the ropes. And if she mailed a note on Tuesday, it might not reach the store till Thursday (in those days the U.S. Mail still worked).

But that first Thursday came and went, then the first weekend and the whole next week. So I was strung all up the road from Raleigh to the Blue Ridge—my nerves were, like telegraph wires in a lightning storm. I'd even told her, in any emergency, to call me personal collect at the store. But no call came and my mind boiled.

You slog through it someway, don't you?—*Christ, how?* My personal memories of World War II in Britain, Europe and surrounding waters still feel to my mind like swansdown pillows compared to that wait. Somehow as I said, I hauled myself upright and in the usual harness from June 16th when Luna left home to July 3rd, a sizzling Tuesday before we'd close one day for the 4th. (Even as late as the 1950s the South paid little attention to the 4th. We were still in a sulk about losing the War Between the States, and the 4th still smelled like Yankees and death.) At least on the 3rd I got a short let up on the daily treadmill.

That day Mother had her biannual eye appointment at McPherson's Hospital over in Durham, and I'd arranged with the store to take her and get back to work as soon as I could. She was due at nine, the drive from her house took roughly an hour, so of course she'd issued the strictest orders that I must collect her no later than seven. I suggested in that case she cook my breakfast. But she said she could barely see to make coffee, and I'd be lucky to get a fast cup—no guarantees.

Punctuality is my only virtue. I knocked on her front door two minutes early and tried to turn the knob—it was locked. That was more than odd for her to be locked in if she was awake, and the hair on my neck stood up and stung. Even in childhood I'd had big scares when she got one of her grim migraines. She'd lie down to rest with all shades drawn. Then when I'd try to ask a question hours later, she'd be so deep asleep or pained that I'd stand on the doorsill and know she was dead. I'd always finally make myself walk towards the bed and touch her chin. I'd rock her head gently and say "It's just Blue," praying she'd look out and know me again.

So now I beat on the dry old wood and called "Mother" loudly. Again no answer. In my drunk days she'd always refused to give me a key; but now I recalled that, years before, a spare housekey was kept hid under the front porch steps. I reached in the spidery dark and found it still on its nail. It was rusty but it turned the lock. The front hall and parlor were dark and clammy, no sound at all. I called "Miss Ashlyn?" Nothing, nothing. Her bedroom was twenty feet off to my left. But I knew to think *Save that for last. Try everywhere else.*

I went down the hall on my right—two bedrooms, including the one I slept in when we'd visited my grandparents out here. I moved like a sleepwalker, scared but hopeful, and stopped in the door. She'd somehow found my old baseball jacket and laid it out at the foot of my bed. It was left from when I played college ball at Davidson; then flunked out, throwing that big chance away. (More than one knowledgeable person claimed I might have had a shot at fame and money. I had a genuine gift for the game—I was deadeye fast—but even that young, it felt too childish to take pride in.) The jacket looked as ready to wear as the day I won it, but I couldn't touch what only belonged to the long gone boy everybody had cheered when the world was green. Maybe Matt could wear it some day down the road or pass it on to her first son.

I went back to the parlor and called again. This time I heard myself say "Please"—"Miss Ashlyn, *please.*" By then I think my mind well knew she was dead or worse, and still in her bed or torn on the floor. One chance was left. I stood a minute and said to myself *All right. You did this. Now take your punishment.* Nothing was left to check but the kitchen and then her room. I tucked my chin, walked back through the dining room and opened the wide black kitchen door that I'd never seen shut.

She was still in her bathrobe slumped in her usual chair at the table. The table was bare as a pond of ice except for her hands that spread out flat and palm down before her. She was staring at them, and her hair was still in a plait down her spine.

I stopped in the door to let her see me. But for ten long seconds, she didn't look up. *She's had the stroke you always expected* (her mother had lived for twenty years after her one stroke, half paralyzed when the last child came, a son that vanished early out west). I started to call her, but that would be painful if she couldn't speak, so I walked over lightly and touched her left hand. It was bluish and cooler than the air around us.

Then slowly she let it turn palm up, and next she closed it round my fingers. She still didn't meet my eyes; but she said "I won't do it, son." Her voice seemed strong.

"What's that, Mother?"

At last she leaned back, stroked her eyes hard and faced me. "I *can't.*" She plainly thought I understood her.

"You've done everything you wanted till now, you're stronger than me, sure you can." I pulled out the chair beside her and sat. She didn't show any sign of explaining, so I said "What is it you can't do?"

She suddenly looked around to the stove. "Lord, I haven't even started coffee—"

"Forget the coffee. You've got to dress. But what's your trouble?"

When she faced me I thought my skin might scorch.

She said "I will not watch you do this thing."

By then I almost hoped she was addled. "This *thing*—please ma'm, what thing do you mean?"

"Your dreadful cruelty—that young girl and your wife and child. I will not watch you do it, Bluford. Forget my eyes. I mean to go blind and put myself in a nursing home with my own money and let you sow your meanness in the dark—my dark at least."

All my life she'd had that brutal edge to her tongue when she saw it was needed. Most times she was cool and kind as dusk. But run up against her absolute certainty of right and wrong, and you'd be lucky to crawl away with your eyes and teeth. I'd seen her turn it twice on my father and once on her brother that struck his wife but never yet this hot on me. I sat and let her watch me take it. Then I stood. "I'm here on time to drive you to Durham. If you aren't going I'll head in to work." I'd never been that distant with her.

And she caught it at once. "You don't even want to hear me out. Yet you were the one that told me the news and drove out of here, leaving me with the mess." She beckoned me to sit.

I shook my head. "The mess—as you call it—is my life, Mother. You've never thought I could put one foot ahead of the other without your help. But finally I've got my own life. I'm sober enough to *feel* it too, and it feels grand—feels like fine *wine*. I'd like to help you see your doctor and fix your eyes when the time is ripe, but I'm not going to wait around and let you slam me back into childhood one more time." Even as the words rushed past my teeth, I couldn't believe them. But I let them stand.

So did Miss Ashlyn. She bent her head in one slow move and laid her forehead on her hands like a prayer. Then she pressed both palms to the table and stood. Her eyes were hard as they'd been before, but she said "You make you some instant coffee. I'll be ready."

I made the coffee, bitter as tin in my sick mouth. And I sat in my old place facing out towards the floor length window, watching the light work round the house and strike the pear tree, then my grandfather's homemade sundial, green with age and its short motto "Time Heals." I'd got a little shaky from the various shocks of the past ten minutes—*Does Mother know even more than I told her? Is Myra somehow part of this? Has Rita called Myra and Myra called Mother?* In the next few seconds, I let myself get thoroughly miserable. And there in a room where I'd passed a slew of sick drunk mornings, I actually felt the floor of my brain beg me for a drink. I knew there was bourbon deep in the pantry, sherry and port.

But I clamped my teeth till I saw stars and told myself *Time heals, old son. Your life has started. Take life, Blue.* I truly believed it, I could have been right, my entire family's life thereafter could have been intended to happen someway that spared us all the heartbreak, agony and blood that came, if only I could have seized it that instant and guided every soul involved on a better path; but I didn't know how. I listened to my body that had been so starved—the body that felt as magic now as a pillar of fire—and I flew onward by its signals, too fast to chase; and I charred us all.

Mother had always left me in the waiting room. I'd offer to go in with her and help her remember what the doctor said (she'd often forget and I'd have to phone him), but she'd just thank me and go it alone. I'd been out there in the midst of blind children, reading wornout magazines for half an hour when Dr. McPherson himself came out and asked me to join them. When I walked into the cubicle with him, Miss Ashlyn was back in the corner on a stool. Her face was rigged in a curious smile like her diminished faculties could see a whole better world with flowers and birds. She didn't so much as nod to my presence, and in another second I was ready to bolt. I can almost manage waiting rooms; but the real insides of a true hospital are rough on me—I think they'll keep me; I know they *should*—so I propped up against a wall, tried to breathe slowly and faced the doctor.

He said "Mr. Calhoun, this good lady has kept a surprise hid back of those cataracts. We want you to know it."

Mother was still not looking at me, but I breathed again and said "All right, sir."

"She's showing the early signs of macular degeneration. That's way inside the ball itself. It's not that rare as we get older. It may not go much further than now, though it could bite down and run the whole way. But this fine lady has lost some vision in the central field these past six months."

I asked what he could do for that.

When he paused an instant, Mother said "Not a goddamned thing." She looked as proper as Queen Elizabeth smelling a rose, but still she put a slow hand to her mouth. "I'm sorry, Doctor Mac."

He'd watched her eyes for many years. I knew he liked her looks and spunk. And now he covered the space between them and laid his slim surgeon's hand on her shoulder.

She reached up, took it; and—the way she'd done this morning at home on her own flat hands—she pressed her eyes against it hard.

He let her use him and with his other hand he stroked the crown of her lovely head. Then he said "I'm sorry as I can be," more to me than her. He knew she could bear it.

We barely spoke on the drive back home or even when we unlocked the house and I walked through all the rooms to check for changes or strangers. Mother knew I needed to get back to work; and as I finished my tour of the place, she stepped from the bathroom and met me square in the midst of the parlor. She suddenly looked five sizes smaller, shrunk and dry. And when she also took my hand, I had to struggle to keep back tears—she'd have hated that. I said the only thing I knew, but it felt like the jackpot. "You know you don't deserve this, Mother."

And oh she smiled. I'd waited all morning for some slight break in the overcast, but now this beaming smile nearly floored me. She said "What's *this* I don't deserve?"

"This world we're in here—the waste and pain."

"I love it," she said and pressed her forehead into my chest. "I love this world more than you've ever known."

To my amazement I suddenly laughed, but I said "Don't tell me how much—I'd die."

"I'd miss you, old Blue." Her voice was still strong. Then she pulled back and faced me. "I've *always* missed you." I understood it was only the truth, and it sent me out the door in pain.

That all stayed with me through the long afternoon. I kept fairly busy with a string of small sales and one good natured old customer, drunk and wanting me to "tune her accordion." But I couldn't shake the thought of Mother. In nearly four decades I'd seen her run through thousands of moods—and as I said, occasional fire storms—but nothing remotely like this morning when she seemed already on the far side of death and blaming me rightly. When the last mail of the day came in at three o'clock, and nothing for me, I suddenly knew that Mother's blame, and now the news about her eyes, cut deeper in me than anything else but the way to have Luna.

I saw I'd walked right past my wife and only child—right through their faces—but one old woman had hurt my brain. And in my mind I argued with her the rest of the day, but the thing I couldn't begin to change was the deep dyed fact that Mother had the right to act like she did. So when I left the store near six and opened my car, I let that stifling air pour out; and I said to myself *Just think about now. Just think about here.* I figured that meant my home and family.

Myra's car was gone from the drive when I got there. That was strange and when I found the back door open and walked on in, I fully expected to see a note on the breakfast table with more bad news. Nothing though. The stove was cold, no signs of supper. I went to the foot of the steps and called Madelyn first. No answer again. *It's coming down. It's sinking beneath me*—I remember clearly thinking such words. I took the high stairs two at a time and headed for Matt's room, a half open door. I stopped just short and told myself *If Matt's here safe I'll aim at her. From here on out I'll do it for Matt.* It was after all the pledge I'd made near two years ago that had seen me through the end of drinking to being a partly upright man.

She was on her narrow bed, turned to the wall. Right off I tried to remember whether I'd ever seen her nap in daylight—not since she was a baby, no. I could hear her breathing, so at least I wasn't faced with another possible death. I crept on towards her and touched her head. It had been a hot day; and at first she felt too warm, maybe feverish.

But when I sat on the edge of the mattress, she slowly turned against my butt, looked up at me, crossed her eyes and launched a big smile.

I put my fingers to her forehead—too warm. "Feeling sick?" It was only then in the mid fifties that the annual summer dread of polio had started to ease. The Salk vaccine had first been used in '54; and as I sat there feeling Mattie burn, I couldn't remember if she'd had the shots. Young as she was she'd lived through several quarantines when the health department would order children confined to their blocks—no swimming, no movies, no public parks. Even a boy in one of Matt's grades had come down with it and still wore a brace.

Now Matt felt her cheek and said "I'm fine. I just got tired."

She's never tired—I well knew that. I said "Then you were right to rest." She was wearing blue shorts and a white blouse, so I took her bare calf and nonchalantly flexed her knee.

She broke out laughing. "*Sky*, I don't have polio! Remember you took me to get vaccinated?"

I said "Of course" but I truly didn't recall the shots. All her life I'd been the one she wanted when doctors were near. Brave as she was about all else, and even if she shut her eyes, Matt automatically fainted whenever she got a shot (by the end of her life, she'd got over that unfortunately—it might have helped her through the pain if she could have just gone *out* every time she got morphine). I'd learned to kneel in front of the chair and prop her gently when she slumped unconscious. Then a nurse would bring the smelling salts, and Matt would be fine.

Lying there now she said "I kind of miss polio."

"Please don't say that. Think about your school friend, the other children, President Roosevelt, iron lungs."

She nodded and was serious. "I just meant the rules they'd lay down for us in quarantines—I loved not being able to leave the yard or the block. I felt like we three were living in a castle with just your car as the only drawbridge. You'd go and come but that was all, and we knew we were mostly safe."

I laughed. "Your brain is frying, child. Don't you remember how the kids came here, and you played cards in the moldy basement and listened to those old records of mine and—"

Matt sang lines from "Stardust" and "Tenderly." Then she started whistling Ted Weems' "Heartaches." I conducted her on to the high pitched end with a waving hand. And when she quit she said "You oldsters had all the good songs."

"You like Spike Jones. You like Peggy Lee."

She nodded again. "But oldsters have the dancing songs—'Begin the Beguine,' 'Night and Day.'"

"Slow dancing?" I said. "You thought that was sappy last time I checked."

She didn't smile. "Last time you checked I was still a child." She batted her eyes, imitating a vamp. Then they shut and she lay there calmer than sleep.

I went quiet beside her to wait till she looked. But when she didn't, the time stretched on. Then—here's a problem known to most fathers but one I've never heard a father speak of. I've asked myself far more than once about the wisdom of setting this down for your eyes now or whenever you read it. I think you'll need to hear it though eventually (maybe too late for me to answer questions), so I write it down in the certainty that it's nothing but true and that it may help you start to see how what your poor dad finally did—under dreadful pressure as Matt was dying—was not entirely a monster's deed, whatever it seemed to all at the time.

A man may be the finest on Earth, with a rough hairshirt and dry bread to eat, but when he lives every day of his life in close home quarters with a budding girl, his soul gets tested instant by instant. I don't say it's an admirable trait in me or any other man, but I say in *spades*—it's the way the male half of the human race is built and wired; and if a man exceeds his limits, it's not necessarily because he's evil, just burdened and frail and sometimes even trying to show—in the whole wrong language—a depth of love that's in his soul.

And not just his soul—there's numerous other parts at stake, starting with his eyes. He has to keep steady watch on himself from head to toe, and it can hurt. I trust you not to think I'm volunteering here as a meaner dog than most of the normal fathers on Earth when I have to say—if truth be told—I sat through those next minutes by Madelyn and fought my skin. My skin and the hungry pit of my mind that kept saying *Touch her. See how far you go.* I've strown a good deal more than my share of pain and confusion but not to my daughter, not that July day or any day after.

Budding she was, though. And somehow my mind had failed to see it till that afternoon—had it just started as summer bloomed? Or had Luna's body, that was three years older, aimed my eyes at sights I'd missed? Excuse me too for saying I shut my own eyes then and thought of the youngest girl I'd known, really known to the quick. I worked back fast and found her face. We were in the seventh grade. *What's that?—age twelve, thirteen at most. I know I was twelve and not really fitted with a full set of works. But all she had from crown to toe, just that winter, had tipped on over the lip of the hill. And she was better than she'd be again, ever in life, though we didn't know it—magic the way her breasts held on when she rose up, no gravity, and those few baby curls down low where I kept looking but was scared to touch. So she led the way. I tagged along as best I could, which must not have been too bad after all—didn't she say I was good to feel? And where is she now—as sad as me?*

Mattie looked up again. "Grandmother's eyes—is she all right?"

You're all but grown, I thought. *Here's the truth.* "Grandmother may be truly going blind."

"Is that what's been the matter with you?"

It stung me hard—since when had she felt that? I lied and nodded. "Miss Ashlyn's got a whole new thing, old Dr. Mac says. The deep inside of her eye is dying."

"Did he say when they could operate?"

"This is new, sweetheart—more than just cataracts. They can't help this."

Matt touched my sleeve. "How long have you known?"

"Today, just now."

"Then have I done something wrong to you?"

What does she know? God don't let her know. I said "You've done me nothing but good since you saw light."

She watched me, serious, a good while then. I thought I could see her believe me finally, and next she said "I ought to do what I said I would." She didn't push on.

"What's that?"

"Live with Grandmother while I can, from now till school starts."

I remembered Myra's instant objection. And sad to admit I thought *Don't leave Myra rattling here in this big house. She'll turn on me.* But I said "If your mother says you can, it's fine by me. You're far and away *my* mother's favorite."

Again Matt paused a long time. Then she checked my face before she said "I wish I could do some great deed for *you*." She slowly crossed both arms on her chest.

Any other day I'd have thanked whatever gods were behind her. By now you know I'd have also wept. But all I could do that sad afternoon was take both her wrists and hold them gently. I said "You've done everything I need on this green Earth." Ten weeks before, that would have been so nearly true as to pass most tests. Now I knew it was worse than a lie.

And whatever Madelyn knew or feared, she shook her head No over and over.

Then the sight of my child refusing that lie broke through the callus on my mind and eyes and very nearly crushed my chest. But when I touched her forehead again, it was cool as normal. What had felt like fever was more likely dreams, and Matt never told her dreams anymore.

When I got back into my bedroom, I realized I'd failed to ask where Myra was. But I didn't call out. I slipped off my hot tie and shoes, lay down to rest for fifteen minutes; and when I finally woke, the room was all but dim—near eight o'clock. I sat up and listened to silent space but was still too groggy to scare one more time this strange day. Then as I washed my face and hands, I heard low knocks and clinks from the kitchen. When I got downstairs there was no sign of Mattie. But Myra stood at the sink washing dishes. She must have heard me, though she didn't look back. I said "You decided to let me starve?"

She still didn't look. "I knew you were tired."

I thought of a thing she'd always liked—for me to come up behind her at the sink and scratch my chin along her neck. She'd always say "Human sandpaper—quit!" But I knew I couldn't do it now. I held my ground and opened the refrigerator. Her usual squared off set of bowls, everything well covered, no spills or waste. I was suddenly mad. "You didn't know how tired I was. You didn't ask *me*."

Myra turned then. "Mattie said—"

"Mattie is not Blue Calhoun, Myra. I'm the *Blue* in this house."

I hadn't raised my voice to Myra in three or four years, maybe longer than that (I was never an angry drunk as I said). And I honestly think it shook her badly. She whipped around to the sink again to hide her tears.

"Is there something in this icebox a human being can safely touch?"

She said "You know your supper's in the oven."

"How would I know that?"

"From fifteen years of marriage to me. When have I failed to feed you yet?"

She hadn't ever. Many's the night she'd go downstairs at three in the morning and softboil eggs for me, make French toast or a white cheese sandwich when I couldn't stomach anything stronger but had to eat. And now she was already bent at the oven, finding my plate. I said "What is it?"

"Blue, I'm sorry—it's frozen fish. I got delayed coming home today, so I rushed this out. Matt seemed to like it."

"Where's Mattie now?"

"Skating with Vicki down the Byrd Street hill."

By then I'd figured I should eat anyhow. But when I sat, Myra moved to the sink. That alone was strange. She came from the final wave of women who watched every morsel of food they cooked, from sink to stomach. Did it go down smooth? Did he smile or frown? How long before the second bite? Too cool, too hot? You were grateful for the tasty end result, but you sometimes wanted to yell and stomp—*It's nothing but food. Calm down for God's sake.* Myra always forgot I'd been in the war; bad food was not my greatest dread. Anyhow I choked down what I could stand of fish sticks tasting like wet newspaper, and then I said "What held you up?"

"Sir?"

"You said you got delayed coming home."

By then she'd dried the last dish and folded her apron. Unhurried as ever she drank her evening glass of water, tall and warm as it ran from the tap. Then she came to the table and sat in Madelyn's chair on my right. So when her gray eyes fixed on my face, I knew she meant to talk about big things. I thought it would surely be Mattie's asking to stay with Mother.

She said "Rita Absher came by here this morning—that door." She pointed past me, the backyard door.

A punctured eye might have stunned me less, but I thought I didn't show it. I said "I didn't know Rita had a car."

"There's a new invention called taxis, Blue. You can ride anywhere on Earth for a dollar."

I wondered, for the first time really, if Myra had ever known Rita back when. *No, Rita's no Catholic.* I said "I've known Rita all my life."

Myra nodded. "She said that." Only then did her eyes look down and wait.

I could see she had no idea where to start, and I suddenly thought I owed her that help. "What else did she say?"

Myra spoke to the table and her own fine hands. "—That you had fallen in love with her daughter and got the child badly mixed up and wild."

"Did she say the child is a full grown woman?"

"Mrs. Absher showed me a picture of her, this year's school picture."

"The child's sixteen. Miss Ashlyn's mother was married at sixteen, my own grandmother."

Myra said "Is Luna planning to marry?"

The name hadn't yet been said in that house. And it batted round the kitchen now like a trapped blind bird. I said "Luna plans to be a musician. She plays the harp."

"That you sold to her—"

"That she learned in school, that Rita brought her in the store to *buy*. They walked in off the street this April, and I recognized Rita after long years."

"Easy as that?" Myra had someway calmed herself—her voice, hands, eyes. So all the rest she said straight at me, no flinch, no fear.

"Myra, nothing in my life's ever been easy. You ought to know that."

"You don't think *I've* walked a primrose path?" She was almost smiling.

"No, I don't—far from it. I've begged your pardon and you freely gave it."

She nodded slowly. "Till now, up to now." Then she stood, walked past me and went to the door that opened on the rest of the house. She called Matt's name once strongly, then again. She was testing whether we were alone. When no answer came she sat back down. "You love this child?"

"I've told her so."

"I didn't ask that."

So I said "I am in love with her, yes." I'd never felt it stronger or truer, though next I sat and watched it scald my wife at a long arm's reach across a table—the woman that no doubt saved my body and whatever scraps of soul I had.

Myra waited for what felt like a year. "Where do we go then?"

I knew that *we* meant her and Madelyn. I said "Nowhere. You're in your home."

Again Myra waited but her eyes caught fire. "Blue, there's a thing I've tried hard to do through all these years; and that was not to tell you the truth if it seemed too hurtful for you to stand. But the way I feel this minute now, I'm going to say it. I feel like I don't want to spend even one more night in sheets that your money paid to buy and that your skin has touched."

It didn't hurt. In an awful way it thrilled me to hear. *She's making it easy.* But then I thought of Matt and her room, and I heard myself say "Don't leave, Myra." I thought I knew her well enough to know she'd ask "Why?" next, and I'd have no answer.

But she pushed on further. "Name one good reason."

I thought and then said "Madelyn Calhoun." I knew I ought to feel deep care for my one child that I said I loved and had changed lives for, but that bad minute my mind was so far off and cold that next I thought *You Catholics will stay. You'll strap me down.* I said "You haven't told Matt a word about this?"

Myra shook her head. "Mattie figured out well before me that you were *off*. I doubt she's gone much further than that. But Blue, she knows you; and since late winter she's kept telling me you were turning sad."

"At least she hit the nail on the head." I could feel a helpless grin try to spread.

Myra said "Can you help me understand the reason?"

My mind went blank as a sheet of glass. But I think what I finally said was right and true to my will. "Honest to Christ, I don't know a reason. A magic person walked up next to my life just now, and everything shifted ninety degrees."

"So two months later here, you're telling Mattie and me to leave?"

I knew it was no good saying again that she and Matt would stay right here. And it still hadn't crossed my mind to wonder where I'd go, tonight and hereafter. So I didn't speak.

Then Myra said "Rita claims you haven't slept with the child."

I figured Luna had told Rita that. I even thought it was literally true—sleep was the last thing we'd done together. But I said "That may not be Rita's business but yes, it's true." Right off I felt the room leak pressure. My chest felt like it had popped a steel band. Myra's frown seemed to fade by a notch, and next I found myself believing what I'd said. Luna Absher suddenly felt as long ago and past belief as the Red Sea parting for Moses' voice. In maybe ten seconds I took my fork and began to eat.

Myra said "That's got to be stone cold, Blue."

Any married person reading this can understand that the whole next hour was bruised but calm. I stayed within five yards of Myra, though we didn't touch and barely spoke. When dark was almost on us, I said we ought to walk down and watch Mattie skate, then bring her back. Myra agreed. We walked the single block downhill and stood on the edge of the Cowdens' walk while Matt and Vicki and three loud boys spun and bumped each other and laughed.

Matt rolled over towards us at last and said "You don't think I'm coming home now, do you?"

I looked to Myra and she said "No, if you're real careful, you can stay till ten."

I'd very much hoped Matt would go back between us. I wanted to hear her slip through the house the way she could on light bare feet, like a well meant ghost that wanted me near. But since I'd turned it over to Myra, all I could do was reach out and wipe two strands of hair back off Mattie's forehead and say "Be careful" again, that helpless.

When Myra and I were home in the yard, I said "I'm going to ride awhile."

She waited beside me a few long seconds, then stepped towards the door. "You've got your own key."

I said I'd be back well before bedtime, and then I knew I actually would.

It took me nearly an hour of roaming through evening streets with a still numb mind before I knew the next two things. *Don't see Rita Absher. Just drive yourself out Ridge Road again and see how you feel.* You recall it was where I went with Luna that first April night and one other time. In those days all that side of the county was ancient woods and uncut fields, not cardboard houses and a runaway mall that flooded in every winter rain. I'd known it by the inch since boyhood. Friends and I used to ride our bikes out there in the summer to swim in Crabtree Creek and hide in woods that felt as thick and endless as Eden but went down dead at the touch of a dollar.

I'd even discovered on my own the two lane logging track that ended in a curious natural bowl of rocks with a steep drop off to the west, a real cliff. I wasn't a very secretive child, but I somehow never showed it to a friend. I kept it for times I needed to be with myself after big disappointments or when I was learning to use my body as it outgrew me. I don't mean to say the place talked back, but it helped me know how far I'd slewed to left or right. Even after I got my driver's license, I never took any dates out there, not the logging track and the edge of that cliff—not even Myra who anyhow stayed very nearly a virgin till we got married.

So I went there that night of July 3rd for no known reason but lonesomeness. I pulled the car in off the road; and with no light but years of instinct, I walked on back in the woods again. After a long stretch of saplings and briars, I was in the midst of the really old trees like elephant legs. Sure as a bat I passed through them in a dead straight line and wound up where I meant to be, the bowl of rocks. The leaves had thickened since Luna and I were last in here, and I could barely see the sky. I went to a certain flat rock though and stretched out on my back to wait. I'd spent whole nights camped out here alone in my early teens, and my body knew every crack in the surface. I'd passed through more than one bad time by trying to rest my swarming mind— just not to think but to let the elements tell me what I was meant to do and how to do it.

I well understand how you're now thinking, he ought to be gagging up his guts in self hate or scraping his eyes in punishment. And I'm very nearly sure you're right. But again I have to say that I felt calmer than not and glad to be me. If you find yourself truly baffled whenever you read the news of crimes and cruelty, try to believe that a human being who's not that far from everyday life—maybe not that far from being *you*—can burn down any number of hearts, then lie on his back in beautiful woods on a clean hot night and soon be free of every pain he's caused or will cause. And he won't need liquor or other drugs or actual blood but his own hot aim to do his will, whether it's murder or intentional ruin to a wife and child.

Me for instance, that July night—I didn't feel sorry for Myra and Madelyn or wonder where they'd be tomorrow, not to mention next year. I pitied my mother's eyes a few seconds but knew I'd stand beside her whatever. Old Rita Absher didn't exist, however low she stooped to block me. And all that mattered on Earth or under was how to think my private way tonight right now into Luna's body that was two hundred miles uphill to the west and love her deep and make her know again how long she'd needed me and always would, and how we'd be together soon.

In maybe three minutes I managed it. My mind moved west by racing through its favorite scenes of Luna at her perfect pitch, bent under me and smiling silent, bearing all I had to give or riding me hard and thanking God. Soon enough I had her all but real in my head. I shucked my pants and opened my shirt and brought my body dark down on her, wherever she lay in whatever cabin with both eyes wide to the mountain night praying for Blue to be there. Now. And I was too, down my whole burning body while I dreamed her face and panted her name—*Sweet Luna, Lune.* (If that disgusts or offends you now, I'm deeply sorry. But since I have to leave you soon and may not return, what I'm after here in these pages—and what you'll need someday if not now—is literal facts on the actual people that stand behind the cells of your mind. If I'd ever known my family story in true detail—who'd done what to whom and when and why—I might have known what demons to watch for in my life, what mines were buried in the core of my brain. I was ignorant though till way too late, and blithely careless; and look what it cost us.)

When I got to the house, it was near eleven. But the living and dining room lights were on. I paused at the drive to see if I could spot anybody at the windows—no. So I pulled in and there at the rear was an old black car. *Matt is sick* was my first thought—*Dr. Brian's car.* It didn't have a doctor's emblem on the bumper, but still I walked through the kitchen door worried. At first I heard nothing, then low voices from the front of the house. *Christ, don't let it be Rita Absher with some of her kin and a Colt .45. Don't let it be Luna in any form.* Footsteps had already started towards me.

It was Matt in a dress this late at night, combed and neat with a hush on her face. She shut the door behind her and whispered "It's Father Scanlon, Sky."

I went ice cold but I also whispered "What's he doing here?"

She stood there silent.

"Who called him, Matt?"

Then I saw she was lost. "He apologized for coming so late; but see, I called him after supper and asked him to pray for Grandmother's eyes. That gave him the idea to bring us Our Lady, but he had to drive to Apex to get her, and that made him late."

If she'd talked angel tongues of flame, I couldn't have understood any less. I turned and meant to climb upstairs, undress again and try to sleep in the front guest room.

But Mattie said "Please come speak to him." When I didn't move, she said "I don't ask you for a lot—" So I let her take my hand and lead me on through the door.

Father Scanlon popped to his feet like a cork, threw out his hand but waited for me to come more than halfway. His grin was tight as a strap on a keg, and I noticed a glass of Coke by his chair. Then again I felt his filleted white hand; and he said "Mr. Calhoun, forgive the late hour."

I forgave him but stayed upright on my feet as he sat again. I needed some quick guarantee that he wasn't here on a marital mission. I could barely believe that Myra would tell him, but still he felt like a huge intruder.

Myra was at the far end of the sofa, and Matt had already sat in the rocker. Both looked to the priest.

So Scanlon invited me to join them—me, in my own living room.

He won't even let me pray beside them; why sit and grin? But for Mattie I also went to the sofa. It was not till then that I saw the statue on the long pine table—maybe two feet tall, the Virgin Mary in what looked like pale beige long clothes, her normal dead-on gaze and open hands. Weird as it was after this long day, I thought of nothing but which Lady was she—the one from Lourdes or Fatima or some other place she chose to appear? (if you lived near a female Catholic in those antique unstreamlined days, you couldn't help learning many such strange facts).

Father Scanlon said "I'm grieved to hear of your mother's plight."

I was still so hazy I said "Well, thanks but is it a plight?"

Mattie said "You bet."

And I knew it was. I said "I'm grateful you take an interest. My mother's a life long Presbyterian."

Scanlon beamed. "Mattie's always made that clear. Our Lady wasn't a Catholic herself! God loves us all as she well knows."

I'd figured out, in my first days with Myra, what a good idea their Lady was—an endless mother that never nagged, never cooked you a morsel or watched you eat it. But there under Scanlon's fat pig eyes, I wanted to say my mother had her own line to God. And if God was choosing to drive her blind, then lay the hell off—she was his to use. But for Madelyn's sake I just said "Thank you."

He nodded acceptance. "Mattie says she'll go out now and be with your mom till school begins."

Mom as the name for the woman that bore you in blood and pain didn't come into wide American use till after TV invented the "family," its biggest lie. And as a name I'll have to say *Mom* is my idea of a childish insult to any woman's dignity. (If I'd ever tried it on Ashlyn Calhoun, I wouldn't be here writing this tonight. I know I've accepted *Dad* for *Father*; but so many fathers are fair game for *Dad*— old Dad, dumb dud.) If we need a substitute for *Mother*, then why not *Moo*? *Moo* at least suggests a creature you milk. But I let it go that night with Scanlon.

So Myra said Yes and now Mattie leaves for the rest of summer. A sudden relief poured through my mind, but I didn't try to think my way through what that meant for me and Luna. I just told Scanlon it was Matt's idea and that I was grateful. When I looked to Matt, she was watching the Lady statue still and looked as wise as any old salt. I said "Have you called Mother yet?"

Matt nodded Yes, not looking my way.

"You going tomorrow?"

She nodded again and since I thought she was silently praying, I said to Myra "I'll drive her out."

Myra waited awhile and said "You will." She was also aimed at the statue's eyes.

I figured I'd interrupted their session long enough—their rosaries were still at hand—but when I stood Scanlon bounced to his feet and said "You good souls need your rest."

I'd understood—and was not far wrong by the Catholic standards of those days—that I wasn't deemed to have a real soul. So for a nice moment I felt promoted. And I managed to show the round priest to his car like I was one more bona fide candidate for crown and harp, though by the time I was back indoors, I felt the howling start in my soul, my brand new tender helpless soul.

Still I slept a good part of the night with Myra there a hand's reach away. But sleep took awhile. As Myra and I'd undressed for bed, we'd acted courteous as strangers—little smiles and nods. But I'd known her so long I could feel the drilling ache in her eyes. For whatever awful natural reason, I was still fairly calm. And when she switched the last light off, I didn't go straight to the Virgin Mary; but for the first time in many a moon, I made my way through the Lord's Prayer— my private version without all the *thou's*. Maybe ten minutes after that, I could hear Myra breathing and still awake. So what came next came sudden and deep from way inside—"You've never done an unkind thing to me in the years I've known you." I was shocked to hear how close it came to what Luna Absher had said to me, but it only felt true of Myra now, and I let it stand.

Myra mostly refused any compliment. Now she lay on quiet so long I thought she refused any answer at all, but then she said "I guess I'm who I've always been."

I said "You are." It was true but I saw I'd opened myself to a hard reply.

She went straight for it. "Then what went wrong?"

Everything I said from there on out came to me from outside or so deep inside I couldn't guess where. I said "Not one small thing went *wrong*. You've given me more than I could name if I had a century. You're a good looking honest reliable wonder. But the world changed on me one April day."

Myra said "You know I can't believe it happened like that."

I said "You believe in Satan, don't you?"

"Mmm."

"Then maybe I'm under his hand right now."

"Blue, please don't make light of this."

"I swear to Christ I'm earnest, Myra. I don't know what's behind this change, but I doubt it's me—I know it's not you or Matt or my job or Miss Ashlyn or money."

"Or liquor," she said. Again she waited so long I thought she'd quit or was sleeping. But then she said "Where does it lead?"

"Search me."

"No, Blue, you *say*. Just say where you want this to lead."

"I do not know."

"You're lying," she said.

In all the nights and days I'd told Myra tales of the filth I'd done with whoever, she'd never yet called me a liar. But in a while now, I knew she was right—I truly did know where I wanted to go and not alone. A whole clear road stretched out in my mind, and I saw its ending plain ahead. Till then we'd both been flat on our backs. I quietly turned to my right side. By then my eyes were big in the dark, I could see the whole good line of her face, but I couldn't begin to call her name. So I said "I want it to lead, and soon, to where I spend the rest of my life with Luna Absher."

"Where?"

"Wherever we need to go."

"Not here," Myra said. "Not Raleigh—God."

"We'd honor that."

"You know I won't think about divorce. There's no such thing for me and Madelyn."

Frankly I hadn't thought about it. But I'd lived next to Catholics so long I wasn't surprised. The road I'd seen didn't just wash out at that light shower. I said "We'd find some way to live."

"*We* is you and the girl, you mean?"

"I think so, yes."

"And all the rest of your *old* life can dry up and die."

"I didn't hear myself say that."

"But you mean it, Blue. It's what would happen."

"Myra, don't undersell yourself. You're stronger than me by miles and years. Mattie's strong as a platinum rail."

At last she rolled to her left side and faced me across the breathing distance. "I married you for all time, Bluford. And somehow I know I'll love you that long. Far more than Madelyn knows or dreams, she turns in rings around your face."

I understand I'm telling you how I chose to crush your mother in childhood. I'm not excusing myself one whit or asking for any least allowance. To come anywhere near comprehending your family's past, you've got to be strong enough to believe I lay there sober that July night and thought as best I could through what I knew my soul really *meant*. And once I knew, again I said "I'm sorry as I can be—that's all." I'd seen deep grades of hell in my time—bleeding full-tilt hell with teeth—but recalling that night and those last seconds before I slept, I know and can tell you here tonight that nothing—human, beast or steel—ever did me a crime to match my words to Myra there in the normal night. I lived to learn that similar words are common as flies—from men to women, women to men, worst of all to millions of children—but most of my waking days here now are spent to pay small bits of my debt.

Next day was the 4th, and the store was closed. I slept a little late, not past seven thirty—some boys down the street had started their firecrackers, ending my dreams. And when I got downstairs, Matt was already at the kitchen table, finishing breakfast. No sight of Myra, though since there was bacon in a plate on the stove, I knew she'd been here recently. When I spoke to Mattie she showed no sign of knowing bad news; but then Matt never cleared her brain till late morning, sometimes lunch. I made myself two slices of toast, stole some bacon, poured my coffee and sat beside her.

After a minute she opened the talk at her usual pitch of real concern. "You don't think I'm in the wrong, do you, Sky?"

I was honestly puzzled.

"—Thinking Grandmother wants my company."

"You talked to her last night. What did she say?"

"She said 'My darling, you're a beam of light.'"

I said "Well then, she wants you a lot."

We both chewed awhile and finally Matt said "Is there something you ought to warn me about?"

"Like lightning and snakes?"

"Be serious please. Is there stuff I shouldn't tell Grandmother, that might make her worse?"

"Madelyn Calhoun, this is the truth—my mother knows every secret I've got from the gizzard out. She'll know every one *you* know ten minutes after you unpack. So talk away to your heart's content."

"But I still shouldn't tell her my Catholic stuff, novenas and all?"

"You can deck her with rosary beads like ivy and prop your statues all over the house. Miss Ashlyn's blood lines to God are ancient. She may be a Presbyterian on Sundays, but in her heart she's a white magician the same as you. And she gets most everything she wants, hook or crook."

Mattie gave that a minute. "She wants to be blind out there alone?"

"Notice she won't be alone now with you. By sheer force of will, she got you to come. But blind? I can't be sure about that. She's watched me do some ugly things—"

"You stopped," Matt said.

I watched her eyes for longer than ever. Big and honest as the help-less moon, they couldn't hide the smallest thought. They were nothing but beautiful now and earnest. Matt knew no more than what she'd seen these recent years—that I'd stopped doping and all that dope meant, that I'd been "sad" a lot here lately. So I said "Don't you good Catholics *know* that people seldom stop their ways?"

"You mean you're planning to drink again?"

I managed to smile. "No ma'm, I'm not. But you keep working on my case, hear?"

She said "I never intended to quit."

I nodded my thanks and sat there maybe two more minutes under the power of her pure face before my mind restrung its circuits for greed and waste.

By two o'clock I'd got Matt settled in at Mother's and eaten tomato sandwiches with them. Mother asked me to walk through the long back field and check on an oak somebody had told her was dying fast and would fall on the barn. It was dying, yes, but just on its east side away from the barn. I'd get the tree man to give it a look and do what seemed best or, doubtless, most expensive. Then as I looped back to the house through buggy weeds, I tried to think my way to the time when I was most like Madelyn now. That would have been before I was twelve and also came out here in the summers to stay with Miss Ashlyn's ornery father, peg legged by then. In those days deep in the Great Depression, adults were still convinced all children were happy unless they turned up bleeding or dead.

And I'll have to say they were more than right about me till I got well on into high school and welcomed liquor into my life, where it stayed. You can take this as actual bedrock truth—my childhood was basically one long grin, though none of the therapists on my case in the world's drunk tanks could ever believe me (so much the worse for midget brains). Oh I had the normal rainy days—I worried sometimes my mother might die. I wondered how you got through time, through all those endless nights and days till you were the kind of tough old coot we saw so many of in those times—deaf as dough and lost in the past but there in your house as live as bears. And early on I figured I might well love my body way too much. Not that I mainly felt filthy and sinful—I was just not sure who ran my mind when it spent so much time south of my navel, submarining through visions of girls laid down like mermaids waving me in.

Otherwise back then I moved like an educated bird through trees. The world *took* me and I took it till the awful day I came to myself and saw that every cell of my mind constantly begged me to help it forget. *Forget?*—when I could barely recall a bad dream, much less hard luck. But beg I did, for years on end. And then of course the whole world changed, the world *I* saw—I'll never know why. And I'm convinced no doctor could even begin to tell me (none has yet). I think the same about most bent lives and almost surely yours, my darling.

Fate's the magnet that draws and wrings you, not whoever tried to down your body and own your mind before you could run to save yourself. And *fate* is just what fools like me, too weak to think or face a true mirror, have chosen to name the hand that started these innocent atoms spinning and then may well have turned away from us and all we have to tread while it swept on to whatever mystery it thought of next, which is why I owe so much to you and you to me— we're what it *left*.

When I got to the house, Mattie and Mother were gone from the kitchen. I knew where they were and made my way through cool dim rooms to the screened front porch. When I stepped through the door, they didn't look up. Their backs were to me in the big old swing— still as the ground with Matt's right hand in Mother's between them. Just that quick sight threw me backward again—the days of hours I'd spent in the same place near that same woman, young and unburdened. I crept behind them and laid a hand on the top of each head.

Matt didn't speak but Mother said "I was wishing for you."

I said "Say why."

She waited and said "Because you used to be mine and I miss you."

It went in deeper than any human words I'd heard in the longest while except from Luna. So I finally said "I'm gone." And I was, more ways than one.

As I came into town on Person Street, nearly the first thing I could see was the back of a big woman dressed in white, toiling along. By the time I could see her hair and neck, I knew it was Rita in her nurse uniform. And the way she moved so painfully, I knew I was going to stop and speak, even if she was just three blocks from home. I pulled to the curb a few yards ahead, leaned over and looked back towards her. If she knew me, she gave no outward sign. So when she was by the car, I said "Here, Rita, let me lighten your load."

Again her small eyes opened as wide as if I'd hit her, and her natural redness flared up high. But she came to the window and said "Blue Calhoun, show me some peace."

"I am," I said and opened the passenger door to give her a ride wherever.

She held back a second and then climbed in like some tired camel folding her limbs.

Before she could speak I pulled away from the curb and asked her the question that just came to me, "You got time to ride to Pullen Park and watch the kids?"

Rita said "I was meant to work today, but then my old lady's nephew turned up (drunk as a skunk—him, not her); so they let me off for the rest of the day."

I took that to mean she was ready to ride. So through the next fifteen minutes, we said very little but pleasantries about the flowers and children we passed. When we got to the park though and saw how surprisingly empty it was for the 4th of July, I pulled up near the merry go round and offered to buy her a cold drink. She nodded, we got our Cokes and sat on a bench uphill in evergreen shade. A long time passed with both of us quiet, but since we each had something to watch—a few kids riding the old wood horses, zebras and lions, imaginary creatures—I thought we were in a likely place to clear some ground and change our ways. I said "Rita, you need to know that I'm not out to ruin your life."

She kept on waiting but finally laughed. "My life was *ruint* so long ago I can't recall."

I shared her fun but I also said "You know what I mean?" By now I recalled a fact about Rita I'd lost with the years—no matter how often she saw your face, she'd search it every time you met like you had drastically changed overnight, or she had buried some hope of hers deep in your skull and was digging to find it. Now at last she nodded and said "I know Luna says you're *after* her."

"After her? Rita, understand—I'm leading Luna." Once I said it I wondered was it true. "Did Luna say that much, or did you ask her?"

"Sure I asked her—she's mine to watch till somebody else starts buying her feed and blocking the hands that try to use her. I can't have her starting off life like me."

"She's not," I said. "She's older and I'm no fly by night to leave her gasping alone in the road."

That called for a pause and the rest of her drink. Then Rita faced me, a pitiful sight. "Blue, I gave you a hard knock yesterday. I'm sorry I had to—I've kept up with you through the years, and I've known you had your own rough times. But now you're strong as an ox, I can see; so I can't let you lean on my child strong as you have. You all but choked her."

I sat there hearing every word. And I understood they might be true, some part at least. But the more Rita said and the truer she got, the more each word glanced off my mind like pea-size hail. I said "Luna thinks I'm saving her life—so she tells me."

"What do *you* think?"

"I think it's vice versa, Rita. She's saving me too."

Rita sent out a whole new search party on me. And by now it was hard to meet her bead eyes without at least a sneaky grin. But I strangled it down; and then Rita said "When I knew you, you were one kind boy. I had many chances through the years to recall your eyes and how you sounded, speaking to me that last day at school when I felt like some scabby cow they were butchering on. But now every night I ask my God to roll time back and keep me out of that music store, that April day."

By then I'd built a case in my mind. I felt like a lawyer in a good crime show—I'd win every round. And I started by saying "Have you talked to Luna since she left home?"

"You know we don't have no telephone."

"Has she written you yet?"

"One postcard yesterday."

One postcard—no written complaint. "Then Luna's never asked you to run me off from her—not in writing, not since she left."

But Rita was quicker than I recalled. "I'm fairly damned certain she hasn't proposed to you by mail. How much have *you* heard?"

"Not a single line."

"Then there's your news. She's shut your door." She paused and waited to watch me crash. But when I just smiled, she tore ahead. "Blue, you've got that mansion of a home, a good clean woman and one sweet child—I saw her picture all over the place, the image of you in your better days. Turn on back now, boy. Treat us right."

I said "I'm not in the seventh grade, Rita. I'm not the tadpole you used to know. I'm one man square in the midst of his life on two strong legs, and till last April it looked bleak as cinders. I might die tonight or sixty years on. Luna showed me how lost I was. Luna *found* me. I mean to fight to stay beside her long as I last."

Hot as I said it, Rita didn't budge. Those eyes held on me. She said "And I can just crawl off and die."

"No, you can wish us clear good luck."

"And your wife and youngun—"

I made it as gentle as I knew how, though I knew it was hard as most of her life. "They're none of your business, girl. Draw back."

With her big grace, that always surprised me, Rita stood up, set her empty bottle on the ground and moved downhill. For maybe ten seconds I saw her clear in all details those years ago, hounded out of the seventh grade and bound on a downhill course for life because one ignorant hot boy had slipped a baby up her flue when she could barely write her name. For one more instant I even wanted to grant her prayer and somehow reel these last weeks back and never meet on Earth again to watch each other try and fail like we'd just done. But then I saw the side of her face. There were already three old men at the busstop. Someway Rita had broken out smiling and was saying words I couldn't hear to the nearest geezer (I couldn't tell which). *One of them's bound to grin her way,* so I let her go.

By then it was nearly four o'clock and blistering hot, but I was cool as the bravest men I knew in Europe. At every corner I'd think of a joke and wish somebody was with me to laugh. I hadn't gone more than eight blocks before I knew I wouldn't be spending tonight at home, not that near Myra. The way I saw it in the next few minutes, I had two choices—I could head back to Mother's with her and Mattie or risk the ride to Bob Barefoot's and hope he'd be in good enough shape to hear me out and lend me a bed. First though I'd need clothes for tomorrow, and that would risk me meeting Myra if she was back home.

She wasn't. The house was still shut, the air was stale, and I didn't wonder where she might be. I found my dad's old black leather bag and packed enough for two or three days. I figured by then I'd have clear plans for how to get from here to there—and *there* was nothing but my hot mind up close to Luna, mind and body and raving soul.

The Barefoot place was farther out from town than now, very much in the sticks—a sweet five miles of trees and fields they still hadn't crammed with mini malls. And Bob was living there alone now that his mother was also gone. He and I'd been in school together from the first grade on, then we roomed together in college till I dropped out, and after that Bob had taken pains to keep in touch several times a year. There'd be occasional late night phone calls with Bob fairly tipsy and always a birthday card (him to me—I mostly missed his). His father had farmed and lawyered his way to big money early, then died in his forties leaving a carload of gold behind. So Bob never married but stayed at home and managed the money, the big old house and his outsize mother—Miss Gin (Virginia), a loaded pistol if I ever saw one.

Miss Gin had read every book on Earth since ink was invented, she'd traveled abroad before her marriage, and she drank like a horse just in from the desert. Never showed it though—she had more wit than any paid comedian. I got a good deal of fun from her talk, her meanness and jokes; and she was a true help in my worst days—when I was groveling in the pit of my life, drunk and dazed, refusing help.

She rode beside me when I first went to an A.A. meeting (the actual start of saving my skin, though Miss Gin gave Matt and Myra the credit). And she held my hand through many more nights when I couldn't think how to put one foot before the other—I was that blind with thirst. So when she died a year ago, Bob found my name on her pallbearer list, the sole white man. And when he called me late in the night and said "Come get her," I rode out there to spend the night in sight of her body and then to help bear her thin bones home—her deep dirt home up back of the house—with five old black men she'd known as a girl.

But strong as she was, Miss Gin had pressed Bob way too hard and ruined his nerve. And though he was full of a gentler brand of fun than his mother's, he'd mostly moved through life like a smile—a broad half smile with long legs beneath it but no will power and no strong dreams. Bob would tell you how he'd done something plain—like taking a two mile walk through the woods or ordering a twelve pound ham by telephone from wildest Vermont—and he'd make the world seem a whole lot grander than you'd ever noticed. But you couldn't ask him to bear much weight, just laugh beside him and thank him for gifts. He loved to give things. I still have cufflinks, pheasant feathers, a pair of Chinese jade bookends and a perfect miniature bird's nest made from horsehair by some smart bird he found in his barn. You just couldn't stop him—gifts were all the life he had apart from his mother.

So it was nearly five on the 4th when I got there. Bob was usually out on the porch by then, sipping rum, but no sign now—not even his dog and the dark windows along the front were all shut tight. I tried to think when I'd seen him last—*New Year's Eve, then maybe March when he came in the store to buy some records.* He must be out at somebody's party—he and Miss Gin had lived for fun—but I parked anyhow and thought I'd leave him a note at least and earn full credit for a social call. But as I leaned to shove my message under the door, I heard slow footsteps and pulled back to wait.

When the door came open, I hardly knew him. Then I saw it was Bob all right—but Bob the way he'd looked in school, too young and lean. It was still decades before men went to plastic surgeons, but I know I thought *He's had a face lift with Miss Gin's cash* (she'd left him considerable money). When he didn't grin or speak, I said "Well, Bob, you're looking rested."

He studied me a long time before he tried to say my name. It wouldn't quite sound in his mouth at first. But then he managed to say "Well, *Bluford.*"

I wished him a joyful 4th; and when he still didn't act like the old gracious Bob, I said "I'm sorry I've broke in here."

Still his mouth refused to speak, but then he put up a hand and beckoned me into the high white hall that was dim and dusty.

I followed him on to the back dining room. Floor to ceiling it was still lined in Miss Gin's books. And now Bob's phonograph records were everywhere, not neatly filed the way they'd been. It suddenly came to my mind he was drunk or on some other sedative. He'd never doped along with me, but had Miss Gin's death left him this addled? *What else has he had? Of course he's wrecked.* Those were still times when you could admit you loved your mother more than the world, and Bob surely had. But now he scrambled to clear me a chair in the midst of mail and old newspapers stacked knee high.

I sat and watched him make the sign of drinking from a glass, then a quick half smile, then he left for the kitchen.

I heard him break out ice and a Coke, and then he was back to pour it for me and take the hard old bench by the window with light behind him so bright I could barely see his face.

He hadn't poured himself a drink. So when I'd downed my first cold swallow, I said "You weaning yourself like me?" (he'd often told his mother and me we'd be "the first to know" when he quit his attachment to rum).

He gave a wide smile and said "I'm weaning myself from life."

So I was right and, if I hadn't been so tied up in my own rope, I might have helped to cheer him on through the lonesome time in the woods out here. At least I might have forced him out to eat barbecue at a place we'd gone to, most of our lives. I said "Bob, take that big trip now"—for years he'd planned a tour through Holland, tulip by tulip, but had scarcely left his yard.

The broad beamed grin was still in place. "I'm *going,*" he said and slapped his thigh.

"Fine. When?"

"In the spring—next spring."

"You going alone or with a tour group?" The country was just start-ing then on the travel jag it's still hooked on—Europe, Asia, the swamps of the moon: boatloads of aging widows in hair nets, the odd old crock who's managed to last, all hauled round the map by air cooled buses and helpless members of the pastel races of humankind.

Bob said "Oh no, I'm going alone."

By now you've guessed what I still hadn't. I blundered on and said "I sure do wish I could join you."

He grinned again—it truly looked wild, teeth long as fangs. "You don't, old Blue. I'm dying, see." He held both hands up, palm out towards me like they were the proof. And in that late orange light through the window, they did look almost like X rays—long bones, no flesh. Then when I didn't break the silence, Bob said "I've meant to call you up; but I understand your arms are full" (he'd never taken to Myra or Madelyn).

I said "Lord, boy, I'm sorry. What is it?"

"Leukemia. Killed my father too, as you well know, but faster than this."

"How long have you known?"

"Eighty six days."

"Are the treatments rough?"

"No treatments—not to speak of." It made him smile.

"See a good doctor. Christ, I'll drive you to Duke Hospital right this minute."

Again the bony hand went up. "I've seen them all. They can't do *nothing* but feed me aspirin and pull up the sheet."

"Is anybody helping you out, out here?" The house was back at the end of a dirt road, no near neighbors.

He suddenly turned his back on me, faced the window, took a long look and chuckled deep. "The *sparrows* are helping greatly," he said. "They eat my meals."

"You trying to cook?" He and Miss Gin had always had a good

man cook and general servant—"Where's Amos Barker?"

"Amos is at his daughter's home, worse off than me—dumb and blind from three hard strokes."

I said "My mother's racing to blindness."

Bob finally turned to face me again. "Then take her in."

I didn't catch it so I begged his pardon.

He lined it out on the air with a finger. "Take Miss Ashlyn out of that lonesome house in the country and treat her right. She gave you the *Earth*." He'd never made that strong a speech in all the years I'd known him. Himself, he had no brothers, sisters, children or nearby kin alive.

I said "Young Mattie's out there with her now. I took her today."

"Mattie's a green child. A child won't do."

"What's she *meant* to do, Bob?"

"Save a soul in pain." Then he smiled too, the best he could—that corpse's grin—and held both palms upright again, flat helpless and hopeless. But when they'd hung in the air awhile, he slowly let them down and pushed both far out in the stale air towards me.

I was five yards off. And when I understood what he meant—for me to hold him—I suddenly felt sweet Luna's skin all down my front under my thin clothes. *Touch him, son. He can't hurt you now.* My mind saw Bob long cold years before, reaching his hand across the space between our desks in a dormitory room and me not laying my pencil down but writing ahead. Next I thought *Don't let him come here. You go the whole way.* So well before he moved to stand, I got to my feet and walked straight to him and took the gift he'd tried to give that long ago. His hands in mine were cold as a rake. I pressed my heat in on him five seconds, then sat back down.

When I could finally look again, his eyes were dry and his head was nodding. He said "Just drink your Coke, my friend."

I took a long swallow, set down the glass and said "I'm hoping to stay here, Bob—you got a spare room?"

He paused like I had spoken in tongues. And his head shook hard. "You got some legal worries at home?"

How on Earth does he know about me? But then I recalled he sometimes spoke of Myra and Matt as my "legal" duties. I said "That's why I need your help."

"Myra taken the veil?" From the days I first began to court her, he'd called her Mother Myra of the Birds—more than once to her face.

I said "I've taken hold of a live wire. It's burned us up. I can't go home, not now at least."

"Who's the wire?"

"A girl, sixteen years old and magic."

"Name?"

"Luna Absher."

"Old Rita's child—Rita Bapp-that-was?" I'd got his attention anyhow; his color improved.

"You remember Rita?"

"*Remember?* Rita Bapp and I have swapped Valentines since the third grade."

"What possessed you to keep knowing Rita?"

"Blue, some people's friends mean a whole world to them. I haven't seen Rita since she left school with that big belly a lifetime ago, but what's twenty four years between deep friends? See, Rita once told me that I was a certified child of God, which guaranteed me room in Heaven if I ever died."

I said "*Rita* Bapp? You're bound to be wrong."

"You know her folks were hot Holy Rollers. She came to school one Monday in spring looking worn to the nub with tangled hair— they'd howled at her church till midnight Sunday—but when she met me climbing the stairs, she held my face in her great strong hands, she brought her nose right up to my eyes; and then she said I was *guaranteed*. I'd done her homework for two years running and always let her copy my tests."

"Ever seen her daughter?"

"No, I told you—none of the family. But I've got her picture." Bob rose to his feet, wavered a little, then looked around and walked to a shelf, a stack of old letters.

My sweaty hair chilled down to the roots. *Lord God, am I ready for this?* I'd had no sight of Luna now for too long a time, and her face had started to fade in my mind. I almost called out to stop Bob. *Don't see her, son. It'll tear you up.*

But Bob had found an envelope and was bringing it to me. "Is this who you mean?"

Once I saw Rita's home address in her childish hand, I felt a big sadness threaten my mind. I pushed on though and took out the homemade valentine. At the top of the page, she'd taped a small school picture of Luna and added a note—something like "Dear Bob, here's the best I've done since I saw you." The girl's face, strange as a hazy moon, wore the kind of smile that always says two separate things—*Stay where you are, no closer, there* but then *I'm here. Why are you so far?* The sadness took me. And I suddenly thought I'd rather die here, helping Bob on his way, than head back into my old life. It was all I could do not to press the paper to my dry lips. I said "It's Luna Absher all right" and handed it over.

Bob took it a moment, then shook his head and gave it back. "A present from me."

Light as it was on the palm of my hand, it felt like the best I'd ever got in a whole life of gifts. I couldn't say "Thanks" but I did face Bob, who was back on his bench. "What can I do for you? Just say."

He waited awhile, then grinned again, then barely shook his lean young head. "*Tardy,*" he said. "Too late, old Blue." But then he said he was much obliged and might well call on me down the road when things closed in. He stood there frail as a dry corn stalk but stronger than me.

Yet all I could find in his steady eyes was a boy I'd known since before I could read, spindly and lost on the school playground choosing me for his friend and still aimed at me here in this room—him there dying next to me now and, in my hand, a visible proof of the livest face I'd met in life or hoped to meet.

I spent that night at the same motel where Luna and I had said goodbye, though I asked the clerk for a different room (I thought Luna's smell might still somehow be left in the air, and I knew it would hurt). I also knew not to take that picture out and watch it. Instead I sat in a tub of water till my skin shriveled, cooling my mind. Then I called Myra to say where I was in case of emergency. It took her several rings to answer, but she sounded calm (I'd left her a note when I got my clothes, to say I needed time to sort my cards). Before I could, Myra even said she wouldn't tell Matt about me leaving till I gave the word. I felt like giving it on the spot. But something stopped me and I said "You try to get some rest."

Myra waited. "Nothing's wrong with me. I'm rested and ready."

I said I didn't doubt it but I was beat.

"Then do yourself a favor—stop hating everything good in your heart."

It barely grazed me and I said "So *long*."

As I was taking the phone from my ear, Myra said "It has been long, old Blue." She was only right. She'd hung on kindly by her lights, and she'd always been there near at hand when nobody else showed hair nor hide to help or cherish the wreck I was.

But she failed on me now. And *old*—everybody was calling me *old*: old Blue, poor child. No fourteen year old locked in a room with his new adult spouting body had ever felt younger—stronger—finer than me that night of July 4th, alone in a hot cinder block motel by a country road in the midst of nowhere far in the pines. I was halfway through an average life. Most of that time I'd poured down a drain or spent on other people's needs. From here on out I'd live for me— me and the soul I planned to love and own for good. As much as I'd done and felt in the world—and a whole World War—I actually thought more or less those words as I lay there stripped and wet on the sheet, feeling young as a colt.

And I slept the instant I turned out the light.

I all but overslept in the morning and got to the store with seconds to spare. The usual slow quiet Thursday traffic—I demonstrated a steel guitar and sold the beautiful mandolin I'd somehow hoped would never sell. It went to a black haired boy from Maryland who said he was passing through on his way to Hollywood and a movie career—he showed me a letter from Bette Davis that said come on; she'd help him out (just to guess from his looks, I figured she would). I started to give him a short request as he turned to leave—to treat that instrument like it deserved—but then I knew I had slim right to tell the rocks in the road to hush, much less guide a boy on his long path. Still it left me sad when he walked out, and I didn't think of much but him—his trip and his chances with popeyed Bette—till on towards noon.

Then just before lunch I made my usual trip to the men's room, way in the rear. And only when I'd finished there and walked back through the dim stock room did my black friend Hobe Pierce beckon to me.

He kept a crowded desk in a corner banked with pictures of tan girl children, all his kin. And when I was near him, he took my arm and said "I figured you wanted this private." Then he palmed me a small gray envelope.

I put it in my pocket at once, thanked him and left. But all the way down the next three blocks, I felt as high as a boy new to drink. I thought I knew the precious thing that rode there hid against my flank as I walked to Belk's Department Store, the quick lunchroom. I was early enough to get a table by myself. And once I'd ordered the chicken dumplings with three fresh vegetables, cornbread and tea, I pulled the envelope back out and looked for the first time at the address.

> *Mr. Bluford Calhoun, c/o Atkinson's Music*
> *The first block of Fayetteville St. at the Capitol end*
> *Raleigh N.C.*

> PRIVATE.

The return address was just

> *L. Absher, Camp Harmony, Balsam Point, N.C.*

I could see she'd lost the street number, but I liked the way she'd worked to find me "at the Capitol end" of Fayetteville Street. And I suddenly saw how much of my thrill came from the fact I'd never seen her writing before. It was tall and headlong, strong as a statesman's in dark blue ink (when ballpoint pens had already wrecked the country's script). A cry in the night, calling my name, would barely have shook me harder than seeing my name in Luna's hand in a public place.

I set it face down beside my spoon and tried to check the room nonchalantly—mostly pairs of local ladies with maids at home and nothing better to do at noon, the two famous Raleigh lesbians of those days (miles of makeup but stylish in bobbed hair and huge picture hats), familiar faces but none really knew me. So I took the clean knife and cut the seal on a letter I'd sweated blood to get. One folded page that I held to my nose, then opened to read (I own it still and it still smells fine).

July 2, 1956

Dear Blue,

This place is all I dreamed and a whole lot more. Everybody is serious and treats me like I've got good sense and enough ability to earn my keep.

The keep is all right, a girls' dormitory with clean pine rooms and iron bunkbeds. We have to sweep and make our beds up neat as the Army, plus we also walk a ways outdoors to the antique toilet through snaky grass but nobody yet has stubbed a toe much less met a snake though some of the boys made a dummy rattlesnake last week and caused the girl in the bunk over me to nearly die.

But like I said everybody is working. I know now I was always right—having music around you the whole day long is the way to live.

There is also music every evening, mostly outside under the stars. So far the music is mostly from the teachers and campers who have been here before. But they have asked me to sing at church this coming weekend, just me and the harp. Church is outdoors too under high old trees. I'm scared but also kind of proud.

And if I make it sound like too much work, well it isn't. I have met more smart friendly people my age in two weeks here than all my life in the Capitol City! And knowing them all day and night against these mountains and beautiful sights is the best thing yet. I feel like finally I'm going somewhere that's got my name on the main road signs.

I bet it's already too hot down there now in the plains and you'll be burning up for the 4th. You drink plenty water and take salt tablets and cooling rides. Say hey to Raleigh from your friend,

                                                            Luna

By the time I read it, my lunch had arrived. At first I thought I couldn't eat a bite. All that waiting to hear some echo anyhow, all the gouging I'd done on Myra and Rita and my past life, and what I had to show myself after nearly three weeks was a letter she could have sent to an aunt. One more time I checked the room—still nobody I really knew—so I read the sentences again very slowly, weighing each one right down to her name. And then I started telling myself I'd missed her point. As the two official lesbians got to their thin legs and swept out past me (I'd always liked them for plentiful guts), I suddenly knew *She's writing code.* And of course I'd failed to see the main point—that in the midst of a new adventure for a girl her age who'd been nowhere, she'd written the letter at all, this soon. Notice too—*Not one word of bad news, no calling quits—no "Adios, Dad."*

So I ate everything and ordered sherbet. And not till then did I trust myself to take out the other envelope—Rita's valentine to Bob Barefoot—and study Luna's face again. Strange, but the first few seconds there, I saw her looks through Bob's sick eyes. He'd barely had a date in college so far as I knew. And looking back I guess he was queer or just as likely stifled by Miss Gin, who soaked up energy from all bystanders. So what he'd seen in this school picture of a teenage girl was the private way time edges on, making a path for every creature where no other creature's gone before. Long past me, Bob had kept in touch with sad Rita Bapp. And he'd have seen how friendship helped Rita crawl ahead through rocks and briars, two husbands, a murdering bastard son, and still come up at the end of all with this fine girl with the miracle eyes and Indian hair, that strong and straight.

I left it there, in public at least, and put the picture back in my pocket. But hidden near me it now felt promising enough to blow up that whole end of town if I exposed it to full daylight and let my mind relive any part of the joy that girl had given, and might yet give, my skin and mind. Still I was back in sight of the store before I saw the *real* deep point of what she'd said. *She's singing in church and it has to be soon, three days from now. I'll take the clue and be there, ready.*

So I spent a third night at the motel, wore the same clothes through Saturday at work. Then Saturday at six I went to Myra's, saw her car was gone and let myself in the kitchen door. I'd wondered how those first steps would feel, back in the place I'd spent my old life. The first thing to hit me was a strong sweet smell—incense maybe. That priest had been here. They'd tried again to pray me back from what Myra saw as the jaws of Hell. It had happened before and at times it worked.

So next I walked to the dining room, and yes Virgin Mary was on duty there. The candles around her were safely out, and I'd guessed partly right at least—at her feet was a saucer of incense ashes. The saucer sat on a neat slip of paper; and while I dreaded to see my name as the soul being prayed for, I picked it up, convinced it would say my full name. In Myra's small round hand though, it just said "Ashlyn Hampton Calhoun" *Mother*—she was praying for Mother's eyes. Even with Madelyn gone—and me—Myra was still at work on my mother, who'd seldom given her cause for thanks. I felt the kind of thanks you feel for a cool dry day, and I set the slip of paper back where it could keep on working, if it worked.

In twenty minutes I'd packed a cardboard box of clothes, the Calhoun family Bible for some reason and an old shaving kit with basic home remedies (like most recovering drunks I was prone to terminal hypochondria). Then with no regrets and well before dark, I aimed my car onto U.S. 70 West that was almost empty by then. I'd barely cleared the city limits when my mind thought *You've died, old son. This is Heaven or Hell. Hold it in the road and soon you'll know which one you chose.*

FIVE

I HADN'T STRUCK OUT for that far west in a good many years. In fact it took me thirty miles—and night was falling on the woods around me—before I thought *I haven't been aimed this far since they sent me home from Europe.* But I drove on through the night, not stopping except for gas or to pee. The best thing was, I seldom had a conscious thought. I listened to the dumb car radio. At first it was local music and logy Christian stations—woozy sermons with detailed schedules for Judgment Day and the timeless thereafter. Then once the crazy locals winked out, I pulled in the distant power-ful stations—Pittsburgh, Cincinnati, Kansas City, with nothing but news—then finally I came on a station from Pensacola, Florida that was playing nothing but upbeat songs from World War II. So I let them keep me awake into Boone—the funny terrible bloodthirsty songs from a part of my life that seemed closer now than it had since Armistice: "Praise the Lord and Pass the Ammunition," "Coming in on a Wing and a Prayer" and of course the dusty old Infantry song that still could raise the hair on my neck, though I'd always refused to sing it on the drill field (no war protest, just a deep reluctance to join a group).

A hardboiled Yankee woman owned the first motel with a vacancy sign. And all she asked after I woke her was "You need a telephone or not?" I said "What's the difference?" She said "Fifty cents" so I took the phone and went to a room that was thoroughly green—green paint, green sheets. It was also cold in the mountain dark, so that and the sight of the ancient phone made me think of a duty I'd failed. It was past one o'clock, but I had to call Miss Ashlyn in case she'd need me. She slept so lightly, you could call anytime.

And as ever she answered the second ring in her lifelong way— "Ashlyn Calhoun."

I said "I'm glad."

"You're glad of what?"

I said "For knowing you're still on Earth."

"What's your evidence for that?" No sign of recognition.

"This is your only son, Miss Ashlyn."

She took a long pause, then "Are you on Pluto? You sound that far."

"Nearly, yes ma'm—the outskirts of Boone."

She said very calmly "I feared as much."

I was sure I hadn't mentioned Luna's whereabouts, so how did she know?—not from Mattie but had Myra told her? I said "I needed a day or two off."

"Are you alone this minute or not?"

"Yes I am." I couldn't help asking "Does that make you happier?"

She said "It does." No explanation.

"Have you talked to Myra?"

"Yes."

"What's she told you?"

"Blue, that'll be *my* business for now. I'll say this much—Myra hasn't tried to smear your name."

"I'm pleased to hear it. She knows you wouldn't let her—"

Mother said "Shame. She's proved her love for you in *spades*, and why would she slander her daughter's father?"

I said "I'm sorry."

"You *are*. You've got that sorry lowdown streak through the midst of your soul; and it came from me—my father at least, another good looker hipped on girls."

"You were a girl."

"I was indeed. And I'm suffering for it."

I wasn't about to follow that up. Even before I got into manhood, I dreaded discovering Miss Ashlyn's past—any possible men besides my dad, any punishing secrets (I had no evidence whatsoever but her hot steady eyes). So I said *"Matt's* a girl. Is she helping you out?"

"No, but that's not why Matt's here."

"Is she bothering you?"

"I didn't say that. I said she wasn't quite helping out—I'm too old to help—but she's good to watch. And she listens to me. Nobody else does."

I said "Miss Ashlyn, I've listened forever. I'm listening now."

She waited so long I thought she was gone—that had happened before. She'd quietly set the phone down on you if you made a false move. Now she said "You *did* listen. I watched you hear every word I said. It drove you wild."

I had no idea what she meant; it was thoroughly new. So I said "Whoa."

"No," she said. "I'm the cause of this. I'd beg your pardon if it wasn't too late and we all weren't lost."

I thought I suddenly knew the truth. Old as I was, it felt like a blessing I'd fully earned and now could give. I said "Miss Ashlyn, this is all meant to be. We'll be better for it—you, me, Myra, Matt. Just trust me and time."

She said "Bluford, listen. I've lived my own wrong wasteful life. I've watched you take a face like a god's and ruin it with drink. I've watched you more than half heal yourself. Now that I'm old and blinder by the hour, you ask me to tend your lovely child while you go chase a fresh damnation in the Blue Ridge mountains. I may not wait for dawn, much less your next foul news."

It hurt, no question. I swallowed hard and when I heard the quiet click as she disconnected, I felt relieved. *Let everybody just* rest *awhile. I'll get this right, in good time for all.* But a minute later in that cheap place with no props near me, panic rose and jumped my heart. I felt worse than I'd felt with German sharpshooters hid beyond me in ditches. So I placed a second call to Mother, the only help I could turn to then, however she burned me.

This time she let it ring a good while. But when she decided to hear me again, she said right off—no word from me—"Bluford, hush and listen to this. When you were six years old and started school in the fall, I missed you terribly at home. The hours from when you left at eight and were back at four were like a big hole punched in my chest—I hadn't missed anybody else like that since my father died. And it took me several days to know why I ached so hard. When I finally knew, I said it out loud to the empty room, 'Your son is gone for the last time, Ashlyn. He can't return. The world won't let him.' I had a long cry upstairs alone, then got my face in good repair before you came through the kitchen door. And you got through the sandwich I fixed as if you'd had a normal day. But when you stood to go upstairs, you faced my eyes and spoke out plainly—'I really won't ever be yours again, will I?' For the previous two years anyhow, like most children before their teens, you'd known how to speak the killing truth. But I'd grown far less brave with the years, so I tried to lie. I said 'Oh Blue, we're here for life.' I meant we'd face each other and share the best of our hearts till death or Hell struck one of us silent. But you smelled the lie and shook your solemn head and left. You never came back from that day on. Not you, not really."

I'd forgot the day but it came to me clear as a streaking bird. I said "What if I leave here right this minute, be there by breakfast and stay awhile?" I thought I absolutely meant it. I thought I'd let Mother lead me now.

But she said "Sleep where you are. You're tired."

"You're saying you don't want me on hand?"

She waited so long I thought she was gone. Then "You couldn't come back—not here, not now—if I were the Queen of Sheba in pearls with balms for every wound you've got or ever caused. Please have the grace to know that now, and don't ask me and Mattie to watch you fail again."

When I thought it through, I saw I could add very little but "All right. You try to sleep."

"I will," she said and her voice seemed strained through a net as thick as the miles between us. Then her phone clicked down.

*

I guess I slept an hour or so. Mostly I lay full dressed in the dark and tried to empty out my mind that felt ruptured now. Even in my worst days when I'd wake up to one more day and dredge the scraps of what I'd done and said last night, I seldom blamed or punished myself. So what I felt that far from home was mostly new. For the first time I took it as fact that now, no way on Earth could I drive back to Beechridge Road and plug myself into that old socket and motor on to the end of my days in my same tracks. I understood I'd almost surely broken something deep in Myra that I couldn't fix nor she with all her beads and candles. I could even hear my mind say clearly *You've damaged Matt so badly now, she'll never trust your face again.*

I hope you don't but if you ever come to lie in dark places watching the scenes that you've destroyed and left to burn, I hope you'll also understand that what kept flooding over me were better sights and hope hope hope. Near as I was to Luna's skin—a few miles off—my mind would cool itself again by running through those precious sights of her near me in April, May and early June with all the sweetness they still gave me. And when real daylight struck my shades, for whatever cause, I let myself see one last sight in my head clear as life.

It showed in color behind my eyes like part of a movie made from the picture I'd always dreaded in my childhood book of Indian tales. It showed too plainly how, if you hurt an Indian child on the Plains, his people might well strap each of your legs to tall bent saplings strong enough to do their will and spring back to shape. Then they'd let the saplings jerk themselves upright and tear your body in two raw halves. You'd seldom walk away from such a righteous fate. And if you did who'd want to know you ever again, much less lie down beside you to rest?

By ten o'clock I'd drunk some coffee, got vague directions to Camp Harmony, found my way out north of town through mountains greener than any I'd known and up a two mile pair of gullies to where

I thought I'd find the answer I needed like breath. There were no name signs, no special gates. But then I rounded one more bend; and there was a clutch of cabins ahead, low log buildings sprawled in the trees. The only sound was a trillion crickets and what felt like a stream to my left, no human in sight and no human voice.

I parked by the second largest building and climbed out thinking I'd found a real ghost town. By then I was almost hoping I had—A *grown man in heat, out here and hunting somebody else's child at camp.* Maybe they'd all gone off by bus for one of the jaunts Luna said they'd make. But hadn't she also said today was when she'd sing? No church in sight but hadn't she said they met outdoors? So I walked on to what seemed like an old baseball diamond with weeds already tall in the midst. Beyond me up the side of a long hill, smaller cabins were tucked away and a horseshoe pit that looked unused. I turned around, half hunting a clue, half hoping something would help me vanish and not be here if a camper showed.

Then suddenly almost touching my hand, a boy was near me, maybe ten or eleven and all in white—white shirt, long pants, clean white buck shoes. He squinted up at the sun behind me, flashing a set of tombstone teeth, the kind it would take him years to grow into. He said "Are you the deputy sheriff?"

I had to smile. "No, I'm the fellow he's dying to find."

"Then I bet you're lost."

I said "You win."

But that wasn't good enough. He turned and pointed back downhill. "You don't belong here." He stayed in easy striking distance, plainly not scared.

Some message from his feisty eyes spread through me like shame. *Get the hell out of here. Pick on your own age.* Then I had to laugh. "You want me to leave, bad off as I am?"

The boy checked me thoroughly. "—Look all right to me. You need you some whites." When I looked puzzled he said "You know—your good church clothes. It's time for church. I slept too late."

I said "I've come all night to be here. Will they let me in if I tie my tie?" I had it slack at my neck, unbuttoned.

Again he checked me, then made a mock of choking himself. "No tied neckties allowed up here." But now he frowned. "Your hair's a haystack. You got a comb?"

I didn't but I took the one he offered and smoothed my hair. By now his hand was back out towards me. I shook it, said my truthful name and waited for his. But he just squeezed my hand and pulled me on uphill. So I went along, liking the matter of fact way he held me and thinking again *I needed a son. Someway I wouldn't be here today if I'd had a boy.* Cold as it felt to think that now, with Mattie alive and a deep satisfaction, it still felt true.

We'd gone a steep ten yards before my partner said "I'm Bert Bertley. I play string bass. You look like a singer."

"How's that?"

Bert didn't need to look. "Strong neck, big jaws."

"Thank you," I said. "But no, I play the musical comb alone at night but not much else. I'm here to see a friend of mine—she sings like the angels."

Bert said "Everybody up here does."

"You too?"

"Yeah. Which one is your friend?"

I said "Luna Absher. You heard of her?"

"Everybody knows her, miles around."

"Why?"

"She's the star." Bert looked up towards me again, dead earnest.

I heard his word in Luna's voice—*star*—and Lord, it rang. I said "I've driven from Raleigh to hear her. But Bert, does she really sound that good?"

"Everybody sounds good, I told you, long as everybody sings together. No, Luna's the beauty."

"She *is* that." Bert couldn't be more than a premature twelve. But something told me not to push harder. He might tell more than I needed to hear. I might yet have to turn my tail and crawl out of here on my flat belly in the tan dust. By then my eyes were cloudy again and I'd stopped thinking. So it came as a shock that, ten more yards, and Bert had led me straight into church—a big oak grove, the long back row of a set of pews and maybe fifty people in white, all looking towards a sheer drop off and a purple mountain past a gorge.

It took my wind, what little was left. And when Bert led us into a pew, I buckled quick as a year old child but not before I'd seen the back of Luna's hair, plaited tight at the base of her neck that still was pale as when I'd touched it last—last month, a century or more ago. Nobody sat to her right or left, not close at least. The space she'd always kept around her before we met was all there now. She was cool and free as she'd once said she wanted to be. So before I could wonder why or to who, I actually bowed my head and said *At least I know when I've been blessed.*

The service was already under way. And I sat quietly, barely hearing the long announcements and the prayer that included every live thing from here to Death Valley, leaf by leaf. I was lost in what I needed to think, this to the newest goal of my life. In the next quarter hour I took the furthest step yet, further than taking Luna's body in a family tomb in afternoon light. Like it was pulling a curtain off a newmade statue, my mind uncovered its next intention. *Take this girl and leave here now.* And when I'd said it twice in my head, I knew it was stronger than any hope—no sweet intention but a hard demand. *Leave and wind up where though?*

I saw a map of this whole country, clear as the trees. And I tried to see us resting in place—Luna and me in our true home. Next I thought the word *Pensacola*—then *Santa Rosa, Walton Beach:* that whole panhandle side of Florida off main roads on the warm slow Gulf, white sand and palms. *Why in the world, of all strange places?* I'd never so much as driven through there. Then I recalled the radio station that saw me through the trip up here with old war songs. Hadn't that been from Pensacola? *But what a reason. Well, good as any.*

That quick and flip, my mind bit in. *We're heading there.* At almost the instant I made that choice, the man who'd been conducting the service—a tall man, thin as a blade of grass—said "Now we worship with our own talents." I realized that not till then had anybody mentioned music—no hymns, no choir, no band in sight. I figured we'd rise and sing unaccompanied. But nobody moved and everybody kept facing the mountain, dead ahead in total silence.

Then Luna rose and walked to the front. A lot of the other women near me were in white pants, but Luna had on a pure white dress and what looked like an ivory bracelet on one wrist. Her dark hair looked like night on the way, and the whole sight took me over again as she faced the pews. There was no pulpit, no platform to climb. She just stood straight on the shady knoll, looked at a high point over our heads and started to sing. So much else of the day and night is still clear to me that it's strange I don't recall the name of the song or any words. I was too bound up in watching and hearing the human sound—not what she was saying but what she *meant* and what was causing her to be here, and not just in my needy life but in this beautiful earthly place with her the star in far more eyes than Blue Calhoun's. I know her voice went higher and farther than ever before in my time with her. I know it felt like every note was fed through her soul by some good power stronger than us.

It all felt like the urgent message of my whole life—*Learn all she's telling you. Use it to save her.* I knew she was safe as she'd ever be, in this green spot with likeminded friends. But more than even when Matt was a baby, I felt like I'd been sent precisely to save this girl. I even spread my hands on my knees to check, like I'd be called on to struggle for her. And as Luna sank to the end of her song, I saw both hands were strong enough. She had that beauty and goodness to give. I had this strength.

She'd sat herself back down again before I wondered where was her harp (she'd sung without it). And I hadn't even wondered if she saw me or not. I knew what I *thought* I knew, and I knew it so powerfully that every note she sang came towards me in love and hope. I more than half knew Luna felt the same or would feel it the instant she saw my eyes and read my mind. We were moving towards that meeting fast—a collection was taken, a few more words from the tall man; and then he held up the longest hands I've seen to this day and said "Bless, bless."

Young Bert beside me nudged my side and said "You think she was worth the trip?"

I was trying to keep Luna's head in sight as everybody stood and mingled between us, but I told Bert "Yes."

"I bet you want to meet her then."

I said "You think that could be arranged?"

"It wouldn't cost but two crisp dollars." He'd seen my wallet during the collection—I had a small wad of dollar bills.

I took him as seriously as he indicated and peeled off two new bills on his palm. He held one up to the sky to check, then stuffed them in his pocket and lit out, yelling "Luney" as he ran.

It wasn't the way I'd meant to do it. In fact I hadn't had a way, though I doubt there'd have been a way too shameful for me to try. I'd thought my powerful taste to see her would blow all obstacles aside. We'd meet the way we met those afternoons back home, like twins with perfectly synchronized brains. But here a kid was spreading our news down the Blue Ridge chain on a peaceful Sunday. I almost turned and walked downhill. At least I could leave and maybe come back when evening fell and do it my way. By then the other people were leaving, and none of them paid any notice to Bert. Then I could see my way to the front pews, and Luna was talking quietly to the boy and nodding slowly. She still didn't seem to have looked my way. I figured she would so I held my ground and let the simple line of her face refresh my memory.

But then she touched Bert once on the shoulder and walked on past him, straight ahead and into a clutch of waiting girls that led her off. Not so much as a glance at me.

Bert slouched back and took my hand as cool as before. We'd walked halfway downhill when he said "She couldn't see you; she's made a promise."

"To who?"

He shook his head. "She's mostly busy."

I stopped in place and freed my hand. "What else do you folks do on Sunday?"

Bert said "I'm not really 'folks' here, see. I'm really too young to be here at all, so a lot goes on that's boring to me."

I rushed on to the worst possibility. "Is she in love with somebody here?"

"Luna? Shoot—" He looked around for the rest of his answer but seemed not to find it.

I'm sorry to say I grabbed his shoulder. "Bert, tell me the truth."

"You're her daddy, aren't you?"

"I'm no kin whatsoever—God's truth."

Bert's eyes had started to brim with water, but he stared on at me. "I like her the best of anybody yet. Don't treat her mean."

I said "That's the furthest thing from my mind. Son, what did you tell her; and what did she say?"

"I said you paid me to show her to you. She said 'You tell him I'm busy till dark.'"

"Did she say for me to come back at dark?"

"No sir, I told you—she's promised till dark."

By then my car was back in sight. "What's on tap for tonight but supper?"

"Just music," Bert said. He pointed to the building I'd parked beside. "We play in there every night till nine."

"And then?"

"I jump in the cot and sleep."

"But Luna—where does Luna go?"

"Oh no, *you* need to ask her that. She lives in the longhouse right up there." He nodded to a curious building back up the hill. It looked like they had started to build a long log cabin, then got waist high and decided to quit. The rest of the walls and the V shaped roof were canvas draped like an Army tent.

I said "They put the women in there?"

"Sure do and don't you walk in either. They're naked as jaybirds most of the time." But then he laughed. "You better be done with me. I got to go rest."

"You said you just got up before church."

He laughed again. "I'm known as the friendly sloth around here."

As I opened the car door, I reached for my wallet. "Old friend, you've done me a world of good—"

But Bert was already ten yards off, calling a stout blond woman in whites who'd eyed us both the last few minutes—he called her "Hearty" or "Hardy" maybe. Either way, I gave her a wave. But she didn't budge till I'd cranked up and started out. *What in the name of all sweet skin am I meant to do from now till dark or later still?* I can't remember a previous time when the clear warm air itself felt like something I couldn't breathe. But when I got to the paved road finally, I turned north—not southeast towards home—and I thought *Just go.*

Remember I was on the downhill side of a normal lifespan. My body chemicals ought to have been in ebbtide at least. More than a few sensible people thought I was worthy of friendship and trust. But here I was this far from any place I'd ever called home on a raw boy's errand, hot as a mink. And thinking about the state of my soul, I plainly saw how close I was to the lunatic edge or even to slashing my miserable throat. I'd come this far to get brushed off like a gnat at the eye of a teenage girl. Still as I drove the narrow road on up through clearer and clearer sunlight, I someway started to think through it calmly.

Luna didn't see you. Maybe not—but then why say she was busy till dark? How many evening plans does she make with total strangers, sight unseen? You ought to be at least as wild as that sick night at the doughnut shop. It went on like that mile after mile till finally I heard the voice I trust in the pit of my mind. It told me *Luna saw your face. She's made a promise to meet you tonight. Wait till nine o'clock. Then climb back up to that church and she'll be there.*

So all the rest of a cool dry day, I wandered up the Blue Ridge Parkway, riding that splendid mountain spine with hazy valleys and almost no other visible creatures—birds occasionally, drifting eagles and what looked like a giant buck as I came round a curve, though it melted before I could see for sure. At two I stopped to eat a sandwich and a fried peach pie. And from then on, every hour or so, I'd pull off the road and sit on a rock or amble down a woody path to pee or ease the part of my mind that naturally leaned too hard on the hope of having all of Luna tonight—skin and bone, time and again.

My strongest memory of the whole quiet day is the pair of great birds—maybe gold eagles—hanging over New River Gorge as still as if they'd been nailed up on empty air. At first I thought they were spots on the windshield or in my eyes. But when I pulled over and got out to check, they were actual living things just lost in doing what I couldn't do, though Luna might when she climbed on through one of her songs.

In the whole new way my mind was working, there alone in sight of those birds, I thought the word *Adultery* again. Suppose these birds were lifetime mates. Suppose they'd already raised their sets of young replacements—what were they doing this close together, this far apart, still as rocks this quarter mile high in bright thin air? *For one sure thing, they're staying their course; and for all you know, it may resemble the loyal course you promised to stay when you were too young to know what* promise *meant or where the wind would take your wings, if you ever got wings.*

And near as those eagles were, I thought for the moment that steady faith with who you choose is likely the best thing in this world, till the grave anyhow. I understood I'd failed completely, now today if never before in my long mess. I knew I was locked in the trough of it too, out here lost on a girl's hot tether, awaiting her will. But then I saw the worst and finest point of all—*No man has ever been gladder than me. Nobody has ever loved the Earth any more than I do, here and now, for giving me these last three months and what's ahead.* I was utterly sure I was right and would stay right. In my whole life, wild as I'd been, I'd never been this far past reach.

At nine fifteen that night, I parked in woods at the foot of the tracks to Harmony. The air was barely dark by then, so I stayed well in the edge of trees and walked on forward till I could see the building Bert had said they'd play in. It was blacked out though. And there were no signs of people near—again just mountain night alive with creaks and yells, scary and sweet. Behind the building, all uphill, was a further thicket of limbs and brush. So I stayed in that and made my way up, past where Bert said Luna lived, to what I guessed was the crown of the hill.

By then it was dark, so I stepped out of the snaky brush and bore due left. And I'd been right—I was at the pews. There was just enough glow for me to see no trace of Luna, but I went on to where I'd sat to hear her this morning. I pretty much knew she'd join me soon. And all I thought for the next few minutes was what to say if a stranger passed. A *family friend of Luna Absher's* seemed like the truth, far as it went. Otherwise I waited in peace (it's one thing to say for fighting a war—you learn how to wait or you die, first bullet). And maybe I waited half an hour. I know some animal big as a pony loped through the clearing, too dark to name. I know there were wings in the air around me—bats or song birds spooked by their dreams. But I never felt a trace of fear; I was the one who was magic now, and I even called out Luna's name in a strong whisper more than once. To my knowledge though, no human passed near me.

Eventually I figured that, if Luna set out to meet me, she'd walk up through that fringe of woods. I went back there and slowly made my way down, with stops to listen, till I got to the back of her weird cabin. No sound whatever but a weak shine lit the canvas walls. I guessed it was ten o'clock by now, and I suddenly knew I'd walk out plainly and knock at the door.

The wood door was open; the screen was locked. All I could see was a dim alcove, and I knocked three times. A human voice yelled a long high "No"—not Luna's voice. Then a few murmurs, then firm footsteps.

And here stood Bert's friend Hearty or Hardy. She was in overalls, a man's blue workshirt; and when she stopped just short of the screen, she looked like a sledgehammer cast in skin—no smile, no word.

I said "Good evening. I'm Bluford Calhoun, a friend of Luna Absher's mother. I've got a message for Luna please."

I've mentioned how much safer those days felt—felt and were—but still the security rules on women were strict as they probably should be now for safety's sake, like every man was assumed to be a roving unmuzzled mad sex fiend (which here at the end of the twentieth century is roughly true). Chaperones, gloves and stockings in public had only just started to fade as the law for girls that planned to survive childhood. So it came as no shock when Hearty said "I'm in charge here. You got some I.D.?" Just from her using those initials, I figured she'd been a WAC in the war.

"Yes ma'm"—I held my driver's license to the screen.

She nodded grimly, turned and pounded out of sight.

And for maybe three minutes, I chilled my heels in the ticking dark.

Then Luna was here, that quick and changed from who I'd seen uphill at church. Her hair was combed out long again, and now she wore a black kimono that stopped at her knees.

What light there was came from behind her, so I was prepared not to see her clearly. In person though, that partial blindness chilled me worse than the night around us.

She finally said "Are you in trouble?"—no smile at all.

"Trouble?" I thought of her criminal brother. Maybe she thought you only drove across a whole state if the Law was on your tail for blood. "No ma'm, I came to thank you for the letter. But it's taken me a long day to say it."

"You could have just written. The mail gets here—it's a whole lot cheaper." She'd shifted a little till her face caught the light.

I could see her eyes were blanker than a doll's, a way I'd never seen them before. By then my mind was sinking through my cold shoe soles. I thought I'd try a final tack. "You sending me back east with that?"

Luna waited a little like she still might bolt. "What do you want?"

I understood that Hearty might be hid nearby. *Bert asked me if I was a sheriff—what kind of people run this place?* I went a step closer but I didn't whisper. "You know I want you by me for good."

She finally nodded. She might have been agreeing to news that dark had fallen or tomorrow was Monday. Then she said. "I want to help you too."

I still doubt I was too far wrong to seize on that as a sign of hope.

I said "I've had these long days, Luna, to think about us. And everything I've told you is true—you matter to me the most on Earth."

She said "I know." It came out clean as a baby's grin, a simple fact—she ruled the world. If anybody else in my whole life had said anything that self assured, I'd have laughed in their face.

But I just said what came to me next. "Let's leave here now." As I heard my words, I went cold scared. But while I watched her think it through, I knew *That's it. That's all you mean. Don't take a word back.*

First Luna smiled and her voice went low. "Leave? *Now?*"

I nodded hard. "Right after church would have been my choice. But sure, right now."

"Where to, Blue?" Her smile had lasted and in her voice my name at least came sweeter than song.

"Florida—hell, down near Pensacola." I was grabbing around my mind like a chimp in a world of vines.

"You got a job there?"

"Not yet but I will."

"I'm still in school—"

"They've got schools down there every block."

Luna actually laughed a note or two but tense, not like she thought I was crazy. We both heard heavy walking behind her and held our breath—was Hearty coming? Then Luna brought her face almost to the rusty screen. "Wait up at the church. I'll do my best. It may take awhile."

I said "Bring everything you need." I meant *Bring all you need for the rest of your life.* And I started to say it. But my mind told me *She knows, she knows. You just go wait.*

Cold as it got by the minute, I waited where Luna said. Again the time didn't seem too long, and one of the strangest facts of my life—I wasn't surprised at her accepting. If I'd been halfway in control, I'd have thought *Of course she's lied to you. Maybe Hearty's already called the Law.* But all my thoughts were looped round me. When I'd first sat—on the front pew now—I carefully asked myself *Are you crazy?* We'd had more than one tragic mind in the family, that spent their final twenty years clawing their faces and screaming to God. *Are you the next in line there, son?*

So I checked my brain several ways. I tried to recite the poems I'd learned in seventh grade—Joaquin Miller, Lord Dunsany and Felicia Hemans. They rolled right off my tongue, word perfect, as I whispered them out. Then I tested the present, always a harder job for me. *What have you done in the past three days?* To my satisfaction I found I could pretty well list my deeds. Then I listed the names and next of kin of every friend who died in the war.

So sure, I was sane. And all I found to snag me was—while I was listing recent events—the remembered sound of Mother's voice on the phone describing what I meant to her when I was young and pure in heart, and she was what I had on Earth. Life was quitting her slowly now, I'd do what I could to ease her way, but both of us knew the world too well to think I could bear the full weight for her. *Stay in close reach of her though. You owe her that much.* Hell, I'd take her with me—or bring her to me—wherever I went, whoever was near. *That waits down the road. Face that when you're gone.* Also Mattie and Myra came up clear in my sight. They looked as strong as the mountain beyond me, lost as it was in thick chill night. *They'll miss you awhile. You'll miss them forever. But what you're doing is clearing* everybody's *path so they can move on.*

Then Luna was here. I hadn't heard her steps in the brush; she must have walked right out in the open. And when she got to the back of the pews and said my name, she spoke in a normal daily voice.

I whispered "Present" and stood in place. By then I could hear her move through the air, though I didn't see a sign of her body till she stood by me and found my hand. Even then I only saw her forehead and chin—it was that dark and she was wearing nearly black clothes. She didn't speak but, since she held just my right hand, I reached for her right—she bent quickly and set something down; then both our hands were finally joined. I told myself *She's brought her belongings,* and I said "You ready?"

She said "Yes, Blue."

I ask you to reach this far with me, however you feel when you get this far—try to feel this *in yourself*. You've waited all your life for two words, *Yes* and *Blue* in the perfect voice at the exact moment in the right surroundings. Think what it would do to you to get that totally usable answer to all your hopes. I'll leave it by saying I never felt that fine again and never will till you forgive me, in acts or words. As far as happiness goes in life, I might as well have quit on the spot; but I said "What's the safe way out of here?"

"Straight back down. I'm not really hiding."

I'd obviously thought we were hiding hard. So I had to say "My car's way out on the main road."

"All right—I only brought my harp." Nothing about us had met but our hands, though I wanted to hold all of her now. But she bent again to find her harp case and moved on down ahead of me.

I followed with two strong voices in me. One said *Son, your life has started*. The other said *Take this minute by minute and never beg*.

When we got to the car, not seeing a soul, we climbed in and sat apart, not touching. But again I thought *Remember all this. This is your new world*. So I finally laughed and said "Some *heat*"—I'd seen Luna shiver and I reached for the heater.

Then she said "I got to be back by sunup. Florida's too far for that, I guess"—all as straight as if we'd planned an overnight jaunt, ten thousand miles to get orange juice, and had thought better of it.

I still believed I was running this; I could turn her gently. *Second by second, son. Move out slow*. I cranked the motor and then I faced her in the green dash light. *Oh Christ, she looks far better than I knew* (lately I'd just seen her in Bob's photograph from before last Christmas). She'd settled herself and looked ahead like we were already gone and safe. So I said "Then where were you hoping to go?"

"They say there's a tourist court a few miles on."

"They?"

"Our cooks—two colored girls."

"What's Hearty say?"

"You know her name?—she didn't say nothing. She was in the john."

"Won't she call the sheriff now you've disappeared?"

Luna finally met my eyes. She held on a second, then laughed very kindly and touched my knee. "It's a *grownup* camp. You met the one kid, and it threw you off—he's the owner's son."

Again this was nearly fifteen years before free love took the southeast states and had normal people talking like whores and pimps to your face. I won't say I felt shocked exactly, but I had a taste of tarnish on my teeth. "So just tonight in a tourist court is your idea?"

She was smiling still. "A deep bathtub with sudsy gallons of steamy water is *my* idea. See, camp's just got these lukewarm showers."

If next she'd stuck her thumb in her mouth, it couldn't have struck me as any more childish. I made myself think back—twenty minutes ago uphill—how fine I felt. *There's a child still in her, son. Push past that. Just find a warm room and watch her change.* I touched the gas and we rolled on.

Luna swore she'd never seen the place and I believed her, but she called every turn and got us there fast—Mountain Mist Cabins, little individual real log huts spread out under trees that were hung with strings of Christmas lights. I went in the office by myself; and the man on the desk said "You won't believe it but we're full up" (a nearby boys' camp was holding a powwow for old boys and parents). The instant he said it, I felt as tired as I'd ever been. I asked him where was the nearest bed. When he said "Maybe in Seven Devils," I must have looked grim. He held up a hand like he meant to ease me and said "You *could* rent the trailer of course."

"Trailer?"

"You know, a home on wheels." He made little boxy motions in the air, trying to describe it. "It's right out back here, warm and dry. Anybody tired as *you* look now ought not to drive."

I knew he was right and paid the seven dollars.

When I asked for the key, he said "No key. Got stole years back.

Folks are tame here mostly. But if your wife's scared, just tell her to push that sofa up against the door. It'll slow the bears if not much else."

And tired as I felt, it turned out better than he claimed. A pre-World War II trailer with a doll size parlor, a master bedroom, kitchenette, toilet and a kerosene heater that looked like guaranteed suffocation. But Luna made a thorough tour, then came back to me and said "I told you. The cooks weren't wrong; they never miss."

I chose not to ask where the cooks had hit bullseye before. I had to say what I suddenly felt—"It's home all right."

Next Luna opened the pink refrigerator, and there was a nearly full jar of grape juice. She found two glasses, we sat on the sofa; and then she said "To Blue and Luna, damned few equals and no superiors."

I knew it was an ancient Air Force toast, and I had qualms about the juice, but I joined her and drank (it was soft as feathers).

Luna drained hers off and then leaned back.

I finally said "This mountain air is agreeing with you. You look even better than I expected."

Her eyes were full and she said "Many thanks."

"You understand I worship your face."

She held a finger to her lips. "That's sacrilegious." But then she whispered "I hate my face."

I'd noticed the first time I ever saw her what simple care she took of her looks—nothing fancy or cheap, just respect for the lovely gifts she'd got from her unpromising family tree. "You've got to know you're a natural beauty."

"Keep saying it but I won't believe you."

"Have I lied to you yet?" We still hadn't touched. I took her right hand and held it lightly.

She ran her free hand along the line of her cheek and jaw, and then she said it straight to my eyes. "If your own father had rubbed his hot thing time and again across your face when you were five, you'd probably hate yourself bad as me."

It crossed my mind again—*Rita claimed he vanished when you were a baby. Was that just a lie?* I had no reason to think that Luna would lie about such a terrible wrong, but till now I'd never had to deal with the subject. Believe me, there in the 1950s such homemade tragedies never made headlines, not to speak of daily discussions on TV and articles in magazines. Back then every month or so you might see an item in the back of your paper—some white trash male accused of "carnal knowledge of a female minor." And I've already mentioned the straits any normal father of a girl must navigate, but Luna had truly sandbagged me. *Act like you didn't hear it, son.* I leaned to kiss the back of her hand. Then I stroked her jaw where she'd just touched. *Show her that nothing's changed about her—not in your eyes, not here tonight after what she's said.*

She shook her head though and moved my hand. "You mentioned Pensacola, Florida. You lost your mind?"

"I *found* it—believe me."

Her face went through a whole new set of shifts. She started smiling, then faded down through pleasantness to dignified curiosity. In these few weeks she'd taken a real stride forward in age—it looked like a face that had been somewhere and was ready for whatever road came next. She said "Then tell me the way you've changed." Her head rolled back against the sofa and both eyes shut. "And make it a story."

I knew what she meant. So I leaned back too, shut out the world and spelled my entire meaning to her. "For a start I've already left home and family. Myra knows I'm gone for good and why. Mattie has already left for Mother's to keep her company till school starts. I've explained to Rita how I love you and how I mean to treat you right till I fall dead. Of course nobody's glad but us. So if we've got any chance on Earth—and I swear we do—it's bound to be somewhere besides Raleigh. I just thought we'd strike on south till we hit sand and warm saltwater. We can dig in there some place in the sun where I'll get a job and you finish school. In two years' time I'll be divorced, and we'll be clear the rest of the way." When I looked over, Luna's eyes were still shut. But tears had run down onto her neck, and I thought her lips were trembling (I wasn't a steady rock myself). I said "Can I just hold you please?"

Her eyes stayed shut but she said "Oh please." When I had folded her into my arms and pressed her close, she said another version of what had meant the world to me once before. "Blue, I *want* to love you now. See, nobody yet has made me feel halfway as safe and clean as you—Blue, oh Blue." My name was like a strap she was holding in a runaway car.

So we stayed together like that a long time, alone as we had ever been, with the woods dead still and the other guests asleep. Just sitting there proved to be enough rest. And about the time I told myself *She's gone to sleep,* my body fired up slow but high. I wanted us in bed and closer still. *Wake her though and you may spoil your chance.*

I kept quiet but let my mind sink through her thick hair far into her brain. Over and over I thought one thing—*Meet me, Luna, on our best ground.* A silent voice spoke out inside me, saying I had no right to her body—she was flat forbidden and what I dreamed was against the law of God and man, plus greedy and cruel. But I found what seemed a fair answer to that. *If she turns to you in the next half minute and says she wants to move to the bed or back to the car, or the tub or the moon, you'll do whatever she asks—no questions.* I went on thinking *Meet me, meet me* and counting the seconds.

I hadn't got past forty five when Luna's head twitched, and she gave a whimper like Matt when she dreamed. But somehow though her face was hid, I understood her eyes were open and seeing the weird trailer around us—"a home on wheels" with lights, water, heat and places to rest: maybe all we'd get, above ground anyhow on this Earth.

Just before I counted sixty, she said "I guess we'd better stretch out."

I actually said, and was proud of myself, "You don't want that tub bath you mentioned?"

"You haven't seen the bathroom then—no tub at all. It's a shower small enough for an ant." Then as simple as if she was leaving for school, she stood up out of my arms and walked through the farthest door, the dark bedroom.

The oily heater had stoked the air to where it felt like pressure on me, a weight that didn't want me to move. I sat still another long minute, giving her every chance to change her mind and tell me. Mainly though I was working to make my soul believe what Luna seemed more than ready to give, not just the splendid body I've mentioned maybe too often but all the hunger her life had whetted. I could finally say to myself what seemed the actual truth—*Son, she's moved two hundred miles. She's known new people and tried new ways. But she's certain now. She's choosing you.*

Again I won't pretend you need or want to know what passed between that minute and daybreak. But let me say this much at least. Fine as our first few private hours together had been, near Raleigh in the old motel, the deeds we managed between us in our home on wheels were finer still. Without being raving wild on the subject, like I said before, I'd known more bodies than one till now. No other body—and no soul in it—ever laid a finger anywhere near Luna's. If God himself gives classes in Heaven on blending souls, he'll have one girl that won't need to learn. Worn as it is, *grand* still feels like the nearest word to what Luna had, so ample, to give. And I knew it from the instant when—there in that coffin-shaped pink room with dim light down the length of our skin—she turned to me and said "I don't have one secret left."

But after all we'd done in that space, to me she looked like one of those rows of sphinxes in Egypt, lined-up riddles vanishing off as far as you see in glare and dust. Any other time or place, I'd have known to doubt her or even to think *She truly believes she's telling the truth; but she's got secrets she'll never know, not to mention me.* So I took it as one more gift I'd waited for—the fact of a person who'll never lie to you, never change to a hateful stranger beside you or set aside her first strong magic that haled you on.

I knew it was all too deep to discuss. And since the steady sight of Luna was more than I could take for long, I turned off the lamp and said "Let's promise we won't ever die." I had no idea where that came from or what it meant beyond the usual human hope to last forever,

young and loved. But it sounded sensible once I said it, almost there
in reach of my hand. And even all these long years since, I can't con-
demn the words or thoughts I committed that night. Luna Absher
was that worth knowing.

When I woke myself at six in the morning, she was still beside me
but so far gone I had to shake her once I was dressed. And even then
she scared me like she'd died in her dreams. I ended up sitting on the
bed beside her and stroking her hand till I reeled her in with the
sound of her name.

It seemed like she couldn't place my looks or know whether I was
friend or foe—she frowned that deep and said "Please tell me where
I am."

It didn't sound fake and it stung at first. I said "I'm the man that's
saving you."

Luna said "I was saved when I got baptized." She still hadn't
smiled.

"How long ago was that?"

"In a muddy river when I was ten."

"Then you'll be needing a touchup today—I left some hot water.
Go shower quick and we'll eat breakfast" (the place had a cafe by the
office). I'd meant the "touchup" part as a joke.

But it struck her wrong. Her eyes flared up and she said the first
harsh words I'd heard from her calm voice. "You get this straight—
everything I do is known to God. He's yet to claim I've gone astray,
my conscience says I'm moving right, but don't you fail to go back
home and read that verse where Jesus says 'Don't harm a child or
you'll be wishing some kind soul would hang a millstone round your
neck and throw you out in the midnight sea.' "

I tried to recall if she'd ever mentioned God or church. *Surely no.*
And it chilled me some, so I kept trying to tease her gently. "You're
no child, lady."

She still didn't break. "Man, you know I'm a minor child. Think
what you've done."

But then she rose to her knees in the cover—she was all-over naked—
and touched the tip of her chin to my forehead, then kissed my eyes
and strode to the bath.

I sat there, wing shot down and sick. I tried to obey her and think
what I'd done. *You're right—you've saved her from a white trash life
with a punk for a mate and wormy kids. You've poisoned her clean
mind and body and wrecked her chance to break loose and run.
Counting Myra and Madelyn and your blind mother—not to speak
of Rita—you've fouled every woman you trust and need.*

Even the sight of Luna again when she came back to dry her hair—
even that privilege hardly touched an awful sadness back of my eyes
that felt right and just.

But when I stopped by the ruts to Harmony and reached for the
door to help Luna out, she put a hand on my arm and said "Blue,
please wait." In the half hour since she turned against me, I'd mostly
thought of missing work—I couldn't conceivably get to the store till
late afternoon. Should I phone ahead with some fast lie or just let
fate sort my roads out? If Mr. Atkinson fired me on the spot, he'd be
within his moral rights (he knew about my drinking days and would
have good reason to think I'd relapsed). And he might be doing me
one huge favor to stun me awake. With Luna taking my hand now
though, I waited and listened.

"I hope someday I get to show you how much this has meant."

"This what?"

"You coming this long way for me."

I thought and said "But you turned me down."

Her eyes looked honestly baffled. "How do you mean?"

"Luna, grow up. I asked you to leave here now with me and start
our life."

She nodded slowly, looked to the road and said "Oh that—"

"That trifling thing—yes ma'm. Oh that."

It took her so long I thought she'd gone into some kind of trance.
Then she swung her body around. At first she smiled but I wouldn't

answer. So she took my right hand and pressed her lips to the big blue veins. "Don't move now please. I'll take my harp and run on back." When her door was open, she put one foot out and said "I know deep in my bones we're *leaving* when the time says go." Before I could even focus on her, she melted into a cedar thicket.

Then I thought *Never, girl. You'll never see me.*

SIX

BUT OF COURSE she saw me and didn't we *go*, to one of the ends of the Earth at least? Still I had to get through more than a month in my old grooves. My boss didn't fire me, though we had a long talk—I honestly think he believed my lies—and I didn't miss another hour of work till the evening I quit. At first I roomed at that same motel north of town. But after a week I suspect Matt prevailed and convinced Miss Ashlyn I was needy and sober. In any case Mother drove herself to the motel—it was almost surely her final drive—and left a message under my door.

Your family home is still yours. Your room is vacant and you can live there, starting tonight.

She hadn't signed it but her hand was unique—I'd know it still in the Christmas rush of the busiest mailroom known to man. Soon as I read it, I dialed her number. Madelyn answered and before I could ask her to call Miss Ashlyn, she said "I'm fixing your supper right now." I still asked for Mother.

She took her time coming, then said "Yes please."

I said "I'd like to take you up on your invitation; but do you understand I'm a sober *man*, not the boy you knew?"

"I've prayed for that since you were eighteen, so I'm glad to know" (I'd started drinking heavily then, my first college year). She dropped to a whisper. "There's one house rule—you don't bring anybody under this roof without my permission."

I accepted her deal. I was that worn out with lonesomeness and cardboard meals, and—don't deny me—I loved her and Mattie. (It's the strangest fact I know about life. You can simultaneously love as many people as you've got hours to spend; and Lord, I've loved five or six at once. But that doesn't mean I didn't hurt all of them one by one in separate ways that wound up stifling their next breath while I stood grinning and telling myself I'd done them good.) From that night then I stayed in my old room at Mother's and got to like the place again. In a day or so I was nearly at ease with her and Matt. And we might have lived there peacefully for years to come if I hadn't told myself every minute that my next course was set in concrete and led due south.

Myra stayed in the Beechridge house. She was solemn but civil when I had to go by for clothes and such. Every Sunday I wrote her the check I'd written for fifteen years, the household funds. I didn't even trim off Mattie's share of the weekly budget, though Mother was paying for all Matt's needs except pocket money which I provided. And twice in the weeks I stayed at Mother's, Myra drove out for supper with us. The four of us sat at the dining room table like a genuine family eating baked chicken and homegrown vegetables and talking calmly like we hadn't smashed into cold black rocks way back upstream.

Me? I managed to put one foot down after the other. I'd have these fits when I felt like howling a name to the trees—*Luna, Lune*—and hoping to bring her back by *will* power to where I mostly knew she belonged. I must have recited her parting words that last morning a thousand times—somehow we'd *go*. All right, we would. I wrote to the Pensacola Chamber of Commerce and got brochures and real estate ads plus a list of all the main stores in the county (six music stores—it's near an air base) and several white high schools.

Just looking at realtors' pictures of the blue Gulf and low white bungalows at reasonable prices could set me off like a boy with a

Polaroid of that one girl he's dreamed to see in the altogether. But mainly I lived a regular life—work, then Mother and Matt in the evenings, going to mass on Sundays with Matt (and Myra beyond her), seeing Bob Barefoot once a week (he was steadily worse), sleeping the best I could in the heat and trying to screen my mind from facts that went against my ravenous dreams.

I'd had no word or sign from Rita since July 4th, so I let that rest right where it lay. Letters from Luna came steadily now, and she didn't mention her mother either. Through the years I've lost all but two more of them. One though says a very great deal to me—and to any normal human who's found him or herself caught in the teeth of desperate love and *shook* till every bone of his body is bruised or splintered. It came right after my trip up there.

Dear old Blue,

I am doing good and I bet you are now. Time up here is speeding ahead and I am already thinking of school. Have to pinch myself to believe I will be a high school junior but it looks that way if I don't die.

Last night I was talking to Hearty Taylor and asked her what she thought my chances were of living by music. I guess you know how tough she is but she then said "They are first rate, girl." She thinks I ought to be writing hymns and gospel tunes. They sell fast once you get to Nashville. But I don't want to be more sacrilegious than I already am so I keep singing the same old stuff dead strangers write and the compliments keep on coming—stuck up! (beg your pardon).

I hope you have got some rest back home. You seemed real strained but then you had driven across a state that's one of the longest. I learned that in third grade geography, a fact. You could turn North Carolina ninety degrees to north and south and we would reach all the way to Canada (if that's confusing look at the map). So thank you again—hear?—and get your beauty sleep.

Love,
Luna

If you set out to hypnotize a grown soul hard in love with you, could you do better? I couldn't, even now with everything I learned beside her over hundreds of miles in the time to come. And I still think she had no plan to keep me grilling over her fire, no meanness at heart. If what she'd told me about her dad was actually true, then Luna might have told herself she'd earned a permanent license to hurt the world more than she did. Back then of course—whatever you'd suffered in childhood or youth—nobody thought you were free to be vicious in the here and now. You were just expected to live in the present. And Luna Absher was no more vicious than a panther cub, learning to use its teeth and claws.

Still, though, I asked her when she'd be home, and should I plan to drive back up and bring her down, but she never said. She kept on writing me masterpiece riddles till finally I called the main camp number, got a woman in the office, claimed I was calling from the Raleigh paper and asked her when the campers would leave. She said it was Saturday, August 11th anytime after ten a.m. And I kept rolling the idea round. I could turn up unasked to bring Luna home and risk getting hot shame thrown in my face, or I could wait till she found her own way and trust she'd call me at Mother's to meet.

I managed to wait. I even went from the store that evening to the A&P, then straight to Bob Barefoot's in the country with a half gallon of peach ice cream. By then it was almost all Bob could eat; and he'd got used to watching me turn in the drive at six on Saturdays, fix him a big bowl and leave the rest for when he roamed the house at night, which he said he did with his skin on fire like a swarm of bees were after his soul (one glance at his eyes and you knew it was true—by then he weighed a hundred and ten).

This one August evening he finally scraped the bottom of his bowl like a blind child. And when I asked could I get him more, he said "I know you're ready to roll."

"I'll gladly sit here till you say go." When the words were out, I knew I meant them, whatever else might wait for me in the night out there.

Bob took it in as eagerly as the cream—I hadn't seen his eyes shine out like that since before his mother died, and she'd be throwing us stinging jokes quicker than we could catch or dodge. He said "I'll keep that in my memory, Bluford. I'm all but sure our memory lasts—"

"Beyond the grave?" I'd never heard Bob nudge that close to anything like a religious thought.

"Oh way beyond." He nodded hard. "You'll be a big star in eternity, friend. More than one invisible mind will run home movies of you through the ages. I plan to be the projectionist."

"Thanks. I won't say 'Cancel the plan.'"

By then Bob's eyes had filled and he stood. With all the caring he'd done through the years, he had less idea of how to show it than any kind man I've ever known. He set the empty bowl on the table and actually pointed at the door. "Rita called yesterday so I know who's due home tonight. You go meet *her*."

It burned my face from four yards off. "What did Rita say about me, Bob?"

"She doesn't know we're back in touch. She's trying to sell me her nursing talents—claims she'll move out here and save my hide for less than half of what trained nurses cost."

"Did she say how Luna's camp had gone?"

"I asked her but all she'd say was 'Luna don't write no more than if I *wasn't*.'" He suddenly grinned. "How did *you* think her camp was going?"

I hadn't told him about my trip or quoted from the letters I got, but now it seemed like one more harmless pleasure I could give. "I drove up there several weekends back. The camp wasn't much, to my eyes anyhow. But Luna—Luna had come a long way."

"In the right direction?"

"Yes sir, towards me."

By then Bob's strength was fading again. He sat down slowly in a chair by the table. "What do you plan to do with her now?"

"I mean to nail her down forever."

He was still smiling. "Christ claims there are no nuptial bonds in Heaven."

Since he'd claimed our memory lasted, I said "Then I'm branding her deep in my memory."

Bob waited, then shook his yellow skull. "Forget you know her, Blue—from this night on."

Mother and Madelyn understood I'd be late for supper. So when I walked in near seven thirty, they were in the kitchen warming my plate. They'd eaten at six but they set my place as neatly as if my life depended on it. Then they sat with me and watched my eyes for signs of need. (I've mentioned how women used to do such things, and none I met seemed to think they were slaves. If they were anyhow they were splendid at it and they looked rewarded.)

By the time I finished we'd covered the tellable news of the day, Mother was up washing my dishes, and dusk was moving towards the house from the farthest woods. Till then I hadn't let myself try to figure when Luna would get to town and whether she'd try—or would get a chance—to leave Rita's place and call me. I didn't even know if she'd come on the bus or catch a ride with some of her teachers. But as I sat there next to Matt and told myself not to ask if I'd had phone calls today, I realized I was actually calm.

Then Madelyn silently reached for my hand. I've said how she'd read a book on palmistry. And young as she was, she'd sometimes make a bullseye landing on one of my secret hopes or fears. The morning after I took what's still my last drink of liquor, Matt had searched my palm and said "You're making room for me in here." Now though when she'd looked for two minutes, she folded my hand and set it down.

"Is the truth really that hard to tell?"

Again I meant it more as a joke, but the nod Matt gave me looked like pain. In all my recent days out there, she'd never said two words directly about me and Myra, not to mention Luna whose name she'd almost surely not heard. And Mother had told me that Matt never mentioned the separation, never asked her a question about our home life. Even now don't ask me why I chose this Saturday night to push for news from behind her eyes. But I reached for her left palm; and when I'd traced her clean lifeline, I kept looking down. "This almost tells me you're very sad."

It was then Miss Ashlyn left the room, whether she'd heard my words or not.

Matt's hand stayed open though and she didn't answer.

I did what came very naturally—I leaned way down and brushed the base of her thumb with my chin.

Through that, she managed not to move. But when I laid my head down gently across her palm, she said "I'm the saddest girl you know."

I hated to look but of course I did. Her face was maybe a little pale, but her eyes were clear and steady as animals frozen in hopes you'll never see them. I'd never seen a human face that looked any stiller, less likely to move. I suddenly knew *She's dead and you did it, son.* I said "You getting a summer cold?"

"No. I'm not getting polio either. I'm sad for us."

"Mother and me?"

"*My* mother, yes—Myra Calhoun and Matt and Blue."

"You see your mother today or talk to her?"

"I can feel my way without Mother."

"Matt, I thought you enjoyed it here—all the mystery books, the old piano, your new bicycle, the girls down the road" (there were neighbor girls about Matt's age).

"I like one thing—the extra time that you and I get."

We'd spent our evenings together lately, taking long walks when the sun went down, making ice cream in Mother's crank freezer, playing card games, looking through pictures in old albums—Mother always left us alone. So I said "I've liked every minute we spent. What else you think we ought to do?"

"You ought to go back home tonight."

"Matt, this house was my boyhood favorite—"

"But you grew up, Sky. You live on Beechridge Road these days. I will too, soon. Mother's there waiting this whole awful time."

Of course it was hurting by the word, the syllable. I knew she meant it all in spades. I also saw no way to help her. I started saying "Some-day I hope you'll underst—"

Her hand came up and shut my mouth. "I *understand*."

"Then tell me please." It almost seemed she knew a way for me to move her anyhow off this burning grate she was on.

She said "We're all in mortal sin." Through all the years I'd been with Myra, and especially once Matt started with the nuns, *mortal sin* was a term I heard every day or so. Was Ingrid Bergman in mortal sin for having a bastard son abroad? Was a man from their church—recently caught in a lady's dress and high heel shoes in the Carolina Hotel drunk as a duck—in mortal sin? It had seemed like one more private sideshow the Catholics ran to keep them busy, like saints' bones and bingo.

But coming from Mattie with this late summer light behind her—and Luna Absher moving somewhere on the west edge of town or already here, ready or not—it hit me dead in the midst of my chest. I tried to think Matt was years too young to judge these questions of love and faith. Her eyes wouldn't let me. *She's nothing but right.* What I said though was "Not *mortal* sin, Matt—not you, not Myra. Just me—old Sky. And I can't change where Sky's headed now." I saw that—whatever she'd yet to learn about hunger, human skin and running for dear life—Matt still knew every truth that mattered here tonight or had *mattered* ever.

She said "I know you can change, this minute. You'd better too—you're drowning fast, and me and Mother are going down with you."

The one good thing I did, that day and the coming night, was nod to Mattie and say "You'll last, believe me," though I could see it hurt her worse than thinking she'd die of pain for me, which she would years later when the chance to help her had long gone by.

Back then most towns had creameries. The name alone would sink a store now; but then when nobody planned to run marathons on their hundredth birthday, the dairy companies would have clean stores that pasteurized milk before your eyes and sold all grades of butter, whipping cream, ice cream and sherbet. The one I'd loved all through boyhood was on Glenwood up near Hillsboro. My dad would take us there summer nights and let me eat till I grinned for mercy. So when

I'd washed my hands at the sink, I called to Mother wherever she was, "Let's drive young Matt to the Pine State Creamery and celebrate."

Mother answered from her room, "What's the occasion?" But before I could think of a cause for joy, I heard her stand and start towards us. When she got to Mattie and me in the hall, she checked us both—"I won't go to ride with two mad people. Have you made your peace?"

Matt didn't speak.

I said "*I* have" and offered my wrist in Matt's direction (she'd always liked to hold my wrist and feel the pulse).

She reached for Mother's arm instead and helped her out and through the dark like a second dessert would heal dim eyes and who knew what other mortal ills?

I can't say for sure but ice cream then seemed more trustworthy than any since. You'd order strawberry and—lo—you'd get thick chunks of berries, garden fresh and naturally sweet. Or gnaw away at a cone of chocolate—it would be so rich you'd feel a pimple start on your nose before you could finish. By the time we'd finished ours that night, in bent iron chairs at a plate size table, I saw we'd all calmed down enough to be tired and not so set to ram the family down our private rails.

So I thought I'd really wear us out; and instead of heading straight to the country, I drove round the Capitol, down Fayetteville Street, then back up Wilmington, slowing whenever Mattie said "Look" at some clothes in a window, and Mother would try to follow her point. I've mentioned before how safe downtown was. I didn't say how many tame people you'd see as late as midnight—relaxed small crowds, young people and old. The movie theaters ran till eleven, people would stop for soft drinks or eats, then windowshop till they were tired.

We were coming to one of the backstreet men's stores that catered to young black men and motorcycle hoods. Suddenly Mattie said "A giant!" and she was right—on the sidewalk facing a window of clothes was a white fellow way over six feet tall in a short sleeved shirt rolled up to his shoulders on arms that looked even longer than him. I slowed a little. Just as we got there, he turned right towards us with out-stretched arms—a long narrow face, clipped tow hair and an outsize grin like we were expected (he must have seen Matt).

Matt's window was open. She gave him a wave and said "Keep growing!" which startled me.

But nothing compared to what I saw the next instant. Off the side-walk—back in the recessed entrance to the store six feet from the giant—was Luna Absher, no doubt on Earth. She was staring at the overdressed window, half smiling and awake like she hadn't crossed a lengthy state this past hot day. And though I saw just the side of her face, it slammed against my cooled down mind like an angel visit or a tiger's leap. I was thrilled and scared and sick as a dog. *Who's her giant?—not the same old hood at the doughnut shop.*

One way streets were fairly new to Raleigh. I quickly tried to think of a way to circle back and prove it was Luna, but I couldn't think of where to turn or what to say to Mother and Matt, so there was nothing to do but drive and slow my heart to a human rate. By then my passengers were bushed. In the rearview mirror I could see Mother struggling to keep her eyes open, and next to me young Mattie had slid back into the speechless ache I'd seen at supper and was helpless to touch.

Nobody spoke till we were back in Miss Ashlyn's yard. Then she said "East, west, home's best."

Matt said "Amen" in the midst of a yawn.

But all I could think was *Somebody help me please right now.* I had no idea who I meant. But like I'd done in deep drunk tanks—when I have actually clawed out chunks of plaster from the freezing walls and chewed them down in search of ease—I somehow had that trace of hope. *Go find her, son. Refresh her mind on who in this whole howling world can bring her peace.*

Well, you crawl on, don't you?—young as you are, you've proved *you'll* last. I envied sides of beef on spits, I volunteered to swap my place with any rock in a gravel crusher, but I made it through. I came up alive and walked - limped - crawled the next ten yards. When Mother had unlocked the door (and even now she liked that privilege), Matt said "The phone!" and tore in past us. The phone was ringing miles away.

Or so it felt. I tried to think Luna had seen me passing and walked to the nearest phone to say the tow haired giant was—Christ!—her resurrected dad or a harmless guy she'd known at camp who'd brought her home and already left for parts unknown. I paused in the parlor for Matt to call me.

But she yelled "Dammit!"—the line was dead.

I tried to watch the late TV news beside them in the kitchen, and I kept fairly still. But when we'd packed Matt off to bed and Mother had poured her nightly shot of apple brandy—one measured ounce knocked back down her tilted head like a chicken drinks—I finally had to speak or split. I said "Miss Ashlyn, ask me a question."

"Beg your pardon?"

"A question, anything—start me talking. I'm in trouble here."

"You are indeed. I see as much." She stepped back and sat in reach.

"You understand why?"

"I heard Mattie start to tell you her news. I left you to it."

I said "Matt thinks my soul's in danger. I calmed her though."

"You didn't. You won't. Mattie knows what's what."

I said "Miss Ashlyn, Mattie is fine. If you live on till the year twelve thousand, Mattie Calhoun'll be strong as a bear. You and she will rule the Earth."

Mother frowned. "You're laughing *your* way to Hell."

"No ma'm, no. You've got me wrong. It's not Matt on my mind right now." Mother's face was patiently settled for whatever tale I had to tell, so I said "You remember when Matt yelled 'Giant!' at a fellow downtown, and he waved at her?"

"I heard it, yes. Matt notices boys."

"Not the boy, not the man. My friend was with him."

"Your friend?"

"Luna Absher. I mentioned her."

"You did indeed. My *mind's* clear, Bluford. I know the name—I've prayed against her."

"Against her? What kind of Christian are you?"

Steady as steel, Mother said "To be sure, I don't wish her harm. I pray she fades off your field of vision."

Mother knew nothing about my trip to Harmony or anything else about Luna's summer. Far as I knew she understood just what I told her the day we went to the doctor in Durham. Of course she also knew I'd left my wife and moved back home, my daughter was sad, I was sober but edgy. I doubted Myra had told her more—Myra learned years back what not to tell Mother. So I said "Acid couldn't fade Luna Absher, not out of my life. We love each other and are moving fast."

"In what direction?—the *altar's* out."

I knew if I mentioned Florida now, I'd spoil her chance for sleep tonight. She'd lie here planning each step of her life when the light had truly shut down in her eyes and she was alone. I told myself *Anywhere you go you'll make plans for her*—I still thought I could. "I'm counting on fate to tell us which way next."

"I can save you waiting on an answer from fate—you want me to? I know right now." A smile was almost curving in the tips of her mouth.

And I thought *All right, this is our old game. Your move, Miss Ashlyn.* I said "Tell on."

As she spoke she drew it out on the table with a careful finger. "You chase this poor girl far as you can—you're no teenager—and then you either *think* you land her and spend the rest of your days in misery, watching a young woman learn to despise you for being too slow, or you do what your friend fate told me to tell you here long weeks ago: *quit* this instant."

On top of the shame of glimpsing Luna in a public street with a lanky punk, Mother's words felt kind and right. But the sight of Luna in a mountain trailer was also vivid in my mind, her face when she looked at my eyes and said "I want to love you for good." I thought *If Luna gives me half a chance, I'll teach her how to love old Blue and every other soul he loves the rest of his life*. But there in the present, I leaned to my mother and touched the rings on both her hands. On the left a wide gold wedding band. On the right a chip diamond and two small pearls.

In the days when she and I would sit on the porch swing in summer heat, I'd ask for stories about each ring. She'd make up legends of where she got them—they were mined in caves by warty dwarves or brought through hail and fire by princes for her alone—but at the end she'd always say "The gold band belongs to your father. If I die first he keeps it safe in case you need it. The diamond's yours and these two pearls that come from the mystic deep itself. They go to your wife or daughter, whichever."

As I touched them now, she finally let her smile arrive.

And I thought, again for the first time maybe in thirty years, *The mystic deep*, seeing those pearls through her dim eyes. I said "Your ancient son is tired."

"Every reason to be. Go rest your soul."

We headed down the bedroom hall; and when we turned apart at her door, it was Mother who put a hand to her lips and pressed a shadowy kiss on my neck.

I said "We'll crawl through this somehow."

She said "We always have before. But as ever, old Blue, there's no *bound to be* rule."

All the nights she'd sat with me, trying to coach me through high school geometry, whenever she'd say "Why is so and so true?" in the theorem at hand, I'd say "Well, it's just bound to be." And her answer was always what she'd just now said in the dark as I was ready to let fate take its course and help me sleep. I tried to smile but I had to say "That may mean you're not bound to be right."

She wouldn't let up. "In your case, Bluford—yours and ours—I'm bound to be right in this anyhow. The whole opinion of the human race is behind me now."

I knew she was right, that far at least, though all I said was "I'm asleep."

And she said "Good."

SEVEN

Bᴜᴛ ɪ ʙᴀʀᴇʟʏ ᴍᴀɴᴀɢᴇᴅ to shut an eye till right before dawn. In the dark I felt as balked and shamed as any thirteen year old caught in the toils of his swollen skin. Harder still—I felt like who I really was: a man in the midst of an average life who'd hauled himself, with others helping, out of eighteen years of alcohol and its blind mess, its intentional meanness; and now I'd spent the past four months acting worse than in the depths of drink. Even so, I'd still gone a time or two to A.A. meetings—a huddle of drunks eating sweet rolls faster than they can chew, smoking like Pittsburgh and telling each other tales as normal for them as coffee and fingernails but that might knock a sober civilian out.

One of the things I've liked from the start about A.A.—they've got good names for the secret crimes most people don't notice. They've sure got the name for people living the way I was—a "dry drunk." If you're a dry drunk, you're technically sober; but you act the way you always did, unmitigated self self self. A lot worse really since now you don't have liquor to blame—it's all your will. You let your mind treat kin and friends like gold one minute and goat shit the next, no rhyme or reason. Worst of all, though your mind is straight, most of the time you can't even *see* the people around you—especially the close ones, your wife and children. You plow right through them like they're clear glass; then they break, to your amazement. And if they're too strong to let you through, they either crack or hate your shadow the rest of your life.

But somewhere after five Sunday morning, I dozed long enough to have a dream than ran its course till it woke me at six. I'd noticed already how odd it was that Luna had never appeared in my sleep. Maybe she hadn't been around long enough to sink really deep in my hid thoughts. In that dream though she came to me vivid as she'd ever been in actual life, in clothes anyhow. I was alone on some kind of beach with high waves pounding too loud to hear. Behind me quite a distance back on a sand dune a carnival was running—just a crap game or two, the merry go round from Pullen Park where Rita and I had drunk our Cokes, a toy ferris wheel, some mangy monkeys. Still I couldn't hear the slightest sound, but people were up there waving my way. So I set out to walk towards them.

Then something knocked on the midst of my back. When I looked it was Luna looking better than ever in the white she'd worn at Harmony to sing. I tried to say "Hey." But she hushed my lips and said "Oh Blue, I finally found her." Right off I thought she meant Miss Ashlyn—Mother was totally blind now, I guessed, and had wandered off. Then Luna took my hand and helped me up through the sand. When we got to the carnival, nothing was left but the merry go round and it had stopped. There were still a few riders clinging though, still on their horses facing ahead. When I tried to climb on a big Palomino, Luna said "You wait."

She was grinning broadly, which I'd never seen (still haven't today); and she led me on to a black Arabian steed—the biggest. A girl was in the golden saddle with her back to us. Luna said "See here" and her smile just broadened. I stepped around to see the girl. The instant I did, I knew it was Mattie young as last night—her hair and clothes, her lean strong legs. But every cell of her face was ruined. She'd been burned out in that one part by some flash fire that left her nothing but a skull with a few scorched rags of skin, two dry eye sockets and teeth that were trying to part and smile.

I've never put much weight on dreams. Once or twice I've been disturbed enough to call somebody I dreamed was dead and check on their health. But no, if you've ever been in a war where actual enemies have your head in their rifle sights, you've dreamed your own death and all your friends' so many times you learn to ignore it. Still once I heard Miss Ashlyn stir this Sunday morning, I knew how glad I was I could join her and drink strong coffee before I had to yell Matt awake and drive her in for ten o'clock mass. That would keep me occupied on through the dinner Mother would serve at one o'clock, then an afternoon nap and then—barring Judgment—an evening and night to survive someway.

Myra met us in the usual pew, and again we sat like the usual family hoping the world won't notice the cracks. I knew that Myra had brought Matt in to confession yesterday. So when they stood to go for communion, I had three long minutes alone. To keep my mind from veering wrong, I tried to think of the last time I'd had real communion—not Protestant grape juice and sliced Wonder Bread. *It had to be way back in the war.* Catholic chaplains, even that long ago, weren't too strict on who they served at the altar rail, not under fire anyhow. And more than once in the thick of fear, I hauled my doubtful heart to the fore and stuck my tongue out like I was Irish for a real piece of Christ.

Even that August morning alone, as Matt got a place at the rail and knelt, I was very nearly compelled to join her in the small mob of priests, civilians and altar boys (there had to be one soul up there now as foul as mine). But Father Scanlon was part of the team, scrubbed and rosy as a poster baby with his bead eyes frisking the gathering faces. I'd always wondered if he'd refuse me after that free Coke at the Beechridge house. And now that he knew my family's news (Myra had said that Mattie told him), I bet myself he'd serve me the bread. He'd break the rule on Protestants and touch my tongue with that round wafer in hopes of a nibble, if no real catch. But if he didn't and turned me back, then Matt would die of humiliation. So I missed a chance to see if I could have bent the fate my mother foresaw.

*

I bent it this far on my own. After our usual leadweight meal and the two hour nap I finally got, I woke with only one idea. I didn't remember any dream, but I sat up straight with a mind as simple as a yard of sand. *Go see if Myra will take you back.* I understood that she and Mattie, fat Scanlon and no doubt numerous nuns, had burned up a gross of rosary beads in recent weeks, praying me back. So I left my room at four o'clock. I was all but sure the phone hadn't rung. Still I hunted Matt to see were there any messages—I'd told her and Mother a fresh lie. I said Bob Barefoot's nurse might send for me anytime and to rouse me at once.

Matt was fast asleep in the broiling parlor on a horsehair sofa, hot as a flue. She'd changed into shorts and a halter top, but her lips were open and leaking onto the arm she'd crushed up under her head. Her hair was soaked and snaky on her brow. And for the first time yet in her life, I heard an awful grating in her throat like she'd aged fifty years since lunch.

I crouched by her head and touched my handkerchief to her hair.

Her eyes burst open and, for six or eight seconds, she didn't know me. Brave as she was, she looked terrified and swallowed hard before she sat up.

I said "You're safe. It's your old pa."

She still didn't speak but stared on at me.

"Did anybody call while I was asleep?"

Her head shook No; her eyes shut again. "I dreamed your face had melted off, and I had to fix you."

It might have stunned me, but I understood—a secret message between us two had crept through these rooms last night and now. *Fate's up to its old cat's cradle games.* But I also thought *Don't ask for details. You're better off dumb.* So I said "Where's Mother?"

"Told me she'd be in her room."

"Let's don't wake her yet." I got to my feet.

"You're dressed again."

I'd put my tie on and was holding my seersucker coat. "I'm making a short trip, but I'll be back by supper at least. If not you'll be the first to know."

"You promise?" Matt's face was a solid block of doubt.

I crossed my heart.

She said "That makes it solemn, Sky."

I had my hand on the door to go, but I said I'd given her my word—"You lean against it." Barring a wreck or apoplexy, I thought she could trust me. I even thought I hoped she would.

Midway I'd tried to tell myself *If Myra's there you'll ask her right off. If not you're on your own again.* Well before I got to Beechridge though, I ruled out the gamble. If Myra was gone I'd set out to find her. But her car was there in the normal place, plus a strange green car parked in the garage. I knew it didn't belong to Scanlon or any known kin or friend of ours. So now I'd face a whole new mystery. *Suppose it's a man that's already shut you out of her mind.* To my knowledge, that was about as likely as Myra drunk on the bathroom floor. But when I finally stood up to move, I paused in the sun to let anybody at the windows see me and do whatever they needed next. No sign of a face and not a sound.

I'd offered my house key to Myra days back; but she wouldn't take it—"This is your home. You were born here, remember?" At the time that felt as important to me as the next car passing on the street behind us. But now I walked through the well trimmed grass round the side of the house to the front door and knocked. While I waited I asked myself *You scared?* I wasn't apparently—I knew every brick in the walls, every rock in the yard. *But what if Myra won't answer the door or comes and sees my face and denies me?*

The door opened. She'd been asleep and, though she'd combed her hair, her face was blurred. She looked beyond me and said "Where's Madelyn?"

"At Mother's, resting."

She kept on watching the shrubs behind me, the empty street.

"Am I interrupting?"

She looked confused.

"—The strange green car?" I pointed back.

"Oh no, that's Lou's from down the block. She's trying to hide from her mother-in-law."

"Then can I step in?"

She said "You may" as firmly as if we were still the children that used to play "May I?" on this stoop—me and all my long gone friends.

I took a giant step and cleared the sill. The air was dim and Myra had already turned and headed towards the kitchen.

As she went she said "I've ironed two of your blue shirts I found stuffed under the sink. They're in your drawer." She pushed through the swinging door and vanished.

I didn't want to do this in the kitchen. Too much old family memory was there—my father dying on the cold tile floor, a million breakfasts and grumpy laughter. I'd planned to do this piece of business in the living room on chairs we'd used very little through the years. That simple plan seemed to matter so much, I stepped through the kitchen door and said "Can I see you in the front room please?"

If I'd said "Myra, this way to the guillotine," she couldn't have looked any harder struck. But she drank the glass of water she'd drawn and said "Yes sir."

Once we were both in separate chairs, I realized I hadn't planned a speech. But Myra had already heard any speech I could possibly give, so I went straight to the absolute start. "I've known you twenty three years—"

She all but smiled. "Twenty two."

"All right then—anyhow most of my life."

Right off the words started making her younger. She sat beyond me firm again and utterly patient. "It was most of *our* lives, Blue—yours and mine—and all of Madelyn's."

That was the skeleton key I needed, the way to break this seized up lock. So I lunged on. "Can I—may I move back here?"

She knew her answer but she held it while she got her own right words. Then she quietly said "Two days' notice please?"

I honestly didn't understand. "Two days?"

"To pack and find a place."

"Myra, I don't want you to budge. I'm asking, will you take me in?"

Again she waited. "We're married, Blue."

"But I've insulted you one more time—and worse than ever—when we thought I'd quit."

She said "I never think *anything* quits this side of the grave." For some mysterious reason she smiled, just to herself. Then she faced me, serious again—"Is it stopped?" When I stalled she pushed. "Rita's child. Is she out of the picture?"

"I'm telling myself it's stopped—*she's* gone. I'm telling myself that right this instant."

"That's not exactly what I hoped to hear."

I realized how I'd missed this streamlined code we could use (we got more done in thirty seconds than the best computer). "No, it's not as firm as I hope to make it; but I think I'm on the right foot again and—"

"Is this for Madelyn?"

"Matt and you and common decency."

"But not for yourself?"

I said "No, friend, I didn't say that. I'm in this too, right up to my mouth. I'm trying to breathe." Warm as it was, even there with the blinds shut, it felt like an iron clamp on my throat relented now and my lungs filled.

Myra had kept herself so calm, it came as a shock when she stood up and took a step forward. I almost thought she was bearing down on me to pay me back—her face was burning. But then she stopped. "I need to get coffee."

"Not for me. No, God—it's way too hot."

"For breakfast Monday. I used the last for myself this morning." She gave her patented short term goodbye, a little downward wave of her hand like a building slowly crashing over. Then she walked to the back hall and took her Sunday purse from the table. She didn't look back but walked straight through the kitchen and out. In half a minute she'd cranked the car and headed out to Peace Street Market for a pound of coffee, first things first.

I stayed in the chair and looked round a room I'd barely noticed for years. Mother had left a lot of furniture with us, and half the pieces were parts of my childhood—the sofa I'd wet several times as a baby, the fireplace where I'd hung my stocking on Christmas Eve, groups of family pictures propped everywhere. Me in a Buster Brown collar at eight, both front teeth missing. Dad in his own drinking days, round as a blowfish. Mother's misty engagement picture—her in a light tan long full dress against a window with white net curtains moved by a breeze. I used to touch it often in childhood, just one finger against the glass—she looked that beautiful even to a boy and always that far past my reach.

I'd make up stories about the window open behind her and who she'd see when she turned to look—me, grown up in a white summer suit with my own car all ready to roll—and if you'd told me "This fine lady will end up gray and going blind six miles from here with your young daughter trying to help," what difference might that news have made? Would I have changed the steps I took, or would time still have sent me down the same dirt road through so much waste?

And once my eyes had toured the room, for a bad instant I thought *I was right. It's all a jail. Run now while you can.* But my legs didn't move, my eyes closed down, my head rolled back, I was still free to breathe. I tried to say "You're *home*, Bluford." I only managed to say my name.

EIGHT

Next morning at the store, I stopped by Mr. Atkinson's office and told him as nonchalantly as possible that if he needed to contact me after hours now, I was back on Beechridge Road. He expressed a sentiment I'd heard before—"Thank you, Bluford. Now hold it in the *road*"—and I put in a fair share of work from that day on. In fact it was extra good for a Monday. My nerves barely called notice to themselves; I felt pretty safe upright on my pins. And by noon I'd sold three hundred dollars' worth of assorted music making goods and was so satisfied to be back on stride that, when I washed my hands for lunch, I hadn't given a thought to the mail.

But as I sat in my usual corner with *Life* magazine, Hobe Pierce stepped over and laid an envelope face down by my hard green apple. This one was white and business size, addressed on an old typewriter and postmarked with nothing but a black smear of ink—no return address. Honest to God, I didn't guess (every now and then I'd get a thank you letter at the store from some kind woman I'd waited on). So I took my knife and cut it open—a neatly folded white sheet of paper—then I spread it out.

Camp Harmony, August 8th

Dear Blue,

My life up here is shutting down and I will be back at Mother's this Saturday if nothing goes wrong. Then if nothing goes wrong for maybe ten years, the people up here say I might be somebody in music, the world of music wherever that is and if I live.

I have decided I will push hard for it even poor as my mother is and with a half brother in the family tree that has just got his probation out of prison.

So school will be starting up in no time and I am going to be extra busy. I will think about you whenever I can and I bet I will always feel like smiling when years from now I let myself look back on the good things you showed me. I am sure you meant to be good to me. I also know I have been the cause of too much worry for you and all yours.

I will not try to tell your family that. My pitiful mother has already ruined my chance of knowing them, I guess. But if you ever get things back together please tell your people I am not a cruel and hateful person.

You deserve a calm life. I bet you will get it. I will pray that you do and hope the Lord hears me after all I have done.

Good wishes from

Luna

In spite of the recent pledge I'd made to Myra and Mattie, I will just say, that letter came closer to ruining my lunch than an H bomb could have—especially the courage Luna showed in not explaining herself or blaming me. My eyes must have filled—I know I couldn't face Hobe for a while—but what I felt was unexpected. I didn't want to run straight out and find Luna to beg for more. I think I mainly felt how much she'd grown this summer and how she was open hearted and fair to say I'd had a part in her growth. They also seemed like the saddest words I'd ever read, not because she'd drawn that line between us but because she'd done it before I could, and done it in a dignified way that reminded me of my own Mattie—all the wise ideas Matt had and could spell out for me.

I did realize I might be stunned, in which case pain and a damage report would wait down the road. But as I slipped that loaded page into my pocket, all that worried me was one new question, *What's this brother going to do to her now?* Then it dawned on me, *That was him downtown with her in the night*—the giant Matt saw, that waved back at her. I sat there still as the baby grand six feet to my right and ate my apple.

When I stood up to take a five minute turn round the Capitol grounds and clear my mind, Hobe said "You still sleeping out at your mother's?"

I didn't break step. I told him "No, I've tucked tail and run." His eyes got wide but I didn't say more. I didn't know where I'd got the words or where I'd get the next that day—assuming I'd be called on to speak, which I always was (no husband and father can play deaf and dumb and not get buried).

Then there was nearly a whole calm quarter from the midst of August on into November. I stayed on Beechridge Road with Myra, and we moved pretty much as we had before last spring. The day seldom passed without me having real reasons to thank her, we seemed to laugh at the same things together (which was no invention but something we'd forgot how to do), we spent several evenings with Mother and Mattie. And one weekend before school started, all of us drove to Manteo to see *The Lost Colony,* swat mosquitoes, eat seafood and risk our necks in a surf off Nags Head as treacherous as any the world provides. We got back though with nobody drowned nor more family spats than usual—Mother insisted on paying for the trip but declined to lay down the law the way she sometimes did when she signed the tab.

Mattie moved back with us in early September, ready for school. Again I checked to see if Mother would let me find a "settled Christian white lady, no home ties" (as the classified ads used to say in those days) or better still, a patient black woman that would know how to buff Miss Ashlyn's angles. Of course Miss Ashlyn refused the notion, saying she'd rather be dismembered and sown to the wind by a den of felons at four a.m. than to breathe some stranger's air and hear them chatter round the clock. So I called her up every afternoon when I got home to check her condition, and I drove out there more than once a week.

I kept on going to mass every Sunday with Myra and Matt, though I got no closer to wanting to climb on their bandwagon, good smelling as it was and built out of hope. I forced myself back to regular weekly A.A. meetings. Don't get me wrong—A.A.'s the only thing yet found except flash miracles that truly deals with drunks and their self serving lies. It's just that what had mostly kept me away from meetings in the past hadn't changed, still hasn't and can't—which is facing the fact at every session that being even a cold sober drunk won't naturally make you a good storyteller. And A.A.'s mostly wall to wall stories of pig shit meanness and self concern on a monster scale. Some of the tales would admit to damage nearly as bad as the worst I'd done, but even those were generally told at a gimp snail's pace and with hot conviction that this is *news* that just can't wait but needs to be rushed to *The New York Times* before dawn breaks.

The musical instrument business picks up fast in the fall with Christmas coming. So work was busy and helped to bleed off pounds of pressure I didn't need to take home with me at night. Not that my heart was involved in my job. To this day now I still can't say I've worked at anything I loved or felt *deep down* rewarded by. I've honestly liked the chance to meet people and watch them play their private hand out plainly in public—I'd say more people that I've dealt with are kindly than not (I'm speaking of the upper South, recall, right up till now); but oh I've dealt with men and women both, vicious as vipers or strictly nuts.

I had one well dressed middle aged gent with slightly pop eyes approach me softly, say "Sir, my name is Ernest P. Tipton. I rule all space." I shook his hand gladly; then he strolled on to a big Skinner organ and played the loudest funniest set of improvisations I ever heard—he said his theme was "Inner Peace." I always tried to remind myself to let the public lighten my load in any way; and they often obliged, which is all you can ask in the way of work and a hell of a lot more than most humans get in a life of toil.

Then the nights. Ever since boyhood I've been a person that waits for night. Mother always said how, even as an infant, I'd often fail to cry at feeding time. And when she'd worry and come to check, I'd just be lying wide awake in the dark exploring the ceiling or my two hands with a big wet grin. Then by the time my body lit out for fun and contact at twelve or thirteen, just the coming on of dusk would have me racing to think how I could touch my goal before day— whoever her name was, wherever she lived. So when I first moved back with Myra, I'd start to worry by late afternoon, *You've got to tread deep water now, son. She's got her plans for what you'll do.*

I don't expect you to feel great ease at the prospect of watching your grandparents' secrets (though as I said, I wish I knew every fact about mine—grand and great grand on back to Eden; they might well have helped me). But by "Myra's plans" I mostly meant what we would do for physical closeness any one night. Myra was not the Brazilian Bombshell of conjugal bliss, but I'll have to say she generally did her cheerful share and almost never pawned me off like so many wives I heard about right through the war. She thought our joining together was holy (we never practiced birth control, and the fact we had only Matt through the years was owing to my having serious mumps and knocking out one of my testicles for life). But that doesn't mean she looped me up in rosary beads at crucial moments. She mostly smiled though, straight at my eyes; and she thanked me by name most every time.

No, my fear of the nights came at me from two things. First was the fear I'd get called out by fate again to track down Luna or some old girl I'd left behind or met at A.A. (honest drunks will tell you A.A. can be as much of a raw meat market as any saloon, if that's what you're after). Next was the problem I hear discussed on TV daily but never back then—how are you going to rouse your skin and mind up high for your same mate that you've known forever and have worn down smooth as a wall in your mind? Or even if she lies there—still and cool, just meaning to sleep, no expectations from you and your nozzle—then how are you going to bring off your big charge of static onto somebody's body you've known so long she might be your sister or a buddy you've driven with to the moon? (I put all that from a man's viewpoint. I have no doubt it works the same through a good many women's eyes, though the women I've known have kinder eyes and can face slack aging skin much better than I used to manage.)

But the weeks piled on. And fate didn't strike—far from it. I felt like the sky had flat forgot me or misplaced my coordinates on the map of joy and doom somehow. And slowly slowly through a delicate patience on Myra's part and luck on mine, we managed to meet in the late summer dark, better and better till we could say we felt we'd found our best selves again—the same young bodies and souls we were for two decades before time swamped us. It was nothing to phone the papers about or run again and again in your head like the bonfire I could always start when I was a boy, just by thinking of the single mole on one girl's belly or even now of Luna Absher's strong dark hair and the way it feathered the place she let me visit first; but when you're past the peak of your thirties, you're grateful for that much mutual ease.

That got me down to early November—me and the three women I tried to do full justice to. Then a Saturday came that was cool and bright as your best dream. I'd spent so much of it shut indoors at the store all day that I called Myra at five o'clock and said I planned a short trip out to Bob Barefoot's, not to hold supper for me, just keep a plate warm. She sounded thoroughly trustful, with reason—I had no crooked plan whatever. I hadn't seen Bob in nearly a week and thought I'd take the last of the sun and check on him before too late.

As ever I bought the quart of ice cream and drove straight out. Since August Bob had gone through several rollercoaster ups and downs in health and pain. But he still somehow found strength to drive himself to the doctor for weekly transfusions. And like Miss Ashlyn he wouldn't listen to any talk of me finding him help or even me sleeping out there those nights he felt unusually weak or edgy. So when I parked and walked towards the house, I halfway thought *I'll ask him to take me in some nights. I'll say I need to think in peace.*

He'd given me a key to the front door weeks ago—"In case I'm dead just walk right in"—and now I walked in and called his name. I thought I heard a muffled scramble like a dog stepped on; then I heard the end of a word in some strange voice. I said "Is everybody decent or should I just leave?"

Bob spoke up then from far away. "No worse than usual—step on back."

The door to the dining room was shut, which was also odd. I knocked one time and opened it slowly.

There at the big old walnut table was Rita Absher in her nurse uniform.

And in his regular chair by the window was Bob, looking better.

I must have showed considerable shock—Rita tried to stand but slumped back down; and Bob said "Blue, meet my oldest friend."

Somehow I couldn't smile and I know I said "I thought I was all you had in the world." Once out, it sounded dumb as dirt.

Rita was facing me, grim as a famine. She said "You are. Bob, don't tell a lie—we're *all* too close to the grave for that."

Bob laughed. "Oh I may yet choose to live. I'm getting new reasons anyhow—all this good company and free ice cream."

That gave me a chance to steady myself in the kitchen while I served up the cream. *How in the hell is Rita out here—no car in sight? Did Bob go get her and hire her on?*

Turned out she'd appeared in a taxi paid for by Bob at the end of her all night nursing shift. They'd had the best part of the day together—watched their favorite shows on TV, eaten a light lunch Rita fixed, then each read magazines and had a long nap. Ever since, they'd looked at old photos and high school yearbooks and talked about everybody they knew. "Your ears are *bound* to itch," Rita said, "with all we said about you, old Blue."

I said "Nobody knows more about me than you two rascals." (I truly meant that—I've never known anyone yet in childhood who managed to surprise me years down the road; children's souls are that transparent and all but never change when they grow up unless they lose their minds entirely.) Then we sat quiet awhile, spooning cream. And it soon seemed like we were zooming through time in backward gear till slowly we'd changed our present bodies and cleared our minds and were young as we'd been long years ago before Rita got herself in trouble or I got drunk or Bob made his slow choice not to live like average people but hole up here and bypass life to stay with a mother that burned him out and then disappeared. The change among us—back towards the old days—felt so real that I kept taking quick glimpses of Rita to see if she was sharing my thoughts.

At last she looked right into my eyes. "Bluford, you're looking a whole lot better." She actually reached out and grazed the lid of my right eye gently. "You look more rested around your eyes."

I didn't know whether she meant a sideways thanks for me leaving Luna alone or whether she'd also felt us sliding back through time. Anyhow I said "I do feel younger."

Bob said "We are. We are, dear souls—safe in each other's heads at least. We'll never die there."

Rita laughed and said "Amen."

And one more time I got the feeling of being somebody younger now and a good deal better—young Blue Calhoun before he started feeding the famished part of his mind and rubbing his skin on whoever stood still long enough, just to cool the burn. So we stayed there a good half hour calling up names and dates from the past—telling old jokes about our teachers, old pains we'd somehow managed to stand, every dream that died. We got so sad and glad at once that present time was nowhere in sight, and none of us missed it.

But finally it was seven o'clock, and I actually wanted to head back home. Before I stood though, I turned to Bob (you always had to ask him directly about his health; he wouldn't volunteer). "You're looking a whole lot brighter to me."

He didn't smile. "If I felt much better I'd vaporize."

Rita said "I told him I'll move out here any minute he says and see him through."

I said "Don't resign from your old lady yet. Bob won't *take* help."

He suddenly got to his feet and stepped behind his chair. Then he leaned on the back and grinned my way. "Not from you—you're spoke for. Rita's free as me."

She nodded hard. "And more so now with Luther home. My match-box house is way too small."

I thought *Don't touch this, son. Get out.* And I also rose to say goodbye.

Bob gave his usual farewell wave.

But Rita stood up too. "Can I thumb a ride?" She looked to Bob. "Is that all right?"

He said "Yes ma'm, I've got your phone number."

"Day *or* night, no hour too late." She went straight to him, folded his skeleton into her arms and gently kissed the side of his neck. When she stepped back she said "You were one good boy. You didn't need this."

"Thank you," Bob said, "but I'm *getting* it, aren't I?—both barrels in the teeth."

I tried to stay polite to Rita but say as little as possible on the road. And she seemed to understand. She was quiet till we got close to town—maybe three minutes more there, trapped together. Then she started in. "I haven't thanked you, Blue."

"No need at all." I didn't look towards her.

"You took one terrible load off my back. Now though I've got a whole new mess."

Stay out of this—all I gave was a sympathetic cluck.

"You don't know Luther?—of course you don't—but child, he's a knife right through my heart."

Again I hmmed.

"And now he's got Luna spinning round after all the sense she learned at camp."

I guessed Rita didn't mean it as a hook, but it cut deep into my mouth, and I said "Luna'd be crazy not to follow her dream."

"Dream?" Rita said. "Christ Jesus, Blue, she's barely slept these last few weeks, much less had a dream."

"Luther's her *half* brother, right?"

"They act like they're no kin at all."

I yielded more ground than I knew was wise. "I saw them downtown the night camp ended."

Rita said "That's when this whole thing started—what did they say?"

"They didn't see me. I was driving with the family; they were windowshopping. Matt spotted Luther and called him a giant. He waved back at her. I doubt Luna saw us."

"Luna ain't seen nothing but trouble lately."

"But she's still in school?"

Rita nodded. "Except I'm scared she's flunking."

"Where's Luther work?"

She let at least a block go by. "See, that's the reason I brought it up. I'm thinking you might know a job he could get. The boy's swept up at the doughnut shop a night or two and answered some ads. He really has made the rounds of cafes, seeing if anybody needs a good cook. He learned short order cooking inside—you ought to see him fry hash browns and make light biscuits. But so far nobody wants to trust him."

"Nothing at Atkinson's—that's all I'd know." But I reconsidered—"Can Luther be trusted?" I'd wondered for weeks how he'd got out after so little time—there must have been some tall good behavior (like ratting on others). So it dawned on me that Bob might pay him to sleep out there, maybe cook a few meals and chauffeur the car.

Rita said "*Trust?* Luther don't know the word. Says we've all let him down so much, he can't stand up. He sleeps through most of the day, I guess. Then once Luna's home from school, they sit in the kitchen and drink black coffee and play honeymoon bridge hours on end. Then when I leave for work, they claim they're going to the show downtown or—like you said—to gawk at windows." All through that Rita faced the road. Then she turned to me. "He's a sweet boy, Blue. He'll notice the least kind thing I do like darning his socks or nailing taps on his worndown heels. And he'll pick me up—big me!—off the floor and whirl around. He'll take little pieces of my scarce money or borrow Luna's nickels and dimes to buy us things—nothing expensive:

new hair barrettes or finger rings—but his feelings are kind. No, for no known reason, he just leaned wrong way back up the road." Rita paused awhile, then played an ace. "Now he's taking Luna." We were back in sight of the turn to her street.

I already knew I wouldn't turn in and stop at the house.

But Rita said "You better stop there at the corner, child. I can't ask you to risk whatever's going on at my place."

For all the questions I'd asked so far, I strained to keep my mind far back from whatever Rita was saying in secret, buried under her actual words. I didn't want to think of whether she halfway meant to lure me to rescue the girl or maybe was driving further nails in my disgust to keep me back on my side of town. But when I'd pulled to the curb and reached to open her door, my mouth went on and said one thought that half amazed me. "You might tell Luther to call Bob Barefoot. Bob might help him out and vice versa."

Rita hunted around my face a long moment. "You honestly mean it?"

Amazed as I was, I said "It couldn't hurt."

"Oh Blue, it could hurt down to the *bone*. But thank you, hear? I'll pray about it." When she'd hauled herself out, she leaned back in. "Bob's pitiful, ain't he? He needs somebody, Jesus knows, but I well understand I'd drive him crazy. He's way too particular to stand my mess."

I suddenly said "Is Luther mean hearted?" and when Rita looked stunned, I said "Is he wild—would he kill again for fun or money?"

At least she was sure—she nailed my eyes. "No, Blue, that was nothing but bad boy luck. He learned his lesson, where *lives* are concerned—*taking* em anyhow. Course I'm not saying he might not pick up a roll of quarters if you dropped it in the road—"

I'd never watched my hand reach out for a drink of liquor against my will with any deeper surprise or numbness than I felt then in that dim car, but again I heard myself push forward through weird country with no road signs. "If you honestly think your Luther can help, tell him to contact me at the store—nowhere else now but Atkinson's Music."

Rita balked and her face went white as pork. Then she gave a funny blear eyed wink and said "God bless you, Bluford, I guess."

It came so straight from her open heart, and was so bang-on my particular target, that I started to laugh and then saw Rita was joining me, but a sudden shadow caught my eye, and I looked out the front windshield.

Luna was standing back at the corner ten yards off. She looked very fine but also changed, maybe two inches taller so her gray school skirt was skimpy now. Her hair was tangled down by her neck, and she had on a shrunk tobacco-spit sweater that barely reached her trembling wrists. They were down at her sides like somebody'd bound her, and she was plainly shaking hard for whatever cause—the air was not that cold or dry. She was watching her mother, not me at all.

So I said "Rita, there stands young Luna."

Rita looked, then leaned out the window and said "What's wrong with you now?"

Luna said "Look, I've been waiting too long—"

And saying no more to me, Rita got out and went towards the girl.

In those old clothes and cold like that—or scared or sorry—Luna looked like a girl maybe twelve years old, heartbroke and hungry. But she still hadn't let her eyes flick towards me so I didn't wave. I just went on towards Myra and Matt—my normal speed, an average dad.

NINE

LUTHER WAITED a week so it was a Friday afternoon when I saw one of the record salesmen point towards me at the back of the store. Then a strange tall man loped my way. I honestly didn't think who he was till he got much closer. But before I could even guess at his name, he put out a huge hand and said "Mr. Blue?"

"Blue Calhoun."

"This is Luther," he said and put out a flat palm at waist level like he was measuring a dwarf beside him.

I let my hand be smothered in his. And then I said what of course he'd heard since grammar school, "How tall are you, son?"

"Six seven, depending on the weather—if it's wet I'm taller. And I'm not too much younger than you so watch that 'son.'" He grinned on a perfect set of teeth.

But I knew he meant it. I hadn't really seen him on the street that night, and I tried to give him a quick runover. He looked less like his mother than I did. He looked no more like a felon than me; and with his lean face and ice pick eyes, he looked like somebody you'd want handy when real trouble struck, that strong and ready to shield your bones from any blast. I'd known a few boys like him in the Army— none so tall or with prison records but with Luther's kind of bullet proof gleam. Everybody always tried to be near them when fire broke out. Since business was slow this day, I took him well aside and said "I knew your mother before you were born."

"So did I!" Then he grinned. "Yes sir, I know all about it. See, I've got several sources on you."

It didn't feel awkward so I kept going. "Rita said you were hunting work. Had any luck?"

"No sir. Not a nibble."

I don't know why it came to mind, but I said "I guess you can't join the service." I meant because of his excess height, but then I recalled they won't take felons, and I must have looked hacked.

Luther kept smiling. "Oh no, I'm way too wild for them. They *train* their killers; I'm just self taught."

By then he looked about as bad as Mattie, which was not at all. Every thread of his clothes was spotless and pressed; his arms were bare and no tattoos, no visible knife scars, steady pale blue pupils that were plainly watchful and liked the world. So I chose to think he'd been a rough kid but had grown in prison, and I took the dive I'd taken with his mother last week. "Your mother and I've got a friend that maybe could use you awhile."

"That's why I'm here. I already talked to my probation officer and then Mr. Bob, and I was thinking I might ride with you on your next trip out. He said he'd send a taxi for me, but I said I hoped to meet you anyhow—maybe you'd ride me out there sometime. Then Mr. Bob could look me over, and me ditto. And you could help us call the play—whether we'd do each other good."

It had already rushed past what I'd imagined and I back pedaled. "Did Bob say he might hire you on?"

"He said he'd about got down to his wit's end—he might need a rescue."

"Did he say *rescue?*"—it sounded thoroughly unlike Bob.

Luther paused to check his memory or brace his lie. "*Rescue*—yes, he used that word."

I guess it turned the tide for me. Any doubt I'd felt cleared off like mist. "Let me tell my wife I'll be home late. Then meet me back here at five forty five." I checked my watch—it was ten past four.

Luther smiled; by now he might have been an honor roll student from the Methodist orphanage, a little overgrown—his face was that clear of previous entanglements. "I could just stay here and practice the organ—"

"You play then do you?"

"Yes sir, I picked it up as a kid."

Again it seemed entirely unlikely, but maybe music ran in the family; he might have taken lessons in prison—we'd have time to talk about that at Bob's. I said "Luther, I'll be busy till then. You leave and come back."

He showed no resentment but nodded and turned.

Rita had told me his last name months ago, but I'd forgot it and something made me say "Is Absher your last name?"

He looked around and his whole face flushed a high red. He spoke out though in his normal voice—"No sir, strictly speaking I'm Luther Ray; but the family mostly calls me Bapp."

It was Rita's maiden name of course. I'd blundered with him and there in public. I was sorry but all I could say was "See you."

He said "May be"—like that, two words. Then he moved his long bones out of the store with old master ease.

Right after that I telephoned Bob. Yes, he'd heard from Luther Bapp. He'd also talked to the probation officer. Sure, if I wanted to drive the boy out, we'd eat ice cream and "look the situation in the face." I told him not to expect a "boy" and that I'd be there if Luther turned up at closing time but not to count on it—if he didn't show, I'd be there tomorrow, my regular time.

Bob said "Blue, listen. Don't worry one jot. You may have lined me up with the right guy to slit my throat, which could be the best deed you've done yet." But then he chuckled and slowed way down. "No, seriously, I - have - no - expectations - whatever. From life or death." He laughed, long and natural.

As ever I asked him what I could do.

"Not a goddamned thing more than you're doing now, my fine old friend."

I said "Till soon."

Bob said "Till forever."

*

And Luther walked through the door up front at five twenty four. He'd been home or somewhere and changed his shirt—a long sleeved navy blue buttoned at the collar and starched stiff as plywood. I led him out through the back and on through the Capitol grounds to where I'd parked off Edenton Street. All the way over he'd point out common facts we passed, the sort of thing I seldom see but that maybe he noticed now he was loose—a dangerous purple moss on the bark of an old oak tree, a squirrel with what looked like a string of tumors down his side (Luther knelt and it came straight to his hand), the first and only indigo bunting I've seen in my life and a genuinely artistic sidewalk drawing in colored chalks of the female organ in scientific detail.

They seemed like valuable findings to Luther; and just the fact that he *saw* the world and welcomed it in seemed like a real commendation to me—Bob would need watching close as a hawk. Just before we got to the car, I even mentioned to Luther I'd noticed his keenness.

He suddenly dropped both arms to his side like a soldier at attention or himself in a lineup. His face went sober as any coal shovel; but he said "The first night you go to jail, you either get real *attentive* fast, or you'll be as full of holes as Mama's best colander before midnight."

I didn't know what else to do but laugh. "I guess that's what they call 'on the job training.' "

Luther laughed too. "It's a *job* all right—I'm still black and blue. But I'm ready for the next one."

So we pulled out and aimed for Bob.

Bob also did the unexpected—he met us at the door (looking worse than anything I'd ever seen on foot above ground) and poured us cups of coffee strong as asphalt in his mother's good china to go with the buttered almond ice cream. I couldn't help watching Luther's hands, and I saw Bob do it. Though they were half again bigger than mine, they stirred and spooned neatly like Luther had trained for a different world from the one he got. Then I thought *So did Luna. Rita tried her best, hard up as she was, and at least they got manners.*

I'd already warned myself not to mention Luna's name or to let the boy remind me of her too often and clearly—the *man*, that is. I figured Luther was twenty three at least, but I knew not to ask and shame him again.

The best thing was, he and Bob plainly took to each other on sight. And once they'd got through the bobbing and weaving of introductions and hollow jokes, they went straight to it, hammer and tongs, on the realistic questions at hand. To my surprise Bob started it off (in his previous life he could take ten years to hint at the fact that you'd forgot his birthday once in the 1930s). We'd barely finished eating our cream when he just said "Luther, you killed a man, did you?"

Luther never missed a beat. "Yes sir. I shot him through his heart, the *end*."

Bob said "What harm had he done you?"

"Not a bit in the world, sir. He just walked in while I was stealing his .38 pistol and I reacted."

Bob was no more fazed than if Luther had said "Red marigolds." He leaned closer to him. "How old were you then?"

Luther said "Fifteen. I told em eighteen so I could get prison, not the juvenile farm."

"What did you have against the farm?"

Luther laughed. "*Work*—they work you outdoors in the blistering sun. You hack weeds out of the swamps and ditches—cottonmouth snakes big as legs all round you."

Bob said "Sounds like you know lots about it."

Luther laughed again—it was genuine fun, nothing crazy or mean. "I may have paid it a field trip or two in my tender years."

I was thinking I'd made a real miscue and was trying to guess a way to retract it.

But Bob said "Well, I guess you've been checked out if they turned you loose—those child experts with all their tests?"

Luther kept up his healthy laugh. "I don't know about the *child* part, sir. But sure, my mind's been all but sliced - fried - eaten by doctors, nurses, social workers, chaplains, female Christians, termite exterminators, Swedish masseurs: you name your brand. They say I'm normal as this ice cream; I just bore left way up the road when others bore right. I can get you their charts—" He pointed back towards Central Prison like it would cough up a sterling reference any instant now.

Bob didn't even pause. He'd listened intently. His face was pale but cocked as any on-duty Marine's. "All right, here's the deal. You move out here as soon as you can. Rita says you can cook, and I need to eat—I'm starving to death. I know you can drive; we'll get you a license if yours has expired. You'll have the whole upstairs to yourself, all the girlie magazines you can read, your own bathroom and flannel sheets when the weather cools off. I sleep down here with a gun and a bell. I can ring when I need you; I'll shoot if you make me—I've already killed my own share of souls, but I'll push on if cornered and forced. Fifty dollars a week and all your meals."

Fifty dollars plus room and board was surely more than Luther Bapp had ever made. He didn't leap to it though. He stood up, knelt—with a rifle crack from both his knees—untied both shoes and retied them tight. Then he said "Time off?" and sat back down.

Bob said "All the time you want when I'm dead." He finally grinned.

And I won't speak for Luther Bapp, if he's survived these thirty years; but I estimated—by the fire in Bob's eyes—that Bob would burn himself to the root by Christmas day, if not before. I wondered still if I'd made a mistake bringing them together. But what I wanted to say here now was "Bob's barely killed a common housefly much less other souls." Who was I though to ruin his story when stories were all Bob had left to give?

Then Luther amazed me. He stayed upright in his chair a long moment with his face blank as milk. Then still very solemn and clean in the eyes as any good child, he leaned far forward and—in what looked like deep slow motion—he folded Bob Barefoot in his arms, firm but gentle.

Bob took the embrace as his natural due, though his eyes were open above Luther's shoulder, staring at me and dry as a grate.

Then they melted apart and Luther slowly looked back my way. "Mr. Blue, I'll stay out here tonight. Tomorrow I'll drive back in for my duds. Thank God for your help." I thought at the time *J. Edgar Hoover would trust those eyes*. And for all that happened from there to the end, I still think he would. What finally happened was not Luther's fault—not all anyhow, not to my knowledge. By his own lights, with the cards he held and the family he had, he tried to be decent, I'm all but sure.

I told him not to thank me. I'd just been the chauffeur that brought him out.

But Bob said "Don't you believe it, Bluford. You caused this whole thing, you and your famous hand of fate. Let's see what we owe you."

I laughed. "Not money."

Bob said "Oh no, there'll be no money—this cancer is wolfing down money by the minute. I meant *praise* or *blame*."

Luther laughed too. "Or years in jail."

I kept on grinning but was already on my feet to leave. Every inch of the way home through chill darkness, I wondered how many lives I'd changed these past few hours—who truly would thank me or blame my name in years to come if anybody still recalled Bob Barefoot and knew of his end, not to mention one Blue Calhoun and his hopes.

By the time I got in, Mattie had left to practice a Thanksgiving show at school. Myra had kept my supper warm and sat with me while I ate what I could. Like most of the married women I'd watched, she managed to be officially courteous to my few male friends; but you couldn't accuse her of enthusiasm. And Bob had always been a trial for her. She halfway understood how years ago he'd been close to me. But the fact that Bob and his mother took me in for six winter weeks when I left Myra the first real time, before Matt's birth—that gnawed at Myra the rest of her life. It helped now of course that Bob was dying. She could pray for a miracle and sympathize with my concern. I guess she also hoped Bob would bleed off any last scraps of my care for Luna (Myra didn't know Bob had kept up with Rita).

So now she could sit, ask calm questions about Bob's case and make small useful suggestions for help. Would he like to come over here some evening and eat supper with us? Would he like to see Madelyn?—it had been many years. Did he need anything her hands could make?—I've mentioned how well Myra cooked and sewed.

I could see she more than halfway cared, but something in her voice upset me. I finally said "Bob hired a fulltime servant today. You stop worrying."

"It's not that filthy old toothless woman that nursed his mother, I very much hope?"

"No ma'm, it's a strong young man that could touch this ceiling."

"Colored?"

"White." Then I knew I'd tucked my head to charge; I didn't want to stop. "You saw him that night last August downtown when Madelyn leaned out the window and waved at the giant."

Myra was in the dark again. "I can't have been with you—you didn't live here in August, recall."

She had to be right, and it slowed me a little—I thought I could see her behind me that night on the back seat with Mother. But once I believed her, I still had to say "We were riding up Wilmington Street after dark, and Mattie waved at a tall young stranger."

"Who is he then?"

"Named Luther Bapp, twenty some years old, strong as a truck and a good cook to boot."

"Where in the world did Bob find him?"

"I found him. In the store. This afternoon."

She frowned. "That quick? How do we know he's trained to nurse a dying man and is safe?"

"*We* don't know at all. We don't know Bob's truly dying either—you keep praying and he might get healed." By then I was smiling and half liking this. "He *is* fresh out of prison for manslaughter—the nurse, I mean."

Myra said "Jesus" and crossed herself. I'd never heard her take that name in vain before, but then I understood she hadn't—she was in dead earnest. "You and Bob just took in a boy straight from prison—no references?"

"We've known his mother all our lives. The Prison Department says he's fine. And beggars can't select their menu—Bob's all but desperate; Luther may help him. There's very slim harm a *human* could do to Bob Barefoot."

Myra's eyes softened and she nodded quietly. Again I want to say it out clearly—Myra Burns Calhoun was as open hearted a woman as I've yet known on Earth (Catholic, Protestant, Jew or heathen). Of course she had little snags down her back, little places where she caught on things I did or said. But though I may live a good deal longer (two of my grandparents made it to ninety), I can't realistically hope to meet a finer person than she was then—she took the secret with her when she died. Good as Matt was, and got to be, even she never matched her mother's heart.

Why in Christ's name then did I take one more step in that peaceful evening air? Why did one vicious cell in my brain demand me to torment this good woman who'd never turned on me with anything worse than a gray eyed look? (Think about it hard as you watch the world; and when you can give a plausible answer, there may be hope for the human race, though don't bet on it.) I said "He's Rita Absher's son. Rita asked me to help him."

Myra's face didn't change at once. She was drawing a complicated pattern on the table, an invisible knot of the kind she sometimes stitched on pillows. But she got it finished. "Permit me to ask when you last saw Rita?"

"A week ago. I took Bob his ice cream, and there was Rita on a social visit—he'd sent a taxi for her. I drove her back and she mentioned Luther—did I know of a job?" I raised my empty hands—that was it, and I thought it was.

"There's nothing else then I need to know?"

"Know for what purpose?"

"I think you well know what I mean—I'd like more warning if you decide against Mattie and me."

I mostly respected her courteous dignity; but there at the end of that full day, it hit me wrong. And I laughed a little. But I touched her shoulder with genuine thanks; and I said "Yes ma'm, I promise you that. God knows you've won it. Don't wait for it though; we're doing all *right*."

"I didn't think I was waiting, Blue, till you mentioned Luther. That family's *sad*. I doubt we can help them."

"I'm fairly sure you're right."

Myra said "But you know I won't stop praying."

Anybody else, you might have wanted to hold your nose at the piety. Not with Myra. She was strictly sure her world was held together by prayer—her world and ours, by prayer and God's unearned deliveries of joy or pain and by those nuns and monks worldwide who prayed for us all day and night, whoever we were and whatsoever our hands were doing or our hot minds. I asked her please to practice what she called "prayer unceasing" for Bob's good death and my strength to help him.

She nodded. "You've got it."

Her word was never less than her bond, so I knew I had. And however short I'd been on certainty about who God was and whether It gave a damn or not what *Homo sapiens* did with his time and his private parts, I thought my wife was well employed to spend so much of her strength and charity hunting the sky for simple mercy to all she loved and the Earth itself.

Even when Mattie got home at nine and pretty much raced upstairs to bed, I went to tell her a true good night and ask her also to think of Bob and do her part to help him out of this world at least. I doubt Matt had seen him in five or six years, but she knew exactly who I meant. She said "The man with the deep green eyes and the dancing dog?" (when she'd last seen him, Bob had a terrier that square danced upright for minutes on end).

I said "He's the man. And he'd have been your best godfather if he'd been Catholic."

She let that slide. "Let me get this straight—you want him to die? You're asking me to help Bob die?"

Her dim light was on, so I showed her a smile. "That's pretty much it—not to *kill* him though, just ease his way. He hurts already."

Her eyes were drowsy and while I watched through the next half minute, she went from being a very mature thirteen year old to somewhere back around five or six—that tired and honest and far from believing the visible world was the main thing to watch. But I could see she wasn't gone yet; she needed to speak. And finally she said "I've dedicated my life to pain"—absolutely those words, I'm ready to swear.

Whatever you think in years ahead, you're not very likely to laugh at any such claim from a child of yours. To be sure I was long since familiar, from my wife and daughter, with the Catholic notion of volunteering to share Christ's pain or of just being singled out by God and tortured so you'd suffer for the wrongs of others, to spare their hides and filthy souls for whatever unknown reasons God had. I'd even suspected—assuming you didn't torture *yourself* but let life do it—they might have a point (I've often thought my mother, Myra and Matt at her death—that they all spared me a world of pain by taking punishments meant for me, and how I wish I'd eaten fire that very night if it could have saved you the harm you took). But I said to Matt "Did a nun suggest that?"

Even exhausted, Matt knew I seldom agreed with her nuns' approach to normal life. "I'm way on past the age of reason. I run my own soul."

However much I wanted to doubt her, it was too late to argue. So I let it go but as I smoothed the covers around her, I had to say "I pray you'll know less pain, my darling, than me, Miss Ashlyn, your mother or Bob. I mean to watch you *thrive* hereafter."

Matt thought about it as best she could, then shook her head. "You're safe, Old Sky. Don't worry about me."

I've always regretted saying "I won't." I wish I'd said *I'll walk through hails of fire for you—you mean that much*. But truth to tell, before I knew I truly felt it years ahead, Madelyn Kirkpatrick (born Calhoun) had already gone through her own white hot needle's eye to whatever waits for generous souls—reward or sleep. And here I'm left with a world of debt that you could help clear.

TEN

AFTER THAT and through the next weeks, Bob's dying brought the three of us on Beechridge closer than we'd been for years. Or so I felt and Myra and Matt give signs of agreeing. Myra quietly asked me to bring her Bob's laundry. Then she washed and ironed it twice a week and sent it back in a willow bark basket. If Luther hadn't been a good cook, she'd have cooked and sent every meal as well (and if you're thinking I make your grandmother sound like a numb workhorse, then I'm at a loss to help you know the deep reward she took in using her plentiful skills and the thanks we felt, whatever I showed in my worst days). Mattie had every Catholic from Raleigh to the sea pulling for Bob around the clock. Even Miss Ashlyn, who'd someway shared Myra's coolness to Bob, would send him detective stories and the homemade raisin bars she recalled he craved in college.

It didn't strike me till the day Matt asked, but none of them mentioned paying him a visit, and I didn't press them. But then on Monday of Thanksgiving week, Bob's doctor finally said he'd done the last he could, by way of home help. Bob should stand prepared to come to the hospital any day now for an oxygen tent and the final siege. Luther phoned me at the store with the news.

I rode out there in the early dusk and found Bob still upright in his chair, still trying to grin, though time had taken care of that—his lips were so thin his teeth showed through like a bucktoothed boy's and kept him smiling. In the three days since I'd seen him last, he'd finally gone completely transparent. I could all but trace the naked limbs of sweetgum trees through his head as he sat by the bright cold window.

But he started in to tell me something he'd just remembered—our joint fraternity initiation in the spring of 1939. Of course he recalled it in full detail; and it strengthened him just telling the words. I started listening out of politeness—college is no good memory for me, who threw it away. But as Bob went on I saw how much this meant to him; how he was seeing our ancient moves, clear there before him like we were boys. So I got interested early on. He started with how, all freshman year, we'd been through hours of dumb pledge training—memorizing the Greek alphabet, learning the names of the pitiful nineteenth century boys at a crossroads college in darkest Ohio who'd founded the club in lonesome desperation one Christmas when they couldn't go home. And on top of all the memory work, we took the endless raw insults our older "brothers" could dream up for us through the fall and winter.

But then came the glorious climax in April, a warm Saturday night with stars. Despite the fact that Davidson was a deep dyed staunch Presbyterian school, the brothers got us knee walking drunk. Then at three in the morning, they blindfolded us, made us strip and throw our clothes in a common pile, then re-dress blind in one minute flat in whosever duds we grabbed up first. Next they split us off into pairs and drove us well out of town and left us, no word of advice but a sealed envelope. Bob and I were a pair of course; so in nothing but matchlight, we opened the message. It said that by midnight the following day, we must finish three chores.

First we had to get to Hickory by whatever means and find the collar from one of the brothers' dog that died the previous week (the dog's name was Slab—I could tell Bob that; it was all he'd forgot). Second we had to locate a penny with a secret mark scratched on the face—it was hid somewhere in the football stadium at Chapel Hill, no seat number given. Third (and the only mystery), we must also bring back "ten thousand dead bodies." Bob said we'd figure that out on the road.

First thing, we hitched ourselves to Charlotte, woke the black man that worked in the locker room at school and borrowed his spotless Model A Ford. Then we drove to Hickory. By the time we got there, dawn was breaking; and we could finally see our getups—the clothes we'd grabbed in the free for all. Bob wanted to quit—no decent man would wear such rags in public on Sunday, but I egged him on. Still it took us hours to find the house where Slab had died and persuade the people that we weren't crazy, just their son's "pledge slaves"; so give us Slab's old collar please. They finally did, plus a huge hot breakfast. Then we drove east to Chapel Hill and spent the rest of the day fine combing every inch of the stadium. We found everything from old shoes to dead bats, took a lifesaving nap and were all but ready to call it quits when Bob discovered the one new penny with our initials gouged into it: *BC/BB*.

That left us the problem of "ten thousand dead bodies." As he told the story, Bob claimed I said I'd "abuse" myself in an old Coke bottle; and that would be it—a million dead lives (from one point of view: the basic freshman's). I had no memory of the weird suggestion; but it sounded like the boy I was at the time. Finally though, Bob cut a foot long limb from a cedar by the road; and we raced back to Davidson as the sun went down with old Slab's collar, one marked penny and the millions of dying cells in one green cedar branch.

By the time Bob got to the end of the story, he had jostled my memory a little; and I could laugh at the clowns we'd been. I also knew that memory itself meant more to Bob than ever to me, even now when memory's the main thing left me. And when he ended by quoting the scalding vow of silence we took that evening in the final rite—"May my lips wither if I reveal the sacred mysteries of I Phelta Thigh" (as we always called it)—Bob slowly dug down into his pocket, brought up a penny and held it towards me.

I rose to take it—bright as new and scratched *BC/BB*. I said "I'll be damned" and offered it back.

"No, you keep it and leave it to Mattie. I asked young Luther to polish it up."

It was far brighter than Bob or me; and it still is, still in my bureau drawer.

Luther had sat through some of that, but mostly he'd quietly worked in the kitchen. So I called back through the open door, "You cooking enough for one more gullet?" It was idle talk; I didn't want to stay.

But Luther stepped to the doorsill and said "Mr. Blue, step in here please." As I moved past Bob, he winked up at me like I was in for a real surprise.

And when Luther led me into the pantry and started to whisper, I did feel a cold wind slap my eyes. All he said though was "I'll try every way I can to keep Bob here at home till the end. But you can help him a hell of a lot by calling up at least once a day and dropping by, every chance you get. It also helps me keep my nerves inside my skin."

"Is he being hard on you?"

At which Bob tried to yell from his chair, "I know you think you've got secrets on me; but I know them all, so ease yourselves—I won't take long."

Luther laughed and spoke at normal volume. "No sir, he's very considerate. But he needs a lot of care in the nights. His blood's so thick it burns his skin like acid in the dark. I try not to let him groan by himself." Luther stopped and swallowed hard, then whispered again. "See, I've never seen but one person die and I killed him. So this is getting real strange for me."

I knew not to let my worries show—that this might be the very last place Luther Bapp should try to tame himself. I just said I understood and would do my best.

Bob heard the word *best* and laughed a high cackle. "Old Blue, you're the best thing I ever knew; and if I get to Heaven, I'll pull you through" (he always burst into rhyme anytime his spirits were good).

I said "That may take big money, Bob—a solid bribe to poor Saint Peter."

"Relax, I've *got* it—money to burn."

Of course he'd recently claimed to be broke. I hadn't believed him but now I was sorry he'd brought up the subject and risked temptation with Luther present. Then I felt ashamed so I gripped Luther's shoulder. "Hang on, friend. You're doing fine."

He nodded but said "Help me" again. "Like I said, I've never seen a good man die—I doubt I've known a good man, Blue—and I'm not sure where we're headed here." It was the first time he'd called me Blue without the *Mr.* But he suddenly looked maybe ten years younger, hardly the boy that killed a man for pocket change.

I assured him I'd keep close watch; I could spend the odd night out here if needed and again to call me at a moment's notice. That seemed to help.

At least his face came back to normal. And for the first time, I could see a trace of his half sister in him—the same blue eyes that, scared or brave, never shut off scanning the world like there was something precious to learn, some well hid secret that might lead to bliss.

When I walked back in the dining room, Bob beckoned me over and said in my ear "You think Luther's bit off more than he can chew?"

I told him No, he was in good hands. I think I more than half believed it.

Bob had to trust it as well, didn't he?—there in the country with barely the strength to sit or stand but longing to die on his own terms. He held the crease of my trouser leg in bony fingers. "You won't let me struggle too hard?"

I wondered how in God's name to stop him when the real end came, but of course I said I'd tend to that.

When I saw that Bob was fighting to hold his grin till I left, I got out fast.

The Sunday after Thanksgiving we were driving home from ten o'clock mass. The air was cool and sun was pouring down from that angle which turns it and all it touches gold. Myra had chosen to sit in the back, but Mattie was on the front seat beside me. And as we turned into the drive at home, she asked what time I'd leave to see Bob. I glanced in the rearview mirror at Myra and saw her eyes go wary. "Maybe late afternoon. Why?"

"I want to ride with you."

By then I'd stopped and Myra was reaching for her door handle, but Matt was plainly expecting an answer. I said "We may have waited too late."

Myra said "You have" and opened her door.

Mattie stayed in place. "I need to go."

I tried to catch Myra's eyes, but she refused and left for the house. So I said to Matt "Want to tell me why?"

"I'm thinking about Bob all the time, and I'm old enough to be learning this stuff."

"This stuff is nothing but pain and death. Life'll break you in when your time comes."

"*This* is my time now." Her eyes held me down.

"Then get your mother's permission by four."

"She may not give it."

"Then you won't go—it's plain as that." I was talking against every urge I had, but I knew I had to respect Myra's rights.

Then it looked like Mattie was searching my hands. They were on the wheel still, and her eyes seemed to think my hands had denied her. At last she said "Coward" and opened her door. Before her feet were on the ground, she faced me and said "You won't quit, will you?"

I knew what she meant, but I still said "What?"

"You won't quit hurting me ever, will you?" Then knowing the answer, she was gone too.

She barely spoke to either one of us all through the meal, but I held to what I'd already told her. And when I was just coming to from a nap, Myra walked in and sat close by me on the bed. From the time I met her in grammar school, she'd always sat with both hands spread out loose on her knees, a little lost; so it felt entirely natural for me to reach and offer my spread right fingers. She took the offer and laced hers with mine. Then I understood what she needed to say, and I knew she'd start in now with a question, not a flat demand.

"You think Bob's ready for Matt to visit?"

I rolled closer towards her. "Bob's barely more than a painted skull, but he's there—it's *him*. He'd be glad to see her; it's been some years. And you could come with us."

She brought our joined hands to her chin, then pressed her dry lips on them firmly. "I'm grateful you ask but I'm the real coward for this go round. I just can't let that hard a sight get past my eyes right now— understand?"

"Nobody knows better, believe me."

"Then if you don't think it'll ruin Matt's peace, I'm willing to let her go this once."

I said "Mattie's peace is already deeper than we've ever had. I hate to admit this worse than anything—and God knows you don't need reminding—but I've put Matt through a hellacious school."

Myra slowly chose not to answer, though when she finally stood to leave, she said "Both of you come back by dark."

"We'll certainly try."

"Don't try, just *do* it. I'm low as a well."

"Any special cause I should know about?"

She shook her head No.

And I knew she meant it. Up till she died, as young as she was, Myra had less taste for self inspection than anybody else I've known. She just took life head on, chin down. If it killed her, it did—she expected that. She trusted her soul could stand what came. And since I'd tested her hardest of all, I knew she was right.

The house looked normal when we climbed the steps. I had my key but with Matt beside me I thought I should knock and give Bob and Luther a chance to get braced. Nobody came though, no foot-steps. A second knock and still no answer. I checked around the edge of the porch—Bob's car was here. Surely they hadn't left by ambulance and not called me?

As I turned the lock, Matt said "Sky, maybe—"

But soon as I took one step inside, I heard what had to be Luther's voice at the head of the stairs right over the door. I stepped in farther and looked above—no sign of him though. I called out "Luther?"

And then Bob spoke from what seemed far away as Nebraska. "Bring that beautiful creature in." So he was still upright or downstairs at least, and he must have glimpsed Mattie as we left the car.

I beckoned her to me, and we walked on to the dining room.

For the first time lately, Bob tried to stand but didn't make it. Still he held out a hand and a smile ferocious as any blowtorch. He said "Oh Mattie—Thanksgiving, *Thanksgiving*."

I knew that, except for magazine pictures and war newsreels, Matt had never seen anything bad as this. But from what she'd said to me back home, I knew not to corner and shame her now. I stood in place and let her cross the room alone.

She did it like Bob's own long lost daughter (if he'd ever had one), dignified but straight from the heart. He kept the hand out shaky on the air; and though she took it, she gently pushed closer and kissed his forehead.

When they were separate again, he studied her. "I knew it. I *knew* it—"

Mattie said "What?"

"Every good part of both your parents has poured into you."

I'd moved as close as the dining table. "Thank you, Robert."

Bob faced me. "No, I need to thank *you* for pleasing my eyes this late in the day. Hell—blessing the world with this grand girl." I knew he was giving his sincere view. Nobody I'd ever run across had shared Bob's outright worship of beauty in everything from ashtrays to angels. He asked Matt to sit in the nearest chair.

She was barely down before she looked back at me, laughed, then said to Bob "Now give me the lowdown on this dad of mine. Was he truly the goldstar boy he claims?" It was pure malarkey but she'd got it from me—you greet people first with some big nonsense to melt the ice—and it turned out perfectly.

Bob started to reel out stories about me from back when man in-

vented steam. Most of them bore some likeness to history, but all were
funny, and he was the butt of every joke. His voice was frail but his
eyes—which now were most of his face—were still as glad as ever to be
in the midst of doing what he did best. I can just recall that the final
tale was about the time when we were Matt's age and ordered by mail
a pink granite tombstone in his mother's name with the date of her
birth and a date two weeks ahead for her death. It was going to be
her birthday present from both of us, but we failed to enclose a de-
posit check, and the tombstone man drove up days later and spilled
our beans across the porch by asking Miss Gin for more details about
the design and the middle name of the dear deceased. As Bob got
towards the end of that, he was starting to wheeze. But he said "Now
Matt, you make this scoundrel visit my grave at Easter with a lily—
this year and for good."

Matt laughed but gave him a guarantee.

By then I'd stopped bringing Bob ice cream—he couldn't eat it—
so we lacked that to keep us busy on visits. He and I'd long since
settled his funeral plans, I'd helped him sort his important papers
and burn everything the executor lawyer wouldn't need, he'd told me
he meant to leave "a piece of money" for Matt's college days but not
to tell her, and we'd told each other every joke we knew. So now that
he sat here studying Matt like she was his roadmap to rest, I thought
she might feel ready to leave. Outside the light was turning brown,
past five o'clock. I said "You want me to call Luther down? We
better get going—Myra's alone."

Bob's eyes went blank, then his head shook No.

I lowered my voice and pointed upstairs. "Everything all right?"

He nodded, whispered "Sunday company" and pointed up.

"A lady friend?"

Bob said "Female."

"But you don't mind?"

"Don't let it worry you. I'm well attended." I'd noticed how Bob's
words and phrases had got old fashioned like he was already far in
the past and easier there.

On the window seat by him was a crystal ball I hadn't seen for twenty years. His mother, Miss Gin, had bought it on one of her trips abroad and said it was Bob's, though she was the only one who used it. One college weekend I spent out there, she gazed in its depths and told our fortunes—Bob's and mine. All I remember is, both of us got our heart's desire and vaporized at age ninety five, no pain whatever and best friends still. The ball itself was the only thing I ever envied Bob—quartz, not glass, the size of a grapefruit and perfectly clear till you turned it one way. Then you saw a fracture right at the core, a slit in the stone that Miss Gin said was the gate her mind slipped through to watch the long years saunter past her eyes.

I said "Matt, notice Bob's crystal ball. He sees well into the future with that."

I'd said it lightly to fill up time, but Matt's eyes seized right on it and stayed. From the start of her life, she'd been a child who didn't crave things—toys or clothes. She'd take what you gave her and say her thanks, but soon you'd notice it was stored in a drawer. Now though, watching that smoky quartz, her eyes had finally coveted something. But she didn't speak.

No need. Bob had already seen her eyes. It weighed almost too much for him now; still he reached for the ball and gave a slight shiver. "This is always colder than the room it's in; so Madelyn, please keep it warm for me"—he held it towards her.

She glanced at me (I nodded *Take it*), then accepted the gift. It lit a slow smile that spread till she was almost too fine to watch. She brought the ball up near her eyes and studied it slowly. Then she said to Bob "You're in good hands."

"With you here, I feel good indeed."

But Mattie said "I mean when you die." From anyone else it would surely have sounded nuts or holy; but Matt was lit by an utter surety that felt trustworthy to me at least.

It clearly stunned Bob but he finally said "Oh Matt, then I'm more than ready to go."

I had to think he actually meant it, for the first time now, and that my daughter had caused his peace.

Matt rose at that moment and this time took the back of Bob's hand and kissed it quickly. "Remember, I'm thinking of you every minute."

Bob said "That's mainly what's keeping me here." He seemed to mean it like nothing he'd said till now in my hearing.

Then I went over and made my own goodbye for the day. I'd see him by Wednesday unless he called sooner.

He said "I want you to watch me go." He'd already told me—he meant his last breath, he wanted me present.

I said I'd do it, bad as I hated to see him suffer.

He said "Old Blue, I've hurt worse than this many nights of my life. This feels like *rescue*"—that strange word again.

I laid a hand on his neck and said what was true and amazing. "You're braver than any man I've ever known."

Bob knew that with my years at war I'd seen my share of outright courage (he'd stayed at home with a heart murmur). And when we finally went through the door, I saw he was beaming.

Because the hall was dim and chilly, I shut the dining room door behind us; and Matt and I walked on towards the front. But when I got to the foot of the steps that led upstairs, I heard again the same low voices. And I suddenly knew I had to check. *I brought Luther in here. He's mine to watch.* So I told Matt to step along to the car—I'd be there directly.

She stayed in place with her hand on the stair rail and shook her head No.

I saw she was bent on seeing it all, this whole dead house. I called out "Luther?"

In under ten seconds a door knob turned, and footsteps creaked towards the top of the stairs. Then there stood a sight I'd have given three years of my life to cancel. Luther was neatly dressed and by his side was Luna wearing what seemed like a new velvet dress—I know it was deep wine colored and long with a wide white collar. She looked a thorough ten years older than when I'd left her that July morning by the road to camp. My heart truly balked and for a long instant I thought I'd fall face down on the floor. I'd never heard such a pounding silence, and I knew everybody could hear my mind as it flailed around for a few safe words to save my skin and get my daughter out of here. But no words came.

At last Luna said "You've got to be Mattie."

Matt said "Yes ma'm."

Luna said "I'm Luther's sister here." She tugged a little at his blue shirtsleeve. "My name is Luna and you're even prettier than what I heard."

I couldn't see Mattie but I heard her say "Thank you."

Luther said "You all have a good Thanksgiving?"

I could finally say "Very bountiful, thank you."

Luna was not exactly smiling, but her eyes had slipped off Matt onto me.

I was flat out terrified of what she'd say, and I rushed to stop her. "We've got to be home by dark so we'll run. I just want to tell you, Luther, again—don't let this *get* you. Give me the word and I'll help all I can."

Luther nodded but then said "Hold on a minute." He slid past Luna and started downward.

I had this awful expectation that Luna would follow. I know I actually put up a hand like a cop at a crossroads.

Then Luther was there two steps above me and starting to whisper. "The doctor says Bob can go anytime. His heart's real fragile; it could snap in his sleep."

I said "Lord, pray it does."

Matt said a quick "Don't—"

Close at hand Luther looked as clean and steady eyed as any drill sergeant. "Mr. Blue, I'll call you the minute I know."

But I said "Sooner. Again just now Bob asked me to be on hand when he goes."

Luther said "Then you better sleep out here. We got plenty beds. We'll make up one—" He glanced back at Luna.

I said "No, just try to call me in time."

Luther said "All right—no guarantees."

I said I wouldn't blame him whatever. I said he was doing a thorough job. I hope I thanked him—confused as I was I felt true gratitude. Then I looked to Mattie, "We need to get on home." When I turned to Luther, he'd already climbed nearly halfway back, though Luna had silently moved from sight. I couldn't stop it—I said "How long has your sister been out here?"

"Today, since morning. Mother's working all night so Luna was edgy at home alone. She's a big help here."

I knew that Bob had agreed to this. It was still his place. When Matt and I were outside though, I felt like I'd marooned a friend in a pitchblack field of strangers armed to do their will. But I felt no backward pull on my own mind. Before I'd cranked the engine to leave, I know I thought *Let him die in his sleep, now tonight.*

Matt and I were turning off Glenwood Avenue two blocks from home when she said a thing that fit my mind like a perfect mate. "I never said a real goodbye till now. Thank you, Sky."

I said she'd see him again someway; and there beside her lovely eyes, I never thought to doubt myself, not that one hour (she was truly that fine in her young life—you need to believe me, no plaster saint). I didn't say more till we were out of the car in purplish evening light. Still in my heart I thanked her fully. *Where on Earth would you have run, son—caught in dread at the foot of those stairs—without Matt to brace you?*

ELEVEN

Monday passed with no more news and likewise Tuesday. I didn't call Luther for fear I'd just get Bob on the line, weaker still. Mattie had made me realize I'd said the best goodbye I could. The way I was thinking in those days, it didn't dawn on me that Bob Barefoot would want me near for his own sake, not to teach me something or punish me. Anyhow I'd promised to drive out again on Wednesday evening, and I meant to do it. But Tuesday night near three a.m., the telephone woke me and Myra, first ring (I've mentioned it almost never woke Myra). Raw as we were we both knew who would be on the line and both said "Bob." I trotted to the hall, and of course it was Luther. He talked like a very excited young boy, capable but stretched to his limits. He spent so long excusing himself for calling that late, I finally had to push the question—was Bob already gone or was he going?

"No, Mr. Blue, he's clear as a bell—in his mind, his *mind*. But he says he won't be here by day, and I don't think he's lying by much."

While I was saying I'd get there fast, Matt came to her door already half dressed, tucking a shirt in her best blue jeans. She'd heard the phone and understood.

That was a bigger surprise than the call, and it really reached me. I even thought *She'll be there for me whenever* I *go*. But when I hung up, I had to say "My darling, no. Not this time, no."

She said "If Bob's not dead, I'm going."

Myra stood in the hall behind me now. I turned towards her and must have looked bad.

So she took over and talked to Matt while I went back for my clothes and keys. All I heard was Matt saying "No" again and again. And when I left she was there in the hall still pale and solemn, watching me fail her.

The front of the house was dark when I got there. But I didn't knock, just let myself in. The central hall was dark as well and cold as ever. I went straight to the dining room door and opened it slowly. At first I thought it was all dark too. But a stifling heat rolled out past me. And then I saw a low shine in the corner and what looked like a huddle of bodies standing up. *Christ, has Luther brought poor Dr. Brian this far out in the freezing night?*

A thin voice said "Blue, don't stop now." It had to be Bob.

And when my eyes had opened wider, I saw him propped up high on his cot in a white nightshirt, waving me towards him. I came as near to bolting out as I've ever come in a sober condition, but I held my ground. By then I'd seen that one face anyhow was Luther's.

Bob said "Is this Blue Calhoun or not?"

Beyond him, sitting on the window bench and holding his hand, was Luna again.

My feet moved forward but as I went I told myself *You'd do everybody—Bob included—the greatest kindness to leave here now.* I wasn't quite sure it was Luna that scared me, but something was clawing down my spine that scared me bad.

Bob's free hand still was hailing me in.

So when I got there I reached to take it. It was nothing but cold bone, a long bone rake.

He said "You kept your word again. Keep this up and you'll join me soon." He had to mean Heaven, and I knew he believed it.

I smiled. "What's the romantic lamplight for?" The only light was creeping out from a pewter oil lamp on the table, and that warm smell was rank in the air as a whole other person.

Luther said "Mr. Bob claims electric light hurts him."

Bob said "I don't claim it does—it *does*."

Luna said "His eyes. It hurts him here—" She shut her eyes to show where he hurt. In her free hand she had a clean rag. She was just at the end of sponging Bob's face, and she looked like she would know what next when the next need came.

I looked at her then; but I couldn't say it kinder than this, "How did you get here?"

"In a taxi my brother sent to get me."

I was wild to know exact details. "A taxi tonight?" It felt like if she'd stayed out here since last weekend, I couldn't stand it.

But Luna was looking at Bob again—Bob was what mattered, not me and my rattletrap selfish fears.

Luther said "Mr. Blue, I ran out of hands. I needed help."

I'd laid Bob's fingers back on the sheet. He reached up now, found me again and set his shining eyes hot on me. "She's a kind child. I wanted her here."

Being me—and me in that bad time—I thought *Bob's brought her here for me, some deathbed reconciliation he's trying to work.* All I could think to say though was "Has anybody called the doctor yet?"

Bob raised a finger to his lips. "I'm running this now. And I want *out*."

I said "A doctor could ease your breathing."

He shook his head. "Luther's got this planned."

I had no choice but to nod Yes to him.

Then Luther brought up a straight back chair, so I sat down on Bob's right side and tried to watch nobody but him. Even with World War II behind me, I'd never been this near to where death was plainly crushing a person I knew (most of my Army friends fell at a distance, and all I did was watch them go).

Once I was settled Bob calmed down some and drifted back and forth in sleep. He'd open his eyes and say a sentence to nobody near, mostly his mother and men whose names I hadn't heard. Then he'd be gone five or ten minutes, breathing hard but apparently dreaming. From what he'd said in the recent past, and from what I saw, I understood he was smothering—his blood just wouldn't hold oxygen now.

My whole life I've dreaded suffocation maybe the worst of any death. But here Bob didn't seem all that desperate. He certainly never mentioned pain or cried for more than we could give him—which was nothing but patience, drinks of water and feeble answers to whatever questions he thought to ask (he kept reminding us of the house, repairs it needed—roof paint, caulking, a man to poison the silverfish that were eating his books). We may have been there another two hours. Whatever it was it didn't feel like any time I'd ever lived through before.

Then as I thought I could see light try to touch the window, Bob turned to me with peaceful eyes. And his voice was almost strong as normal. "Has Mattie used her crystal ball on you yet, son?"

Son? He'd never called me that. But I told him she was practicing daily on neighborhood friends before trying me.

He said "She'll need a thousand years—"

I'd tried not to do more than nod at his talk (to spare him every possible breath), but to that I said "Am I such a deep mystery?"

It seemed to reach him. He pushed up slightly, stared at every cell of my face, then lay back in silence.

Luna took his left hand, bent to his ear and told him plainly "Blue's deep as a well." She was almost smiling.

Bob gave her a look that was harder than buckshot, then tried to laugh. "You *know* him, don't you?"

Luna said "I do."

Far back in my mind, I thought *You did, long ages past.* I didn't resent her. I just felt a million miles from her now and long cool years.

But Bob still had his eyes right on her. He waved his head back to indicate me, and he said "Blue tries to walk alone. I've been telling him sixty years—all our lives—he's deep down *wrong.*" Then he seemed asleep, the calmest yet.

Sixty years?—we weren't forty yet. I told myself his mind was gone, a mercy by now. And then I thought he spoke my name. Somebody did—one long high *Blue.* Bob's entire head looked shut as a stone, and finally I looked at Luna.

Her lips were parted. It might have been her that spoke but I doubt it. Anyhow she met my eyes—no smile, no fear, no actual word.

So shortly I was peaceful again. I thought of all the times Bob said he "lived for beauty, the only goodness." And I told myself *Nobody beautiful as this girl here has been in this old room before. He's dying high on the hog. Lord take him.*

Luther laid a heavy hand on my shoulder, then said "I think our job's about done."

I took Bob's wrist and felt for life. I waited maybe a whole clock minute. Then it felt like everybody's job here anyhow was finally done. I thought I knew just one grim thing, *You're left without a friend alive* (and it's all but the truth three decades later, which is no cause for pity; and I don't ask it).

When I could manage to look again, Luther was moving to switch on the light.

And Luna was laying Bob's arms straight down by his sides on the sheet.

I said "Luther, hold off a minute with the light." I someway knew we should wait for day. *Let daylight find him.*

He nodded and moved to the thermostat to turn that down—everybody but Bob had sweated hard. Luther stood in the dark far over by the chimney and said "Keep telling us what to do."

He didn't sound mad but I was confused.

So he said "Bob told us you'd know what next."

It almost hurt to think this was why Bob ordered me here, to be drum major at a bachelor funeral. "He told me his funeral plans—that's all. I know which undertaker to phone."

By then Luther stood in reach of the lamp. He looked like a giant in the Brothers Grimm that's either your finest friend or your curse—he can't decide which. He said "Bob claimed you'd own all this." Luther's long arms made a wide slow sweep of the room, the house and the woods outside.

I thought *Oh Christ, please Bob, don't do it.*

But he had. Luther's next move was to go to the kitchen and come straight back. Then he handed me a white envelope with just my name in Bob's small script. Luther said "He wanted you to read it now."

I looked across Bob's body for Luna. She'd vanished without me seeing her go. I've always hated a torn open letter, so even now I took my pocket knife and slit the envelope. There was one sheet of lined white paper, and in Bob's hand it simply said

My sole heir and the executor of my estate is Bluford Calhoun. May it give him ease.

Robert Brick Barefoot

Near the bottom was yesterday's date and below as witnesses the names and address of Luther and Luna.

Right off I knew *This won't hold water. His lawyer's got the real McCoy in his safe downtown.* But that didn't stop me suddenly facing Luther Bapp and crying out "Can you believe this?" I meant *This pitiful bastard's generous heart, that I never helped and waited way too late to try.*

Luther nodded; he believed it with no sign of doubt. But then he'd spent in these few days more closeup time with Bob than I'd put in since boyhood.

With no real thought but exhausted thanks, I said "You won't go begging here, Luther. You did a good deed."

"Mr. Blue, I can tell you now, I owe the world way more than I've paid."

I guessed he was right but few felons know it; so I said as much (I consider myself a felon too, though unapprehended). Then we both looked up at the sound of the door.

Luna was here and window light reached her (the sun was up). She'd washed her face and fixed her hair. She said "People, we need to eat or we'll fade." Then she walked on past us into the kitchen and drew fresh water for coffee at least.

All my life I've noticed how people get raging hungry once death's passed through. Luther joined Luna in the kitchen while I called Brown's Funeral Home and then spoke to Myra. I only told her that

Bob was gone, that I'd stay here till the undertaker came and then head to Beechridge to dress for work (no point in mentioning Bob's estate till I talked to the lawyer).

Myra said "He made you a loyal friend. Please know I'm sorry."

Since that was the kindest thing she'd said about Bob in years, I felt relieved and asked if Matt was still speaking to me.

"She will be when she hears the news, but she's got another half hour to sleep."

So I let them be, ate a big hot breakfast, watched the undertakers roll Bob out of his lifelong home, asked Luther to stay a few more days till things got settled; and then I had to leave for work. When I stood up from the loaded table, I wanted to say a genuine thanks to poor Rita's children who'd done their best. But when I tried to find the words—just grateful words—my throat choked up; and I stood a long minute shaking hard.

It was Luther that got up and tried to ease me. He said "Bob thought you hung the moon."

I guess I'd privately known that forever. But I managed to thank this giant beside me and say he'd done an excellent job, which so far as I knew he had. The strangest thing in this whole visit though—I'd truly forgot that Luna was with us, quiet here at the end of the table like some leftover dark trace of the night.

Then she stood too and said "I guess I feel a lot older." Right then fresh daylight fell through the window beside the stove. And as Luna rose, light struck all down her hair and face. She was right—she even looked thoroughly grown and strong as she'd actually proved to be. She said to Luther "I guess I ought to go on to school."

He said "If you want to—"

"Will you be all right out here alone?"

Luther laughed. "I've been alone for the past hundred years—on Earth anyhow. Maybe I won't crack."

So she looked to me. "Mr. Blue, can I catch a ride to my mother's?"

When I said "Yes" it felt as normal as saying "Hello" to a dead telephone.

*

And all the way into town in the sun with Luna beside me on the front seat, she felt more like a formal friend than the woman I'd gone stark wild about this same full year. I even thought how she felt a little like Bob's cool body after he died, the scene of a big storm funnel but calm. We said very little. At least I'd had a few hours' sleep before Luther's call. She'd had none whatever, and here she meant to go on to school. When we got in sight of the turnoff for Rita's, I figured I might just stop at the corner. But when I thought how hard Luna worked for Bob all night, I made the turn and pulled up by the small white house.

She looked at me then. "I'm real sorry you've lost again."

At first I didn't follow her. I heard her saying I was always losing so I laughed. "I already know I'm a loser, don't worry yourself."

She frowned. "No *sir*. I mean, I never came back to you and now Bob's gone—" She'd kept the strong grown look I'd seen awhile ago.

But I was still hearing her words as childish—*Blue lost because Luna never came back*. I had to swallow a mouthful of meanness. Then I said "Thank you, hear? And give your mother my very best. I hope you don't fall asleep in class."

She said "Me too" but she hadn't smiled.

So I was still safe. I'd left the motor on and was aimed ahead.

But when she'd got herself outside, she stopped an instant and bent to look back. Her face was still fine as I'd ever seen it; she was trying to fight against a smile.

I said "You don't have to grieve for Bob."

"I'm mourning for you, my old friend Blue." Then she was gone also.

Right off I thought *It's you again, son, alone as the hills*. I tried to think it was my normal state, that I could walk through forty more years of this here now—this being a man stuck down in a field with no firelight, no human voice, no skin but mine to touch and praise through many more years. Then why did I feel like stopping right now in the midst of the road, throwing my head back and bellowing hard at the blind deaf sun?

*

By the time I was home, I'd told myself such thoughts were nothing but dust in the wake of the night and Bob's last struggle. I shaved, got in to work on time and then phoned Bob's attorney to ask for a noon appointment (he was Foster Phillips, a boy we'd known behind us in school). I'd skip my own lunch, show him the final handwritten will and see if it had any value at all. Turned out it did. By state law a simple handwritten will is valid if two acquaintances of the deceased can swear the handwriting's genuine. Foster was ready to take his secretary (who'd known Bob too) and walk with me to the Clerk of Court where the two of them swore the hand was Bob's; so the will was legal, then and there.

I'd never inherited ten cents before. What my dad left went straight to Miss Ashlyn. He'd kept an account of all he spent on drying me out at expensive clinics and deducted that from my share of his money, which left me well in the red but rightly so. Bob's gift was the first money I ever owned that I didn't earn on my two feet. A whole year later when everything was clear, I had possession of twenty thousand dollars; and that was no joke, not in real dollars in the 1950s. But that runs too far ahead too fast. I had the hardest part of my life before me now but also the happiest, as I've kept claiming.

After supper I called Luther, and he answered the second ring. It surprised and relieved me, and he sounded all right (I don't know where I thought he'd be but not in the house I'd left this morning with the memory of Bob still loose in the rooms as any trapped bird). He said he'd napped in the afternoon but otherwise had "cleaned things up with a fine toothed rake," was watching TV and awaiting my instructions. I told him to turn in early tonight, then start tomorrow on pulling the years of old newspapers and magazines from the second floor plus giving the yard a lick and a promise for the funeral Friday.

Then I asked if he had money to buy anything he might need—cleaning equipment, milk, food, funeral clothes for himself. He said Yes, he had twelve dollars; and he guessed that might be the last he saw for some long time (having lost this first job so fast to death). I said I'd reimburse him tomorrow when I came out to check on things and that I might yet have work for him out there, fixing the place. All his answers were straight and polite, and it wasn't till we got down to the end that I suddenly asked him how Luna was.

He said "You've seen her since I have."

I said "Is that so?"—just for something to say. I felt exposed.

But Luther jumped on it, still courteous but fast. "You didn't think I had her out here, did you?"

I still didn't know if she or Rita had mentioned me to him or how much of that old story they'd told—whatever tale they'd made by now out of me and Luna an eon ago. So I backed out the feeble way. "You're a grown man, Luther. Use your best judgment."

"In that case—yes sir, I already have."

But when we were done, I thought I heard footsteps behind him as he hung up. It could have been the old dry floorboards creaking of their own accord. Still from then on out through the night, that trace of a clue cut my mind deep to the painful quick. *What do these children mean to each other, and what earthly right do I have to ask?*

TWELVE

I GOT OUT to Bob's before dark the next day, a clear cool Thursday. From way down the drive, I could see what a good job Luther had done on the yard and that wilderness of mountain laurel that hadn't been touched in God knew when. The place looked better than it had since Bob buried Miss Gin out back. And just this much of a change made it easy to walk on up, not dreading Bob's yellow skull anymore. I knocked, turned the key and called for Luther.

He answered from upstairs and trotted down clean in a white shirt and starched dungarees.

"Who did all that good yard work?"

He grinned. "Me, myself and I." But then his face clouded. "You still thinking I can't do everything out here *alone*?"

"No, no. I was trying to joke. It looks like the White House lawn, but you're so clean and neat—who did it?"

"Well, I didn't have Mamie Eisenhower to help me" (she was First Lady then). "I finished in the yard by noon and have been upstairs weeding coathangers, paperbags, old bars of soap—Mr. Bob collected soap. Must've dreaded another war and him dirty. That got me thinking I'd take a bath—first actual long tub bath I've had since 1949. Just showers in prison and that's one place you can truly get killed. You got some enemy that's made him a knife, he waits till you're naked with soap in your eyes—you're *his*, old Blue."

As I moved past him into the hall, I thought *So now he's named me old Blue too. But what the hell?—I'm breathing and never spent a whole night in jail.*

We sat and drank coffee in the dining room. I told Luther what to expect tomorrow. I'd leave a little early and be here by four with Bob's ashes. Myra would pick Mattie up from school and they'd come out. Plus whatever friends of Bob I could reach. In recent years he'd seen so few people, nobody much cared. He didn't want a preacher involved but had asked me to read the Ninetieth Psalm and lead the Lord's Prayer. Then he asked that everybody present take Miss Gin's big silver ladle (the one she broke out for Christmas eggnog) and one by one help scatter his ashes in the grass of the Barefoot family graves— some stones went back to the 1820s.

When Luther had heard the simple plans, he shook his head. "I very much doubt I should be here then."

I said he'd earned full rights in the matter.

"No, I don't have a suit of clothes. Your wife's so fine—"

I told him my wife was a kind person.

He took awhile to think that over like he'd heard otherwise. "Can I wear one of Bob's two thousand neckties?"

"You can wear anything in the house that fits."

Then he changed his tack. "No music at all?"

"Bob loved it, sure, but he never asked for it—not in my presence."

"Can Luna sing?"

I'd seen right off where he was headed. "Luna can sing like the angels of God but—"

When I balked he held up one long finger. "*But*—no *buts*. Bob told me before you came Tuesday night that he hoped somebody sang at his grave."

I halfway thought he was suckering me. But for whatever cause I said "You're saying you want Luna here."

"See, you claim I earned my rights—then she did too."

"Luther, I told you my wife was coming."

"You said your wife was kind and strong."

"Then let's just say I'm not cruel enough to ask her to bear it, not this week at least."

Luther said "She knows everything you done. What news would she learn?"

So now I saw he knew a great deal, from Luna or Rita plus his own eyes. All he'd said, he said very calmly with no trace of meanness; and it made me see he was more than half right. Then my mind went back to Tuesday, deep in the night with Bob barely gasping and Luna beside him close as if she'd known him for life. It was hard to say, but I knew it was fair—"I'd want your mother here with Luna then."

"Mother belongs here—Bob loved Rita."

"Can she get off work?"

He consulted a watch I didn't recall, a nice gold watch. "Sure, she doesn't go in till eight."

You've watched me come this far that year, so you won't feel any hard shock now. I leaned towards Luther and said "Take Bob's car and ride in behind me. Ask Luna if she'll please sing one song—she'll know what's right. Then go to a phone booth, call me up and let me know if she will or won't." If I'd had sufficient control of my mind, I could have just stood up, gone straight to Rita's, knocked politely, told Luna to pack her toothbrush and comb and the two of us headed south by dark. Likely I would have if I'd really known she'd say a quick Yes. But Christ, she'd cut me off months back like a poisoned leg. And here she'd been these recent weeks, tied up in whatever knots with this tall capable brother that might be making big claims on her body or might be trying to give her the gifts of dignity and tardy care that she'd never known, not from her own kin nor lately from me.

Luther still hadn't answered or got to his feet. We were both still huddled down like spies.

"What's your claim on her, son?"

He let the word "son" pass this time, and he took a long pause, but he finally held both palms up empty.

It was dark by then, and we headed to town.

*

My family got through a whole quiet evening—a hot supper that Myra had plainly worked hard on, and then I tried to help Matt do arithmetic but ended up confusing her (as I mostly did since the nuns used totally different methods from what I'd learned). A spot on the upper right side of my head knew I was waiting for the phone to ring, but I stayed fairly calm. And nobody called, not even for Matt; so at ten o'clock she went to bed. Myra was "reading" in the dining room (which generally meant she was praying at their shrine, though she always did it invisibly—if I walked in she'd just be sitting on the old loveseat with a book on her lap and maybe a rosary loose beside her). Back in the kitchen I finished paying the monthly bills. Then just as I gave up expecting word, a ring broke out of the phone like thunder— I know I *shook*.

Myra got to it first and called for me. When I got there she only told me "It's Rita's boy," then handed him over.

Luther said "We're set."

I understood him and not till then did I see what I'd undoubtedly done—or let be done. My mind just shorted out entirely (Myra was ten feet away with her book). And all I could finally say to Luther was "Your mother too?"

"Yes sir, old Blue, if you'll pay the taxi—you could use Bob's money. He'd be glad of it."

I wanted to say *You knew Bob Barefoot fifteen minutes. Shut your goddamned mouth and disappear.* It wasn't all true but if I'd had the guts to go that far in words (plain words would have done it unless Luther had it in his soul to kill me)—if I'd just said *Many thanks, now leave,* where would the rest of my life have gone—mine and at least six other lives including your own? I didn't say anything near it of course. I managed "You rest. I'll see you tomorrow."

When I hung up Myra didn't speak. I knew I couldn't risk talking yet, so I went straight to the downstairs toilet. It wasn't until I'd washed my face that a wave of nausea rose deep in me and slapped my chest. I thought I'd either faint or vomit. Then I thought *Go on and die,* but I slumped on the stool, and the wave passed through.

My mouth was bitter but I said to myself *Tell Myra the news the simplest way. These children helped Bob Barefoot die. I have to thank them. Please understand,* which is what I told her a minute later in a very few words. I also said "If this shames you I beg your pardon; I'll understand if you stay home. It'll all be over by dark tomorrow."

Myra didn't look hurt but she took her time. "You know how much Matt wants to go."

"I can get Matt from school."

"Then she'd ask questions about my absence. I also told your mother I'd pick her up at four."

I pulled out a chair and sat close to her. "Don't make yourself a victim in this. These children trapped me. *Luther* asked his own half sister to help—it was *not* me." That wasn't entirely true but nearly.

Myra said " 'Children?' I very much doubt Luther Bapp's a child— the girl is, surely." But then I saw her eyes crouch down the way they did when she'd run out of good sense or kindness. She mostly tried to spare me that look. So she stood up fast and went to the kitchen.

I heard her draw cold water to drink.

Far in the night I woke up completely, knowing I wouldn't sleep again. Since I'd been sober such times were rare. When they came I'd mostly creep downstairs, read a magazine or watch early morning television. In those days that was generally lectures on Shakespeare's plays or how to grow soy beans for personal gain. But when I woke that Thursday night, I could hear Myra breathing awake beside me. At first I dreaded how she might turn and ask me questions to ruin us both. No, she lay on quiet and separate. So then I turned to see her in the dark (the street light slatted in through blinds).

Like all the world she was different at night. And now she looked so young and free—the line of her face turned up to the ceiling—I asked myself if I hadn't been right, back in August, thinking she'd be far better without me. It somehow felt like I could hand Myra her whole life back, just reach out now and cancel our pain (fifteen years' worth). The longer I watched, the younger she looked till I even thought *Hell, ask her now. Just ask her, son.* I brought my left hand up to her chin, nudged her head my way and said "Aren't you much better off without me?" Now her eyes were lost in the dark, but I guessed they were on me. And to my surprise I welcomed them.

Finally she said "How did you know I was wondering that?"

"It didn't take a college degree, not tonight."

She gave a pleasant sounding sigh, then went so quiet I figured she was gone. But next her hand came up to my arm and rested on it. "Yes, I might well be better off, for peace of mind."

"Then tell me when. I'll leave when you say."

She actually laughed, just one high note. "You'll grow to the sheets."

"Ma'm?"

"If you lie here while Mother Superior Myra Calhoun makes up her mind to say 'Get gone,' you'll grow more roots than poison ivy."

"It's mainly because you're a Catholic then?"

She gave me a genuine knock on my hipbone.

"Why else would you want me?"

She knew right off. "Because there's such a thing as love."

I'd heard her say it more than once with me in far worse shape than now. I'd watched my mother, long before that, sit ten feet away in a cool dim room and meet my young hot baffled eyes with a patient care that she called *love*, which I have reason to think it was. But not till now—with Bob in ashes in a box downtown, his funeral scheduled hours from now with one walleyed poor practical nurse named Rita Absher and her two kids (a killer and a girl that knew the outer limits of skin), me and my family plus birds, mice, owls and larger beasts— not till here this Thursday night did I think I glimpsed what Myra meant, and Mother behind her and now young Matt. You could stand or lie that close by a person all your life and never once—not seriously—want to rise and *run*.

You can give one person all your life and not be hungry or bitter or broke—not ever, right on, far as you go. For that long moment it seemed so fine, so far past me and my pitiful reach, that it cored me out dead hollow again. Again I could feel the night blow through me. And when I reached for Myra's arm, I found somehow just her warm flesh, her powdered shoulder and down from there, no shirt or gown. She slid in closer and we went on, slow and in full possession of our wits, towards an actual end, a destination, like people that trusted each other in darkness—people that knew the secret paths to every pore of their starved hides and their minds that longed for the plentiful help we gladly gave each other again.

THIRTEEN

THE NEXT AFTERNOON was also clear with a chill keen edge. I stopped by the undertaker's at three, picked up Bob in a metal urn as ugly as any bowling trophy. I'd wanted him packed in a plain wood box, but it was his money, so I paid for the trophy and headed out for the scattering. All the way I thought how long he'd have laughed at his tacky new surroundings; I barely thought of the Bapps and Abshers. But soon as I parked I saw a new touch. Luther had put tall branches of magnolia leaves in the two old churns that stood by the door. At first I balked—*Bob wouldn't want this*—but then I thought *This is not for Bob but us. Let them be.* As ever I knocked, then turned the bolt and called to Luther. There was no quick answer, so I set the ashes on a hall table and went towards the back—he was probably uphill at the graves, still clearing and raking.

When I opened the dining room though, right off I smelled a change in the air. It had been so musty through Bob's last days, then clean and dry. But now it felt like pressure was leaking through some ragged hole. *Is a window broken?* I stepped forward anyhow and then I saw in the midst of the table a vase with one more branch of leaves. The vase was set on a sheet of paper with a handwritten message. It didn't surprise me. Luther had stepped out briefly for something he thought we'd need. But as I saw the first three words, I was truly stunned.

Pardon me, Blue, but I'm checking out. At Rita's last night things came all to pieces, they act like I am worse than I am—which is going far—so here I will give them the peace that matters more than their blood kin ever can. You were fair to me, I'm glad I helped Bob die near friends, and I know I helped him leave you his stuff. I hope it eases some of your burdens. Since everything is yours now I took the liberty of helping myself to the clothes you mentioned, one suitcase and fifty silver dollars I found stuck back in Bob's bottom drawer in his old bedroom plus a wristwatch. He forgot them long since and I do not guess you will be hardup for fifty now or a dented watch. If you ever get broke though down the road I hope I live to see you again and bail you out plus interest and a very sincere handshake for all you did to this

Old Giant, a friend
Luther Ray

My first thought was *He left without his check*—he had a check coming later today (I'd already written it). But then he had the silver dollars. Well, he'd seen Bob through his final breath with decent patience; and he started the cleanup drive on the place. He was welcome to fifty dollars on me. But now I'd have to tell Rita and Luna their boy was gone—the only problem he'd left me really—unless he'd already told them last night. I stood and went to the kitchen to look uphill at the graves. Had he finished the weeding? And there on the table he'd laid out boxes of saltines, peanuts, a slab of cheese and a second note.

Thinking somebody might want a nibble after you have strowed Bob. Good luck to all,

Luther

It felt like the kind of whistling-in-the-dark last wave I liked to give in my drinking days when I checked out on kith and kin for parts unknown, and I folded the paper neatly to keep for some strange reason.

By then it was nearly four o'clock. And before I had time to think again about the sadness of all Bob's pain or even of how much Myra and I had said between us deep in the night, I heard the front door knocker blam. That would either be Myra, Mattie and Mother or Rita and Luna—*Not all at once please.*

It was Luna by herself on the porch with a Yellow Cab leaving the drive. She wore dark blue with her hair combed down as long as it reached like a mane around her. And in her hand was a small clay pot with a red begonia bright as a torch.

"Where's Rita?"

"You know," Luna said.

"No ma'm, I don't."

Then I saw how solemn she looked—her eyes were either scared or offended. I said "Don't say Luther beat on his mother."

"Can I come in?—I'm freezing out here."

As we walked back to the dining room, I told her my folks would be here shortly and that Myra understood who'd be singing a hymn at the grave. I meant it of course to ease her nerves.

But when I finished Luna said "You don't give a good goddamn." Like a lot of women in those days, she used profanity so very seldom, it made a big effect when she did. Two degrees higher her eyes would have flamed.

I said "I'm lost—"

Hot as she was her voice was calm. "You've been lost, far as I know, for years." She looked round the room and towards the kitchen. "Is my brother here?"

I wanted to ask her to use my name—*Say "Blue" just once*—but silently I gave her Luther's letter.

And once she'd read it, she said "Thank Jesus."

I told her there were some snacks in the kitchen if she felt low.

But she said all she wanted to do was sing her piece for Mr. Barefoot and get back to Rita.

"Rita's not hurt bad?"

"A knife through her heart—how bad is that?"

"Great God, then she's in Rex Hospital?"

Luna shook her head. "Not a real knife but what Luther said to her *and* me—how we caused every wrong he suffered by not understanding his mind through the years."

I heard myself say a foolish thing. "I'm sorry for whatever part I played."

"I hope you'll tell my mother that."

Dread was already moving my way. I felt my mind start to hunker down—*Stay back, stay back*—and I didn't answer.

Then Luna said she'd go wash her hands "from the filthy cab and sort her thoughts" and that I should call her when the others came, if I still wanted what she had to give.

When she left I walked on up to the graves. And yes, Luther had done a neat job. The ground was rocky but clear of weeds, and the tallest headstone stood clear in the midst—BAREFOOT with small sunk footstones naming his father and mother and then the older stones nearby (two or three were just rough field stones that marked the graves of household slaves). If Bob had wanted his whole body buried, he'd have had to lie behind the big stone apart from his parents. But now I could sow him all round the space with only the low brick wall to stop me. I came back indoors hoping my family might have arrived. No, just the same gray emptiness—not even a creaking board overhead from Luna's feet. It was quarter to five. Something had to be wrong—*Matt's hurt at school. They found Mother dead*— so I dialed home expecting no answer. *Call the hospital, fool.*

Matt's voice answered but then in the background, Myra said "Mattie, I told you I'd get that." They both went quiet and I could picture a tug of war.

Then Myra spoke, again at a distance. "Madelyn, leave me here alone. This is not for you." A door slammed hard and finally Myra said "Bluford, I'm sorry—"

"What's wrong, for God's sake?"

"I thought I was brave enough, but then the day wore on, and I kept thinking till I knew I couldn't face what you planned."

I guess I wasn't completely surprised. I even almost felt relieved, but something snagged in my mind, and I said "You made this choice on your own?" I think I wondered if Mother had swayed her.

Myra waited but, truthful as ever, said "Father Scanlon came by this morning."

I flushed hot. "You called him, you mean."

"He tapped on the back door of his own will."

"And you told him what?"

"I told him the very deep trouble I felt."

"And he said 'Don't go near the strumpet.' "

Again she gave an actual laugh. "No, he said 'Forgive her and go. You'll bless everybody.' But once he left I still couldn't stand it."

"Did you call Mother then?"

Myra said she did and then she whispered "I met Mattie at school like I promised and told her you had asked us to wait—something had come up. You'd take us out soon, and we could bring flowers."

Once she'd calmed me about fat Scanlon, I felt again we were all maybe lucky. So I just said I understood. I'd see them for supper and for her to tell Matt some harmless story to cover the change.

Myra waited. "Just tell her you changed your mind. I feel like lies have stacked up round us till we can't breathe."

I honestly had no idea what lies she could mean—*I've quit the lies*—but I said "All right." When I hung up I turned and was shied by Luna beyond me, back in the room with no sound at all, though her good smell reached me.

Her face was calmer and she looked maybe five years older than when she first arrived. As we stood there three yards apart, she gave no sign of needing to speak.

So I said "My folks can't come out. Looks like we're jinxed—it's you and me."

Luna said "That's how it started, I guess. Let's move fore it's dark."

I got the urn and she got her flower, and we walked up in a slant brand of light that played deep chords far back in my head. I kept seeing Bob's thin face years back dreaming up one more joke for me. And I thought how much he'd have loved this mess and how late

Miss Gin would have stayed up to phone every friend she had with the white trash news. But also I was mad and hurt. *Bob deserved a lot more respect than this. Rita at least and Mother should be here.* When we got to the graves, I must have seemed confused.

Luna said "You want me to sing this late?"

Even as I faced her, the light was sinking faster and cold. It lit her hair and the line of her shoulders, and I know I thought *Who'd willingly leave a world with this in it?* But I told her my plan—I'd say the psalm, then she could sing while I strowed the ashes and then I'd pray. She nodded, I set the urn on the stone and started off, " 'Lord, thou hast been our dwelling place in all generations.' " Like everybody in those days, I'd learned it by heart in grammar school. And lately I'd heard it at A.A. meetings when a young drunk lawyer made us sit still nearly an hour while he explained it word by word when everybody knew it worked like music or not at all.

So I had no trouble skimming along. I kept my eyes on Luna at first. But by the time I got to " 'Thou carriest them away as with a flood; they are as a sleep,' " the only thing I was seeing was Bob—Bob so young you couldn't imagine him tortured and dead in the prime of life, thirty six years old. To my eyes then Luna Absher might have been on Mars. And when I'd got to the final verse, my eyes skipped back to the page before, Psalm Eighty-Eight—" 'Lover and friend hast thou put far from me, and mine acquaintance into darkness.' " My mind came back to the here and now in serious trouble, and I nodded to Luna.

She stood where she was with that red flower and raised her head as she always did. Her lips barely opened and her first notes were "Rock of ages, cleft for me." I realized she lacked her harp, but that didn't slow her. She gave what she had, and oh God knew she hadn't lost one thin atom of strength. It poured out easy.

But fine as it sounded in that much stillness, I know I thought *Can she still harm me?* I started walking a wide circle inside the wall, strowing the tannish gritty remains. I made one round before Luna finished. Then I started a second, but her eyes stopped me.

She held both hands out cupped and said "I get a real part in this."

She stepped on forward so I agreed and poured the leavings into her palms—a few spoonsful. She stooped and sifted them onto the dirt around her flower, then set it firm between Bob's parents.

I said "It's bound to freeze tonight." I meant *You're killing a harmless plant*.

"It'll serve its purpose, hot or cold. And *I'm* bound to die too. What are you trying so hard to save?"

I might at least have said "My daughter"—I'd kept seeing Matt all through the strowing, how moved she'd have been and the lesson she'd have drawn. But my eyes couldn't move off Luna's face, brave now as an arrow on fire in the night that fell so fast around us. Before I could think how the Lord's Prayer started, she brushed on past me and trotted down.

So all I said was "Amen, Robert." Then I went to find her.

She was in the kitchen slowly washing her hands at the sink. Her face looked peaceful. But when I walked towards her, she turned straight at me. "No sir. Stay there."

I said "Whoa, Luna. Don't flatter yourself." Then I heard how stingy it sounded, like she'd misread me and thought I meant to grab her somehow. I went to the table, opened a box of cheese tidbits and held it out. "Luther laid these in, in case we were hungry."

She said "Luther laid in a lot more stuff than you ever guessed."

I wanted to rush at her mouth right then and force that back—just the plain words, whatever they might mean, were something we didn't need to hear. But of course I couldn't.

And next slow tears were rolling down her face, no sound. I must have put out an offering hand, but her head shook hard, and she walked past me to the dining room.

I gave her a minute, thinking she might head upstairs. But there were no footsteps. And when I followed she was there on the bench beyond Bob's cot, facing the window and near full darkness (Luther had said he'd move the cot back where it belonged across the hall, which he failed to do, though he stripped the sheets). I sat by the table and took the first step. "Is there something I can do to help?"

She didn't hear me.

All I could see was the side of her face. And I'm glad to say I could watch it now and not call up those real pictures of her and me that I'd fingered through so many times. I understood there was some new hurt, that it featured Luther and Rita at least. My whole mind said *You can't take this. Don't take it, son.* And for ten more seconds, I fully obeyed. Then I stood and took one step her way.

Her hand came up to stop me in place, and she finally faced me, but she still didn't speak.

I stayed upright there next to the cot, and I said "You've got to tell somebody." Then I knew *If she answers now she trips a landslide.* I wanted to say "Let's head for home," but I thought *Someway this is home here now.*

And it seemed Luna someway felt the same. She touched her eyes and went very calm. Then she spoke right at me. "My brother has got some sterling traits, he always has, he's been good to me when nobody was. But see, I hadn't laid eyes on Luther for several years—Rita wouldn't let me visit in prison—so when he turned up free back in August, I tried to pay him for all he'd missed. I suddenly liked him that much, Blue—"

The sound of my name in her voice right then was at least as strong as any music, so I sat back to hear her out.

"See, I'm trying to tell myself that you and I brought me to life, straight out of all that miserable childish time I had and told you about. And when I gave you back to your wife, we left me grown but stranded bad. In so many ways you'd rushed me to be as grown as you—kindly, I mean—but suddenly there I was with kids again; in school, on dumb dates and that was rough. See, I had everything I felt for you, just humming there in the air before me but nowhere to land. Then Luther showed. He's not mean, Blue. He's just been pressed to where he barely can breathe clean air."

My mind was begging not to move past that, and it took a broad jump. I heard myself say "Tell me please that you're not pregnant."

It didn't faze her. "I wouldn't know that this soon, would I?"

I tried to think about time—how long since Matt saw Luther downtown that first night, since Rita asked me to get him a job, how long since Luna's first night out here? By then though, all I seemed sure of was *She's right. You caused this. Help this girl.* I said "Luna, you're a decent soul. You helped Bob Barefoot end his pain. You sing like angels at the top of their stride. I've hurt you bad and I'm deeply sorry. I don't know how—I'm blind here tonight—but Bob has left me all he had. It's a nice piece of money, and I'll find my way to help you someway—maybe send you to college or a real music school."

"Not a red cent, no. That'd make me a whore."

Blind as I was from grief for Bob, anger at Myra, the sight of this girl and whatever else, I hadn't foreseen I might offend her one more time. I said "I'm sorry as I can be. Tell me one thing I can do to help."

"You can hold me, if that won't shame you."

I honestly think she meant just that—*Hold me a minute to ease my ache.*

I hope you'll understand that I went, and she stood to meet me. I circled the cot and folded her in where now she felt so different from back in the spring and summer. By August her skin had outmatched mine; today she seemed no bigger to hold than Mattie Calhoun. She even seemed no more of a mystery—*Show this child she'll change with time and run her own life.* And we stood there by the unshaded window a slow quiet time before I knew my body had started to shine deep down like a spark in hay. Full as I'd felt last night with Myra, I felt like now my feet were funnels draining all my strength and hope. My mind remembered how she'd fed me time and again—Luna, this same girl here and now. I leaned back, hoping her eyes would meet me.

They did, long instants, with no sign of blame.

In unison then like a chord that shakes the pit of your mind and seems like an answer to your last question, we sank on down to the bare striped mattress and started from where we'd quit that night in the mountain trailer. Every step of the way, for me anyhow, it felt like some benevolent hand was pouring blood back into my body—fresh blood ready to make me new, though I told myself *Just this one time here now, no more.*

FOURTEEN

THE DOCTOR'S WIFE had looked in twice to ask if she could fix me a Coke or coffee or even a "snacker"—her reindeer Christmas cookies would be done any minute. She looked a lot like my Aunt Daisy, dead for years—that soft and ready to help any way this side of the Law. But no, I told her, I was holding up. The second time as she was leaving, she said "Your daughter's a striking child." It was bound to happen early in our trip; and honest, I thought she meant young Mattie. It threw me for a temporary loop—*How on Earth does she know about Matt?* Then she went back to the kitchen so I followed her. "Is it safe if I take a five minute walk?"

Her mouth pursed up. "I can go ask the doc—"

"No ma'm, I'll just step out in the yard if you don't mind and take a deep breath."

She thought about it, then nodded. "Poor child—"

I didn't know if I was the child this time or Luna (I felt as worn as Grandfather Mountain), but I got out fast to stave off questions. Ten yards from the house by a huge fig tree was an iron table with a rusty chair. I slumped down in it, faced away from the house at a wall. Then I asked whatever was driving my life if I could stand and walk out now this minute—clean, for good? I'd leave every dollar I had under this seashell on the table. The doctor's wife would see it and guess who I meant it for. I'd leave the car keys, trot to the corner,

flag a ride to the highway and—just one more old tramp on the lam—
I'd follow my thumb wherever it led. If Luna lived—*Of course she'll
live*—she might even rest here overnight, then drive herself and the
car back home (she'd taken Driver's Ed. in school).

Just thinking it out was enough to stall me. It came to this—and
you're welcome to howl—I was too well brought up to leave a girl flat,
even if the baby was none of mine. I was too deep dyed a coward to
face my true deserts, which surely would leave me lone as a snake
behind some road sign, dead by New Year. I was too ashamed of my
weak soul to meet Luna now, take her back to the Mildew Motel,
help her pack and aim us both where we belonged—a capital city,
three states north. *Where somebody knows the sight of our faces and
may yet pardon Blue at least* (I thought Myra would take me back; I
thought it was more or less her business as a God fearing soul).

And being who I'd been forever, next I thought *Go phone Miss
Ashlyn and let her call it.* I still hadn't let Mother hear my voice since
we left Raleigh, though I'd stopped in Georgia and sent her a wire—
SOBER AND SAFE WILL CALL YOU SOON. CHECK ON MATT. YOUR LOVING
SON. "*Loving Son?*"—*Christ, spawn you a geek; you'll get better mile-
age.* Even so I was suddenly on my feet to walk back in and ask the
doctor's wife to lend me her phone, charges reversed. I took two steps
and looked at the door.

Behind the screen but plain in the shadow, Luna was standing,
trying to smile. It seemed like a squad of dwarves was behind her
milling and shoving. She raised one palm and held it towards me, an
Indian sign.

I had no idea what it meant, but I saw it was steady, so I moved on
in. When I got to the screen, the dwarves turned out to be the doctor
(five foot four), his stunted nurse and the wife of course. They met
me like the welcoming team—no laughs or cheers but cooing grunts
and limp handshakes. *Congratulations, you killed a kid but the mother
may last.* In money alone it had cost three hundred dollars, by check
(which the doctor confirmed by phoning my bank). And though that
put a scratch in the funds I'd finally get from Bob's estate, when Luna

opened the screen halfway and turned her cheek for me to brush with my dry lips, I said to myself *You don't feel it yet, but you're as happy as you've ever been.* Right off I made myself forget it, and then for some reason I thought of the time poor Bob and I went hunting that lost dog collar in the night and how we watched the moon as happy as if we'd never die but roam the world forever green. Even now this near the gruesome midget doctor, I guessed that meant I was happy again.

What had happened was—after we'd scattered Bob to the wind and tried to make up for it with skin—Luna and I went back to town and parted ways. You know I vowed not to touch her again. I even meant not to set eyes on her but by accident and then at a distance. And I managed better than you may think. I told myself it hadn't much mattered that Myra balked at standing beside me to scatter Bob. Maybe I'd asked too much of her. I drove Mattie up to Bob's that Sunday and let her lay down a wheat straw wreath she'd made in school. She propped it on Luna's red begonia that weirdly enough was still alive despite the frost (Matt said "I wish I'd brought that color").

You'll know I had to rassle my mind to stifle the brand new sights I'd stored on Bob's bare cot. Idle time on my feet in public was always the hard time for training my brain—my brain aimed to *wallow.* But of course the Christmas rush was starting, and I didn't have too many free hours. Not in the daytime anyhow. Nights could get a little hot and bothered, cold as it was. But then I'd take the family for rides to see the Christmas decorations. I'd work with the figures from Bob's estate and estimate what to do with the house—sell it quick, as was, or fix it up and sell it next spring or rent it out.

I'd sit at the kitchen table with Mattie and help her with the annual handmade Nativity scene she'd put together from colored paper, modeling clay and scraps of a shattered mirror she used for rays of light. I kept on thinking my mind would get its feeling back and start to hurt but it really didn't. At A.A. meetings I even mentioned how I was giving up one more craving, and all my fellow juicers would nod

We know—we're down in the pig shit with you. But I never broke down in public or private; so I started telling myself I was grown—a grown man, finished as any fine red oak floor in a brand new house all ready for traffic.

I was pretending to be just that, one Saturday evening in the midst of December, when Myra answered the phone upstairs and called down to say it was Mother for me. With the Christmas rush I'd neglected her. And before I even touched the receiver, I thought *You owe her better than this*. It even flashed across my mind to move us all into Bob's big house and fix up a downstairs apartment for Mother, come spring anyhow. But then I heard her masterly voice and knew she'd burn up Myra in a week.

She said "I trust you've had a prosperous week" (I hadn't told her about Bob's will).

I laughed. "Bingo! Sold the last harmonica east of the Rockies at noon today."

"Shoot, I was longing for one myself."

"Maybe it'll be in your stocking then."

"Santa lost my whereabouts centuries past." But her voice was young; I could hear the smile that tugged at her lips.

"Will you pardon me playing hookey here lately?"

"You know I do. I haven't needed to see you though." She still would talk about *seeing* and *watching*, though I guessed her eyes were fading fast.

"I'll make it up to you by New Year at least."

"Tonight," she said.

"Ma'm?"

"I need to see you a minute tonight." I guess I stalled a second or two, so she said "Is that too much to ask?" She didn't generally tighten the screw unless it was urgent.

I asked if it had to do with her health.

"Not mine, no sir. But it's pressing or I wouldn't call you this late."

I told her I'd be with her posthaste.

*

Halfway there I knew what it was, and I guessed what I would try to do when I heard the news and went to Luna and she agreed. It didn't scare or even depress me, but it sure God made me feel important. Mattie's love for me, Bob letting me help him die in friendship and now this big load coming right at me—it was long years past since I'd been trusted to bear real weight. *You've never been trusted till these last weeks. You've been everybody's pet cripple with a cane.* Good as I felt by then all the same, I felt the danger barreling at me. And I sped up to meet it.

It was eight thirty sharp when I tapped on the door, but Miss Ashlyn was already in her robe. When I kissed her forehead, it felt too warm. I said "It's not flu season yet."

"It's not, no." Then she led the way to the kitchen.

On the table at my ancient place was a clean white napkin, a fork and spoon and a plate with slices of datenut bread, my boyhood favorite. As I sat she brought out the cold creamed cheese and poured my coffee, then stood to watch me take the first bite. Only when I groaned in pleasure did she sit too.

I took a few swallows, then said "Miss Ashlyn, your babe is all ears."

She of course didn't smile, but she said "I wish you *were* just ears."

"How's that?"

"I had a phone call tonight."

"From Rita Absher—"

"How did you know?" She seemed amazed.

"I didn't really."

She said "Is it yours?"

"Whoa—"

"Luna's child?"

That hadn't dawned on me. I held off, trying to figure the dates. *No way it's yours.* I said "No ma'm, most certainly not." But I wasn't about to forge ahead and mention Luther—I guessed Rita hadn't.

I was right that far. As Mother laid it carefully down, it turned out Rita had called this evening—in tears, to be sure—to build a bridge back onto me and ask if I could help her out by finding a way to "fix Luna up," which didn't mean a date.

At least Rita hadn't called me at home or stopped by the store, not to mention telling Myra again. So once Mother got to the end of her tale, I knew a serious question and asked it. "You think I'll ever get free and clear?"

"Of what?"

How to say it? "Christ, clear of my *life*. Everytime I think I've cleared the vines, they just grab onto my legs again."

I meant it in earnest but Mother smiled. "You never were much of a yardman, were you?" She reached and, just with her dry finger, drew a star on the back of my left hand, which was flat on the table. It was how she thanked me years ago for little chores or to ease disappointments—"A star for your pains!" like a gold star in school.

To my complete surprise I sobbed. Sobs humped up in me, and I let them rise. Till then I'd thought I was flat homefree.

Mother stayed still but laid both hands on top of mine and waited me out. When I looked up finally and wiped my eyes, she said "Now finish your snack—that's next in your path" (she'd always told me to visualize my "path through life" and see which things came first or last in the underbrush).

The snack anyhow truly hit the spot, so then I could face Miss Ashlyn and say "You telling me I owe her this?"

"Owe Rita?"

"The girl, the *girl*—though I'm not the cause."

"The girl's name, son, is Luna—Luna Jane."

I'd never heard her middle name. And hearing it in Miss Ashlyn's calm voice gave *Luna* a better sound in my mind—nobody I'd ever known named Jane would harm a fly. So I forced Mother onward—"Answer me please."

"Yes, son, you owe this child your help."

"I could get in trouble, fixing a baby" (it was still illegal in North Carolina and most of the world for decades more).

"You know anybody?"

"No, I don't." One of the wrongs I'd failed to buy, thanks no doubt to my one dead nut, was a kitchen abortion—the main way then, with a straight coathanger and a handful of cash.

Mother said "I've got the money here." I'd always known she kept money stashed in jars and crannies.

The thought of Miss Ashlyn funding this for Rita's girl—great God, I know I had to laugh. But then I made a real mistake. I told Mother briefly about Bob's will and finally said "So from now on—you'll be glad to hear—I won't be begging at your back door." Before it was out I heard how lowdown cheap it sounded, and I reached for her hand.

She was way too fine a woman to jerk it back and refuse. She let me take it and give it a squeeze, but then she said "You truly mean to slouch on through your life to the grave still hurting the very few people that love you?"

I knew it was true as the law of gravity. But I said "Am I truly loved by *few*?" I was trying to smile.

Mother knew right off. She nodded hard, took her hand back from me and held up two straight fingers in the air. "Two people exactly— three at most—from the *human* race."

She was utterly right. I knew I'd left warm bodies behind me years down the road to live or die the best they could. But I'd never quite whittled the list that slim, and the news fell on me. I heard myself take another wrong step. "I'm planning to fix up Bob's house and thinking we all should move out there and rescue the tribe—"

"*Tribe?* Come to your senses, Blue. What you and I, Myra and Madelyn constitute is not a tribe. It's four people trapped in rubber bands so rotten they'll snap the moment we lurch."

I thought she was wrong. *Son, you've tested the bands forever. They hold like steel.* "Is it truly that bad?"

"If Rita's girl has a child that shares your blood and grows up aimed at murder like his uncle, you won't even have God's love to count."

I said "You want me to sit down here with the calendar and prove to you it can't be mine?"

She said "I'd rather die tonight."

"Maybe you will. Maybe I ought to."

Mother said "You'd never have the nerve. Death'll take you, thrashing like a day old baby."

All I could think was *Run for it. Breathe.*

Which is what I did as you know—*we* did—in two more days, Luna and I six hundred miles south, huddled around a baby smaller than any pet goldfish that I hadn't caused but meant to stop. You don't need or want to hear me lay it out in roadside detail. Of course I went from Miss Ashlyn's to Luna that Saturday night. She and Rita both were gentle but bruised. Rita gave me permission to take Luna riding for a private talk. You'll know we ended up off Ridge Road having each other, weeping to boot and making a final tidy plan that would free us to leave tomorrow night and have us back at our separate homes in two days maximum.

I honestly think we both believed that would be *it*, two days and back to our own lives—I know I did and I was cold sober. For reasons you can also guess by now, I told nobody about my part. First, I knew they'd never trust I wasn't involved in Luna's baby. Second, I couldn't believe anybody would truly care. That's a lie—I didn't give a hot goddamn. I was that hell bent on saving this girl I'd been the occasion of ruining again by trusting her brother with a house full of beds. I doubt I even thought of the *names* of people I was leaving behind. And I told myself when I was back I'd beg off sick for that day's work. Then Myra and Madelyn would watch me walk in free at least two days from now. After that we'd be set for long years of life.

So Luna and I left Raleigh at sunset, telling ourselves we'd drive to Winston or maybe Charlotte and find a helpful woman or a doctor. Back in college I'd heard plenty tales from boys who'd had to cross the tracks and ask no more than one or two people before they found the help they needed for whatever girl was crying in their car. But we were literally in sight of Winston when Luna recalled a Negro girl who'd worked at Harmony and ditched a child. All she knew was the girl's first name; but since it was something outlandish like Sophronia, she wanted us to push on to Boone and find her—there couldn't be two black Sophronias in town.

We actually found her by four in the morning. Sophronia didn't seem dazed at all and said she'd gone to her great aunt's in Spartanburg to fix her problem. She gave us plentiful baffling directions, hugged us both and said "Happy landing." But when we were back in the car and moving, Luna looked at her hands and slowly said "You'll think I'm crazy, but why don't we go on now southward and do what you were always hoping—Pensacola, sun and sand, just a day or two? With all those sailors' and pilots' girls, they're bound to have crooked doctors on hand."

It sounded crazy as a bat in your mouth; but her voice was serious and a little less sad than she'd been all night, though I checked her face and saw she was solemn as she needed to be. I guessed she'd gone to the breaking point and was on the far side temporarily—I knew she was strong. So from that instant I aimed us south and barely slowed but to eat and pee till we pulled up in panhandle Florida, one grim sight, where we did our miserable medical errand by surf and sand.

The evening after we left the doctor's, Luna was naturally low as the ground. Whenever I asked she'd say "Oh no, I'm feeling safe, just peaked a little." I felt as sorry for what she'd been through as if I caused it, which I partly had. And watching her fight to brace herself—not to cry, not to give in to grief for what she'd lost—I saw how hard she'd worked through the years to keep her hard luck from outright killing her in her tracks. By dark that night she'd had a short nap, and I knew she ought to eat a little something. But I couldn't persuade her to eat a morsel, and I knew it would be wrong to order room service and gorge in her presence. But truth to tell, I was hungry as I could remember being. I hope you understand how that's not extra proof that I've got no more feelings than barbed wire—recovering drunks in general eat like young hyenas, no matter how many years they're sober. So I stepped down to the lobby, got the moron bellhop to buy me a burger; then I sat out on the hood of my car and bolted it down.

Low as she was, still Luna couldn't sleep. After we'd watched TV till midnight, she asked if she could use the other twin bed for just this once. I turned down the spread and helped her undress, cool as a sister. When she'd washed and climbed in the covers—and I sat down on the edge to thank her for being so brave and sensible—she listened calmly. And when I stood to brush my teeth, she turned her face to the wall and said "You think you'd want me in your life any longer than these few days down here?"

I said "Oh darling—" but I couldn't think what words came next, not to mention what hope.

Luna said "You won't really get a fair sample of what I am, not sad like this and us on the run."

Here she was saying what, months ago, I'd have died to hear. Now all I could actually think was *Sleep—just let her* sleep. *Don't answer now, son.* But then I said what flooded my mind, too strong to hold. "Luna, I've got all the proof I need," and I thanked her for it. It felt that true and it felt built to last as long as me, which looked like forever from here tonight, strong as I felt. There in a muggy motel room the size of a crate, I felt as free as any Spaniard lost from his troop on the ancient heights of the Andes mountains but unafraid. We'd turn this whole thing to good somehow wherever we went, and no live humans would suffer an instant because of us.

Where we landed was Bob's old house in time for Christmas. We'd been away for six gray days—the whole panhandle was battleship gray and drizzling rain. I'd spent the best part of six hundred dollars, lost my job at Atkinson's Music and stunned again the three good women I'd vowed to guard. You'll likely say you don't believe I went through with it, or else you'll now consign my soul to the hottest Hell if you haven't already. I won't attempt to stop your judgment, assuming you think you've earned the right to judge a flea much less a human who may be careless but never draws blood.

Still if you find yourself in trouble accepting the facts—what I did and the way I did it—then read the daily paper closer or watch those daytime TV shows where men and women confess the best and worst they've done from cheats and lies to beating their own blood children to pulp. It curls *my* hair; I won't speak for yours. And that's not asking for easy pardon because a good deal of the human race is common as germs. It *is* to claim, with all jets blazing, that anything you can't believe about anybody can *happen*—believe it—and in your home on your new kitchen counter in daylight if not black night.

Excuse my steam there. It built too high and is not meant for you.

When we got to Bob's it was near dawn Saturday. Luna was still understandably sad and deeply exhausted, so she climbed straight upstairs to rest. But though I hadn't shut an eye for more than a day, I understood I wouldn't sleep again, if ever, till after dark. It's actually cheating to say I felt any doubts or qualms. I didn't. Even once they're sober, drunks like me—and a slew of drunk women—can tell themselves outrageous tales of glorious dreams just up the road round this next bend. I've even got to where I felt like any minute my fingers would sprout green leaves and flowers to cheer the world, in a manner of speaking.

Anyhow once Luna was fast asleep in Miss Gin's tall four poster bed, I made some coffee, waited for sunup and then called Mother. I still hadn't called her since my wire, so I was ready for a frosty welcome.

But no, she was mild. And once she knew I'd accomplished the errand and was safe nearby, she sounded ready to start her day—no questions about my job, my family, my general plans.

I had to say "Mother, I'm not at home."

"You just said you were."

"I said I'm *back* but I'm out at the Barefoots'."

"Alone?"

"No, Luna's here resting. It's been a rough trip."

I thought I'd lost her, she took so long. "How long will her nap take, would you say?"

It was such a perfect sample of Mother, I almost laughed. But then I ignored it. "Did you call Mattie like I asked you to?"

"More than once."

"And she's all right?"

"Blue, you be the judge of that."

"Can I call her now?"

"You called me. Your finger still works—dial Mattie's number."

It was six fifteen. Matt and Myra would sleep till seven, then rush to confession. I might try then. So I signed Miss Ashlyn off by saying I'd try to see her this afternoon.

But she wouldn't quit. I'd broke her composure. She said "I have to refuse your offer. Don't come here now."

"You got the Christmas blues already?"

She said "Son, Christmas is not involved; but one Blue *is*—you well know that. You've spread your meanness one more time on me and all your loyal family."

"Mother, recall you asked for this? It was you that passed me the news on Luna."

"I know I did and I ought to be shot. Any fool should have known you'd get it wrong."

"Wrong how?"

"You know." Her voice was shrinking back like it did when she got cold. "You left here to do a hard short chore that needed doing. You stayed gone a week with no news but one wire to me. Your daughter could have been cut to bits in the city street—you couldn't have helped her. I could have died a thousand times. And now you're back in the absolute wrong place but close enough to open every wound you've made—*count* them, Bluford." She seemed to stop and I thought she'd finished. She hadn't. "Matt will probably see you if Myra lets her. But no, I'm giving you up for Christmas and as long thereafter as I can foresee."

Christmas. Christ, it was three days off. I didn't feel mad or seriously hurt. I felt historic, the way I did when I took my last drink. I'd been in the kitchen on Beechridge Road. It was way in the night, and Matt had waked up yelling just now in the grip of a dream. I'd been on the downward spin of a drunk for maybe ten days (they mostly ran their course in two weeks), and I headed downstairs to find my bottle—Myra had managed to stay asleep. I poured myself a shaky two ounces, then threw my miserable skull far back to slug it down and maybe sleep an hour.

But at that moment it dawned on me what Mattie had said as I tried to ease her back from her nightmare. She said "Sleep hurts me worse than light." And I finally stood and told myself I could either change that much at least or die in the effort or push my life on out of sight off a tall enough building or down a deep well. I poured my full shot down the drain, rinsed the glass, set the bottle in Myra's pantry. And then I saw myself through the eye of a first class camera hung in space—*This man's gone dry*. I thought it was true; and it turned out he had. He'd truly gone dry and it's lasted till now, half a lifetime later.

So here at Bob's in cold December with Mother's blistering breath at my ear, I heard myself take a similar step. "Oh Miss Ashlyn, Bluford's grown now. Blue goes his way." I tried to keep a smile in my voice.

But Mother said "Then don't ask me to watch you please."

That was Saturday morning. I waited till late Sunday afternoon, and then I drove to Beechridge Road. Myra's car was in the garage. But instead of walking in through the kitchen, I went around to the front and knocked—I owed both of them a chance to refuse me. They'd hung up a skimpy evergreen wreath with a big red bow. And in no time I heard steps coming, slow and firm, and thought they were Myra's.

Matt opened the door. I could see I'd waked her—her face was flushed and her cheeks were creased. Matt's naps were scarce and, though she was still in a dark church dress, I wondered if she might not be sick. She finally said "Hey" but held her ground.

"Merry Christmas."

"Not yet, no sir." Now her color had drained, and to me she looked frail.

"Sweetheart, are you sick?" I put out a hand to feel her forehead.

But she drew back and said "Yes sir."

"Don't stand here in the cold door then. Can I come in?"

"Suit yourself." She turned and headed away down the hall.

I stepped in. "Madelyn, come back here." When she finally looked I said "Let's sit in the living room."

She said "No thank you" and climbed the stairs. Even her back seemed under the weather.

So I tried to think if she'd ever refused like this before—*Surely not.*

But I kept quiet and she was halfway up when the kitchen door swung and Myra was here drying her hands. She didn't look shocked but she didn't speak.

And then I couldn't. I didn't fill up but I went blank.

So Myra said "What's this visit for?"

"Did Mother tell you where I went?"

"She tried to tell me *why* but—" Myra stopped.

"Mother was right. She knew the truth."

"Blue, I didn't marry your mother—I thought it was you, and you didn't give us the grace of a *word* when you stole off." She started to turn.

"Please let's sit and you hear me out."

"I've heard every one of your songs forever; they don't work now."

"You haven't heard this—I'm innocent this time." I thought I was; it was simple as that. I thought the fact that I hadn't laid a hand on Luna since right after we sowed Bob to the winds—I thought that kept me clean in this.

Innocence was never my old alibi. I'd seldom denied the truth to Myra, so this was something very new, and maybe it truly caught her off guard. She said "All right. I need to hear this" and moved towards the kitchen. When I got there she was already in her chair at the table.

I took Matt's place and first off said "You got any questions?" I meant it politely—*Don't tell her what she already knows.*

But she took it wrong. "*My* questions? Bluford, there's not but one—when are Madelyn and I moving out of this house?"

"Never. Of course not. What happened was this—a week ago Rita asked Miss Ashlyn to get me to help poor Luna out. The girl was pregnant with no known father. I hope you realize how I felt responsible for some at least of the trouble she was in—not the baby though. It was not *my* baby! I can swear that to you with utter conviction. But your whole religion says 'Help thy neighbor'; and since I was all the available help, I set out to drive Luna Absher to Charlotte. That plan didn't work—no help to be had—and we wound up in panhandle Florida before I found the help she needed. It's no pretty picture, I freely grant; but this time it's true. And now it's *over*."

I give Myra this among much else—she'd listened calmly. And when she spoke her voice was steady, no tears to sway me. "If the child wasn't yours, then tell me why you had any duty to stop it coming."

"I doubt you want me to spell this out."

"I don't, no sir—I want a billion more things first. But I've got the rest of my life to lead and Mattie to raise, so I think you'd better."

I'd never asked Luna one question about her pregnancy in all the miles. Nor Rita nor Luther. But now I had to say "My main thought was just this simple—I got Rita's Luther the job at Bob's, Luther called for his half sister Luna when Bob got bad, and that threw them together alone in grim surroundings. The rest just followed."

Myra shook her head gently. "Wrong, wrong."

I raised my hand to swear sincerely. "It was *not* me."

"I hope not," she said. "But there wasn't time—from out at Bob's deathbed till now—for a baby to show up, much less die."

I truly hadn't counted through it, but I couldn't stop to do that now. Luther anyhow had been home since late August. Whatever the facts I knew one thing. "I haven't told you one single lie. I have not touched Luna. Whoever helped or forced her to bear it was some man you've never laid eyes on."

Like so many other Catholic laws, the ban on abortion was sacred to Myra but not to the point of human torture. And I'd known her long enough to think I felt a cloud lift gradually, not all the way. Whenever she couldn't think of words, she'd mostly study her hands intently—the backs of her palms and her short clean nails. The nails looked like they always had. The skin of her hands was as speckled now as a partridge egg. She picked at one spot till I had to reach and quietly stop her. Then she said "I'm just so numb, Blue—I'm scared I'm dead."

"You're who I've known these thousand years."

"And who are you?"

In those days people didn't just sit around and ask such questions. The idea that you might not *know* yourself, right down through the rind on your callused heels, was as foreign then as the fact that—just a few short years ago—there were more aborted fetuses in Washington D.C. than live births. But I went on anyhow and told what seemed like the simplest truth. "I'm everybody I've always been. Maybe that's the problem." I meant the way I shifted course, but even then I thought it was normal—slightly worse than normal for the man of the species but no cause for war.

Myra said "Are you hungry?"

I was but I thought that didn't come next. I said "I need to speak to Madelyn."

"You do," Myra said. "I hope you can."

I didn't try to think what that might mean. You've seen by now that, most of the years of Mattie's life, she and I'd liked each other's presence. Even when I'd be at my worst, sick and depressed in the bed for days—or back from a ten day vanishing act—Matt would grin to see me and dive right in to bring me up to date on her life. Till that one Sunday in late December '56, I don't recall she'd ever said a hard word to me, whatever I'd earned—none of those words that stand upright in your mind forever like shivering knives. Matt seemed to think the way I lived was natural as air, which included storms; and she never shamed me. So when I stood in her bedroom door, I thought we'd take up where we left off. I said "Tell me how the Christmas play went."

She was back lying down with a light blanket on her, and her eyes were on me a long quiet time. "How would I know?"

"Your eyes, your ears."

"I didn't go."

Since Myra hadn't mentioned it, I had to think Matt wasn't sick. But I didn't know better than to say "Why not?"

"I knew they'd laugh at me."

"Who would?"

"Everybody at school, nuns included."

Dim as it sounds I hadn't completely lost my mind. I just couldn't think the news of my trip had reached Cathedral School that fast. So I had to say "What have you done funny?"

Matt's face shut on me like a slammed car door. "Not me. *You*."

Hard as it hit I stepped on forward and sat on the edge of her bed. She slowly turned her whole self away and curled in tight.

I laid my hand on the blanket where her ankles were.

But she said "Don't."

Can you believe me if I say truly that her one word left me all but desperate, then and there? Drunks, old or new, don't have many secrets. They manage to spill their beans on schedule night after night—how hard they hate you, what scares them to death, how they wish you'd vanish (or just be there to use like a doll when they get ready to rub or strike you). But every drunk I've ever known—me included, as you understand—has got one secret he'll fight like a rabid pitbull to keep. *If the truth be told, which it finally is, we don't give a pickled goddamn on Earth for the harm we do. Any pain you feel in the wake of me is your tough luck. You likely deserve every tear you shed. Sit there and eat it. You'll get to like it. It may do you good.*

Those "you's" don't mean you at all, my darling; but they did apply, years back, to your mother. You also know I could watch my mother's bitter pain, my wife's and any other's including Luna Absher. But just this sight of Mattie wrenching herself away from my sight or touch was harder than I'd have ever guessed. It was years before I could understand how she stirred me deeper with every year she moved in closer on womanhood. But I still said "I'm back here, Madelyn. I'll be here right on through till *you* leave, God willing of course."

She said "You don't believe in God."

"That's really not true."

"If you did, you couldn't act this way."

"Mattie, believe me this minute now. I ask God to pardon me. I ask you too." I felt as certain as I ever had that something somewhere, buried in fate, heard me and nodded.

Matt took a long time, and she stayed turned away. But when she spoke her voice was utterly steady and strong. "I pardon you, sure. I have to do that. But I don't want to see your face."

"For how long please?"

"Forever."

"Please, no."

"Forever," she said.

That instant a tight and crucial nerve in my mind broke in two for good. I heard one part say *Fine. Now son, you're free as you were the day you were born. Go get the life they've all kept from you.* The other part said I could stay here and heal my own bad break and all I'd wrecked in Matt and Myra. *You can but should you? Won't it harm you worse?* I set my hand back on the spot where my young daughter's ankle had been, and I said "Are you saying you want me to go?"

"Forever."

I tried my hard goddamndest to obey her.

FIFTEEN

I T TOOK ME through that whole long winter to another spring. Through the rest of Christmas, I didn't try to get a new job. I lived off Bob and stayed at his place day and night, finishing up what Luther left—throwing away every scrap I could spare, painting the eight rooms, waxing the floors and letting the daylight shine where it hadn't for many long years. My friend Hobe from the stock room at Atkinson's lent me a hand some few weekends, but otherwise I just had Luna for help. And oh it was *help*.

Once we were back from Florida, and Matt had shut me out of Beechridge, Luna went back to Rita's long enough to get her clothes and school books and to tell her mother she'd stay with me till further notice since I'd been kinder to her already than anybody else in seventeen years—she'd turn seventeen in February. By then Rita had good reason to trust I kept her daughter's welfare at heart; and she stopped complaining, for the cold months at least. No sign of Luther's whereabouts except a postcard Rita got from Texarkana but with no address, that said

I'm moving still and fast. Will call you when I know any more.

So by the middle of January, Luna and I had made a life we could live by the day. We'd wake up early, she'd fix a real breakfast, I'd drive her to school, come back out and work on the house, then pick her up at four o'clock; and we'd spend one more evening together and then a long night, both peaceful as doves. She'd sometimes help me paint window frames; but mostly she'd cook a delicious supper, then start her homework in the dining room with me working round her—sorting Bob's books and thumbing through for bills and checks (I found four hundred dollars in cash and several antique checks I managed to get reissued). We'd watch the TV news at eleven, then climb upstairs to sleep once we had thanked ourselves for all we meant in each other's minds.

To my mind even this far after, Luna meant and still means a miracle—all the more so since you took to her and also found what a help she can be. In those slow months I didn't lay eyes on Myra or Mattie, though I mailed them checks. I saw Miss Ashlyn once a week and talked to her daily but otherwise saw no other woman I truly knew and very few men. Still if you want the truth, I know how to tell it—I never missed another soul from my past life. Luna Absher took up where she'd left off late in the summer, and she went nowhere but deeper on into every room of my head and heart. She fed every need I'd ever known. Fed it *daily*, I mean to tell you, with no leftover hunger to howl in dreams by night.

And didn't I try to thank her by the minute, the way I'd never thanked anyone else? I wasn't scared she'd vanish again. I didn't try to make long plans for us together till we both fell dead. But every part of me wanted that girl to know my feelings at every milepost, day or dark; and the feelings were keen and healthy as any I'd ever known. For maybe the first time except when I was a boy with mother, I'd find myself sending my whole mind out of my body to hunt through Luna's brain and heart and actually *learn* her, top to toe.

It got to where we could work in the same room a silent hour, and then I'd think *She's hungry or thirsty or needs to yawn,* and two seconds later she'd stretch her arms and yawn like a baby. In a world where men are constantly told that women are more mysterious than caves, I finally thought I'd understood one female creature. Better still, with her at Bob's I thought I'd finally reached one human I *wanted* to reach. Luna seemed to agree I had, and she reached back many times a day. At least she'd actually tell me I mattered in ways you hope to hear from the saints in ultimate Glory, not here on Earth.

One of the finest things that happened night after night—Luna would take a pause from her school books and say "Let's sing an old favorite here." I'd pick a tune from long ago or one of the idiot songs of the fifties—I never picked one she didn't know—and whether she played the harp or not, we'd start together on the words and tune. Then I'd have to stop when I ran out of words; but she'd keep on, which was really the point—watching her clean voice climb the air. It gave her the only practice she got towards that great life she still dreamed of. And of course it gave me a peaceful blameless joy every time, though for once I knew not to beg for more than she freely gave.

To be fair to her and not to lie, I have to say that I'd sometimes find her fast asleep on Bob's old couch with tears on her cheeks or standing at the sink gazing uphill and looking lost. I'd never ask her what was wrong. I'd take it upon myself right then to do her some kindness, even if only a little joke or a memory of something funny I'd seen in the war or childhood. Maybe fifteen times in all our weeks, one of us got rubbed wrong by the other—always about some piss ant thing that mattered not one gram of weight. But hard as I'd been on women before, and little as Luna had known about men, we mostly found ways to step back cool before we burned.

Except for one night in late February. By then I'd had a new job for a month—music sales again, two rungs down the ladder at Poole Music off Fayetteville Street (the stock was mostly electric organs, the weepy kind)—so I don't blame our pain on idleness. Nor tiredness either. When I stopped for Luna at Rita's that evening (she always walked on to Rita's after school), I felt really calm and ready to *glide*. She seemed fine too, though worried as always about geometry. It wasn't till we got indoors at Bob's, and I asked her to make some coffee, that the first break came. I plainly saw she was deep in her Spanish, but I asked her still like I lacked hands, and she got up right then to make it—instant coffee but it took her five minutes.

When she brought it to me and I said "Oooh, bitter," she stood in place and said "Oooh, *bitter?* You've got no idea what bitter is."

I said I thought I'd tasted my way through miles of gall. But then I smiled, which was my mistake.

Luna didn't weep or run upstairs—rare for her sex in those old days, she didn't have that kind of blackmail in her. She sat at the other end of the table and said "Here, *listen.*"

Young as she was, still I knew I was in for punishing news. But I braced to sit through it.

Her face was almost peaceful the whole way. She never flared her eyes as hot as I knew she could. She was not out to pain me. She just lit in—"You think you know me. Blue, you don't. You haven't so much as scratched the surface. What I told you last spring and summer was all I wanted you to think. I knew the whole truth would run you off." She paused to let that sink in us both.

So I just said "I don't plan to run, but maybe neither one of us needs more yet."

She said "*I* need it, it's choking me, you got to know everything, then you can choose."

Most of my life from early boyhood, people have trusted me to listen to their worst news. I guess it goes with the face I've got, open as a church door and seldom frowning (also the fact that, for some reason, my eyes blink less than normal eyes—I can watch you steady through the darkest confession you need to make). But that night with Luna, I barely kept myself in place. I guessed I'd hear about one or two boys using her body to help them grow. I might hear a few more facts about Luther and how far back he'd leaned on her, but that would be no big revelation. I thought I was way ahead of my time, thinking such childish touch didn't matter. I was way off course.

Luna said "You wouldn't think a girl less than five years old could take your body—take a grown man's dick—up into her womb. Would you, Blue?"

"No ma'm," I said and tried to hide the cringe that started deep down in me.

"Well, you'd be wrong. It'll hurt her bad, though she might not bleed. But oh she can take it if the man loves her up first and greases her skin."

Believe me here—I've already mentioned how, that far back in American life, we hardly knew such crimes existed outside our own shameful dreams or newspaper items with, again, that strange but accurate name: "carnal knowledge of a minor child." Like me, you might have known a school friend that told you such and such a woman or even a man had asked to see his private parts but nothing worse. And not till late in the 1970s did droves of people start telling their own bad memories or calling the Law on present offenders— child rape, child porn, wholesale violations of the trust of blood kin children in all kinds of homes.

To this day now I can *not* watch those TV pictures of battered children, bruised and torn—my eyes refuse. If you're even trying to understand me, you need to hear every syllable now. With all the toughness I've earned in life, I can *not* deal with actual cruelty to children's bodies; and I don't know where my weakness started— neither one of my parents laid a heavy hand on me in love or anger. It may just come from a full awareness of the harm I did to three young minds—Matt's and Luna's and yours years later. But being too gun shy to watch the subject doesn't slow me from wanting to *stop*, by any means, every single man or woman that strokes a child in longing or strikes it in anger.

So try to guess how fierce it was that winter night to hear such news from a face I loved like the hope of Heaven. I sat there trying to make us both dissolve and reappear with Luna's words gone and the deeds that caused them. I prayed that Luna had told me the worst—the harm was loose in the black night now and could sail away. She could ease on back, and we wouldn't have to mention the matter ever again. But when she took a deep breath to continue, I knew I couldn't leave or stop her.

She said "Exactly that much happened to me from four years old till shortly after my eighth birthday—the man that everybody said was my father, my mother's husband anyhow, whoever else he might have been till God struck him dead."

I thought again of Rita's own story that contradicted most of this, but of course I couldn't bring that up here. All I wanted was to reach and warm this hurt girl's hand, but I thought I knew better. I said "I understand it was hell. I trust he's burning wherever he is." I didn't mean that. I've spent enough time in Hell myself not to wish it on the vilest soul, though I do believe in stern detention for true offenders.

Luna thought a long time, then met my eyes. "You sure you're ready for the rest of this truth?"

I thought *Christ, no* but I said I'd hear whatever she needed.

She said "After maybe the first few months, I didn't hate it. What I mean to say is, to keep from losing *all* my mind, I told myself it made me special to one of the two grown people I knew. I told myself it amounted to love. He *said* it was love, time and again with his eyes stuck on me while he did it, slow. And even now I'll dream it sometimes and hear him say it over again—*Luney, Lune, you're all I love.* Then my eyes will open in the dark, and I tell myself he thought he meant it; it really was love from the man that helped to start my life. So how can I pray he's suffering now, when I know how—young and small as I was—I'd sometimes smile and try to help him ease it in?"

When she stopped talking the house felt thoroughly dangerous like the walls might buckle and smother us in. I still remember it was my first chance for absolute hate, pure blind refusal to *think* about mercy. I mentioned killing four German soldiers at distant range; I never hated a thing about them. But now on the spot at Bob's old table, I wanted to grind the whole male sex up and ram it on some no return rocket to the far rim of space.

If Luna saw how hard I took it, she couldn't let up. She said "You just know a little on Luther, the recent news."

I had to nod.

"You know he didn't use a pistol on me?" Before I could answer she pushed ahead. "You know that night you saw us in August downtown when Mattie yelled at Luther and he waved back? That minute then, I was happy as I'd ever been in my life—Luther was home and said he still loved me; and you all saw us, clean and proud of each other's company. See, ever since I was ten years old and Luther left, I'd let boys finger their way around. Some took it farther in broad daylight. And I liked to watch—just lie and watch their eyes get glassy and stuck on me to where they didn't know who they were but sure God knew where they meant to *go*." She stopped. By then her own eyes were scarey as any I'd seen outside the war or the worst drunk tank, and they held on me like I was either the cause or the rescue.

So I told her, if she meant to punish me for something, she'd gone way past a normal beating. But if she had some other purpose, I failed to see it. I said "Help me please or I'm asking you to quit."

It seemed to surprise her. "Oh Blue, I had to do it, see. And I'm not done yet—"

My hand went up of its own accord, and I told her—far as I was concerned—she was done for *good*. I wouldn't hear more. I even got to my unsteady feet.

She nearly smiled. "I guess I needed to see how soon you'd run off too."

"Well, it looks like you found out," I said.

She was still at the opposite end of the table, six feet off. But her whole right arm came up in the air and tried to reach towards me.

I thought *If she stands up and comes here now, I'll need to move.*

Then slowly her arm went back in place, but she said the worst I'd heard till then. "I liked it, Blue—" Her eyes were filling.

"Of course you did." I meant it gently by way of helping her pardon herself for whatever feeble part she blamed herself for playing in so much hell. The way I heard her, she'd said no more than a starved child says to the first crumb you throw it.

But when we turned in, way in the night (she'd studied late), Luna left the lamp on by our bed and asked me to watch her "do her best." I'm sad to say I told her "Sure" and lay there watching as long as I could till my skin all but boiled away, and I came hard as any pile driver in cold concrete. I'd been in the dark with German whores in 1944 when it seemed like they were trying to cancel all our mutual years of pain, plus their own shame at the same hot minute, with just their mouths. I knew one girl in Düsseldorf who worked the meanest streets in town where G.I.s went—she wouldn't take a penny; it was *sacrifice*. And through the years right here in Raleigh, I'd begged some women to stretch way past where they aimed to go. A few obeyed me to my long shame.

Yet till today—porn movies included—I've never watched any woman but Luna *work* to hide herself inside a man's body by force of will or else to lick his skin and bones from off the Earth. At the same time it felt fine as wine, it also felt as scarey as all she'd told me about her past. This child had been crushed—back when she hardly knew *No* was a word—and I wasn't helping her heal, far from it. I was feeding some blaze that I hadn't started but that well might gut her before she was grown. And several times through that whole night with her asleep, I'd wake and try to see her in starlight. More than once I asked myself, *Years from now, if she survives, will you be one more hurt in her story—one more blind set of hands and teeth?* And more than once I thought *I'll deserve the worst she can say.*

We never mentioned that again and never put ourselves through a night that punishing and somehow grand—oh nowhere near it, though we went on pleasing our skins like before (I know I pleased myself most times, and Luna gave no contrary sign). By early March with the weather still gray, we'd settled into a life that felt like normal business, the kind your mailman likely lives—perfect attendance at work and school, eating and sleeping, me still fixing up the house, occasional trips to see a movie (never at a place we'd run into Madelyn). We even drove to the Outer Banks on the only bright weekend for weeks. The beach was all but totally empty; we found a flimsy motel open and spent two days just strolling the sand and eating seafood—Luna loved shrimp and I never saw any woman welcome food the way she would when they brought on the shrimp, cooked any way.

For the time being now, you've heard the worst. I tried not to make it any more honest than it had to be so you could start knowing where you've come from and why you suffered what you did. The one other thing you need to know from that old time is, not even once in all those weeks—those times as private as any lifeboat—did Luna and I speak once of marriage, whatever we thought. Me, I'd moved on past my spring and summer wildness. I'd lie awake some nights and miss big parts of my life with Myra and Matt. I truly believed that Myra would fight divorce like a panther, though I could have got one if I'd been desperate. Many nights with Luna sleeping in my arms, I'd lie and miss Madelyn—her eyes that were so much like my mother's, way back in my boyhood, and the jokes Matt used to bring home from school like five dollar bills to cheer me up.

The bones of my skull would ache for just a glimpse of Matt's forehead and her auburn hair, not to mention her promise of growing straight and taking the wheel of her own life. And far more times than I'd have guessed, I wanted to watch Myra cross a room as dignified as a fine show horse and hot inside with all her faith that every step we took was watched and every move of our hands was seen by God in person and noted down pro or con in the Book of Justice. So frown if you will but that's the way I lived by the minute one whole dark winter—suiting myself and the one other soul I meant to suit in that strange time I knew would end, and long before death.

It ended at Easter, which was late that year—April 21st. I'd asked Luna if she'd like to take a trip to the mountains and see the dog-wood, maybe look up some friends she'd made at camp. But she turned the tables and asked for a favor. On the Thursday evening when we'd finished supper, she stood at the opposite end of the kitchen and said "Do this for me—" (she'd never stand near you at any such moment, no strokes or smiles).

I told her I'd try.

"Ask my mother out here this weekend. She's got all Saturday and Sunday off."

From where Rita worked (the old lady's house), she'd call up Luna every few days; and some nights they'd talk long after supper—the meals they'd fixed and who'd enjoyed them, something on TV they liked or didn't, clothes they'd seen and envied or hated. Young women now don't want a man to say it, but in those days that brand of background music at dark could ease a man's mind like Swedish massage. If they ever spoke a word about me, I didn't hear it. And if they mentioned Luther once, they spoke in a code I couldn't break. Rita even wrote occasional letters that Luna left out but I never read. And as I mentioned, Luna stopped by her mother's most days after school. Still I had to grant that Rita kept well out of our business. So what could I say but "All right. You ask her"?

We picked her up at four on Saturday. By then the days were lengthening out, and the air was warm. So Rita was wearing a short sleeve dress that showed her stocky mannish arms. Her luggage was just a shopping bag, but I insisted on carrying it, and that seemed to please her outlandishly. I had the feeling that Luna had warned her of what not to mention and how to act in general around me. Not that I planned to be hard to live with. As I said way back, I'd had a warm spot for Rita since she got canned from grammar school. Any crossed wires between us in the past year were perfectly understandable to me. Whatever kind of results she'd got in motherhood, it did seem Rita had tried at least and worn herself to a nub in the process. If she'd come up with a fugitive felon and a daughter living with a man her dad's age, up to his eyes in adultery, well, that was hardly worse than the average human deal in the years we're in now when having kids in the U.S.A. is at least as risky as Russian roulette with more than one bullet.

Of course Rita hadn't seen the house since before Bob died, and she and Luna spent at least an hour looking things over. I stayed outdoors raking the graves with the thought she'd want to visit Bob's ashes. But when they never came outside, I went back in. And there was Luna, starting supper and no sign of Rita. Turned out she'd stayed upstairs to nap, a luxury she seldom got. Luna seemed pleased just to know she was with us even one night. And she went great lengths to fix a supper her mother could eat (Rita claimed ulcers).

When she started serving it up near seven, I went to the head of the steps for Rita. She didn't answer my first call, so I walked to the shut door and gave one rap. No answer still. I called her name—nothing. So I turned the handle and tried to see in. You recall this brand of situation had hit me before with my own mother and others since. I've even suspected that my strange luck has thereby tried to tell me something I've yet to learn, though it could be a joke (I'm convinced fate jokes as often as not).

Anyhow that Easter a little spring light still crept through the blinds; and Rita was in her slip on the bed, facing the wall. I stepped back out and spoke her name loud. When she didn't budge I thought *Lord God, another woman's threatening to die on me here. This seals something.* I didn't ask what *seal* might mean; but the moment felt entirely important—a hairpin curve in all our lives, which it turned out to be. I thought I'd call downstairs for Luna. But then I knew *It's your place, son. Rita's your old friend. Step on in there and meet the news. Woman are dying* off *on you.*

I called again, then rocked her shoulder slow and easy. She was cool, not cold. I could nearly hear breathing, so I just kept on rocking slow.

And after a while Rita said my name without looking up.

I said "You've been in dreamland, sister."

Her hand came up and covered mine, though she still didn't look. "I have," she said, "and it's been rough."

"I was hoping you got the rest you've earned."

She finally looked and found my eyes, but it took her a minute to recognize me. Then she said "Old Blue, you were ever a friend."

"Absolutely forever. You feel like eating Luna's good supper?"

"Lord, has that child already cooked a meal? I told her to leave the kitchen to me—she can't melt lard."

"She can now."

Rita half nodded and almost smiled. But when she got up on her elbows, she said "I had this awful dream—she was killing you."

I had to ask "Who?"

"You know—my child."

"Not Luna—she's brought me nothing but sweetness."

Rita sat to the edge of the bed, still watching. She reached down to slip on her worn blue pumps. And when she stood to slip on her dress, she leaned out towards me and whispered "Blue, you got to help me."

I said "Say how."

Again she nodded. "Not yet, not quite."

She didn't tell me at supper either, and we were never alone after that—not Saturday night or Sunday morning. After we'd finished a big Sunday breakfast, with some Holy Joe on the background radio, Rita finally said she'd like to see Bob's resting place. I thought this might be her excuse to talk to me further (by now I halfway dreaded a talk), but Luna quietly walked out beside us. Rita shed an honest tear as I set down the Easter lily that Luna had asked me to buy. And when we all stood back in respect, Rita said "Won't it be the best thing, children?"

Luna didn't speak.

So I said "What?"

Right off, no warning, Rita went fervent as any snake handler. "—Soaking deep in the ground like this with your loved ones near."

I didn't know what Rita's faith might be, this year at least (Luna said her mother shifted churches so fast she'd about run out of brands to try). So I figured I better not answer her claim.

But Rita could take your silence for an answer and read it her way. I felt her watching my profile hard. "I hope your poor mother's got good help, not just some hired hand shoveling food at her."

I said that Mother still lived alone, was managing bravely and that I'd be seeing her later today—a grave mistake for the happiness I was so drunk on then.

*

After we'd taken a long loop ride round half the county with Rita pointing out house after house where she'd watched so and so perish at eighty six pounds without a tooth left but talking to Jesus there at the bed as real as a brother—after that and some more to eat back at Bob's, I had to say I was off to see Mother. And Rita jumped on the chance to join me (we'd thought she'd stay till Monday morning, but she claimed she couldn't sleep in the sticks—the wind in the pines was spooky and sad; she'd ride back with me, if I didn't mind). That left Luna out.

By Luna's own choice she'd never met Mother—Mother, I know, would have met her politely—so she said for us to ride on to town. She'd rest out here and start her homework.

Rita and I were within sight of the fork in the road where left was the way to Mother's place and right led to Raleigh. She suddenly said "I sure would love to see your mother. Haven't laid eyes on her since the fifth grade picnic. I might could help her—"

"Mother won't take help."

Rita said "She will or she'll drop dead soon on the lonesome floor."

I thought *Well, all right, take Rita with you. It might help everybody's future.* At the same time I was still feeling an ending, I saw a shaft break open on the future—me and Luna someway together, harmless for good and acceptable to all sides. It looked so fine from where I sat, I could barely drive for thinking ahead; but of course we got to Mother's safely.

For her own unstated reasons, Mother had recently lent me a key; so when Rita and I stepped into the hall, there she was in the parlor in sunshine reading the paper. She'd expected me in late afternoon. Now here I was a little early and hauling an unexpected guest. But as ever she was ready, this time in a new black linen dress. And she'd washed her hair, which was very nearly too white to watch—like her mind was radium burning slowly. She stood right up and smiled towards Rita, which meant she could see that far at least.

I said "Here's somebody you used to know."

Rita went to hug her; and while that was hardly Mother's style, she let herself be squeezed and kissed. And she kept on smiling as she asked us to sit.

I said it was too nice to sit indoors.

But Mother said "The light's too bright. I need to wait till the shade leaves come" (strong light swamped her vision now with the cataracts).

So we sat and muttered our pointless way through half an hour of easy memories, funny tales we'd shared or watched and deep regrets for the world's sick present. Mother truly seemed to enjoy us. But just as I was thinking *This worked*, she calmly said "Son, don't forget it's late in the month. I've laid all my bills out on my desk. If you'll just write the checks for me, I'll take Rita out and show her my garden" (her old Negro yardman had planted late, but a few things sprouted, and the deer had spared them).

It seemed untypical but then I figured the light was lower than when we arrived. I said "Please, neither one of you fall. All we need is a broken hip." Out they went and I sat down to write the checks— pittance sums for lights and phone, more for doctors and the most for groceries (trim as she was Miss Ashlyn cooked three full meals per day and ate them with relish, mostly alone). When I finished I noticed she'd left a small packet of letters face down on the desk.

They were tied with wool yarn and looked antique—*She's dug out something else of her dad's*. But when I picked them up, they were mine—letters I'd written to her from college in the Old Stone Age. I'd forgot that, though my dad was alive then and held my respect, they were all to Mother—few mentions of him. You know by now I'm not a man in love with his past, not unless it weighs on the present. Still I didn't resist a look. She'd set them in chronological order by the postmarks. And being me, contrary as always, I read the last first.

Dear Miss Ashlyn,

Brace your knees. Here comes a curve. As of two o'clock this afternoon, I am not a college man anymore. The Dean says I am entirely too burdened with baseball and girls to "do my duty to the Holy Ghost and humane learning." So I will oblige God and His books by clearing out and putting full time on girls hereafter. I guess baseball is finished for now since I don't plan to beg the bush leagues to hire me on as waterboy, though you might like me being in closer touch with drinks of water than I've been for some time.

Myra does not know about this yet. So if she speaks to you about me, just wait till I can soften the blow. She thought she had a future lawyer lined up for life and a likely convert. She and I both will be lucky if I stay out of jail and manage not to get expelled by the Presbyterian church to boot at the rate I'm going. Right now I cannot see two yards ahead but will be home in a day or so and will trust your guiding hand again.

Your truant,
Blue

Till that Easter Sunday I'd never asked myself whether fate had shipwrecked me that day in college, as opposed to numerous other bad days. But there in Mother's clean bright room, I told myself *It tried to kill you then and you let it. You can back up, starting now, and live.* I have no idea why I thought it now today of all times when I felt so richly happy with Luna despite her memories that I couldn't cancel. But I know I stayed at Miss Ashlyn's desk another few minutes scanning the letters and wondering where to seize my life and turn it right if this way was wrong. Before I'd retied the letters though, I understood it was much too late; and neither my brain nor heart was in it. *I'm a man way up to his ears in luck*, though again I felt like this bright Easter was somehow trying to shut me down. *To hell with it then*—I'd go find Mother and Rita, settle them, then get myself back near Luna Absher before sundown if the Sunday drivers agreed to spare my neck that far.

I was more than halfway down the hall before I saw Matt there at the window, and I know I thought *Not this. I can stand anything but this.*

She was in a remade version of the dress she'd worn last May Day; and she faced the road out front, not me.

My mind just quit, though I guess my feet kept moving on. *It's what you've known was coming all day.* And when I could think again, I told myself *Go back. You don't have to take this, son.*

But Matt was the one that turned, towards me. She looked a lifetime older than when I'd left her turned away on her bed before Christmas, and her eyes were nowhere near to smiling. Still she said "Happy Easter, Sky."

I was so knocked over that like a stunned fool I quietly sang two lines from the chorus of a hymn I'd taught her years back. She'd always loved its bumpy beat with Christ resurrecting like a jack in the box.

> *"Up from the grave He arose*
> *With a mighty triumph o'er His foes."*

I don't know what I thought that would do; but it didn't make Mattie smile, not then.

I came on down the rest of the hall and waited to see if she would move.

She kept her place at the window but facing me four yards away. It looked more like ten thousand miles.

I finally said "Is your mother here?"

"She brought me, yes sir." Matt pointed vaguely to the yard and the garden. Then it looked like she also wanted to bolt.

By then I knew I had to stop her. "I've missed you worse than you can know."

"No," she said, "I *didn't* know; and you sure picked a weird way to show it. It's felt like you didn't ever know me."

I wanted to say "My darling, no." But then I saw I had no right on Earth to call her anything but somebody else's loving child in a graceful dress. I said "You're looking finer by the day."

She said what much-loved children say often when you compliment them. She brushed her hair back off her forehead and said "I know." But you of all people know she was a genuine beauty; so even as tense as we both were, it didn't sound too proud or funny. She looked down to straighten the sash of her dress. It was still Mary blue; the crown of her head was darker still, deep walnut now. And Matt's whole life in this bright room was as unconceited as a tree in blossom.

Remember this still—I was a man who'd killed other men, though under orders in a worthwhile war. So I had full knowledge of the kind of spite that levels whole nations, but I took a long step towards this calm serious child and said "Don't hate me please anymore."

I saw her lose hold on her dignity an instant, but she seized it back and said the word "*Why?*"

Then I saw she'd come on purpose, or fate had brought her. I knew I'd waited a long time to tell her, but now I felt compelled to claim what felt dead true. I figured she was old enough to hear it. "Why?— because you're keeping me back."

She was brave enough to say "Back from where?"

"From you, where I ought to be this instant."

Matt nodded. "You ought to."

"Has Myra told you where I've been?"

"At Bob's, yes sir." I could see right off it was all she knew.

I needed to push through one more question—did she know about Luna?

But before I could ask, Mattie clasped her hands at her waist like a child about to recite a school poem. And what she said seemed memorized, "I want to ask you to come on back."

First I thought how with all her years of Christian training, she might have asked my pardon for driving me off that last grim December Sunday. But then the bigger part of my mind saw how she'd acted right both times—driving me off and calling me back. "Did your mother tell you to ask me now?"

Matt stopped me fast with both hands up. Then like a kid she suddenly bent to scratch her knee. "No, I told *her* to bring me out here."

"To see just me?" I could hardly believe that Myra had let her one child risk it. *Suppose they'd run into Luna or, worse, me drunk again.* And I had to wonder if Mother had somehow given the signal.

Matt nodded. "I came just to see you, Easter day. Or you mainly, yes sir."

"You knew I'd be here?"

"I guessed. Then I called Grandmother this morning."

So Madelyn Calhoun had canceled her old iron orders. And Myra Calhoun was out in the garden air this minute with my blind mother and Rita Absher. *Christ, won't Luna materialize any instant now? All these women have planned this out. And what if they have? They may be right.* It came down over me easy as that (and hard as a seizure). All day I'd heard that distant engine grinding hard to shift my gears. And as ever fate worked more engines than mine. So here I stood in a family place late in the day on a late warm Easter—some kind of axle in somebody's wheel or, truer maybe, trapped again in my old tracks. I felt calm though. More likely stunned. I thought *Don't say any more than you mean.* Then I said to Mattie "Can I step over there and hug you, you think?"

Matt actually waited to think it through. Then she looked out the back window onto the garden and pointed that way, firm this time. "Let's get outdoors." She brought up a hand to fan her face like it was hot in here, which it wasn't.

I said "All right" and we went on out Indian file.

The three women were moving towards us from deep in the garden with dark woods behind them. They were all in their best Easter clothes; but from where I was, it looked like all their hands were green right up to the wrist.

As they got closer I could see they each held heads of early lettuce, Mother's pride. I said "You look like the Three Rabbiteers."

And when nobody else spoke up, Myra said "We're three lucky girls, that's what—these sweet young greens."

All three of them faced each other and smiled.

A half hour later I stopped in front of Rita's house. She and I had said very little on the drive from Mother's; and no big thing had yet been broached, not to mention settled. Rita had her shopping bag of clothes between her feet with the lettuce on top. And soon as the car stopped, she reached for the door—"Blue, I *thank* you." She hadn't faced me.

Since I was braced all afternoon for somebody other than Mattie to spring, I'd fully expected Rita to fire some parting shot in our short time alone.

But now she even opened the door.

"Rita, sit. I'll play the gentlemen and help you out in a minute here. But first I need an answer from you."

When she looked her eyes were blared and shifty. "Blue, I don't know night from day. Don't ask me nothing." She gave a fake laugh.

"You know who set this whole day up."

"Sir?" Her eyes got worse by the second.

"—You announcing you'd go home early and asking to stop by Mother's place, then Matt and Myra turning up in time to meet us. Don't tell me that all fell from the sky with no human aid." As I spelled it out, I thought *You ought to be furious, son.* But I knew I wasn't.

Rita made a wide cross on her bosom. "Swear to God, I'm clean." Then she tried to prove it. "It's natural, Blue—your friends and family. Raleigh's not all that big a town. You're bound to see us."

"You haven't been calling around or visiting any of my close kin again?"

She said "I harmed you that last time, and I ask your pardon all over again. So no, I haven't said diddley, friend."

Her face had always been transparent. I still remember the day she walked into school, a Monday in mid October when God was young; and young as *I* was—twelve years old—I could read through Rita Bapp's weak eyes that she'd let some boy "go all the way" the night before: it showed through her pupils like a crow in the woods. And now again I saw she was telling the helpless truth. I reached across her, shut the door and said "Help me here."

"Every way I can—"

I said "My daughter wants me home."

"It's *your* home for sure."

"I know you think I've misused Luna."

Rita took my wrist in her strong grip. "No such of a thing. That was months ago. You've been better to Luna since than all the rest of the world she's met."

It came to me suddenly to spring it on Rita—when *had* her second husband died, and was Luna telling the actual truth? It was way too late. So I said "You think we belong together—Luna and I?"

"Far be it from me—"

"You think Luna loves, really loves, me now?"

"Blue, I've never known what Luna thinks, not one whole hour of her short life. She's deep and still as her poor dead daddy."

Oh here he comes. "I understand we'd have all been safer if he'd died sooner."

If I'd hit Rita with a cold iron pan on the flat of her face, she couldn't have looked any worse for the moment. When she finally got control of her mouth, she said "*I* still miss him round the clock."

I thought *Son, keep her from dodging now. Make her tell you all.* So I turned my wrist from out of her grip, then held her plump hand. "If God asked you to vote in this car now—vote whether I drive back out to Bob's and ask your child to marry me tonight or whether I bring her to school tomorrow and leave her duds on your front porch— what would you say?"

Just hearing the words had filled her eyes. Her free hand went up and smeared her cheeks. "I'll leave my key in the mailbox, hear? Set Luna's things back in her room on the left of the door. I kept it clean."

I still held her hand, so I bent over and brushed my lips on the palm. It was dry as sand, but it smelled like my mother's spring salad greens.

When I got to Bob's, the sky was black. But the house still showed no sign of light. If Luna was here and trying to study or fixing supper, how could she work? It chilled me to think of the chances—*She's already gone. She's in there now with Luther waiting to show me worse things than I've yet dreamed. She's killed herself.* Even last night I'd have been truly worried, but now I saw I had just two real choices before me. *Go in and face whatever you find. Or turn right now and go to your home.* I knew I still loved Luna Absher so strong I'd walk bucknaked through a snake cave, with bats on the walls, to watch her face in near pitch dark if no other way. I also knew my daughter had faced me after four mean months and opened the door I ought to walk through—wherever I needed or pined to go and with whoever near me.

I let myself in and fumbled in the dark till I found a flashlight on the hall table. I didn't call out but walked towards the dining room and looked round the best I could with dim batteries. Nothing but Bob's old stuff on the shelves and Luna's school books neat on the table. *Try the lamp; maybe the power's off.* No, it worked and when the lamp shined out through the room, I finally saw Luna back in a corner. I'd long since moved Bob's cot upstairs, but we'd kept his old leather couch down here to remind us of him and for catnaps.

She was stretched out there on her side with an afghan over most of her body and her eyes full open now on me.

"You sick?"

She shook her head.

"Rita wear you out?" Strange as it seems I still hadn't guessed the real shape of this day.

Luna sat up then and hugged her body like she was freezing. I'd taken a seat at the head of the table before she said "I'm just real scared."

"Of what?"

"Just you."

I said what I had to think was true. "I'm harmless, darling. Nobody above ground loves you any more than Blue."

She let me see she understood that. But then she said "I've done this big thing, and now you'll hate me."

"Not likely," I said, "but what 'big thing?' "

She couldn't believe I didn't know. "Me calling up Madelyn."

My mind split down the absolute middle and heat rushed in. "You called Matt when?"

"Last Thursday night."

"And told her what?"

"The plain truth—about you, not us."

I knew I ought to be foaming mad. You recall how this whole past year I'd dreaded Matt and Luna crossing paths and hurting each other worse than they already had. But hot as my mind was, I felt deep calm. "You planned this Easter then with Matt Calhoun—this whole weekend?" *It can't be true. It was too complicated.*

Luna's face was still pale and drawn. I saw she was still afraid of me and what I'd do. She had the guts though to say "Not *planned*, no sir, old Blue. But I told your daughter how much you needed to see her again."

"And Mattie being at Mother's just now when I was there with Rita—you didn't plan that?"

"You just saw Mattie?" Her surprise looked real.

"Matt and Myra both, an hour ago." My own eyes must have cooled by then.

So Luna managed the start of a smile. "And Matt said what?"

"She didn't mention you anyhow." That sounded stingy and I tried again. "Matt said I might need to come on home."

Whatever that did to Luna Absher's mind or body, I never knew. But I can swear it flushed out whole new rounds of beauty all over her face. In her old outgrown blue housecoat, she looked dignified as an Indian princess, that self possessed and suddenly that far gone from me forevermore.

My throat shut down. I thought all kinds of words and hopes, but I couldn't speak them.

Then Luna showed her bravery again. She said "You do—you've needed your home for a long time now. You need to leave this dark old house and get on home."

That freed me up to think about her, her own whereabouts from here on out. "My darling, where does that leave you?"

"A lot better off than where you found me. I can thank you for that." She stood and slowly folded the afghan.

"You can't leave now—"

She smiled again. "Oh Blue, I *can*."

At no one moment in my long life to that warm night did I ever feel so utterly lost and helpless and lonesome. I even tried to think of names, just simple names of friends and kin I could count on to save me drowning alone. Nothing, a blank. I was finally where I'd feared to be the whole ten days my ~~troopship~~ took to get to Europe—in the gray wide sea light-years from land and no ship near, no human to hear me. But I said "Please let me take you on to school tomorrow and then—"

Luna said "That's - fine - by - me."

Fine then. Fine. I spent maybe half a minute there, hearing my chest pound out so hard I thought any second I'd crash down dead by her feet on the floor. I didn't of course—you generally don't, like I already said. I somehow managed to say I was hungry, and in half an hour we both sat down and ate like humans starved for days in desert sand. And all the rest of that long last evening, we moved through our old natural steps and words like somehow, somewhy now, we hadn't just chosen—with both our pairs of eyes wide open—to end the life that I at least craved most on Earth in the time I'd had.

And way in the night when I had lain in the dark awake for maybe five hours, Luna turned towards me from her deep sleep and—with no more words than a tree can speak—she showed every piece of my mind and body how she also knew we were quitting *cold* a place and a dare at some new life that we could never try again, however long we lived or hoped or begged to return.

At the end I told her what I hadn't quite said for months, "I'll love you every minute I breathe."

She echoed Mattie from that afternoon and said "I know."

Stronger than ever before I thought *She's a* child, *Bluford. Don't balk her growth.*

But then she said "I'll see you too any time it's dark."

I knew she meant just in her mind—she'd see me in her memory some nights. And I knew I ought to say *No don't. Let my face go.* But all I did was draw her closer in again and hold her there while she slipped back into sleep and dreams till daylight broke.

So my darling,

Myra and Madelyn took me back the best they could. For weeks we moved around each other like children in the early grades of school, testing each other for meanness or trust. You can likely guess I was numb a long time—not pained or hungry but numb as the hand you've pressed beneath you a whole long night. Still I did my job at the store and slowly began to notice the rest of the human race (in my time alone with Luna, I'd pretty well watched nobody but her; and even now I don't regret it—one thing the world will do is *wait* till you get back, when you're young at least). I gradually settled Bob's estate, got two men to shingle the roof, install an oil furnace and finish the painting Luther began. Then I rented it out to a family of honest tree surgeons that had worked for Bob and treated it gently as if they didn't live there. The remains of Bob's money went into savings for Madelyn's college education; and I went on the way I'd gone all my sober life that stretched by the day. Or so it might have looked to the world. What *I* knew was, the absolute core of my spine had snapped like a stick when I left Luna by her mother's house on Easter Monday.

And Luna? Oh I saw Luna Absher before my eyes all day and night for a long time there. I truly seldom missed her body or things like the smell of her hair in the dark. I guess I'd learned those facts so well, and stored them so deep, I almost never felt the panic you feel for a soul you've lost eternally—on Earth anyhow. But I missed the songs she'd sing in the evening, I missed the way her eyes could last through all you'd give her and still not blink, I bitterly missed some further chance at giving her back the life her family tore away before she held it—a life I thought I'd done the last damage to.

But I never tried to see her again. I never drove past Rita's corner or past Broughton High School at quitting time. Whatever power had let me walk away from liquor and drugs on a given day, that same strength let me draw another line in the dirt and stand behind it till here tonight all but thirty years later. Raleigh was no metropolis then, and I kept thinking that she and I were bound to meet on the street someday. All I hoped was, Luna would be entirely alone or just with her mother—no strange man please, no musical group with her the main singer.

But I never saw so much as poor Rita, not to mention Luther or the doughnut hood or even Luna's name in the paper, though I didn't trust myself to read the list of commencing seniors the June I guessed she'd graduate. And I never heard a trace of news about where time had led her to go. It couldn't have been to the heights of musical fame and fortune, or a town as small as Raleigh then would have made a big noise and staged a parade. I should have known it from World War II—that the ground can open, swallow dear souls and leave no trace—but I'd mostly been a small city boy and used to knowing my townsmen by name (or their looks at least—till the 1960s I seldom saw a face on the streets I didn't recognize as familiar). So it took me years to believe I'd never see Luna again, even that splendid crown of hair across the street and maybe her husband and normal kids.

Where time led *me* was side by side with Myra and Madelyn on down the years. You'll need long stretches of time yourself to comprehend how strange it was but utterly natural that Myra and I lived better in harness those last nine years than ever before. Not that we set any records for bliss or earned any medals from God or man. But give or take a sulk or tear, we made it through in dignified fashion till Madelyn also finished high school and started Woman's College in

Greensboro. And once her mother and I realized she was not just gone till Thanksgiving weekend but actually gone for the rest of time, barring short glimpses, we slowly settled in a whole new ease we'd never known, a laid back trust.

By the second year Mattie was gone, Myra and I were doing things I'd never thought could hold my mind—planting bushes to replace shrubs of Mother's that died from age or ice, stripping the paint off two cherry washstands Myra found at a country auction, walking to Five Points mild spring evenings to watch a rerun from our young years (Jean Harlow or Fred Astaire or Gary Cooper's early face, that Myra thought was the finest sight this side of the Pope). Then I tried to give her my full strength in the last hard weeks of her own mother's life—your maternal great grandmother, who'd moved to Kentucky and that you never saw.

And Myra changed in ways I'd long hoped for. She'd never been a steady complainer or one of those female district attorneys that shakes you down every night of the week for the smallest facts of your tame day. But once she saw I was truly *back*, she slowly relaxed to where we'd spend whole weeks close side by side and never ask each other for anything more than salt or pepper at the supper table—that restful, not bored. And Myra said much the same about me.

So by the time Matt finished college and left to work in Washington D.C., my wife and I made as good a pair as men and women manage to make when the time arrives to bank your grates and burn on low if you burn at all. I hadn't turned into a whitewashed monk in a New York minute—my mind could still rear back on me at awful times and threaten to strike the nearest soul or say *Son, clear your ass on out. You're dying here like a milkfed gelding.* But I'd grit down on my back teeth or go to an A.A. meeting that night and hear the worse off drunks moan on about the pageant of their miserable souls; and soon I'd have my one horse wagon back in the road, clocking the miles.

And clock them we did, Myra and I, till she woke me up cold one dawn in January 1966. She didn't speak but her eyes stayed on me while she led my hand to her left breast and a birdegg knot, hard and dug in deep. She'd known about it more than a month but had kept it from herself and me till that dim morning when it bore in on her that I would suffer if she left first, so I had to know. The moment I felt it slipping tight between my fingers, my mind said *Dead* and was dead on right. From that day onward it flung out roots and burned up high and ate her to the mortal ground in agony with no minute's pause in nine quick months like one last baby sheltered and fed. Among the several amends fate owes you is a huge return for hiding your grandmother out of your sight years before you came. She'd have lived for you, she'd have got young again to follow you and teach you strength, and you'd have prized her before you could talk.

When Myra was gone and I was there on Beachridge alone, I wondered if I might stagger again—turn to drink or pills or self neglect to hustle me to my own grave. But then Miss Ashlyn needed me, or so I let myself believe. After she had her cataracts out in 1958 and got new glasses, she held her own against the loss of much more vision. In spite of having to hold her book to left or right, not just in her lap, she managed to read right on through the years and to keep a clean house with no great help, not indoors at least.

Of course she had to give up driving, darning my socks and trying to shoot the fiendish squirrels at her bird feeder with my dad's pistol; but TV helped her pass more time than I'd have guessed. She mainly loved the news programs, the male comedians—Gleason, Skelton, Ernie Kovacs—and any glimpse of an ancient movie was sure to keep her up till three, purring deep and phoning me maybe once or twice to see if I was watching too, and didn't I think the world was better in black and white than anything since, and did I feel like driving out then and there to finish an icebox chocolate pie she'd made that evening?

When Myra was in her final days at Rex Hospital, if I didn't sleep in a chair in her room, I'd give the nurses Mother's number and drive out there to lie in my old boyhood room (I'd barely nap) and let Mother cook the kind of breakfast she always ate with no sign of harm—scrambled eggs as light as down, Canadian bacon, toasted biscuits, maybe cheese grits and hot apple sauce with endless cups of coffee strong as a lumberjack's. She'd lay it out and watch me eat it; and mostly before I'd head back in, she'd touch my hand or brush my shoulder and say a true word or two, always different, like "Son, this ends. Believe me, grief *ends*; and you'll be standing straight when it does."

In spite of all I watched, she was right. It got to where a woman strong as Myra Calhoun would need to howl through whole long hours. And that endless final night, when Matt had driven back to work, I halfway lay on the bed by Myra and held her close as I could bear (by then the cancer smell was rank as burning sulfur). More times than one she'd find my eyes and stare deep in me, wild as any horse in flames, and say some terrible version of this—"You could stop this, Bluford, by raising your hand; but I know you won't."

She meant her pain; I could stop her pain. I'd raise my hand and hold it before her, so she could see how weak I was, till she clamped her eyes and drifted off—at least it seemed to help her drown for a few hot minutes in the horse size morphine shots they gave her, not often enough. But I never told her my deepest thought—*I caused every volt of what's frying you; and it's way too late for me to quit now, girl.* From there till she breathed her dreadful last, I called her *girl* in every thought, which was how I saw her—so thin and young.

I lived at Mother's some months after that. And slowly we worked ourselves partway from the here and now, with both of us stunned, back towards the early ease we'd made for one another—just simple ease in the way we'd cross a room to meet or the way we'd tend each other at the table, checking each other's plates for need. I might have gone on that way for good till one of us died too. But once spring got itself underway, and I had set her tomato plants, Miss Ashlyn called me in one night after she'd gone to bed. She asked me to sit at her straight desk chair, and then she said "I'm running you off." When I looked puzzled she said "A week's notice—then you go live your own new life."

*

It didn't feel new. A long month after Myra's funeral, old Mr. Atkinson called me one night, expressed his regrets and said he'd like to give me my job back at good pay. Bob Barefoot's money had mostly gone for Matt's college years and a cancer death, and I'd made very little progress where I was at Poole Music, so I thanked my old boss and took his offer on the spot. It was not till way in the night that I woke and thought *Lord Jesus, I'll see Luna now.* I guess I figured she'd stroll in one day to buy harp string, and the prospect scared me through the first weeks back. But no, no Luna—nor Rita nor Luther nor any other messenger from that world I'd been so *live* in, years ago, though the memory still could flash up in me if I lay down and shut my eyes to say Luna's name in the stillness around me.

I just went on with my old selling, laughing with customers I'd been serving since they were children or former schoolmates that half recognized me and somehow knew I'd had a wild life and put others through it but was harmless enough to joke with in public. The women often knew about Myra and would hook my eyes—"Blue, how *are* you?" When I'd say fine, which was not a huge lie, they'd say "No *really*, Blue. It's rough, I know." Well sure, I had the odd grim dream. I got tired fast of warming canned suppers and the gruesome TV dinners of the time. But for the first stretch since my own war, I took a real interest in the world beyond me, which was mostly civil rights and Vietnam.

I don't claim any special credit from seeing well before Kennedy died that we'd do nothing but pour live boys into one vast murderous greenhouse if we chose to fight that far from home. We chose and fought; and that gave fate its postponed chance to notify us it had never forgot how, a century before, we U.S. citizens exterminated all but the last American Indian (every one of whom were migrant *Asians*, as we'd forgot). So numerous thousand boys and girls were blindly poured out till the debt was paid. Thank Christ, not one of them came from my family. With civil rights I have to admit that, in the early days of the uproar, I took an old fashioned though genteel view of black people—if they'd been in such hot torment for three hundred years, why in God's name had I never heard an honest moan from *one* black mouth—not from one that was standing anywhere near me, and I'd stood among them my whole life.

All they'd ever showed me was kindness, beautiful music and the strength to pulverize granite hills (with occasional grumbles at the heat and mosquitoes or somebody's dog that barked at the sight of any dark face as white dogs will). Then when the real demonstrations started—the fire and blood—at first I felt that all those feverish young marchers, with ranks of solemn old women behind them, were personally insulting the care that I and my family had tried to show in the narrow quarters we'd often shared with Negro people around us at work—and not just me but all my honest forebears behind me, to hear Miss Ashlyn tell it at least.

But when I'd watched the evening news for a good long while and kept on hearing young Reverend King with his gold tongue for bitter truth—still and again in the face of thug cops and Southern mayors my age and station but vicious as jackals—by then I'd slowly figured out what had truly gone down, what my kindly people had stood and *let* go down down down for endless ages, thinking they were kind when the plain fact was this—very few white trash in hoods and robes had done much worse in the eyes of fate than me, my mother, my dad and wife with our full white hands limp at our sides. And anyone of us that called himself "Christian" ought to find sackcloth and ashes quick, or better still, a fireproof vest for Judgment Day.

It was even a young black woman and child that brought my sad mind back to life when Myra had been gone fourteen months. To be sure, several widows my age had brought me frequent covered dishes with baldfaced offers of steady service. But not one of them had rubbed so much as a cell of my brain. My own body rose and fell as normal for a man near fifty; and I dug out a fact I'd mislaid in college—I could handle most of my dumb body's needs, no outside help. But after those last nights with Myra, the cancer stench and the dreadful skin that shrank on her bones, I couldn't make myself want to touch another woman in more than pity—not for years to come.

Then that next fall one Friday noon, a tall brown woman came up to me in the store and said "My son won't give me a moment's peace."

It shot through my head for no known cause, so I said it—"He wants a flute to play."

And she broke into a smile so fine it brought me to tears, though I think I hid them, even from her big beautiful eyes that held right on me. It was truly a flute her son had requested for his birthday that coming Sunday. And the young woman's voice was so consoling to my old wound that I hauled off and gave her my best discount, though flutes were selling like discount gold by then (the late sixties) to flower children and homemade Hindus. I also somehow managed to speak of my loss and how I was hoping to snooze through Christmas. The woman listened, nodded politely but said very little till I gift-wrapped the flute and handed it over. Then before she left she showed me a picture of the boy. He was ten years old and had her eyes. They were trained on the camera in a wide grin, innocent as any pup. And before I handed the picture back, I finally had to wipe my eyes and tell his mother that, yes, I was all right—just impressed (once Myra was gone I never shed another tear in grief but only for joy, which is still the case).

In under a week I drove to her house in Chavis Heights, invited to supper with her and the boy. I'd knocked at the door and donned my smile before it fell in on me like bricks—I'd never entered a black household to eat their food at their own table. Close as I'd been to various black men and women since birth, as many thousand meals as I'd eaten from their skilled hands, I surely felt no physical qualm. What I felt was what till then I hadn't felt that often in life—blistering shame. Not shame for any special wrong and, God knew, not for harmful thoughts against this woman that I still called by her full name—Dr. Sandra Bedford, Ph.D., of Shaw University, a history teacher.

It had been her upright smiling kindness that caught my mind, that and the fact of her stylish dress and beautiful speech and me never selling a flute to any black person before. Then four weeks later she'd called the store and asked to speak to that "well set up gentleman in the camel's hair sportcoat." I hadn't heard the old expression "well set up" since my childhood, but nobody'd seen me in that light since long before Myra got too sick to watch me—nobody I could care about knowing. So I went to the phone with an open heart.

It was Dr. Bedford politely asking me to visit soon and hear young Wilkins play a tune. I couldn't have been any more surprised, and in my confusion I must have stumbled. She quickly said "I'm sorry—I've embarrassed you." By then I'd got my breath and managed to say I'd be pleased and what about tomorrow evening? She said she forgot it would need to be evening; but certainly, why not come for supper?

So there I was and after a slow first fifteen minutes, I started feeling useful again—in the world, I mean. In *touch* with somebody, mentally speaking. The boy Wilkins was in a new blazer, and he looked a lot like his handsome mother (no father in sight). When I'd got his confidence by giving him two first books of flute music, he calmly went and stood by the window and played straight through "O Holy Night" without a flaw, then made a formal bow to the room. It was early December and I'd been selling Christmas presents for several weeks, but this was the first time I'd done more than dread the actual day itself.

Mattie had phoned me shortly before and asked me frankly if I could get through the time without her—she honestly felt like home might kill her this near Myra's death. It was so entirely unlike her nature that I knew she was earnest. And once I knew she wasn't sick too, I said that of course I understood—I'd be with Miss Ashlyn anyhow. But the thought of the day kept bearing down. And I'd asked Mother if we could just forget the season, to which she said "No way on Earth but we'll do our best." And now this near a bright young child, I thought I saw a path out.

After a bountiful old time supper, when Wilkins stood to do his homework, I heard myself say "Son, on Christmas Day how about you and I go hunting in the country?" I hadn't fired a gun in years, and hunting had never been my line, but squirrels had got in Mother's attic and cut big holes in the weatherboard, so I'd been saying I'd thin them out.

Wilk glanced at his mother.

She said "Say thank you" and the boy obeyed.

I'd said my own thanks and headed home before I started to feel a strangeness take my chest. First, it hadn't yet dawned on me that I'd be forty seven, Christmas Eve. But that hit me too as I drove along, and I wondered if I was coming down with the flu or worse.

Turned out, no. What I was doing was coming back to normal life from way down deeper than I'd ever realized I was dead (or burned to the root by Myra's pain). And what I suddenly knew I wanted most of all, for the first time maybe in my whole life, was a child beside me on a regular basis. Some child that was young enough still to treat a man my age seriously. I also thought of a fresh sad question that you may not yet understand—*If Myra and I had had a son along-side Mattie, would I have let him see me dazed for all those years before I quit? Would a boy's clear eyes have shamed me sooner (me being a man)?*

Anyhow Christmas afternoon Wilkins and I went to thin out Mother's squirrel population. Of course the minute they heard us arrive, squirrels flew out of the attic, all directions. And I was loping around the yard for the next half hour popping off shots at chattering squirrels with Wilk behind me. The fact that I never hit—not one—somehow endeared me to the boy, though when I offered him the chance to shoot, he said "No thank you. I can't kill things." So I gave up and led us into Mother's kitchen for hot refreshments.

After he'd finished, Wilk came close behind my chair and whispered "Let's keep doing this." Till then he'd never actually smiled except in the picture his mother showed me. But when I said "By all means, let's," he couldn't refuse the powerful grin that took his face.

Even Miss Ashlyn saw it spread and broke out laughing.

So Wilk and Mother and I spent numerous times together all that winter and into late spring. If the weather was bad, we'd sit inside and talk or watch TV. Otherwise the boy and I would hunt through the woods for arrowheads, or we'd wade in the creek and do odd jobs on Mother's house or the shed out back. Sometimes Wilk would bring his flute and demonstrate how fast he was learning—it soothed Miss Ashlyn as much as me; I doubt he played more than three wrong notes in our presence ever, and he begged our pardon for every one by saying "I'm not a professional yet."

But mostly he seemed content to let me plan our visits. And they were as calm as broth in a bowl till early April when I took us all to Ringling Brothers Circus at the State Fairgrounds—Wilk, Miss Ashlyn and Wilk's mother Sandra. The boy sat by me and kept his usual dignity till near the end when the clowns played their ancient trick with a car. You know, a midget car drives in; and one by one three dozen clowns unload themselves and wave at the crowd. As the last clown slowly unfolded himself—he was eight feet tall in a black top hat—it finally got to Wilk's funny bone, and he set up a helpless laugh that lasted till everybody round us was helpless.

I could honestly tell myself *You've done completely right by one human being finally. You could quit tonight.* I meant I could quit my own life now in peace and vanish. So far as I know, for the first time ever in my grown life, I shut my eyes and thanked my fate. When I looked again the boy was watching nobody but me; and I thought *If it wouldn't land us all in endless meanness from the outside world, I'd beg your mother to take my hand tomorrow noon.*

Maybe Sandra picked it up someway in the air between us then and there—I never asked—but when I'd driven them both back home at nearly midnight, Wilk had gone straight to bed; and Sandra asked me to sit down a minute. Till then she knew very little about me except my job, that my wife was dead and that I had a grown daughter in Washington. Any man would have seen how fine she looked, how warm she sounded. And I was still young enough to feel her draw from yards away, though I'd strangled even the quickest thought of asking her to take me in.

So when we were there in the room alone, I suddenly thought *This is somehow the end.* I thought we'd got to a jumping off place. We'd all three been too kind to each other to risk going on. I don't mean to say Dr. Sandra Bedford was drawn to me in any way beyond friendship. But I was scared that if I kept on seeing Wilkins, I'd spread confusion to the point where none of us knew what to hope from the other.

And what she said was "You know where we've got to, don't you?"

I couldn't be sure of what she meant, but I nodded my head.

She said "I started it all, I know; and it breaks my heart."

I said "You're speaking of me and Wilk?"

She waited a long time. "Yes—say that at least for now."

"Wilk's brought me a whole new lease on life." I felt this whole broad life raft sinking, and I was fairly well panicked at the moment. I knew my care for both these people was utterly true, I couldn't see any way it would harm them, and I was scared I'd beg any instant. But though Sandra met my eyes straight on and said she was glad and that I'd helped Wilkins, I held myself in and started to think I could let them go. Just to have seen Wilk beaming tonight with all his clowns, and him eyeing me as the cause of it all—I suspected the boy had already turned my life on a path towards spring (the first spring for years), and I didn't feel up to pleading for more. I'd look elsewhere. I got to my feet and thanked his mother, and then I felt I ought to say "I've had no designs on you whatever—" She actually came on towards me through the room and took my two hands hard in hers. Then she said "I guess I'm the old timer here—me being a scholar of history. I guess I'm just two shades too dark to watch my boy love you like this."

It ought to have hurt me, but again I was calm. I thought it was maybe what I owed on the white man's mortgage (my dad had always called it that—"the white man's mortgage," by which he meant what we'd owe God eventually for slavery and all its remains). But if so, I knew I was paid in full. And when I'd bent and kissed Sandra's cheek, I told her to tell Wilk I'd moved north to live with my daughter, and then I left with fewer regrets than I've left most places in my life.

By the next Sunday morning I knew two more things. I missed the boy like a fresh lost leg. And in the past week, my skin had grown new nerves again and was telling me *Women* for the first real time in more than a year. You won't need to hear much more about that. Try to believe I meant to be decent; so when I called on one of the widows I mentioned before, I let her know I had no plans for more than mutual adult kindness after work—one on one, an hour at a time. And I always took us out to eat so as not to let her feel leaned on for more than I meant to ask or give. The woman was smarter than me by far (they've absolutely always been, even Rita Bapp); and she suggested we take short trips to worthwhile places in reach of Raleigh—Appomattox, Roanoke Island and Sir Walter Raleigh's Lost Colony, Heathen Valley in the Great Smoky mountains and Charleston (three long fine spring days down there).

It was Charleston that put the tin lid on it, on me and my hungry skin at least. We stayed in an old hotel that had been tuned up to high class taste; and when I woke up there the last morning and watched the ceiling fan spin slow, I heard my kind friend breathing beside me still asleep; and I felt my mind click firmly shut. It said *You get this lady home safe and thank her fully, then tend to your own needs hereout.* God knows where such an idea came from. I've mentioned that I was near fifty by then—a full head of hair and most parts working if called upon. With all the self centeredness of any old drunk, still I'd never thought of living alone. I guess I'd thought, once Myra was gone, I'd let life take its normal course and that some appropriate mate would appear. In her worst pain even, Myra had gripped my hand and said "I want you to find somebody to love you."

Now I didn't want it. Once I'd walked away from Wilkins with what he'd given me, I started finding that my life was *enough.* And what my life amounted to was days at the store, maybe two full evenings a week at Mother's, an A.A. meeting every ten days; and every few weeks a friend at the store would ask me to supper, or we'd go see a basketball game at N.C. State or to watch Little League with some of their kids (none of whom I was tempted to like). Then Mattie would fly home every few months for a good weekend; and I'd drive up there once a year at Eastertime, my lowest point. That was pretty much it; and it served me nicely, soul and body.

By then in America, and even Raleigh, there were several new brands of whore on the market. The outskirts of town had sprouted a ring of "All-Girl Staff Massage Lounges" and "Movie Mates for Tired Tomcats," and more than once my car nearly drifted off towards one, but then I'd think *You'll pay fifty dollars for something you've had far better and free. You don't need some poor country girl's hand to haul your happiest memories back,* and the car would drive on. My body had served its time in love and parenthood and hot-down rut for more than thirty years. It was thankful to all, but I guess it was *fed,* so it just wouldn't gorge for the sake of fullness.

And then you started drifting towards me. Not right away after I left Wilkins, but that next year your mother got married in Raleigh from the old cathedral, and I stood by to give her away (the closest I ever got to that altar). By then I'd all but learned to trust in my lone strength. But when I passed Madelyn's hand to a tall young man named Dane Kirkpatrick—and saw the utter faith in Matt's eyes, knowing she'd kept every promise she made so far in life—I wavered slightly and thought my knees might buckle and shame me. But I heard Miss Ashlyn plainly clear her throat behind me, so I thought about her and what she'd borne, and that got me through the swapping of rings and the rest of the day.

If you'll really think back through your life, you'll know I truly liked your father, even if he was from Pennsylvania. I'd known him almost as long as Matt had. She'd only met him a few weeks before my Easter visit the previous spring—she was working in the Pentagon then; and so was Captain Dane Kirkpatrick, in public relations—so while I was there, they showed me round the place together in the awful pit of the Vietnam years (Dane had served his year in the thick of the worst). They also took me to museums, restaurants and more than one church (they were shopping around for their family parish). Matt of course was relieved, finally knowing a Catholic she liked, and I could understand her feelings. She'd said to me the year before that every Catholic boy she dated was drunk at the time or well on his way to a soaked career. And while she didn't draw connections with me (her Protestant souse, dry for years), I sympathized with the sober hopes.

Dane and I had some good times together when Matt was busy. I recall a trip to the National Zoo which was when I first saw Dane with animals and realized how watchful he was of their least move and how the sight of his pale eyes *drew* on them like a prey or a master. He never acknowledged how rare it was; but he could barely stop by a cage before the creature zoomed in on him and sidled near—every ape in the place, the larger birds, a golden python and the female snow leopard, blue eyed as Dane (she struggled to reach his hand through glass like her lost mate). I started to tell him how gifted he was, but some child screamed, the leopard bolted; and I never got the chance again.

I'd also noticed how Dane would clamp his square jaws taut and how his light eyes went a shade lighter if I touched Matt or brought up our happy past together, but I put that down to normal envy of the people who knew your loved one first. And as much as any admiring father is able to like his daughter's suitor, I gave Dane the benefit of every doubt—from that beginning in '67 through nineteen years till after Mattie was at her worst, as you well know. And right to the awful end of his life, I doubt we passed a cross word between us (*powerful*, yes, but never cross)—Dane and me, a pair of men who maybe were way too much alike where it came to hunger.

When you were born, the best part of two years after the wedding, your parents were still in Washington, still doing well for all I knew. And once they sent me your first picture—not the very first, parboiled and purple, but one where you were an actual person six weeks old with eyes like saucers of the best old brandy I used to buy from a country bootlegger out near Cary—I got the idea to take Miss Ashlyn and drive up there for a personal meeting. When I called Mattie to get permission, at first I thought she sounded stunned and I backed off. But she spoke some muffled words to Dane; he yelled back and I thought they were mad. Then Dane took the phone and said "By all means, Pops—rush on up." I'd pretty well lost the urge by then, but I already had Miss Ashlyn primed, so up we drove.

And it went all right. Mother and I stayed at a motel nearby, and everybody acted like a well raised family. You've guessed by now I didn't expect to be bowled over by one more kid, even my own blood. The thing was though, you somehow set your heart on me. Even young as you were, across a whole room you'd pick my voice to listen to and my face to watch. Matt saw it at once, I could tell; but in the cause of family peace, it never got mentioned. Your dad was so busy court-ing Miss Ashlyn with tales of his family, and how they'd all known William Penn, that it took him awhile to see you'd somehow chosen me to love on sight. But I'll hand it to him—when he saw you grin-ning in my arms, he spoke right at you. "Sweet girl, you've made a safe choice."

Recalling it now I wonder if Dane didn't mean to sting me—*safe*. Safe was something men didn't long to be, not then in the death throes of Vietnam when hateful people of every color roamed the streets with guns and dope and two by fours to club young chil-dren's skulls to pulp and the country to dust, which they all but managed. And anyhow *safe* was the last thing I proved to be to Dane Kirkpatrick.

Miss Ashlyn loved you right away too. But she always needed time to show her deep affections. She was not one to fling herself at your feet, at least till you proved yourself trustworthy; and time was what she didn't have left. More than I can tell you now, I'm sad to think that you don't even remember her voice from our first visit, that was Mother's last. Her voice and mind were the things about her that never changed by one iota in the years I knew her till she took one seamless final breath and said "Oh Blue, I've enjoyed *my* life" and then lay back on the pillow and quit. It had been her heart—no long condition, just a sudden pain down her whole left arm one stormy afternoon in the fall. She had the time to call me at work and ask me to run out please if I could; she thought she might need to see her doctor.

By then in America doctors would no more make housecalls than treat you for free; so when I got there, she was fully dressed for a trip to town, though her face and eyes were more than half dead. Since she was seventy six years old and had often said she was ready to leave, I took it on myself to ask her whether she wanted to head for the doctor's or lie down here and rest awhile to see what happened.

She understood I was trying to simplify what might turn out to be her end, and she gave it more than an instant's thought. Then she met my eyes as straight as a spear. "You think you're strong enough to carry me to my bed?"

I had the trick back that most men have by the time they're past fifty; it crossed my mind to say "No ma'm," but I raised her up with the gentlest tug. And yes I managed to bear her lightness with no great effort back to the bed where she and my dad had started me (so she'd told me the previous month, her final news).

Her eyes never shut and every few minutes she'd tell me something I already knew—where her will was stored, how the waterheater was knocking at night and would soon explode if I didn't call a plumber, how she didn't want to be embalmed ("No chemicals please"). The only word of warning she gave was not to eat the chicken salad left in the icebox; it might be sour. Then as I said, she expressed her pleasure in the time she'd had and slipped on off with her old best grace.

Turned out she left a bigger estate than I'd ever guessed. I knew my dad had left her fixed with a tidy nestegg to see her through; but she had managed her funds so shrewdly, without ever seeming stingy or strapped, that I had my hands full again with somebody else's land and *things* and serious cash. It kept my mind from too much grief, sorting through her business affairs and getting the old house ready to sell. I asked myself if I didn't want to move out there and live in my old innocent tracks but No, I didn't. It was way too late to live alone in a country house that needed care daily, and even Madelyn said she'd never move back there to live, and I should do what I thought right. What I thought was, if I ever moved out of town I'd likely go to Bob Barefoot's, a sturdier house. For all its hard memories, it still felt like somewhere I could stand; and it feels that still as I write this line, with even more hope.

By the middle of winter I'd sold the homeplace to a Pakistani surgeon just moved to town; and I banked the money, thinking the principal would go to Matt when I died or sooner (though Dane was well paid). Then I finally had the time to start feeling sorry for myself. Mother was just a hole in the air, the courage I'd got from Wilkins had faded, I had enough money to quit daily work and do whatever I wanted on Earth, but I couldn't think of a thing to do that wouldn't roadhog on somebody else or bore me blind before a week ended. So how in hell was I going to wade through twenty to thirty odd years more of this?

None of the old codger makeshifts attracted me—fishing, collecting garish seashells, birdwatching or nailing yourself to a La-Z-Boy rocker and watching sports on television till the light erases your mind completely, and you and your popcorn are gone by dawn. I was too young to go to the Senior Center and jig round the dancefloor with spry old bone dry gals that would make you a pink ashtray in Arts and Crafts, then call you up in the dead of night a few days later to see was it broken yet and couldn't you use her newer model?—I hadn't smoked in twenty five years. And lately I was too restless to read, I couldn't concentrate on cards, I'd enjoyed golf in college but couldn't bear to hear what men my age talked about as they rounded the holes ("niggers" still, women's anatomy and how much they hoped such and such a liberal politician got shot before he bought his way to the White House).

A few more weeks then, and always after A.A. meetings, I was asking myself if I might now want to just start drinking. Not pills this time—they were too hard to get and would damp me down to where I might well shoot myself, which for Madelyn's sake I didn't intend.

I went so far as to buy me a pint one Friday evening—Jim Beam, my old standby. As I paid the clerk, a man in his sixties, I could see him searching my face for something. So I said "Yes sir, you know me. I used to shop here years ago before I knew better."

He never gave the slightest smile, but he counted my change a second time and said "Welcome back."

Strangely it thrilled me. I could already taste that safe old world of numb confusion opening for me, to take me back with all my ancient privileges restored—*me* and nobody else alive. I went on home, put a frozen chicken pie in the stove and poured three fingers of bourbon in a glass I'd bought after Myra died (it seemed important that she'd never touched it). I cut the bourbon with plain tap water, walked to the den, turned on the TV and sat to test myself against the news, thinking it would easily drive me to drink if my hand flinched. The news was sadder and funnier than usual. The sadness of course was American men being scythed right off at the ankles in Asia and not one goddamned sane reason for it, except a scared handful of leaders too blind to see how every road runs two clear ways—*in* and *out*.

The fun that evening was watching a family in coalmine Kentucky waiting for their soldier boy back from Nam. He'd called them from San Diego four days earlier, saying he'd put his thumb in the road and see them directly. And though they hadn't heard again, all fourteen sisters, brothers and toothless Ma had strung crepe paper from his bedroom window to every tree and shrub in the yard. A drop of rain would have dyed the county red, white and blue. The Yankee reporter, with one of those upper midwest accents that sounds like Kraft cheese trapped on your palate, asked his mother how long she planned to stay up waiting—she hadn't slept a wink since the call. And she said "That's the foolishest question ever asked on this land, son. Ain't you got *kin?*"

Next the sight of your clear eyes in that first picture Mattie sent me, a picture I'd framed long since and set on the TV—you reached out at me like the strongest hands I'd felt for years. Not begging, just reaching. I laughed, got up and poured the drink on that old rubber plant I hated so long (it of course thrived on it). Then I called you up—your mother at least—and asked her to visit me soon as she could with you in tow.

I'd almost never leaned on Matt, not since she got married. But now I was truly needy and shameless; and she said "Sky, that hits the spot. I'm worn out with this gray winter up here. Let me talk to Dane. If he says Yes, then we'll be down."

What it came to was, Dane hadn't yet told Matt he had to spend a month's duty in Germany, showing our H bombs to various senators itching to devastate the Earth. So down you and Madelyn came to stay three weeks from the midst of February on into March. And that was when we *really* chose sides—you and I truly chose one another in a way I'd never known before, except in my own secret heart for my young mother, who never quite knew, I honestly think, though she loved me back the best she could with her cool eyes.

No doubt about you then—you *told* me in numerous ways, and I told you as steady as time. By then you were starting to jabber on and were well underway to being the person I know tonight—the one that's in you now at least, that I still hope to see again with clearer eyes. Most of all, like Dane Kirkpatrick, you were one strong watcher. Back when you couldn't even sit up, you'd find a thing on the ceiling to watch; and your eyes would track it for whole long minutes, solemn as owls, before you either sneezed or laughed. The laugh was your second most welcome trait. My whole life I've prized good laughers and have tried to keep at least one nearby, all times of the day. But nobody yet has equaled you—by breaking down the way you did in helpless chuckles, you showed me early you trusted the world. And when joy struck, you were ready to leave yourself at the mercy of the nearest hands (I worried sometimes that you trusted too much and weren't shy *enough*). Even here lately when we've barely trusted our own tired selves, the fact you've managed to laugh occasionally—more and more lately—has done a great deal to see me through our mutual pain without giving up.

So by the time your dad was back from Germany and ready for his family near him, I'd built you into my mind so deep it almost choked me to think of you gone. I worked it out a hundred ways and all but asked Matt to leave you with me—I'd get a capable black woman I knew to live right with us and help us on into real spring at least, just a few weeks longer. Then I'd bring you north on my usual Easter cherry blossom trip. Honest to Christ, I almost asked her; and I know what stopped me—the thought that Dane Kirkpatrick had real blood claims that were stronger than mine (my first mistake about Dane and blood, and it just kept growing in depth down the years).

Still as we got to the night before you and Matt would fly north, she was standing at her own mother's sink, rinsing your bottle.

I came through the door and saw her shoulders—they looked forlorn, I knew that much—and I did what seemed the natural thing. I went up behind her and hugged her towards me. She didn't shy but leaned into me, and next I said "Oh Mattie Calhoun." Her old name just came naturally to me. And I thought I felt her tense a little, so I said "I'm sorry—Mattie *Kirkpatrick*."

Still turned away she shook her head against my chest and said "*Calhoun*—God, oh I *wish*." She let that sink in the room like a stone. Then she laughed and wiggled, and I dropped my arms. But I knew I wanted to take her words as the utter truth. And her smiling eyes never tried to stop me, then or ever again in the life that was left her.

Four years went by like a calm afternoon. However old you get to be, if you're watching a child in the midst of your life, time will at least not weigh on your hands. It's one of the secret things kids are for—processing time. I don't mean to say I went softminded and haunted the shopping malls showing your picture to bored strangers or bronzing your shoes. Again I had my music sales job; and because I felt too privileged maybe, I took to working in a rescue mission in old South Raleigh. The sum of public misery then in the late seventies was way less than now. But still I'd put in two nights a week making peanut butter sandwiches and talking to winos, outright lunatics, small time crooks, the occasional minor who'd seen more hell at age fifteen than me in all my reckless years and could do your mind a permanent hurt just with a sideways look from his eyes and then—by way of comic relief—the old time tramps that were far from desperate, just hungry for freedom and cold fresh air between their bodies and whatever wives and kids they'd ditched.

I got into that, believe it or not, from Father Scanlon at the Cathedral. He'd been a world of strength to Myra in her hard months; and he kept up with me through the years after, not pushing exactly but letting me know that the Catholic church had changed a lot since he first knew me and might well be "my ticket" now. I'd thank him, take his pamphlets and knickknacks and say I wasn't going anywhere yet; I'd even enjoy his Irish nun jokes. Still nothing I'd met with yet on Earth had nudged me back towards a church door, not for more than visiting hours. I was leaning on God—if one was there and listening—to count my slim handful of decencies. If they didn't satisfy my debits, then to hell with it all. *Let him fry me forever.*

I won't deny it—for the time and place, an independent widower that cooked a number of his own sparse meals (with just a cleaning woman one day a week) and showed no signs of being crazy or burying orphans' bodies in his crawlspace, once he'd gnawed their fingers to the bone, was scarce in my old part of the world. If I hadn't lived on Beechridge Road most of my life, I might have got even fishier looks from the neighbors than I did. And I won't try to make you believe that times didn't come when every pore of my body moaned at the midnight air like a creature gnawing its one good leg off to flee a steel trap. But then I'd ask myself again the same old questions, *What do you want? How the hell would you use it? You've had everything you ever needed. Be glad or thankful and serve your time.* Or something equally down, self pitying and dead-on honest. It always amazed me that here I was, alone as a lightning rod in a storm but still more or less upright and serving. *Serving who though, for what possible good and sufficient reason?*

Then you'd turn up and, not even knowing it, wind me back like a kite on a string. Swear to God, it almost always happened. Let me get truly low in the soul; and either that night or the next few days,

Mattie would call up to talk awhile, then put you on. And you'd be full of your headbent news, but you'd also have lots of questions about me (in fact, you were truly the only child I ever knew who took a real interest in the adults round you). Better yet, Matt would call and say she was driving down for two or three days with you in tow.

You'd pile out of the car at the end of a five hour drive and shine at me like an airport light, that strong and *aimed*. By now I had a box of toys in your own room, which had been Matt's before you; and you'd play with them, but the plain fact was you liked my company a good deal more. If I'd been sober in Matt's childhood, then later not so choked on guilt, she might have given me what you gave. But of course I wasn't in my right mind for most of her childhood, though she turned out better than those rare children with ideal parents (or the few I've known).

While Mattie went out shopping in the evening or visiting friends she'd known in school, you and I would read the same books over and over (reciting them blind). Or weekend afternoons we'd roam the yard making what you learned in kindergarten to call "nature tours," collecting leaves to press in scrapbooks or beetles in jars. And when Matt heard you say your prayers, I'd sit by the bed and watch you say them mainly to me. I can't remember what you'd ask for; but I do recall I'd always think of what I'd give you if I had half the power I wanted then—*Perfect safety, endless* joy. And for years to come it seemed you were safe. Nobody doubted you were evermore glad to be on Earth, wherever you'd come from.

Then Madelyn called one Friday night to say that Dane had been promoted and posted to Europe—near Stuttgart, Germany—to keep on currying official guests and other licensed crooks (Matt left it at "congressmen"). Dane felt it was his best chance by far and had said he'd stay for at least two years, so of course she and you would move over with him and set up house for however long. She managed to sound glad of Dane's luck and sorry to leave me all at once.

But it didn't exactly bowl me over. Dane had told me about his ambitions many a night after Matt turned in, so I'd expected that sort of news for some time now. And while I felt the ache begin before I could speak, I just asked her to come down with you one more time before you left.

That was when we went to Myrtle Beach—even Dane asked to go. So I rented a cottage for the last week in June; and the three of you flew straight down from D.C. Dane hadn't been south of Richmond in years, not since you were born; but he tucked in and enjoyed himself eating seafood three times a day at least. You were six by then and had learned how to share yourself among us so nobody felt left out or pressed. You'd also learned to stay by yourself; and sometimes when I was with you outdoors, you'd say "I'm going up there alone. You watch me from here in case I need you." Then you'd go dig in the sand half an hour. You could find prehistoric shark teeth by the bucket—none of us adults ever found one. I would catch Matt watching us both sometimes and smiling slightly. I knew she saw I was offering you what I couldn't give when she'd been needy, but she never showed a trace of resentment.

I did get to take you to Brookgreen Gardens alone one day to let your folks rest. And there in the shade of those huge live oaks, much older than time, we finally sat on a granite bench. And by yourself, no coaching from me, you looked at the ground and said "Well, Sky, my new life starts."

It sounded so ancient and wise, I laughed.

But you said "I don't like it a bit."

I said you'd like the world overseas, your mind would stretch, I might come to visit, you'd be back here in two years at least.

You wouldn't have it and you faced me finally. "You could keep me here at home with you." It's one of the tragic facts of my life—can you recall?—that I laid a hand on the crown of your head and said "Lyn, Sky's getting too old for you."

That was the summer of 1977. I was going on fifty seven, your mother was thirty four; and Dane was thirty six, I believe. I know we all sat out on the porch our last beach night and actually talked about our wish to freeze each other right where we were—no older, no wiser, no richer but *thus*: the way we were, glad and satisfied as people get to be. It was Madelyn that said it first; but all the rest of us agreed, one way or other in our own words. I still think we meant it, even your dad with his hot taste for the spotlit ring in the midst of all rooms. Your dad, my darling, was not born wrong. What happened to him, I all but *know*, was not because he was skewed inside. It was what time brought him with its worst hand, like it brought me you eventually through so much pain.

I've mentioned working at the rescue mission. Once the three of you were gone, I put in even more time down there—still spreading the peanut butter sandwiches, or bologna and mustard if some meat packer had made a donation, and hearing those men tell their own side of where they'd been, what they'd done and—more than half the time—what had been done *to* them. You could draw a line down the midst of the mission and put up two hand lettered signs, just *Doers* and *Doners*, and ask the men to choose their side (the *Doers* are always tougher, funnier and likely to last, though the *Doners* generally tell better tales—they've had to watch the world much closer to know where to run). In two minutes flat you'll know which ones are likely to live through the next hard freeze and which will die from blood so thinned with dollar wine that their thick skin will just dissolve at the touch of ice under some crate or railroad bridge.

It also made me understand, for the first time ever, a useful fact about myself. I'd got this far in working order because I'd mostly *done* my life, not had it done *for* me or *to* me, not often—or so I'd felt. But I don't mean that as personal praise. Up till now it has been my run of luck with the hands time deals me.

And that next winter with you far gone at Christmastime, I tried to keep my whole mind set on ways to prop those lonesome men through the worst of the short dark solstice days (they'll almost always tell you they dread the shortest day of the year much worse than ice storms six weeks down the road). The way they could always reach me was by meeting my eyes. A soul on the road won't generally meet you eye to eye—he tries to spare you his bitter news—but every few nights an exceptional man will nail his black eyes right to mine. Then as I sit there hot in the gaze of some gray codger or blistered kid, I'll sometimes feel my spine screw tight and my hair rise—*Is this somebody I've known before, and am I part of the blame for this?* Till that first Christmas you were gone, the answer had always been a firm No. I'd laugh and talk on.

But then December 23rd, the night before I turned fifty seven, I was there extra late on towards the time the dormitory closed and shut down the lights. I'd been with an elderly colored man from the Shenandoah Valley long years back; and as I watched his gentle features tell the tale of where he'd walked for most of his life—it was all on foot—and what he'd accomplished (four or five entire families), it slowly came to me that this strong soul had to be near ninety or else he was lying. And if he was ninety, well Lord, his parents had been born slaves and knew that curse in their own bodies. I was on the verge of finding a way to ask him if I'd guessed correctly when a heavy hand gripped my shoulder from behind and a deep voice said "Santy Claus, old friend."

The instant I looked I thought I knew him. But the name wouldn't come—I just felt like he was what he said, an old time friend in his own late forties, no serious harm to me or mine. So I put out a sincere hand.

He looked surprised, then set down the mug that was in his left hand and offered me that. "Long time, Mr. Blue—"

Strange strange—I still couldn't think who he might be. But then as I touched his hard left hand and realized he'd lost his right, something told my mind the truth. It was Luther Bapp, old Rita's son, gone these twenty years and missing a hand.

He asked the elderly black man's permission, then pulled up a chair and threw me a grin. "You down here looking for me again?"

I laughed. "No, Luther. You look too prosperous to be here at all." His clothes were neat, just wrinkled and mended along the sleeve. The strong face he'd had in his twenties was stronger still and leaner now. He'd stood beside me at his young full height.

He said "Warm thanks for the compliment. Years ago I promised myself I'd be as good a looker as you by age forty five—I've got a year left, but I doubt I'll make it." It was just malarkey; we both knew it. But before I could stretch the truth and say he looked young and well, he staved me off. "I'm just on my way through, bound to Tampa. Stopped in for the john and a cup of coffee."

That had to be some form of a lie, but he truly did look thoroughly traveled—streamlined in his bones. I still didn't feel any scare or ache; but I told myself *Don't ask about Luna. Let it come, if it comes.*

We talked half an hour; and it didn't come—not Luna nor Rita, nobody we'd known in common but Bob Barefoot and his last days. Luther had the clearest memories of Bob, and they all were kind. He even remembered I'd had a young daughter and asked after her. When I said she was grown with her own child and living in Europe, Luther said "Dear Europe—you seen it yet?"

I wondered if he'd been overseas somehow—the merchant navy— but I knew not to ask if I planned to go home alone, which I did. And I didn't mention my war experience but said I was hoping to see it this summer—Germany, the Rhineland at peace.

By then the black man had melted away; and when I said that last word *summer*, Luther flinched and snagged my eyes with his, like long meat hooks—that sharp and deep. Then tears poured from him in silence a minute.

His one hand was out between us on the table. I made a fist and tapped on his skin, the back of his hand.

He turned it over though and held out his palm. "You can *touch* me," he said. "You won't catch your death."

They'd warned us here in orientation not to touch anybody we could easily avoid—there might be germs, occasionally lice; and the homeless might not know how to handle a truly sympathetic gesture. The rule for touching seemed to be *If mercy requires.* So sure, I laid my palm on Luther's. "You got something you need to tell?"

First his head shook a definite No. But then he thumbed the tears away and got his voice back. "You mentioning summer was what threw me there—you hoping to see your people abroad. See, I'm hoping to just see *summer*."

I missed his point and agreed it was cold for this early on. But when

Luther held himself still before me, not blinking or budging, I suddenly saw behind his eyes right in through his mind. *This boy's dying.* I said "You seeing a good doctor, son?"

It seemed like *doctor* was a foreign word to him, and I suddenly knew he'd long since warned me not to call him *son.* But he let it go and waited a minute, then shook his head. "I'm guessing it's something I caught from Bob."

Now Bob had died twenty one years past, and I'd never heard leukemia was catching. It came to mind that Luther was asking for some of Bob's money, though nothing was left but rent from the house. So I didn't try to set him straight on cancer or money; I just said "Tell me what way I can help." As the words crossed between us, I thought *You've done it. They'll drown you again* (by *they* I meant his long lost family strewn behind him).

My hand had been flat on the table for some time. It was Luther's turn to touch me now—he tapped my thumbnail. "No way on Earth to help young Luther, but thank you for asking." He launched a wide grin, his one fist opened; and there was a small rock, a flint arrowhead—somehow I knew it and leaned to see.

But Luther laid it right before me. "Merry Christmas, Blue—my personal thanks."

I took up the flint, still not knowing.

"Remember you gave that to young Rita Bapp when she got knocked up and kicked out of school? She gave it to me when I got paroled, the first time at least. She said 'Lute, here's you a harmless weapon.' I've managed to bring it through thick and thin. It's yours again."

"No, it's your good luck piece—keep it."

He finally laughed. "Christ Jesus, *luck?* Then more than ever it's yours again, Blue."

I put the flint in my inside pocket and saw how just that close exchange had improved his looks. His color seemed too healthy for cancer, so I asked if it might not be tuberculosis.

"I don't really want to know. I just want the sun."

"You're truly bound for Florida then?"

When he nodded Yes a chunk of the past slammed back at my face. *Did Luna follow my lead somehow and actually go back down there to live?* It seemed the natural thing to ask—"You got friends there?"

He pointed at the roof and smiled again. "The sun, like I said." Then while I was struggling with whether to ask for any more news, he said "But you—you're looking real sturdy."

I said I was doing all right for my age; and then it poured on out of me, helpless. "Is she still alive, Luther?"—she'd been so dead to me for so long. I dreaded him laughing.

He didn't though. "She's a young woman still—it's you and me that's worn to the nub."

"You know where she is?"

He looked round the room like she might be lurking. "I knew two years ago, last time I looked. She was in Mama's old house same as before."

I went cold as any old tramp nearby. "Is Rita alive?"

"Alive and staying with one of her shut ins—last I heard, my birthday card she sent me in August."

"But Luna hasn't been here all this time, not in that same house—"

Luther said "Oh no, she was taking a breather last time I looked—you know, between husbands."

"Any kids?"

He waited and shook my face down hard as any warden. But when I kept quiet, he said "Oh no, you took care of that, or don't you recall?"

Whatever he meant, it was harder to hear than any word since Myra's last. I wanted to shut down tight as a tomb and not give more, but I heard myself say "I don't know anything of the sort."

"When have you seen her?"

"Easter Monday two decades ago." All of a sudden it felt like a day, an hour ago. It felt like Luna might be at the main door waiting to stride in on us now at a signal neither one of us knew.

Luther said "Go see her—if she's still around. She mentioned you last time I saw her."

I guess my head shook automatically.

"Suit yourself of course. She was a *view*, wasn't she? I see her right now." It shook him slightly and his eyes shut.

But all I could think was *Leave here fast*—leave the mission and Raleigh and every place where I might glimpse one more live soul ruined by me.

I stayed of course, though I called my substitute and skipped the mission for a night or two. What I did was try to clear my mind, get it calmed down and then let it—or whatever drove me—plot my course. And I managed to hold out against what felt like a reckless lunge till New Year's Eve. Then I made the mistake of turning on TV at ten p.m. and catching the start of the big hoorah in Times Square and elsewhere round the world—1978. I shut it off fast; but what I'd done was start the tune up in my head, "Auld Lang Syne." It was one of the songs Luna had sung me night after night at Bob's place in those quick months we had together. She'd always stand by the window to start it, where Bob had kept his final bed; and her voice would pitch the melody higher than you thought she could stick with through to the end. But just as my nerves would threaten to snap, she'd take every note as pure as spring rain. And by the time she'd come down a little and claim we'd "take a cup of kindness yet," I'd be seized up in thanks and hope as she walked on towards me.

So first I looked in the telephone book—no number for Rita or any more Abshers. To strengthen my balance I even went and looked at your picture, the new school picture you'd sent from Germany just that fall. I didn't mean to ask you to praise or blame me; I wanted to see what holding your likeness would do to my aim. Nothing at first. Then I kissed the dry glass above your forehead; and all I could think was *Go, son, now*.

When I stopped on the street, it was ten forty five. At first I thought there were no lights on. But when I'd sat another short while, it seemed like a faint gleam came from the back where the kitchen had been originally. I thought *Luna may be dead or in Tulsa. Rita may be in*

*there with some old man, both drunk as monkeys and armed like
bikers. Or Luna herself—Christ, bearing down fast on her thirty
eighth birthday, locked in here with whatever brand of thin lipped
geek she's washed up here with to meet a new year.* But in twenty
more seconds, I climbed those same steps and tapped on the door.

Silence like nothing I'd heard since the war when bombers passed
over and the smoke hung on.

I thought *That's your gamble. You apparently won. Now haul ass
out.* But of course I knocked stronger one more time.

Finally I thought I could hear leaves blowing down Rita's short hall,
some weak dry rustle. Then I knew it was feet in stockings or bed
shoes. Then a clear voice said "Is it you again?"

I thought *Christ, yes. It was always me. Where the hell have I been?*
What I said was "It's Blue Calhoun. Is this Luna Absher?"

More silence, so long that I thought whoever stood there had either
fainted or died. Then the same voice said "Name a music camp in the
mountains near Boone."

"Harmony, Harmony"—I almost sang it.

A hand worked awhile at a chain on the door, then a deadbolt lock.
Then a lightbulb switched on over my head, maybe twenty five watts.
Then the door came open.

It was Luna unchanged by time or distance.

I said "Happy New Year. How in God's name?—" I meant to say
"How'd you know it was me?" but my throat shut.

She said "I didn't but I've prayed a few times."

Twenty minutes later in the kitchen by lamplight, we sat at Rita's
old porcelain table with coffee strong as I'd drunk since France; and
then I could see how Luna had likewise paid her share of tolls to the
years. But nothing had cut that powerful shine like early light on
moving water which came and went. We'd asked each other the easy
questions—the births and deaths, where so and so was, our present
health. I filled her in quick on Myra and Matt and the good you'd
done me in the past five years. Luna had gone through two bum mar-
riages like her mother; but she said she had one son age nine that she

lived for, named Anson Adams, asleep down the hall. By the time we got to the end of such questions, we both shut up and drank the coffee, which was cold by now.

And I got scared. I knew—however much she'd changed—that whatever part of this woman had drawn me, it was still in place, still young enough and strong. But nothing in my mind felt that high old humming begin, that hellbent lunge to know her all from crown to toe this instant now. And I couldn't think how to use up any more time in her presence. So I thought there were just two ways to go, tonight at least. I could wish her well and bow out or suggest we switch the TV on and watch Times Square. By then it was pushing half past eleven; and being that near Luna's fineness again, I knew I couldn't see one more year in with me alone in an empty house. I bet on the TV, and Luna said "Sure"—it was there in the kitchen on the old green cupboard.

That got us through into '78; and just as the drunks on Broadway were yelling and goosing each other, I was fool enough to think *Now son, here's a whole new chance.* I guess I meant a chance at life, not just touch or any quick fix but a better life with company. I didn't move though or look towards her.

In another few seconds Luna stood up, walked round the table and bent to kiss the top of my head.

It was like a child's kiss, that fast and finished; but it meant a very great deal to me at the time.

Then she stepped out, saying she'd be right back—no sign she wanted me to leave—so I waited peaceful as I'd ever been, watching a bucknaked teenage girl run up 42nd Street, and glad I was here. When Luna was back again in her chair, I finally said "Are you truly doing as good as you look?"

That helped her laugh and she moved over to stop the TV. But before she sat she said "I guess these legs'll haul me down life's road awhile yet."

That made me feel at least as old as the Appalachians. But I laughed too. "You keep yourself happy though?" That came unexpected—I doubt I'd thought of Luna as *happy* before this night—but it came from her eyes. They'd deepened and calmed, though were far from tame.

"I've been through the usual slugging, sure, but I keep on. My skin won't hardly bruise, remember?"

"I know for a fact, *I* never struck you."

"Not in meanness, no."

I had to correct her, to my knowledge anyhow. "Never, child. You were way too precious."

She took it and nodded. But then she said "This child, old Blue, has seen the world."

"How far did you go?"

She laughed again. "To tell you the truth, no *farther* than Charlotte, Atlanta, Chattanooga, smaller places round there. See, once I got my high school diploma, I climbed on the bus and went to Charlotte where a boy I'd known at Harmony was starting a Christian gospel group to tour the South and then make records. You don't need to hear the ins and outs of those four years; but I will say that, if we didn't get to Europe or Asia, I at least got to the depths and heights of where you can go this side of the stars, inside my head I mean, not famous. And true, it was maybe more depths than heights; but that's about average as women go, right? The boy said he loved me and we got married. For the first two years he honestly thought we were happy as clams; and we sang together like genuine pros till the very last note in Opp, Alabama which of course was the very right word—*Amen*. But we never made an actual record, just cheap demos that got nowhere except to sick Christian music producers with a lot of gold chains and wandering hands where I was concerned. And towards the end the boy was loving the alto (and sometimes the baritone) a lot more than me—in buses and bathrooms, alleys and gullies. I had enough pride to check on out after too much looking but not before I'd stored up a life share of humiliation to add to the past you know about." Before I could stop her, she said "Not us—not our past, Blue. You know what I mean."

I figured she had to mean her father. "You truly don't have to go on with this."

She said "I *do*. I need you to know it."

So I didn't try to stop her again, and it didn't take but twenty more minutes—a two year stint in motel bars and cocktail lounges through Arkansas and east Missouri. Then a second marriage to a much older man that said he held the original patents on aluminum siding but, when he suddenly died of stroke, turned out to have twelve thousand dollars in life insurance and little else (his funeral ate the money).

Then in Nashville, Tennessee there were jobs she didn't want to specify—beyond insisting they were decent work that involved no singing—but no more men except her son. Then two years ago she'd come back home when Rita was down with a broken back (from lifting one of her stout old ladies) and had just stayed on "since the schools are good." Right now she was ringing up checkout lines at a grocery store on Bloodworth Street, not six blocks off near Oakwood Cemetery, our old stand—she didn't mention that.

She's got a son—good. From the time Luther said it a week ago, his poisonous notion had worked in my mind—that I had ruined Luna's body for children. I still believed that what we left behind that sad day in Pensacola was not my child, and I felt convinced I couldn't have given her any sickness to balk her body—I'd never been sick in any such way and still never have. But since she'd told me this much now, I asked for all I needed to know. "Who's your son's dad, Luna?"

She took it hard, which in her case mostly meant she'd shut her eyes and wait out the trouble. When she finally looked she said "You still know me too well. You go to my *quick*."

"I'd far rather hurt myself than you. Forget the question."

But her hand made motions in the air to stop me. Then she took a long breath. "He's not ours, Blue—you well know that. If you and I had made anything, any living child, it would be grown now—Lord, *think* about it." She stopped to think, which in my head I refused to do. Then she said "No, Anson cames to me from God." She was smiling when she quit.

I thought *Her gospel singing got to her. She never would lean on God back when,* and I just nodded at her.

She went on though. "See, Chub—who invented aluminum siding—

he and I adopted Anson right before Chub died. Chub's favorite granddaughter had the boy; but being fifteen they wouldn't let her keep him. We took him on gladly—I took him; Chub watched—and once Chub was gone, I came on back here faster than I might have. I wanted him out of his mother's range to keep her from getting her feelings involved—it seemed wise for all."

"Has he turned out right?"

Luna glanced at the wall clock, then checked her watch. It was way past twelve. "I'll wake him up if you've got time—"

I thanked her but said I wouldn't disturb him.

She said "He's all but the joy of the world."

It was one of the better compliments I'd ever heard, though I saw she didn't know quite what she meant—it just felt true to her. And I was the last one to doubt such a claim, not with you in my heart in recent years. I asked her when his birthday was.

"March the 3rd."

"Let me leave him a present then." I took out my wallet and held it low, not to look rich and kindly. I had a twenty and a few small bills, so I folded the twenty and held it to Luna.

"Won't we see you before March 3rd?"

It hadn't dawned on me she'd want that. The whole time there I'd told myself *This ends as you leave. Make every word count.* But now I said "That's for you to decide."

And Luna waited. She honestly thought—I could see through her skin, still clear and firm except at the eyes where pain or laughter had left a few creases. Then she touched my hand to press it back. "Keep your present till March the 3rd; then give it to Anson here at this table, his tenth birthday."

I said "It's a promise" with no real scruples of mind or body, though my body was calm as I hoped the boy must be, in his sleep, when I bent to pay back the kiss his mother had risked on me as the new year broke.

Believe it, I got through the next two months in no big struggle with the notion of Luna. She moved in and out of a dream or two, way deep in the night; and I drove past her store one afternoon and nearly stopped till I knew my pantry was groaning full. It wasn't till late in February that I recalled the old picture of her, the one Bob gave me. I could see it still as plain as my hand—I could tell you how there were nine strands of hair, dark and separate, on her left shoulder and where the light glanced off her left eye to make it look like she'd moved that instant just to see you.

Then it struck me cold as a bayonet—*I know exactly where it's waiting.* I'd hid it in a crack between the living room mantel and the wall. And I went there now, half praying that Myra had found and burnt it ages past or that silverfish had made their weird lacework all through it. But when I got the bathroom tweezers and dug at the crack, it came right towards me, eager to serve. And oh she was still there, Luna young and the finest thing that happened to me till you, my darling—right up till you. But what I felt was thoroughly changed. She seemed more like a child I'd known in a previous life, some lovely girl I'd wished well to, then watched her drift on out of sight into her grown life nowhere near me. I wished that clear face well again and hid it back in its old place.

It had been eleven years since I took Wilkins Bedford to the circus, and in that time your presence and the thought of you filled my need to watch a growing child—you'd simply opened a path where I'd seen nothing but a concrete wall. So on that evening of March the 3rd, I went towards Luna and Anson Adams, thinking more about him than her. Ten years old—would he turn out to be a third kind child, a welcoming utterly frank human being that I could show care for and help to grow?

The moment I met him was strange enough. Soon as I knocked he opened the door—no Luna in sight—and said a long "Hey," as earnest faced as a probation officer greeting a con. He said his mother was in the kitchen cooking. Then he led me there and even pulled out a chair at the table and waved me towards it.

When I'd spoken to Luna and taken my seat, Anson stepped back and stood by the icebox, not shy maybe but watching me like something that might flame out and char this room if he blinked once. So I talked even gentler than usual and thought my way ahead like a blind man tapping his road—it meant something to me to get this right.

His mother had smiled and said "Hey yourself." But she was busy at the stove bending over in a pink housecoat (which didn't seem like her) to pick up biscuits out of the oven and nest them down in a straw basket lined with a napkin. Just as I wondered if the housecoat meant she'd started letting go of her looks, Luna set the basket on the table near me, stepped to the corner, took off the robe, came back to the table and said "Please Anson, will you seat your mother?"

Before she sat I got one look at the change she'd made. The housecoat must have been for protection because beneath it she'd worn this handsome dark blue dress that did its best for her pale face, her hair that still was dark with gray strands and her body that was full but lean as ever. Again I felt very calm, just friendly and grateful someway for the past—how it had kept itself alive and growing on beneath our feet in the unseen night till it bridged its way here in peace. For confirmation I almost brought out Luther's arrowhead. Anson surely should own it next, but then I thought Luna might not know about Luther passing through town before Christmas, so I kept still and surveyed the table.

I recalled she'd learned to cook at Bob's, but those quick months neither one of us had big appetites for food as such. Anson's birthday supper though was huge and the same as what Miss Ashlyn fixed in my childhood for festival days. There was cold crisp celery in a glass boat with glass salt cellars by every plate, then broiled chicken, English peas, creamed potatoes, baked yams in their skins, sage dressing, gravy, spiced peaches and sour cucumber pickle with strong hot coffee and Anson's cake. The three of us ate like well brought up but long starved children. And it wasn't till we got down towards the cake that any substantial words were exchanged.

That started when Anson looked my way and said "Don't get your hopes up any. This cake won't have a candle on it." When I asked if he was hiding his age, he said "I'm ten but everybody knows, so I just told her to cut out the flames in this firetrap—I'm too old to put you all to the risk."

His eyes did look way older than ten but not like somebody beaten and crushed. He had that look your mother had before she was married—and that you've worn right from your birth till now—the kind of eyes that can watch people move in very slow motion and see exactly what we *mean* deep in our core. That look had shied me more than once in my old life. But by the time I met young Anson, I was finally somebody able to bear it. So I said "Son, I just brought you a dinky present from the music store. I'm asking you though to name one thing you actually want, that I can find and bring you soon."

He didn't speak till he'd opened the small harmonica and played a scale. Then he looked to Luna. "Can I tell him?"

"You're grown, Anson. That's up to you."

He faced me straight. "I've been hoping some man would take up time with me."

I understood that his old stepfather was long since dead and that he surely hadn't known his real father, but had this notion really come from the boy? I checked Luna's face; she was watching Anson. So I asked her "You approve of this?"

Her eyes were honest as a heartpine board. "He asked me about it an hour ago. I told him not to bring it up, but then you gave him this new chance."

I said "Son, this *time* you mention—what would you want the man to do?"

He held off a good while, and then he smiled for the first full time since I'd walked in. "I couldn't tell him till he makes me a promise."

The smile surprised me as much as Luna's, her first time twenty two years past in a whole other universe that somehow was back in reach tonight. And if she hadn't told me the story of the boy's adoption, I'd have truly believed he was her blood kin. He showed that same glow giving in to too big a gladness. I said "I might just offer my services if I could be sure I wouldn't get hurt."

He shook his head hard. "I can't tell you that."

Luna laughed. "*Anson*—"

But he told her "You can just never tell."

Of course I thought I heard pain behind it, pain he'd been through at some man's hand. My next thought was that tomorrow was Saturday; so a little sooner than I'd intended when I drove here tonight, I said "If you've got time tomorrow morning, I'll give you a job."

Anson said "How much you paying?"

Luna pulled his hair.

But I liked his spunk. "A dollar an hour."

"Doing what?"

"Raking leaves." Late as it was now, almost spring, nobody had raked the leaves at Bob's. And the lame tree surgeon that had lived there ever since I moved out had lately gone to an old folks' home with his wife beside him, babbling the Bible.

Anson took his harmonica, looked my way and played a scale in the other direction from his first attempt. No word or nod.

"Is that my answer?"

He said "It means Yes."

Luna said "Thank him, you wild galoot."

But Anson said "Better wait till we try this thing out."

It felt strictly sensible to all involved, so Luna rose up to get the cake—caramel, three layers, clearly homemade and big as the wheel of an old dogcart. Whatever agreement we'd just contracted, it hadn't ruined anybody's appetite. We still ate onward like birds in the snow.

Anson and I raked leaves from nine on Saturday morning till three p.m. with a sandwich break (Luna packed the lunch). We were having a run of premature weather, bright and sixty degrees; so we made time fast on the tons of leaves. Then after too many negligent years, I got the urge to clean out the old Barefoot storeroom—a locked dry room that had once belonged to Miss Gin's cook, a stumpy woman strong as a wrestler that drank like a fish and cooked like God. I'd never given the tree surgeon a key, so it took us awhile to coax the lock open, but we both worked at it. Not till the bolt moved and Anson said "*Go!*" did I suddenly think there might be things he ought not to see. I couldn't think what; but very few families, not to mention lone men, would welcome a strange child's eyes on their trash. It was too late though.

He led the way in; and once he stood in the midst of the room and saw the *stuff* piled ceiling high on all sides, he broke out laughing till it bent him double.

I'd seen him smile but never laugh, and I looked round to see what caused it. Two or three ancient toys of Bob's—a black tricycle, a small pool table, a Chinaman mask with a long mustache. I said "Whoa here, what's tickled your gizzard?"

It took him a minute, and his face was still shining; but he said "Lord, man, I've been waiting for this."

I guessed he meant the whole boy's goldmine of secret stuff, and I said "Steady now. This is mostly a bonfire ready to happen. We've got to get ruthless."

Anson looked like a shot balloon, but then he walked in a dead straight line to a crammed bookcase and took down a shoebox. He put it to his ear, shook it a little (it sounded empty), then held it out. "Can I have just this?"

I recalled how much I'd loved a good box when I was a boy; so I said "One condition—if it's stuffed full of money, we split the take."

He shook it again, then carefully put it back on the shelf—no sign of regret, just no compromise.

Of course I said "I'm kidding—it's yours."

He turned his back on me to open the lid, and then he stayed turned till I had to say "Empty?"

When he faced round slowly, he was holding out, not a doll exactly but a ten inch statue of an Indian brave in actual buckskins, real hair and feathers, real beadwork.

I knew it right off—Bob bought it out west on one his early trips with his mother. For years it had stood on the dining room mantel; and even as a grown man, I was sometimes tempted to ask him for it. It was that realistic and dignified. For an instant now I almost said "No, put that back." But then I wondered *How on Earth did he guess?* He'd gone to it like a shot from the bow. I said "That belonged to my old friend that owned this place and gave it to me. Your mother knew him and even helped him die in peace."

Anson nodded. "She mentioned about him."

"Did she mention the Indian?"

"No sir, no. I love shoeboxes—"

"You a good caretaker?"

He grinned. "Real fine. You got to see my corner at home. Everything's lined up."

So I said "You found the best thing here. Congratulations. The rest is junk."

He nodded solemnly but took a long look round the stacked newspapers, orange crates, Mason jars, old brass bedsteads and a world more of boxes. "Blue, I wish I lived here though. This could be my cave."

He'd never called me Blue till then. But when he faced me and made a deep bow like a boy in a picture of olden days, I very nearly gave him the place and all its mysteries, sight unseen.

He naturally took a big place in my thoughts for the rest of that year on through Thanksgiving. I'd collect him Saturdays and we'd keep working at the Barefoot place (I was in no hurry to rent it till I'd made some repairs). We went to the movies a number of times in the afternoon—Anson generally picked science fiction and would poke me awake anytime I snoozed. We also visited the Natural History Museum, especially the live snakes; the State Zoo with gorillas he'd watch by the hour till it got to where they plainly recognized him and would imitate the movements his hands made, telling them things (I never asked what), Civil War battlefields in easy reach and the Indian mound at Town Creek with its spooky temple and a million bones.

Luna never came with us, but often as not she'd have supper cooked when we got back unless she was working a late shift. A few of those times Anson came home with me and spent the night in Matt's old room. Despite him being entirely a boy, he got fascinated by the scattered remains of Matt and Myra's religious shrine and by the pictures of you through the years. He asked me enough about you to build a lifesize working doll if he'd chosen to. But when he finally asked the question I'd waited for—did I love you or him the most?—I told him what felt right at the time: "Both the same" (I hadn't seen you in nearly a year, and he truly was that helpful to know).

Looking back I can see that Anson and I got everything dead right for all those months. We never said a harsh word to each other; and in the times we might not meet for a week or two, he'd always call me up on Wednesdays to tell his news. *It meant the whole world*—you'll understand that if you get as far along as me, and your family's gone and your mind is aching to teach somebody the best and harmless things you've learned.

Luna seemed glad that Anson had picked me to focus on. And almost all she'd say when I brought him back at dusk was "Don't let this wild tapeworm *drain* you" (he was called Tapeworm from his appetite that was bottomless, though he never gained weight). But I never felt drained, and after a while even old Rita would join us some evenings at a family meal. She'd long since quit thinking I was a threat, so after supper we'd all relax and let her tell us stories from her endless career as a practical nurse—astounding bone chilling true life stories of the rich and senile that always ended with her triumphant in a room with a corpse she'd bathed and dressed to meet its Maker politely.

For months I'd planned to fly to Europe for two weeks at Christmas with you, Matt and Dane—my first trip over since '45, the end of the war. Anson knew about it early in our friendship; and dignified as he generally was, I could tell it nagged him. He cranked up a whole new blizzard of questions about your size, talents and school achievements; and he'd always end by saying some form of "When did you say she was moving back here?" I'd say "Maybe never," which was only the truth; and that would end it for now at least.

But as we got further into that fall and the days stayed fine on into November, he called me late one Sunday night and, whispering low, asked why didn't we go spend a night somewhere before Christmas. When I asked if he had anything in mind, he knew right off—"The Atlantic Ocean." He'd never seen waves.

It had been too sunny a day to feel lonesome, which I'd still felt; so I heard myself say "How about Thanksgiving just like the Pilgrims with the surf behind, wild turkeys out front and armed Redskins?"

He broke down laughing in his patented way.

I said "Sure, you ask your mother and we'll talk tomorrow," my first mistake.

Anson thought I meant *You ask your mother to ride along with us.* And when I called him on Monday, he said "She's ready as me. You just say when."

I told myself *No problem, sure. We're solid friends,* my next mistake—mine, not Luna's.

One of Anson's hobbies was airplanes—models and pictures. I'd driven him out to the airport several times to watch real flights; and however many times he saw a plane lift off, the thrill of it lit him up like fireworks and flashed onto me. So I got us two rooms at a year-round motel in Kitty Hawk where the Wright Brothers flew. And the three of us headed out Wednesday after work (I'd got a retired friend to spell me at work, and Luna made a similar deal). We got there late in the night exhausted.

But Thanksgiving morning was fine as any day I remember from my whole life—the sky was like a perfect shelter from dawn to dark, all one deep blue and not a cloud. Once you've watched a child you love having outright joy in a beautiful place, you'll know what those few days were like—how much it feels like you're repaying every debt of your life, to the living *and* dead, with cash to spare. There were no big events but a calm string of satisfactions on the empty beach, in small cafes with just the locals and a huge turkey dinner, TV in the nights till we were all tired and of course the trip to the Wright Brothers' monument, which Anson climbed three steps at a time and didn't want to leave.

Luna slept a lot—she'd worked double shifts to earn the time off.

So the boy and I were alone together most daylight hours. But when she finally woke and dressed, she also seemed to go with the spirit of the time and place—low key but strong. In fact by the end of Thanksgiving day when we said good night to each other, I watched her and Anson turn towards their room; and my mind thought *Old son, you've really* done *something now*. I guess I meant I'd caused this peaceful rest among us.

As ever time had a different idea. Friday was set to be our last night (Luna had to work Sunday), and we ate supper together at a place way up the road where they roasted oysters on a flat iron grill and served them to you with melted butter till you died of bliss or burst your sides, whichever came first. Luna ate a respectable lot before she confessed that oysters had been in her worst nightmares most of her life, and these were her first—"Not bad at all." They were Anson's first too, and he loved them like me. So by the time we finished dessert and walked on the beach in a strong warm wind, the boy was as bushed as a three year old. But not too bushed to make me deliver on a promise I'd made—that he could sleep in the other twin bed in my room tonight.

Luna turned in at her door with just one word said twice—"Glory, glory."

I more than halfway understood, but she was gone before I agreed or even said "Thanks." Anson had already opened our door so I joined him; and once he peed and was under the cover watching me fiddle with the television, he finally said "I need to tell you something please."

Things had gone so smoothly till now that first I dreaded what he'd say. But then I knew I'd yet to make a real error with him anywhere on Earth so I said "Tell."

"I'm glad my old stepfather died."

No. I thought I just couldn't stand to hear another monster father story, not anywhere near his mother now. But I knew not to stop him. "You almost surely shouldn't be glad of that."

"I am all the same. He was real old; he had a long chance. Then I got you."

I said "I can't fail to say 'Many thanks.'"

I doubt he heard me. Before I said the word itself, he looked fast asleep.

But I walked to the foot of the bed and said it again very plainly. I hoped someway his mind would hear it better asleep and keep it for good. It felt that true and would have stayed true if I hadn't gone the natural way for hours to come. By then I was still so wide awake that all I wanted was a walk on the beach right by myself to set these days in memory.

I walked half an hour, then figured I must be ready for bed and climbed back over the dune that shielded our rooms from the sea. As I got to the crest, I saw Luna standing outside her door in the dim light of an overhead bulb. It naturally made me think of the night I first went to her—April '56—with her on Rita's porch and just the one light. Now she still wore what she'd worn at supper with an extra shawl around her arms. One arm was up against a post; and the best I could see, she was watching the road. It came to my mind *She's leaving us, here safe and peaceful. She's leaving me Anson.* I think I actually hoped it was true. I know I waited a long time to give her the room she needed to work her plan, whatever. But she stayed on there facing the road, and the wind was stronger and cold so I walked back.

It wasn't till I was almost there that she heard me and looked. Her face was in some deep kind of pain.

I said "Nothing's wrong with Anson?"

"Oh no, not really. I phoned your room and when nobody answered, I figured you were out for the air—a bomb won't wake him."

"Something's wrong though." By then I was one long arm's reach away.

She tilted her face and I saw she'd been in tears for a while. "I hadn't left home in so long, Blue, I didn't guess how rough this would be."

"Rough? Lord, I'm happy, child. Anson's had the time of his life."

She nodded hard. "Like I said, it must be the quick change of scene. At home everything's so gray and samey, I don't have to think."

"But you're thinking what now?"

She waited and finally smiled. "Don't ask."

I couldn't stop there. "I've earned this, Luna."

Her smile was gone when she met my eyes. "I think I've made a bad mistake by letting my son get this close to you."

At first I honestly misunderstood and in one instant I was mad as hell. "I haven't touched a hair of his head—"

She frowned deeply and put out a hand that almost reached me. "Oh no, Blue, no—I well know that. But he's leaning harder on you by the day, by the *hour* out here. And you aren't exactly holding back with the kind attention."

"He asked for me—you remember when. I don't plan to fail him."

"But you're *bound* to. Somehow or other you'll go your road or we'll go ours and Anson'll pay. See, I run his life for a few years yet; and I can't let him get burned again."

I shivered in the colder wind. "Can we sit down inside for a minute?"

Luna turned and actually studied her door like it might say *Stay Out* or *Stop*. Then she opened it slowly and walked on in.

Right off I noticed how neat it was—not a sock out of place, all but ready for the next tired traveler. Then I recalled how she'd arranged Bob's house the winter we spent out there—all Bob's clutter simplified and laid out neatly in parallel lines and right angles, not a speck of dust. It had made me learn to love that kind of half crazy order, though I couldn't maintain it once we split up. I suddenly knew I wanted it back, her whole world around me.

There were two straight chairs at opposite ends of a small table. Luna had already sat in one and pointed to the other. I sat and, honest to Christ, felt this—*All this happiness is leaving you now, son. Let it go.* I said "You planning to move away?"

She nodded. "We might."

"Far?"

"Real far."

I knew I'd long since lost the right if I ever had it, but I said "Is some man calling the shots?"

At first it hurt or made her mad—her eyes went narrow. She let it pass though. "Won't that be just *my* business, Blue?"

"Ab-so-lutely." Again I thought *They're all but gone. Get out with your pride.* Still, pride's never been a strong goal of mine. So I said "I've got more than one big reason to hope you and Anson can stay on peaceful the way we are."

"I'm about as peaceful as the Airborne Army in a damned fire storm."

Luther came to my mind. I'd still never told her about seeing him at the rescue mission a year ago; but something told me he was in on this, some part of the cause. "Is Luther troubling you again?"

It offended her badly. But then she said "To the best of my knowledge, he's on the moon—where'd you get that notion?"

I begged her pardon. "I was hunting a reason for you leaving home again. Look, I like Anson at least as much as he likes me. I think we've done each other good" (I'd let you and Wilkins be carried off from me with no protest; I was fighting now for something more than one child's presence—I thought I couldn't live single again).

Luna nodded. "Oh I know you have. But I'm here too and I'm broke *down*."

In the next long wait, I finally truly saw her again for the first time since Easter '57. She'd made herself much finer to see—I don't mean makeup, style or clothes but just in the way she'd met her hard life and let it firm her bones and eyes. She was still a quietly amazing sight, and to be that near her felt like almost too much luck. But I didn't hear that high pitched sound like a magnet humming that had poured out of her when she was sixteen. What I felt most was mainly this—whatever mistakes she'd made or suffered, she looked as worthy of care and kindness as any cold child. I knew if I moved on further now, I might trip locks and safety valves that I couldn't mend. But I heard myself say "I can't believe I let all those years fall between us."

"Oh Blue, you did."

I still felt a century older though. "You weren't waiting for me, I very much hope—"

"No, not that I knew of."

I said "Good, because this is the truth—I've pretty well gone past love completely, not anything like the love *we* had." The instant it left me, I knew it was wrong. The words themselves had fanned more heat than I'd known was here in storage inside me.

Luna said "You misunderstood me again. I'm not begging you for a teaspoon of air. I'm doing all *right*, Blue. The last thing I—or my son—want is for one more man to rock my boat." Looking back from tonight I think she believed it—may even have meant it.

But then I was suddenly too close to her alone in a motel room as secret as the back wall of space. I scratched a spot on the back of my hand. "My skin's so lonesome it's howling—listen." I held it towards her. "Hear it? It's *sad*."

She nodded Yes and waited a space that felt as long as the years we'd missed. Then she said "I'll send it a sympathy card."

I tried to laugh but felt too earnest.

So Luna laughed for me; but it wasn't genuine and when she saw I still couldn't join her, she said "We ought not to be in here."

"Look, the whole Atlantic Ocean is waiting. We could go walk by it." I'd forgot the wind.

"I can't leave Anson alone asleep."

For a second it shamed me—I'd flat forgot Anson. And even now I tried to bring his face to mind and let it guide me. But no face came except the deep eyed girl's I craved so long ago, who was here again.

An hour later I was back outside. The wind had quit but the night was cold for another walk. Since I knew I couldn't sleep anytime soon, I went to the car, cranked the engine and sat in there with the heat on awhile and the radio low. I was trying to guess how much had changed—in me, in the world, in Luna and Anson. But starting with me I couldn't feel like I'd crossed any river I couldn't re-cross on a normal day. I felt very much like the middle aged man I'd been at supper and for some years past with just this change—I'd tried at least to reward myself and one other creature for good behavior, two decades of decent life.

I even felt so much the same that I worked to find the way my mind and body had felt the April night I first knew Luna Absher deep. That wouldn't come, no more than who I'd been in the cradle. *No use, old son. No cell of your skin or mind's the same as you were then, hot as a spike in the blistering sun.* I was even so calm I didn't feel a trace of need to beat on Luna's door and beg back in. I didn't imagine I'd sabotaged Anson and his idea of me till now. No person or thing—least of all my famous blundering fate—was marking vicious time at the window, waiting to hear me say my regrets and beg a full pardon. But I thanked the highly visible stars beyond my windshield for one big blessing—the boy had slept on sound, right through. *The deed his loving mother and I, and millions more our age tonight, have just worked through means no more to him than trees on Mars, if Mars has trees and water to wade.*

When I unlocked my room door though, I heard low voices and saw dim light. I could read the face of my watch—one thirty. And on his side with his big eyes wide, Anson was curled up facing me. I said "You find you an airplane movie?"

He shook his head No.

"A boogerman dream?"

He still didn't speak so I brushed my teeth, stripped down to my shorts and climbed in the far side of my own bed. I'd seen he had the TV remote control by his hand. "You plan to be awake much longer?"

He said "Yes, till we get home tomorrow."

It chilled me quick. "That sounds like a mighty long time off."

"I know it is. I've stayed awake long nights before, since I was a kid." When I didn't speak he said "One time I stayed awake all night, all day and the whole next night. I was home by myself protecting things."

I'd have rather had him run an icepick through my eardrum, but I lay still and asked my mind to say the words he needed now. After a while I said "Have I hurt you?"

He suddenly cut the TV off, and the room was black. I heard him struggle with his covers some, and then he said "Don't you know nothing?—I don't *get* hurt."

I lay there waiting for some better word from me or him, but silence poured in on us so heavy that all I heard was the surf a hundred yards away and then short hours of bitter sleep.

I never knew what Anson took wrong. The motel walls were too thick to hear from room to room, Luna's door had been locked, her curtains drawn (I checked them myself). Thinking it over in later times, I've mostly thought he just woke up, found me gone and hated that—a man had *quit* him one more time. But he had dug his heels in deep and he stayed put. All the way back to Raleigh on Saturday, he acted more or less normal, just tired. He'd answer me if I spoke directly—was he hungry? Need to stretch? So I don't think Luna noticed the trouble, though in the five hours, he never started a conversation with her or me. And when we were back in front of their house, he just picked up his pint size duffle and said "I had a nice time."

When I said "I'll hope to see you next weekend," he waved behind him but still didn't look.

Luna said "He's whipped. He'll call you soon."

I nodded. "Please."

By then the boy had vanished indoors, so she reached out and touched my wrist. "Blue, I want to thank you myself—you're a gentle heart after so much time—but about last night. We're too changed, aren't we?"

I had no more than a dim idea of what she meant. Neither we nor time had waited exactly; still my new mind—and hers, I'd guessed— had met in recognizable bodies with the same deep courtesy we'd known at our best. But sure, I said we'd changed a lot. Then I stood on the pavement to watch her walk back through the door she'd first walked out of to change my life and all those round me, including your mother and now you.

*

Anson nor Luna, nobody called me. I ached the better part of two weeks, then told myself it was all for the best. Three days before Christmas I stopped by the grocery store, bought a few things and lined up at Luna's checkout counter.

She didn't see me till I was right on her, the way I intended. Then she flushed deep. "Well, stranger, hey."

I let her ring the items up; and while she was bagging them, I said "Does Anson still feel bad towards me?"

She finally paused and met my eyes. "He won't say your name. I can't make him call you—I'm sorry, Blue."

"Don't be." Of course I wanted answers to *why?* and whether she thought I could do anything to mend his feelings. But there I was in a grocery line, and Luna's face was politely shut. I said "Please tell him just this much from me—'Merry Christmas, boy, and spend this for fun.'" I handed Luna an envelope with fifty dollars sealed inside and just his name.

She could see through the paper enough to know it was bound to be cash, and she handed it back. "Give it to some poor hungry person— he won't take this from you or me."

"So he hates you too." The word was too strong.

"No, he's got to have somebody—see?—and I'm what's left."

An ancient colored woman behind me with two pounds of fatback and dry navy beans said "Move on, man, my *heart's* hurting me."

I said "That makes two or three of us then." But I smiled to Luna and moved on out, sad as I'd been in many long years.

I made it through the dead winter though with only one long siege of bronchitis; and Matt kept calling from Germany to keep my spirits at floor level anyhow, though hardly the ceiling. I'd got a sizable bonus for Christmas, selling the most electric keyboards (that I hate to hear); so when Matt said on the phone one Sunday in late February, "We're waiting on that old promise you've broke," I said "How about I come for Easter?—they owe me ten more days of vacation." Mattie whooped Yes and I made my plans. That had me involved in buying a new suit, cleaning out the basement on Beechridge in case I died in the air or, for that matter, on the ground I'd fought through once already, there next to the Rhine.

But when the night came to pack for tomorrow, I took the key to Doris next door and said if she saw flames at my windows, just keep it a secret and let the place go. She thought I was kidding of course, which I wasn't. Then when I squeezed my suitcase shut and figured I'd watch TV till it tired me, I suddenly thought of unfinished business too big to wait—*Go call up Anson and say goodbye, ask him what he wants from abroad.*

It was past ten o'clock, and I knew he might be asleep, but the phone rang a long time, and I let it go. At last somebody broke the ring, but no voice spoke so I said "Luna?—Anson—who's there?"

Turned out it was Rita on her night off, and I'd waked her up. "Damnation, Bluford, you may be rich; but I have to work. Leave me *alone.*" And when I asked for Luna or Anson, she just said "Gone. Too late. They're gone." Wouldn't say where either. "I still don't know. They're not settled yet."

"But they left for good?"

"Good or bad, they're out of my way. God only knows what'll come of that kid."

It sounded so rough I said "Your grandson."

"Wrong, wrong. Not a drop of my blood in his pitiful veins—thank Christ above."

A considerable part of the rest of the night, I stayed on the phone with Information trying to find a Luna Adams in any sizable town nearby, then the bordering states. But nothing, no. If they were alive together still, they weren't on the phone—not in their own house with their own names. I was wide awake heartsore till six in the morning, which was time to head for the airport and you.

You were going on eight and fine to see. Since I hadn't laid eyes on you in nearly two years, I'd thought you might be in some standoffish phase like so many boring children. But no, you came right towards me at the gate—*ready* the way you'd been as a baby—so I cheered up inside an hour, bushed as I was from the first long flight I ever took (the Army of course had conveyed me in boats). You're bound to remember those days still—the trips we took to castles and parks, the splendid zoo and all our shopping at your dad's PX where I bought you that first camera, then taught you to use it to keep me posted on the family's progress. The main thing you have no way to know is what your mother told me one day while you were in school and then what your dad said the last night. I don't know which one burdened me most.

But your mother first—she'd seemed very much herself right along, a handsome woman just past thirty six that had kept all the better traits of her childhood and added only an adult dignity and slow laughter of the kind that nobody has but the "pure in heart"—without a whiff of sanctimony, she'd kept her old lines open to the sky and what she trusted were steady gifts of trust and patience. You maybe won't know till you watch your own child; but through the first week, I knew Matt was holding me back at arm's length. It felt like watching your dearest friend through thick plate glass, not hearing their voice. But then this afternoon I mentioned, we'd eaten our sandwich and sauerkraut lunch and were still in the kitchen—mine and her best place to meet in whatever land. When we got to a silent spell in our talk, Matt stepped to the icebox door and said "I'll ask you a favor. I'm going to pour me one glass of wine and let you watch me drink it—just one."

Till then she'd drunk no more in my presence than water or coffee, though your dad drank wine with most of his meals. Since I quit liquor I'd had no trouble in watching people drink nearby. But I felt a little uneasy with Matt. So when she'd sat and drunk a long swallow, I asked the question that came right off. "Remember saying you wish your name was Calhoun still?"

She nodded hard.

Then I recalled at church on Easter how she'd sat in the midst of me, you and Dane and let tears spill down her cheeks untouched. "Are you bad off, some way I should know?" My hand moved towards her hand on the table.

But Matt pulled back and halfway smiled. "Don't touch me, Sky. I'd just break down."

I told her I'd be leaving soon—if she knew any way I could help, then tell me now.

She shook her head.

"Is it Dane? Is he cheating?" I guess I showed my own colors there, but it's what most men would wonder first.

The tears had made her look a lot younger, but now she wiped them and moved backward fast—not actual distance but her mind retreated to where I didn't feel the right to follow. And all she finally said was "Sky, I'm *old* now, see? I'm halfway to seventy. I wanted at least another chance to give you a grandson—it seems like I won't get him now."

That didn't answer the question I'd asked—no way I could tell—so I just said you were more than I'd hoped for, not to consider me on that score. But she still looked so young and abandoned, I had to ask if Dane was opposed to children or marriage itself or what?

Matt said "He claims not. I—" Then she stood up and rinsed her wine glass, dried it carefully and shelved it away.

I felt like she'd showed me one of her childhood Catholic pictures again—Jesus parting the skin of his chest with two fingers, displaying a heart in scorching flames. But all I knew to say to her now—the daughter I loved but too good a Catholic to run from pain—was "You've got a home in Raleigh, Madelyn, long as *I* live and the rest of your life. You don't even have to phone me first." Then I said what hurt even more. "With the father you got, you may want to keep an eye on that wine."

She called me "Darling" for the first time maybe in all her years— "Darling, that's the last thing you need to fear."

I didn't believe her then, though I should have.

It was not till you and she got to Raleigh two years later that I realized it. She was dry as a bone, but by then she was dying. I knew it the instant you walked off the plane. You were ten by now and a whole foot taller, but Mattie was, lean as a stick and pale. I honestly think she didn't know it—all through those three weeks you were with me, I'd gently urge her to see a doctor (I've never trusted Army doctors, which she'd been seeing; they're fonder of death than civilian doctors and that's going *far*). But she'd just say the German winter had got her down, and she'd snap back when spring arrived.

Towards the end of the trip, old Father Scanlon came by at Matt's request to visit. He didn't mention your mother's looks, but towards the end he asked about Dane. I hadn't probed in that direction because she'd barely mentioned him, so I listened close and what Matt said was "Dane Kirkpatrick's a colonel now. He's on his own really." When Scanlon looked baffled, she calmly said "No, Father, I don't mean we're apart—just that he's busy and gone a lot." Again when Scanlon asked us to pray and Mattie knelt beside her chair, I saw—not tears but a dark look spread out from her eyes like she was watching a soul in the pit.

Turned out she was. But I didn't know it for the longest time nor try to think who the soul might be. By the day you two went back to Germany, Matt's color was better; and she'd gained a few pounds. Then she didn't call me for weeks (by now like most Americans, we'd pretty well stopped writing letters at all). I didn't think too much about it since I had a few postcards from you and you seemed well. Then a letter came addressed by Matt. It was thicker than any she'd sent in years, so I knew it held substantial news. My bet—a father's normal bet, maybe even his hope—was that she'd decided to part from Dane, move back here with you of course and cut a new path where she was wanted. So I went in the kitchen to read it by the last daylight (somehow I wanted to read it by sunlight).

You may know the rest. She'd found the lump in her breast that last week here at home but had not said a word. The resemblance to her mother's history may well have stunned her. Then she'd waited a month in Germany to see if it might not dissolve on its own. It hadn't and now she'd undergone a double mastectomy with "guarded hopes." I know she said "I won't be Mother, Sky. I will *not* leave you." Anyhow she was set for chemotherapy and radiation once her scars had healed, and she asked me to vote for what color wig she'd need to get when her hair fell out (the choices she gave me were pink or blue).

Try though she did, I smelled rank death all through her words—
that and the care she was taking to ease me—so I knew her hopes were
guarded with every ounce of faith she'd kept through the years. I also
knew what had given both her and her own mother such endurance—
they never expected the best to happen. They let God know their
personal hopes, then took what came as his full reply.

Strangely for me—when I'd sat at the kitchen table too long reading
and reading her hard words—I went for the phone and called Father
Scanlon to set him praying before sunset.

He said he'd have it in the hands of Our Lady before I hung up
(the church may have bailed out on Virgin Mary, but not old Scanlon—he still knows where the power lies).

That night I called my doctor at home, told him everything Matt
told me and asked for his absolute honest opinion. Like most of the
younger doctors now, he'll tell you true—so true it can split your wisdom teeth at pointblank range. He asked a few questions, then asked
her age. When I said she'd just turned thirty nine, he gave a helpless
long low whistle. "That's against her, Blue. Time's badly against her."

I've heard a good deal of grim news in my life, maybe more than
the average middle class man. With all the waste of near thirty five
years at the start of my span, then World War II, then Luna Absher
and Luther and Bob, then Myra and Mother and more than one
friend—with all that, I've watched too many people die: die or burn
in my helpless presence. I mean I've stood in reach of their hands as
they quit life cold or melted down to the ready Earth or vanished off.
But nothing I'd seen or heard till now was harder to bear than those
four words, *Time's badly against her*. I guess I'd somehow thought
deep down that a soul who lived through my drunk meanness, my
year with Luna and whatever troubles Matt had with Dane—that
surely she was good for a long ride, surely way past where I'd turn off
and join her mother in the dry crabgrass of Oakwood Cemetery, our
last home.

Another hard thing was, I wanted to climb on the next plane over
and see for myself how Matt seemed. But I knew her well enough to

know she'd think I was rushing to say goodbye while I could. So I relied on calling her up when I thought she'd be alone at the house, daytimes when you and Dane were gone. And before much longer she sounded normal with just one difference. She wanted to talk about the past, the truly good times, and about her mother. She'd sometimes start to list Myra's good points like she was trying to keep me mindful of who I'd lost. I'd join in, trying to tell her things she didn't know about her mother—how Myra would purposely hide dollar bills in curious places around the house, then yip with glee when one turned up years later maybe in an old milk bottle. Or how her voice would change through the day till by bedtime it would be so soft you'd strain to hear but then would find she'd said something too true to say out loud with the world slowed down.

Of course I couldn't let Madelyn suspect the other grief that weighed me down. When I saw the first snapshot she sent—thinner still and in a dark wig with you behind her, both trying to grin— again I could smell her pain and death as strong as if she stood here beside me. And then I started to punish myself. I knew I'd caused her suffering. Little as I've ever thought about God, I still believe in some brand of justice bigger than our poor cops and courts. And if you believe in that kind of balance, then how in Christ's name was I not due to be cut down for my long blindness? And what could I do now to try to break its grip on Matt and you?

You're rich in sharing your mother's faith, trusting that prayer can actually shift our loads or lift them partly—or anyhow that your personal words reach a powerful ear that may reply. And I know you worry for heathen me. But please believe an honest man—again I don't doubt you or your mother's early bookkeeping on God and Jesus. I'm just shut out and oh was shut a million miles from my one child through all that scorching trial she had. The only thing I could see to do was somehow try to find a way to recompense her heart for the pain I'd caused her then and still.

I'd call, like I said, when she was alone. I'd send her frequent personal presents—newspaper clippings about her old friends, butterscotch Lifesavers she couldn't get, a silk scarf or a picture book of old

Raleigh houses. And she seemed grateful. But short of canceling her past life and running it over with no big failures, or at the least, bringing her home and getting the best American care, what could I do? She had a husband and a needy daughter. She might even *be* cured—she claimed she truly believed she was, though I could hear the risk in her voice. Like you and her, with a lot less comfort, I waited and tried hard to trust. It got to be the main work I did—sending powerful thoughts towards her, which I more than halfway guessed were futile.

I'd told myself for a long time that I'd retire at sixty five, then modernize Bob Barefoot's place and maybe move out there and spend my old age growing vegetables, feeding the birds and polishing my last skills as a hermit (one with a car and color TV). Then as that birthday came into sight, I knew I'd be a miserable fool to give myself so much spare time with something as grim as Madelyn's chances on my mind. But as months went on and she began to sound a lot stronger, I found a young team of hippie carpenters and set them working on Bob's house anyhow—the porches and steps, a whole new kitchen and the upstairs bath. I might yet need it—if not for me then maybe for you and Madelyn if time somehow brought the two of you home.

Then time kept going, Matt kept sounding well; and since Dane was soon resigning from the service and planning to start his old ambition—an "entrepreneur of transatlantic promotions"—she said she just couldn't visit right now. Wouldn't I fly back over soon? I still can't tell you what held me back—maybe the fact that Dane hadn't said more than "Hey" to me on the telephone since I left Germany. But something strong said *Blue, keep still. You may truly have some blame in her trouble, and you can't know what the sight of you that close to Dane might cause inside her healing body* (I'd read here lately how people can actually give themselves cancer by picking away at old resentments; and though I doubted it, why take the risk with Matt at stake?). But I went so far as to ask if the two of you couldn't fly to Raleigh for a summer visit. Matt said No, that with you moving in on your teens now, you were deep in the phase of spending every ounce of your energy on children your age; so she wouldn't move you.

*

It was you that brought me the last hard news—that call I placed on your thirteenth birthday when Matt had let you skip school a day, then got her dreadful word from the doctor. You said she couldn't talk to me right then, but late in the night she finally reached me to say the cancer had spread to her spine but that she was going "to beat this yet." Her mother's face and voice came at me so strong that instant, I nearly moaned. But I managed to keep a hold on my feelings and said I felt very confident she not only could but would beat it all. Then she asked me to make her a promise. She didn't just say "Come see us anytime." She said "Once I'm back up from this shock, I may be needing to see you, Sky. Will you come when I call?" I said I'd leave any minute she gave the sign, and I truly meant I'd pull up every stake it took to help or heal or die in less pain than her mother took.

That was May '84. We stayed in close touch from there on out— phone calls, letters for the first time in years, even those tapes Matt asked me to make of the old time poems I'd memorized in school and taught her to love before she could walk. But it wasn't till eighteen hard months later, Thanksgiving '85, when she finally called to pay me her thanks and tell me to come for Christmas please—polite as it was, it was *telling* not *asking*, though even that late she tried to pretend it would be my sixty fifth birthday party. But under every word she spoke, I could hear the empty cave around her—her voice echoed and sounded burnt; even on the phone I could see her eyes get bigger till they were the last thing left.

They were. *Matt was.* By the time I got there, December 20th, she'd got much worse than I realized from talking long distance. The tumors had gone to her liver now, and you know what her color was like. In fact you know a good deal of the rest. But I'm writing it still with the hope that when you see my whole story through my eyes, then you may stand a chance of knowing the entire shape of those dark days—why Dane and I did what we did, and why I'm asking you this way for total mercy or all you can give.

But know this first. Three days before I flew to Germany, I read the

morning's obituaries (a real sign of age) and saw that Rita Absher
had died. Of course my mind was already dazed, but I sat at the
kitchen table now and truly broke down—first tear I'd shed in all
Matt's troubles. Once I got through that, I went to the phone and
sent some flowers to her old house (the paper used that old style line,
"Burial will be from the home" and gave the address). I guess I did it
without much thought because of the timing with my own sadness
but also because—even that late and with all my waste—I felt some
thanks for Rita's life and the happiness her daughter brought me so
long ago. But I thought I wouldn't go to the funeral and take the
chance of being unwelcome with whoever might be there these days.

After supper that night though, the telephone rang when I was
down in the black sub basement of lonesome grief. The woman's voice
said "Blue?" but I didn't recognize it—it sounded young and faraway.
I said "Speaking—"
She tried to say "Thank you," but her voice quit on her. Then she
couldn't say anything else but "Wait."
I waited and finally a man's voice said "Well, stranger, we sure
would like to see you."
I had to say "Who's speaking please?"
It was Anson Adams—Luna's son. The woman's voice that sounded
young was Luna herself.
It seemed like they were both sincere in wanting to see me. And
since I knew I was leaving anyway in thirty six hours, I drove to Rita's
and climbed those steps that by then felt historic to me. It had been
an unusually warm month, and the front door was actually standing
open when I got to it. But I couldn't hear any voices inside, so I
tapped on the screen. And then at the far dim end of the hall, I saw a
tall man facing my way, both arms at his sides like they were strapped.
I thought *Lord God, it's Luther back from the grave himself.*
But no it was Anson, six feet high in a dark blue suit with his white
shirt open at the neck on a little gold cross hung on a chain.
For some weird reason I suddenly thought *Luna's made us a priest;*

but I didn't call him "Father" yet, not young as he was, though he looked full grown and plainly a gent.

He stood behind the screenwire a quiet instant, then opened it outward and folded me into his long arms. "Blue, we're just glad you turned up."

I chose not to doubt him but said I'd pay my respects to his mother, then I'd have to leave since I was packing to fly overseas.

He said "We're back in the kitchen—come on."

We. I dreaded who that might be. Luther again, with more parts missing, or Luna's new husband or somebody worse—this roof had seldom sheltered anything normal by way of a human. But I followed the tall man Anson was becoming (I'd figured he was seventeen now). And when I stopped on the kitchen sill, I saw that the *we* was him and Luna and a black Lab retriever that seemed to know me—no bark at all but a family welcome.

Luna stayed in her chair, and her eyes filled up.

Anson touched my shoulder and said to his mother "He hasn't changed all that much, has he?"

She shook her head slowly. "Not a minute's worth."

So I went towards her and held out my hand. No thrill or jolt flew up my arm; but soon as I touched that skin, I thought *I'll never get out of here without a good cry.* Luna felt that much like my oldest friend, which she almost was—I'd shared more with her than with anybody else in North America: that much was sure.

She said "Dear friend, sit here" to confirm it.

So I took the chair I used to take when Anson was young and tried not to stare at Luna too closely while she told me about Rita's stroke and peaceful end at three a.m. two nights ago right here at home. Like my own mother she'd had time to place a call to Luna and tell her goodbye before she called the rescue squad. And long before Anson could drive Luna down from Lynchburg, Virginia, Rita was gone with her earrings on (Luna thought she'd had time to fix herself up, stroke or not).

By the time I heard the news, I'd more than registered the change in Luna. I knew she was forty five, and she looked it—not haggard or slack but seasoned and wise across the brow and in her splendid eyes that hadn't dimmed a watt but still knew more than she'd ever tell (because it might kill you—she knew too much). I was starting to feel a kind of pride in how she'd lasted.

Then she said Anson claimed I was bound overseas. It seemed like more bad news for her now. Her face got paler.

And when I'd told her about Matt's trouble, I thought for a while I'd told her too much. There were no more tears; but she gave her old sign of serious pain—she spread both hands and watched just them like they would know the best way out.

Anson had sat down with us by now, and finally he reached out to cover her hands. "You might need to lie down awhile."

Luna nodded her thanks. "I can't leave Blue. No way—he's *worse* off. Rita *had* her life."

So Anson said if we didn't mind, he'd drive to the funeral home and check on things (Rita was laid out there till tomorrow). He rose behind me and brought both hands down on my shoulders. "Try to stay till I get back."

I told him I'd need to go very soon, so to my surprise he leaned and pressed his chin on my head. He said "I feel like I saw you last week" and was gone out the door.

In the next half hour, and because I asked, Luna told me where they'd been the last seven years—various towns between here and Lynchburg with her doing mainly hostess jobs at motel restaurants, trying to keep the boy in clothes that he outgrew like a calf on cream. Lately she'd started taking a course in data processing at the local college and thought that was bound to better their lot. Anson had never been less than honest, good at his lessons and his part time job, backup pitcher for his baseball team and still in hopes of being a pilot, though he might have to join the service for that. So how had I been?

All I could say was "The absolute same." At first it felt like my biggest lie in recent years, but then I saw it was utterly true. My body might be thoroughly flushed of the man I'd been the year I went for the brass ring with Luna, but my whole mind could sit here now and find her young beauty where it lay under what time did and feel her draw as strong as then but with none of the reckless lunging that scorched us and all bystanders. It didn't make me want to touch her. It didn't even make me want to stay here watching her now. What it called up though was a powerful wish to help her someway, some useful way—not *change* or save her, just help her on in her normal life, her and the boy.

I had the money that Mother left. Except for my one trip to Europe, I'd let it grow in several banks with no clear plan for how to use it— old age and sickness, any big need of Mattie's, your own college days. *Should I just ask Luna what help she needs? No, son, that could strap her to you in ways you both would very soon hate.* Then I thought of a natural way. I said "I'll count it a serious favor if you let me pay for Rita's funeral."

Luna looked amazed.

"I might not have seen her for too long now, but she was my last childhood friend." It was only the truth.

Luna said "She left a small nestegg—three thousand dollars, believe it or not; I thought she'd eaten it all in doughnuts. That'll just about cover her last expenses. Thank you though." She was still watching her hands, uneasy.

And now I wanted to cover them close; but since I was leaving in two more days, I knew not to put her or me to that strain. "You keep the money for Anson's life. Let Rita be mine."

So Luna accepted with dignified thanks. Then she said "I'm selfish, thinking of me—are *you* going to make it?"

I said I guessed I'd last awhile yet—I had to now for Matt and you.

Luna took a long breath, then met my eyes. "Are you thinking what I'm thinking now?"

I understood her. "Yes ma'm, thinking *hard*—"

"That we brought all this down on our people—you and me three decades past."

I shook my head. "You were still a child."

"Not so," she said and her eyes plainly meant it. "I was sixteen years old; I knew the Commandments."

I nodded and said "I'm bracing to pay back the last thin dime I can to Matt Calhoun."

"But there's nothing I can give her, is there?" Luna stopped now where the words had left her, tired and grieved but grand as anything known to me.

I reached for her hand and held it lightly. "Not now. Don't worry. Strong as Matt is, she's ready to go." I believed myself.

And all those first bleak days in Germany, it still seemed true. Just before I got there, Matt had gone to the Catholic clinic and was feeling calmer. Her use of German was good enough for mild occasional jokes with the nuns; and far as she let me see at first, she was not in pain. I'd sat with her mother through the same kind of death though, and I kept waiting for her face to say she was in the fire. But right through my birthday and Christmas, she was even-keeled and gave me the strength I needed to watch—she'd got so thin the light cut through her, and I could see the girl deep in her, volunteering for agony. I'd stand by the bed when the priest came in every morning to give her communion and pray for healing. And I want you to know that when she'd take that bread on her tongue, she'd look exactly like she did the day I saw her take first communion—that clean and eager, that welcoming to fate. That child was still inside her, strong, and would lead her on through whatever came. All I could do was try to keep my eyes on her and trust her path.

New Year's Eve at nine o'clock, I was there alone with her—Dane had taken you to some school party. I was trying to read a magazine and had thought Matt was sleeping.

But in a low voice she called me "Sky."

I started to rise and move towards her, but she waved me back. Then she said "I wish to God I wasn't *punishing* you."

I swore I was bearing up all right and was just relieved she wasn't in pain.

She'd barely let me see it till now, but her head shook hard, and her whole face said "I am. I am. And it gets far worse"—she'd watched her mother enough to know.

I said "Tell me one thing I can do." I meant one thing that might ease her even for a minute—a cold cloth, some ice (she could seldom drink water).

Her head still shook.

"Then let me beg your pardon for every hurt I ever caused you."

Times like that, people get the power to say things they've put off for years or never known till this hot instant. Now I think Matt understood what a world of recompense I owed her and how I could pay it. She said "Take Lyn."

I said I'd watch you as closely as I could. I'd help Dane every way I knew, that he could use.

But Madelyn's eyes held onto mine. "Sky, *listen* to me—I already told you. You take Lyn" (I ask you to trust my memory here. I'm strictly certain she said those words).

I couldn't imagine how I'd take you anytime soon with an able bodied father in charge, but I told Matt "Yes. You count on that."

I could see she tried to let it go, but her mind wouldn't leave it. She said to me "Swear."

So I looked right at her terrible eyes and swore I'd take you. I figured time would show me a way, though I never guessed the answer would come when it did and how soon.

Then the end time started. Because it seemed wise to Matt and Dane, you were spared that one sight anyhow. In years to come if you ever wonder how your mother left this world, take this from me as simple fact. She lived through pain that, even in my darkest nights in the State drunk tank, I know I never came anywhere near. As it did with her own mother before, it got to where the strongest drugs the nuns could give her were useless as water. And all Matt had from then on out was that daily communion, the prayers she'd mutter between the grindings, and both my hands that she'd press on so hard I thought my actual bones would pulverize. She'd sent for me explicitly across a whole ocean; so I stayed with her every minute I could, sleeping by her most nights on a cot the nuns were glad to give me. It was my deep wish and Matt's dire need; and then Dane had to stay at home with you, just making short visits when your neighbors spelled him.

So I was there when she died at sunrise, January 10th of this same year, which is already way the longest I've known; and it's barely half done. She knew my face till the last breath left her, and she'd said your name a short while before. Nothing I'd watched in sixty five years, not even the burned exploded children in the streets of France and Germany in the worst of the war, struck me like Madelyn's final eyes. They'd never aged a day in all she had to bear. And though there was no spare ounce of flesh on her, they met me the way they always had—that steady and clear and truly that fearless. She said "I remember—" and may have tried to smile at something, but her mouth had long since forgot how to curve, and then she was gone. There was no nurse with us, and I didn't call one for some little while.

I sat on the cot till I'd got back the power to see her in childhood days. I knew I had to do that now or only watch her this final way the rest of my life. And eventually my tired mind got her back, fairly young and straight—no mark on her skin anyhow, no frown. I watched thin daylight find the window and take her whole still body once more, the only thing I'd ever helped build that wasn't a wreck and that here I'd destroyed. A part of my mind now says that's false; but this last minute near Madelyn's body, I *knew* it, right or wrong, deep down—don't doubt me ever. Then I went to find the nun that had always been her choice, a strong dwarfed woman named Sister Hilde, who seemed too young to spend whole nights in the midst of agony and still be ready and helpful at dawn, which she always was.

Some days before, on one of the rare times Dane and I were with Matt together, she'd told us both to cremate her body and bury the ashes in Raleigh by her mother (till then I didn't know the church had raised its ban on cremation). At first I thought *No, her place is with Dane wherever he'll be*—I hope to lie next to Myra, not Mother.

But of course you don't try to argue with somebody made out of pain the way Matt was by then anyhow. So when I called Dane up the last morning and said she was gone, he came straight over, pale himself, and quietly took charge of all arrangements. With his years of service, he was fine at that.

He also gave me a long hug and said he couldn't have stood it without me, for me please to stay now and live with you two. To this day still I believe he meant it. I think he was that sad and desperately sorry for what he'd already done against his suffering wife, not to speak about you and your long torment that *only* he caused. I think he realized most of all that he needed somebody halfway decent and tall enough to stand between his body and you. Then he naturally wanted what any parent wants—a trustworthy person to watch his child when he was away on business trips, more frequent than ever now the money was coming.

Before I left Raleigh I'd told young Mr. Atkinson, the new boss, why I was going and that I might well be gone for months. He was sympathetic and said all I would need to do was send him word of what to expect. Then if I ran into something too bad, he'd arrange my Social Security papers and set me free to do what I must from there on out in full retirement.

So once Dane asked me to stay nearby you, I figured nothing stood in my way. I was needed by my only close kin, and you were the thing I prized on Earth. Cool as he'd been in recent years, I had no cause to think Dane was anything more than he seemed right here in my eyes—a smart, ambitious, overworked widower with heavy new burdens in his own grief and in raising you. I looked straight at his stunned blank face and told him I was no butler, cook or child expert but that I would gladly do what I could for now and the immediate future.

But it lasted just those few fast weeks. Dane thought it was right to have a funeral there for Madelyn's friends and his associates, and I agreed it made good sense (we'd take her ashes to Raleigh someday).

You recall how we got through those sad motions, and it wasn't till I looked over at you in the midst of the service that I realized I'd made another big mistake.

You looked so frozen and so shut out, even from the rare sunlight this day, that I saw how I should have made a way for you to say goodbye to your mother in person, not here in the midst of adult strangers watching to see how hard you grieved. Sister Hilde would have fixed a way for you to touch Mattie while she could still see you— she'd ask for you like I said to the end, and all I'd say was that you were fine and praying for her. So one more time I had a new reason to think I was going on helpless as ever, passing my hurt down the years to you.

Dane himself had waited till now to let his grief out. In the years I'd known him, I watched him keep his feelings cooped in the same tight Army-issue box that I recognized from junior officers in my war. In fact till Dane broke up in church and let sobs shake him, I'd never been sure he had what most humans have for feelings—not normal traits like love and loyalty, joy and sorrow. So to me that came as a kind of let up in my remorse, and I trusted him more as I also tried to free my pity for Madelyn now and let it run towards him and you. My object of course was mainly you, but Dane after all was half of you. And since I prized you the way I did, I felt I owed him thanks as well.

That way we got through the darkest weeks I ever saw—I mean it literally as well as otherwise, those German days when the sun didn't show till nine in the morning and set at four on buildings colored gray and gray. Struck as I was from those last sights of Madelyn, I tried to keep upright for you and to let you know you were ringed around by the same safe care you'd always known, so far as I saw. By early February I thought it was working. Someway I let myself believe that you and Dane both had slowly begun to show new life and to look at the world like it would last, just the outside world of people and things—the outlook for spring even that far north.

So after a week of February thaw, I secretly told myself I could leave for Raleigh almost anytime. Dane was already hunting a live-in maid and companion for you—he had some good prospects. And though he was courteous. as always to me, I understood I was not his father nor one speck of real kin but just the living cause of a wife he'd been unable to save, even soothe, who would shame him till death (which we both must have thought would be years on). But I also knew in my bone sockets, I was all you had by way of blood tie to your lost mother. And everything that's happened since, I firmly believe, came out of that knowledge—that and the care I'd built for you since I laid eyes on you the summer you were born.

There are two more nights you need to know. On Friday evening the 14th of February, you'd got back from that Valentine show and gone to bed when Dane walked in from his regular trip to Amsterdam. He was so exhausted as he stepped through the door, I thought he might slump right down on the rug; and I tried to cook him some eggs at least. But all he said he wanted was a drink and then just to sleep "till the split of Doom." I was tired myself and still low from the weather, but I saw he needed company, so we sat up at the kitchen table, and Dane talked more in the next two hours than I'd heard from him in all the years. I knew it was partly because of the vodka— he made a serious dint in a pint before he quit—but from my own drinking, I also knew that now he was down to the true brass tacks, no more of the public relations line he spent his work life spouting to clients.

It started with how he'd loved your mother better than the moon and stars and how he felt completely gutted. I never tried to contradict him or doubt he believed every word he said—I still don't doubt it; you can love two people if you're stocked that richly as I said before. Then he started on about you—what a beautiful trustworthy genius you were, and did I think he was doing you wrong to stay abroad, or should you two come back stateside so you could go to American schools? I'd long since known not to give any fellow drunk an earnest suggestion—if you say *right*, he'll turn due *left*. I just said he could count on me for whatever help he needed wherever, if it was in my power to give. *Power* turned out to be the wrong word.

Dane sat glum awhile, then met my eyes. I realized I'd barely seen his eyes before—he seldom truly faced other men. He held right on me though and said "Your *power*, Blue? Don't worry, stud. You've had all the power here all this time."

I guess I smiled and shook my head to change the subject.

No stopping him now. He kicked the word *power* around awhile longer like it was a low slung vicious dog that was lunging at him. Then when he'd worked his brain too hot, he faced me again. "You know you ran my whole damned marriage from the first night on— Matt lived for you every step of the way; I was just her chauffeur. And now young Lyn is feeding off you like a day old calf."

A drunk like me should have known not to try it, but I tried to joke. "Whoa, Dane, that makes me a cow. You called me stud a minute ago."

"Oh no no no, you're the bull around here." Then he went on in that weird direction till he'd said things about my relations with Mattie and you that cut me deep—how I had also constantly tried to corner your love and nearly succeeded.

By that time though I'd got myself pretty much in hand. I knew if I answered, it couldn't reach him; his addled mind just wouldn't accept it. I said I was going on to bed, and I stood to leave. I thought *I'll let him find that woman to stay with Lyn and then I'm out.*

Dane let me get as far as the door before he said "I know you'll really enjoy your dreams. Christ knows you've got the *makings* for dreams."

I knew what he meant—and you will too by the time you're grown— but I went down to my bedroom and lay full dressed in the dark till morning, even after I heard Dane snoring loudly. All I could think by then was *Maybe you can't leave right now, son. Stand and fight for her.*

Two weeks more we went on calmly, or so it may have looked to you. Anytime you were home, Dane was on good behavior—to my eyes at least. And he showed no memory of what he'd said to me that night. He even asked me in a sincere voice to stay right on as long as

I could, "for life if possible." He hadn't traveled any that week; but from what both he and you had said, I thought you were going home from school with your friend Tillie to spend the last Friday night of the month. So early that evening I went as far as to leave a note on his bedroom door and bus myself downtown for supper and an awful, typical German movie about a legless woman that forecasts the end of the world correctly.

It was my first night outdoors alone in Germany for forty one years. And I'll have to say it was sadder than any I'd spent under fire, though nothing compared to what came down before sunrise. I didn't get back till past eleven in hopes that Dane would be asleep or still out some-where. (By now he had mysterious chores to do after dark. I suspected they might be what he thought of as premature dates—I wish to Christ they had been, in spades.) Anyhow however late I stalled, I was early from the point of view of Dane Kirkpatrick and most of the dreadful strength in the air of Stuttgart, Germany that one night.

I let myself in with my own key as quiet as I could. And when I saw the lights were out in the front room and kitchen, I tipped on down the hall towards my room, praying the carpet wouldn't squeak. Then I saw a dim light under your door and paused beside it. At first I thought I heard an animal breathing rough in its sleep or dreaming. I knew you'd asked to replace old Gyp when he died last summer and that Dane had told you to wait till a new dog wouldn't pain your mother. I thought he might have just brought one in and left it for you to see when you got back tomorrow morning—that may sound crazy but I swear it's true.

For long days, Lyn, I truly didn't think you knew what came next. I turned your doorknob—not a sound—and pressed it open by maybe a foot, enough anyhow to see the whole room, dim as it was. You were home already, your bare back was to me, you were facing the wall be-hind your bed with rock and roll posters all beyond you, your head was tilted back a little so you were almost watching the ceiling. A grown man sat on the edge of your bed; but your body hid him, his face anyhow, though I guessed right off he was known to you—his hands were on you.

Turned away from me, you looked like a freezing orphan in the dark, left bolt upright at the whole world's mercy. Since you never flinched I thought you hadn't heard me behind you. But something told the man to look. His head leaned round you and saw me standing five yards away. No other eyes I've met on Earth—not even my own eyes in mirrors when I trapped somebody I craved up an alley and took some nourishment they wouldn't give—were worse to see. If any knowing soul had warned me, I'd have prayed till my skull powdered to dust that it might have been anybody alive but Dane Kirkpatrick looking stupefied as any drowned creature hauled back to light and worse than pitiful—if I'd had pity in my heart, which I didn't, not then. Not then, in time.

I shut the door, still no noise, and went to my room. I had to put one arm on the bureau to brace my legs. I even tried to think of a prayer, but nothing would come; I'd waited too late. Maybe I stood there two or three minutes or half an hour—I was that sealed off from the actual world. I also knew that next I might do anything possible on this planet, anything an able bodied man my age might do; and it scared me badly.

Then I heard somebody run water in the kitchen and unload silver from the midget dishwasher. I someway knew it couldn't be you, not this late now; but I didn't think it was up to me to go there first and see Dane's face—whatever it showed—especially not in a room that full of knives and bludgeons. I might have killed more than one person on the spot or made a hard try. I'd turned that wild in that little time.

Something half sane though told me next to sit on the bed and try to breathe deeply. I tried it awhile and also tried to think of other faces to cancel Dane's, the way he looked trapped there against you. The only face that kept arising was a small relief—Luna's boy Anson and all I could do was to pray he hadn't been offended like his mother or like you now, my darling, and that both of you would yet be safe, maybe under my care. That surprisingly calmed me or gave me the strength to stand up, walk to the kitchen and meet whoever was there.

*

Dane of course. He was in his green sweatshirt and pressed Levi's; and it looked like he'd just showered and shaved, though I knew he hadn't had time for that. But he'd made a pot of coffee and was drinking at the table. I poured a cup and sat at the far end hoping someway he'd speak out finally and help me know I'd been in a dream that was over. I knew I couldn't begin to speak, not first anyhow.

After what felt like a scalding hour, Dane said "Run across any prospects in town?" He'd joked for weeks about finding me a frisky fräulein.

"I didn't speak to one human being." The words felt like they were coming from far off, not in my voice, and might turn into a howl any instant.

You know what a keen mindreader Dane was; he had to know I was in dire straits. But for all his years in public relations, next he made the tragic mistake—with me at least on that one night. He said "Blue, I doubt I can live alone. I'm not strong as you."

I said one of those old fashioned things you wish you'd forgot. "Your wife's barely cold."

He actually smiled. "This is painful stuff but understand—Matt went cold on me more than five years ago."

Tense as I was and still half wild, I understood him. Mattie had spent those winter weeks with me in '81 with you beside us, and right after that came her radical surgery. So I even tried to sit here and think of myself as Dane, through his own eyes. He was forty three years old and suddenly on his absolute own after long years with a soul warm as Matt. At that age I'd been back with Myra seven years from the time with Luna; but my body still could flash up on me any minute and wail at the moon for extra women of all descriptions, though I stayed true to Myra. So no, however hard I tried I couldn't understand Dane, not this night. And I went for his throat, in words at least. "Is Lyn sick?"

"No sir. Lyn's asleep."

"I thought she was spending the night with Tillie."

Dane was calm as glass or seemed to be. "Lyn thought so too but

Tillie's mom got a migraine headache, and Lyn called me to come bring her home. She can go next week."

I had no warning I'd actually say it; but out came "No, she's going with me."

Dane's eyes crouched back; then he smiled again. "Sure, take her—I may need to be in Munich."

I said "Home, Dane. I'm taking Lyn home." I saw I'd reached him, though he tried to look puzzled.

"Sky, whoa here, you're way out of line. You've got me wrong."

So he granted that I'd seen something anyhow, however I read it. Another two words and I might have calmed down or started to. But he'd called me *Sky*. Dane hadn't addressed me as Sky five times in the years he'd known me; and since it was Matt's old name for me, it made me worse. "My eyes still work. I know what I saw. You're beneath contempt."

I'll give him this. He was stone cold sober. He looked as righteous as any judge, and his eyes stayed on me. He drank some coffee and his color came back till he seemed near normal. But then he spread his fingers before him on the white enamel and watched them like they might move against him or vindicate his name entirely. Then while I watched not two yards off, Dane folded on himself like a building slowly crumbling inward. It made no sound but his whole body heaved; and though his eyes had come back to me, they were awful to see. They stayed right on me and never blinked when he said the last thing—"Blue, I love Lyn every way you *can* love; she loves me too and it's cost us a lot." It had burst out of him like the absolute truth; and it left him old and slack all over, young as he was.

I knew his pain was utterly real. I'd been there myself, not this exact place but near enough in the selfish harm I caused every woman near to me in the whole first half of my lifetime. And if I hadn't done what he'd done—reached that last entirely shut place—I'd fouled Luna Absher's body in her childhood. Wasn't she a baffled middle aged woman now—a borrowed son and no live husband, none of the musical life she'd dreamed but struggling to keep two people fed, no hope of more? If anybody *live* gets the blame for that, it's also me.

And hadn't I otherwise spoiled your mother's early life and maybe tripped the single cell that turned one instant and ate her down to the agonized ground?—not even to speak of Miss Ashlyn and Myra, too long gone. I don't mean to sound like a direct descendant of Judas Iscariot and General Sherman volunteering to bear all the loose blame on Earth. I still think what I've claimed is *mine*, and I acquired it with both eyes open. But however botched my own past was, I couldn't reach towards Dane Kirkpatrick this night here, not even a tap on the back of the hand. I couldn't find mercy in any form to act on or speak of—not this night, which was all we had to rescue things, though at that table neither one of us knew it, I'm all but sure. With my worst brand of dry drunk blindness, I'd shut my doors in the face of everything a man could do to jump start life—Dane's and ours, the three part family we'd still had among us a day ago.

I stood and went back to my narrow room. Not even my room but Dane Kirkpatrick's, bought and paid. I've never been much of an angry soul; I trust you've seen that all through here. Even in my worst drunks and dazes, I seldom flailed around me badly. I was mostly the one that slunk home sick, fell on the bed and waited for strong and heartsick women (your mother and Myra) to nurse me back with baked custard and warm rice pudding. For all I knew this February night, you were in black trouble behind your door. For all I knew you'd knotted your sheets, climbed out your window and gone forever. I might at least have tapped on the door and said good night through thin gray wood, just to hear your voice and know it was there and let you know how nothing was changed in my care for you—you'd live to win everything you'd earned and be a strong soul.

But no. I noticed your light was out, and I chose to think you'd managed to sleep and you needed that more than any live visit. I left my own door cracked slightly open, so I must have thought I'd hear Dane's movements and could stand between you and him the instant a need arose—which I thought it wouldn't, not after the words I'd just poured on him. Colder still I took my shoes off, lay in the dark staring up at the ceiling and grinding my teeth till I someway went unconscious awhile, planning our hard trip home tomorrow through all my dreams (I remember your body kept sliding away in the packed airport like mist through my fingers, that you couldn't speak, your eyes couldn't cry and I couldn't understand or use a word of the language that crowds of strangers were babbling at us while the planes roared off and left us dumb). Trapped in those hot useless stories, I stayed asleep too long to guess what happened next in the actual world eight yards away through a plywood door.

There was never a real sound, not that I heard from the actual world; and the least sound wakes me. But my eyes opened in pitch black night, and I knew some permanent thing had passed like a great black ship—something was done and ended now but still here to face me. I stood up in my cold sock feet and went towards the bathroom— the front hall bath, not Dane's and Matt's. Like I knew it would be, the door was locked. At first I thought you were both in there; and my whole mind was so crammed with the fact, I could hardly see. But when I'd pressed my ear to the door, I knew no two live humans could stay that quiet for long. Then I couldn't speak. I went to the kitchen and found an icepick—you know it was one of those "privacy" locks a child can pick with any sharp point. And right till the moment I reached inside and found the light, I didn't know which one of you I'd find or in what shape.

Hard as this seems I'm setting it down like I said before for the day and year you need to know what your father did that final night and what your grandfather did after that. This anyhow is all I saw. Dane had changed his clothes again—a clean black polo shirt, black trousers and those black shoes he'd only just bought for Mattie's funeral. He'd leaned himself against the wall between the sink and the low commode, so he sat boxed in where he couldn't flinch from his full intent. The commode lid was shut and his right arm lay on that with a pen in his fingers still. No paper though. He must have wanted to say a last word to you or me but waited too late. Still he'd had plenty time to do all the rest.

I went over to him and leaned towards his face. I could feel he was cool through the air between us. I know that next I said three sentences—something like *I never meant this, poor son. Sleep deep. She truly forgives you* (I guess the *she* meant you and your mother). But I'd said things like that forty years ago in this same country to two of my friends who died beyond me in sniper fire, though I'd never offered forgiveness before for somebody else—you and Matt both. I still don't know if I had the right. I'd had real practice for the tender words, though nothing in a thousand years could have fitted me to bless two hands that had just offended the soul I love above all else.

Dane had carefully doubled two of Matt's old trousseau towels on his lap and under his powerful arms; then with his long straight everyday razor, he'd cut deep through the tender skin inside each elbow there at the hinge. It had plainly worked fast, and the towels had nearly spared the tile. So I had very little washing to do before the rescue squad got there with nothing to save.

When I met them at the door, I asked for silence to let you sleep. And they gave it to us. They were two young Germans like the kind I'd killed, but they took your father's body up with decent respect. And ten minutes after they entered the house, they had him in their van and were gone.

You didn't turn when I opened your door and switched on the lamp; you were that far off till I called your name. You sat up slowly and hugged yourself in the damp chill. Then you saw my face for the first time since the previous morning when you left for school.

After the two disasters since dark, I couldn't imagine how you'd look or what you'd say, especially to me who'd seen less of you in Matt's last weeks than was good for us both. I'd got through the past quarter hour in fair shape. Now I couldn't even speak or nod.

But can you remember what came down next? However I looked, after what I'd seen, you said "Sky, you look like Dixie sunshine." Then you halfway smiled. Christ knows where you got the strength to do it; but you *did*, though I can swear for a fact you haven't smiled that plainly since, not to me nor anybody we've met this winter and spring.

When you finally knew your father was dead—there was no way I could lie about how, but I made it gentle as I could—you plunged straight into a shock like nothing I'd seen since the worst combat. I'd got Tillie's mother on the phone before I woke you, so at least you could stay with them while I took care of that day's worth of the complications caused by any unusual death, especially in a country as hipped on details as Germany. But the self explaining nature of Dane's wounds, and news that his wife had died a month back after years of ordeal, were explanation enough for the men who examined his body. They issued the license for another cremation with no long wait.

Since Dane's office staff was just the one Air Force captain's wife that typed his mail, at least there were no more humans to tell, not that day. I gave her the facts of how he died, not why or where, and asked her what I needed to know about his business (he'd always been mysterious about it, but my main guess was more or less right—"international investments and contacts"). She was sad too but, when she saw I had no intention to run the business, she admitted that Dane had "worked from his briefcase and wouldn't take help." She was clearly far more competent than me; so when she suggested I let her write the final letters to various clients and send a few bills, I told her Yes. Then she said the thing that surprised me most, "Mr. Calhoun, this is no news to me. Dane was in anguish where I couldn't reach him for long months now."

But according to her Dane's business debts at least were nil. He'd run a tight ship, which didn't surprise me—meticulous files on everything he'd done or hoped to do in the future. Ever since dawn I'd tried again to tell myself how I understood him, now too late. Strong as he always tried to look, he'd lifted more than his back could bear— for too many years like he said to me. And at last he'd buckled, his legs and mind and maybe his soul, the way I'd buckled years ago except I failed with a person that my own family never saw; and poor Dane failed in your presence and pressing on you. But with every try I'd come up against a wall my feelings couldn't clear—he'd likely smothered your young mind, a thousand years too young, God knows.

Then I tried to tell myself I was calm, that what I planned was not in panic. I told myself it was all for you, to clear you out of a place I thought you were bound to dread. And I know for a true fact, the thought of your heart was on my mind in every scared move I made—your strict welfare. But I rushed you through unimaginable hurt like you weren't burnt all over your body right down to the spine. And I've paid ever since, though no more than you.

I'd told Dane's secretary she and I could meet tomorrow and make arrangements to shut down the office. She kindly offered to help you and me pack up at the house and think about whether to sell it or what. She even said she'd turn it over to a rental agent if that seemed best. So what I thought was, I'd take Tillie's mother's offer to keep you with them while I packed what I thought you'd need in the first days back home before we could shop. Then once I'd got Dane's ashes with Matt's, I'd lock the house and cars down tight and let them wait till I had you calmly settled in school (I'd get a housekeeper to stay with you and fly back to Stuttgart no later than spring to finish closing down that life, the tangible part, and starting our own). It seemed that simple or possible anyhow. Or maybe I was just that simple minded. Maybe my similar past experience misfitted me to help you rightly. I kept seeing you as Matt or Luna, even Myra and Mother—too seldom as *you* with your own scars that might never heal and that naturally blamed me for all the loss. Even now though, I doubt I was crazy; and I knew who I loved.

But I'd already harmed you badly as anybody you'd yet known, by letting your father die alone with no word to slow him. You *felt*, and still feel, that. And I understood how feeling was the main thing now in your life (and the world's for that matter). You *thought* you loved your father more than anything left, and you *knew* he loved you more than all—he'd told you so more than once here lately, he'd told me too, and I don't doubt him even tonight these slow months later. By the second night in Stuttgart though, your shock had begun to fade a little; and you let me know it.

I may have had worse times than the hour we sat outside Tillie's house in Matt's car—if so I forgot it. You looked as strong as an oak in the wind when you told me plainly I'd killed your father and made me believe it. I couldn't ask where you got the idea. I couldn't tell you what I'd seen with my own eyes and what Dane said to me after that at the kitchen table in normal light. I couldn't even try to call to mind our happy old time days in Raleigh when you were a child, or us together at Myrtle Beach or how your mother had shown her final love for me in so many ways and had left you to me for her own powerful deathbed reasons, that now I thought I understood, though how long she had had to bear them I still don't know.

So once I'd sat there silent awhile, you said the hardest thing of all—that Dane had told you that last night how I'd glanced in your bedroom door and misunderstood. (I haven't told you this till tonight; but Lyn, there's no way on God's Earth that I was wrong in what I saw—it lasted too long. What I *didn't* know was when it started and how much havoc it had worked all through your eyes and mind by now, with you fourteen). Once you'd condemned me, as I recall, the only thing I managed next was facing you blankly and saying we'd fly home in three days and that I'd already called Father Scanlon and got you into Cathedral School for the rest of the year.

But when you said home was where you *were* this minute in Stuttgart, and Tillie's mother had asked you to stay until your school term ended—and you were *staying*, whatever I thought—didn't I shake my head and say No—nothing better than No? I'm fairly sure it was all I could give you that bleak night. And one more reason I've written this—these sleepless nights—is to say that, sure, I was sixty five years old and tough as a boot; but I was burnt too, deep into the quick after waiting helpless beside your mother and then discovering your ordeal, though what has hurt the most till now is you refusing me the pardon you've always given so freely before.

Still, look—we've lasted an endless winter and a rainy spring. That's more than I thought we'd last many times as I sat writing this ancient story. For a person who's seen and borne so much, you've done more at school than I could have dreamed. I've tried to say what an honor your classmates paid in naming you to succeed your mother and crown the

Virgin this past May. Nobody ever deserved it more nor looked any worthier there at the altar. *Believe* it—it's true and it actually means that time is healing you and that your future will be far stronger for what you've undergone so early. Father Scanlon says you're stauncher than Matt; and he well knows—in confession he heard your mother's secrets through most of her life.

I can even gamble on asking if you don't think we've come a small way in winning back what got lost between us in that hard place we left behind when the plane took off—believe me, *behind* us. I know our time with Dr. Bailey, together and separately, has started to help us. She hopes that now with summer on hand, you'll take the time to see her steadily and learn she has your peace at heart. Talk to her, Lyn, till it's *out* of you. Everyone of your family was a seasoned talker and true storyteller. It saved more than one of our lives, mine included (if I'd been mute I'd have died long since); and it could well be what lifts your burden. If I'd had a counselor tough and kind as Maud Bailey fifty years back, there's no telling what I might have spared the world around me—people, I mean, and occasional trees I plowed into. So keep her appointments, for your sake first but also mine.

See, until I can meet your eyes and watch you try to believe I acted to save my last blood kin from ruin—*nothing* but that—then I'll stay balked in my old Hell, where I kill a big portion of what I touch. And we'll be cursed with having no chance to make a useful life together these few years till you leave home on your own road, the life your mother would want us to have and Dane himself in his right mind before time broke him—time and bitter lonesome grief.

With school behind you for the next three months—and you turned fifteen with me in Germany for however long it takes to finish there—I trust you'll have long warm spring days to watch the world revive herself and to know your life is likewise finding its deep bedrock: the good you got from Ashlyn Calhoun, Myra and Mattie and Dane Kirkpatrick in his best days. Since you'll be out at the Barefoot place with those durable pines and beeches, that pure well water and Luna and Anson agreeing to stay till I'm back at least, I leave in the hope that (by whatever time I'm home) you'll start to feel an actual family round you again and will want it to last—a family that's safer than any you've known, with a chance of lasting till you're the woman you're due to be, that straight and strong at passing up every chance you get to inherit the brands of waste and pain I laid on Myra and Matt forever, on my own mother and at least two other honest women who never showed me one whole mean day.

For all the waste I've shown you here, I hope you've also seen the grace of every woman that stands behind your mind and body—three generations of bravery, wit and open armed mercy. And for all I've strictly owned up to, I'll even risk claiming that your grandfather may not be cause for total shame. Look at his hands in all these pages—see what they've done—it was not all harm; it won't be again, not if luck gives you and him a half even break between tonight and the day you stand and walk out of here into your grown life, with him as a cool-headed watcher from home. Christ knows he means to watch every step he takes hereafter to clear your path as far as he can. So Lyn, no woman I've watched—live or dead—is literally *backed* any stronger than you.

And now you've got Luna Adams as well. From the hours you've spent with her since May, you know that she has lifelong reasons to understand you better than most souls left above ground. The fact that you took to her so truly from that first Sunday we drove to Lynchburg has meant a lot to her and me, more than you guess (she's mainly back in Raleigh for you). If you read this far with me away, there may be something you won't know yet. I've asked Luna to be my wife if I come home alive and moving—my wife and the person that sees you through the tangled places I can't go. She says she needs these coming days in country air to sort her thoughts, then talk with you and Anson about it before she gives a firm reply. Since it may be more like weeks than days till I get back—what with selling the house—she'll also have free time like you, plus this to read.

She doesn't know I've dug this deep and brought this much of our past to light. It may turn out I've gone too far. She may think I've not only stolen her oldest secrets but proved my monster heart again by thinking a soul your age needs this or could bear to use it (when what I know is, young as you are, you've already faced more than most generals). She may want to burn it, and me, for good. That's her move to make—there's just this copy. But if Luna chooses to show it to you—and you read to here with her to guide you through such a wilderness of lives—then I beg you'll join me in hoping she finds her own way clear to tell us Yes.

Till when, dear friend, your
Blue Calhoun